Captured
by the
Highlander

JULIANNE MacLEAN

St. Martin's Paperbacks

This is a work of fiction. All of the characters, organizations, and events portrayed in this novel are either products of the author's imagination or are used fictitiously.

CAPTURED BY THE HIGHLANDER

Copyright © 2011 by Julianne MacLean.
Excerpt from *Claimed by the Highlander* copyright © 2011 by Julianne MacLean.

Hand lettering by Iskra Johnson
Cover illustration by Gregg Gulbronson

For information address St. Martin's Press, 175 Fifth Avenue, New York, NY 10010.

ISBN: 978-0-312-36531-8

Printed in the United States of America

St. Martin's Paperbacks edition / March 2011

St. Martin's Paperbacks are published by St. Martin's Press, 175 Fifth Avenue, New York, NY 10010.

10 9 8 7 6 5 4 3 2 1

For Stephen and Laura, who fill my world
with joy and laughter.

Acknowledgments

Special thanks to the librarians of the Halifax Regional Library system and the Dalhousie University Libraries, for keeping the kinds of collections a writer of historical fiction requires. You are treasures.

Thank you also to my agent, Paige Wheeler, for your continual support, and for always saying the right things. It's been thirteen years. Thanks for helping me stay in the game.

Thanks especially to Deborah Hale, for sharing not only your books about Scotland but your imagination and creativity as well. You truly helped me find the heart and soul of this story. It wouldn't have been the same without your contribution.

Kelly Boyce, you always step up to the plate at the right moment and drop everything to lend a hand. Gayle Callen and Laura Lee Guhrke—you were both very generous, inspiring, and supportive at a most important time. Thank you.

To my cousin and soul sister Julia Smith—thanks for inspiring me with your daily blog, A Piece of My Mind, which celebrates art and life in the most eloquent way. And to my cousin, soul sister, and critique partner, Michelle Phillips: You are a true friend. I cherish all that we share.

Finally, thank you to my parents, Charles and Noel Doucet, and my darling brother, Charlie, for being the best that a family can be.

Some say he fights for Scottish freedom. Others say he is a bloodthirsty savage. I know him as the Butcher of the Highlands, and you will know him only by the gleam of his axe when you draw your last breath.

—Anonymous

Chapter One

Fort William, the Scottish Highlands,
August 1716

Monstrous and mighty, teeth bared like a feral beast, the Butcher rose from his battle lunge and watched the English soldier drop lifelessly to the floor at his feet. He swung his damp hair away from his face, then knelt down and removed the keys from the dead man's pocket. The Butcher continued in silence through the cold corridor of the barracks, ignoring the stench of stale sweat and rum, while he searched for the staircase that would take him to his enemy.

The chilly haze of death flowed through him, steeled him viciously, and compelled him to the top of the stairs, where he stopped outside the heavy, oaken door of the officers' quarters. The Butcher paused briefly to listen for the ill-timed approach of yet another tenacious young guard, but there was no sound other than the noise of his own ragged breathing, and the beat of his heart as he savored this long-awaited moment of vengeance.

He adjusted the shield strapped to his back, then squeezed the handle of the sawed-off Lochaber axe in his hand. His shirt was grimy with dirt and sweat from days in the saddle and nights spent sleeping in the grass, but it had all been worth it, for the moment had come at last. It was time to cut down his foe. To slaughter the memory of what had occurred that cold November day in the orchard. Tonight he would kill for his clan, for his country, and for his beloved. There would be no mercy offered. He would strike, and he would strike fast.

With a steady hand he inserted the key into the lock, then entered the room and closed the door behind him. He waited a moment for his eyes to grow accustomed to the darkness, then moved silently toward the bed where his enemy lay sleeping.

Lady Amelia Templeton was dreaming of a butterfly, fluttering over a hazy field of heather, when a faint noise caused her to stir in her bed. Or perhaps it was not a noise, but a feeling. A sense of doom. Her heart began to pound, and she opened her eyes.

It was the nightmare. She had not had it in years, not since she was a girl, when images of the massacre she'd witnessed at the age of nine still burned hellishly in her mind. On that dreadful day, she had pressed her tiny nose to the window of her coach and watched a bloody battle between a band of rebel Highlanders and the English soldiers sent to escort her and her mother into Scotland. They had been traveling to visit her father, a colonel in the English army.

Amelia watched the dirty Scots slit the throats of the soldiers and bludgeon them to death with heavy stones they picked up on the road. She heard the screams of agony, the desperate pleas for mercy, quickly silenced by sharp steel blades through the heart. And just when she thought it was over, when the screaming and sobbing faded to an eerie silence, an ugly blood-splattered savage ripped open the door of the coach and glared in at her.

She had clung to her mother, trembling in fear. He

studied Amelia with burning eyes for what seemed an eternity, then slammed the door in her face and fled to the forest with his brethren. They disappeared into the glistening Highland mist like a pack of wolves.

The sense of terror Amelia felt now was no different, except that it was mixed with anger. She wanted to kill that savage who had opened the door of her coach years ago. She wanted to rise up and shout at him, to slay him with her own bare hands. To prove that she was not afraid.

The floor creaked, and she turned her head on the pillow.

No, it could not be. She must still be dreaming. . . .

A Highlander was moving toward her through the darkness. Panic swept through her, and she strained to see through the murky gloom.

The light sound of his footsteps reached her ears, and suddenly he was above her, raising an axe over his head.

"No!" she cried, reaching out to block the strike, even when she knew the heavy blade would cut straight through her fingers. She squeezed her eyes shut.

When the deathblow did not fall, Amelia opened her eyes. The brawny, panting savage stood squarely over her bed. His axe was poised and gleaming in the moonlight from the window. His long hair was wet with grime or sweat or river water—she knew not which. Most terrible of all, his eyes glowed with the boiling furies of hell itself.

"You're not Bennett," he said in a deep, growling Scottish brogue.

"No, I am not," she replied.

"Who are you?"

"I am Amelia Templeton."

He had not yet lowered the macabre weapon, nor had she lowered her trembling hands.

"You're English," he said.

"That's right. And who are you, to dare enter my bed-chamber at night?"

She wasn't quite sure where she'd found the courage or sense to inquire so boldly about his identity when her heart was pounding like a mallet in her chest.

The Highlander took a step back and lowered the axe. His voice was deep and terrorizing. "I'm the Butcher. And if you scream, lassie, it'll be the last breath you take."

She held her tongue, for she'd heard tales of the brutal and bloodthirsty Butcher of the Highlands, who committed grisly acts of treachery and left a trail of murder and mayhem in his wake. According to legend, he was descended from Gillean of the Battle-axe, who had long ago crushed an invading fleet of Vikings. The Butcher was never without his morbid death weapon, and he was a Jacobite traitor, straight to the bone.

"If you are who you claim, why have you not killed me?" she asked, fear and uncertainty burning in every pore.

"I was expecting to kill someone else tonight." His sharp, animal eyes surveyed the room, searching for some hint of the person he'd come to slaughter. "Whose room is this?"

"There is no one here but me," she informed him, but his heated gaze swung in her direction and compelled her to answer the question more thoroughly. "If you are looking for Lieutenant-colonel Richard Bennett, I am sorry to disappoint you, but he is away from the fort."

"Where?"

"I don't know exactly."

He studied her face through the moonlight. "Are you his whore?"

"I beg your pardon?"

"If you are, I might slice your head off right now, and

leave it here in a box on the table, for him to admire when he returns."

A nightmarish queasiness churned through her belly as she imagined her head in a box. Where would he put the rest of her? Would he toss her headless body out the window?

She struggled to breathe evenly, in and out. "I am not Colonel Bennett's whore. I am his betrothed. My father was a colonel in the English army and the fifth Duke of Winslowe. So if you mean to kill me, sir, be done with it. I am not afraid of you."

It was a bald-faced lie, but she would not let him see her cower.

Something in his face changed. One large, strong hand squeezed the handle of his axe, and he lifted it to rest on the edge of the bed. She found herself staring mutely down at the dangerous hook at its tip, which was pressing against her thigh. She noted the huge broadsword in a scabbard at his side, and the flintlock pistol in his belt.

"Get up," he commanded, poking her. "I want to look at you."

Amelia swallowed over a sickening knot of fear in her throat. Did he mean to ravish and abuse her before he killed her?

God help them both if he tried.

He poked her harder, so she carefully folded the covers aside and slid her legs over the edge of the bed. Eyes fixed on his, one hand clutching the neckline of her shift, she stood.

"Come closer," he commanded.

As she moved forward, she noted that his face was drawn from elegantly sculpted contours and sharp, flawless angles, and his eyes unveiled a passionate fury—the likes of which she had never seen before. There was a spellbinding intensity there, and it gripped her by the throat, held her captive in its power.

The Butcher backed up, and she followed. She could smell the masculine scent of his sweat. His shoulders were broad, his biceps heavy, his hands rugged and enormous. They were a warrior's hands, roughened by years of battle and butchery.

Her eyes returned to the fierce expression on his striking face, and she felt her insides quiver. As brave as she wanted to be at this moment—and she had always *dreamed* she would be brave—she knew she was no match for this beast of a man. There was little chance she could ever overpower him, no matter what she tried to do. If he wanted to ravish or kill her, he could. He could knock her to the floor with one swift swing of that deadly battle-axe, and she would be powerless against him.

"When it comes to your fiancé," he said in a coarse voice, "I have an axe to grind."

"Do you intend to grind it on me?"

"I haven't decided yet."

Sheer suffocating panic squeezed the air out of her lungs. She wished she could scream for help, but something was paralyzing her—a strange, almost hypnotic power that turned her muscles into useless pools of liquid.

He moved slowly around her. "It's been a while since I've had a woman." He circled around to the front, lifted his axe, and touched the hook to her shoulder. Her mind flooded with alarm as the smooth steel slid over her flesh.

"Are you his beloved?" the Butcher asked.

"Of course I am," she proudly replied. "And he is mine."

She loved Richard with all her heart. Her father had loved him, too. And God help this dirty Jacobite when her fiancé learned of this. . . .

"Is that a fact?"

She turned her raging eyes to meet his. "Yes, sir, it is a

fact. Though I doubt you would know the meaning of the word *love*. It is outside your realm of understanding."

He leaned close until his lips touched her ear. His hot, moist breath made her shiver. "Aye, lass, I have no use for tenderness or affection, and you'd do well to remember it. So it's decided, then. I'll kill you instead of him."

Terror swept through her. He was going to do it. He truly was.

"Please, sir," she said, working hard to soften the animosity in her voice. Perhaps she could distract him with a desperate plea for mercy. With any luck, his entry to the fort had been noticed and someone would soon come to her rescue. "I beg of you."

"You beg of me?" He chuckled grimly. "You don't strike me as the begging type."

He was enjoying this. It was a game to him. He had no compassion. None at all.

"Why do you want to kill my betrothed?" she asked, still hoping to delay the inevitable.

Please, God, let someone knock on the door. A maid. My uncle. The cavalry. Anyone!

"How do you know him?" she asked.

The Butcher lifted the axe off her shoulder and tipped it upward to rest on his own. He continued to circle around her, like a wolf studying its prey. "I fought against him at Inveraray," he said, "and again at Sheriffmuir."

The Jacobites had been defeated at Sheriffmuir. It was the battlefield where Richard had saved her father's life. It was why she fell in love with him. He'd fought with courage and valor, with unwavering honor to the Crown— unlike this savage moving around her, who didn't seem to understand the rules of war. He seemed bent only on exacting some dark, personal revenge.

"Do you intend to kill *all* the English soldiers you fought against that day?" she asked. "Because that may take you a while. And there were Scots there, too, fighting for the English Crown. Campbells, I believe. Are you going to butcher all of them as well?"

He circled around to her front. "Nay. It was only your beloved I wanted to slice in two this evening."

"Well, I am sorry to disappoint you."

Visions of war and murder spun before her eyes. How unfair it all was. Her father had been dead for only a month, and she had come here to Fort William under the guardianship of her uncle to marry Richard. Her protector.

What was going to happen now? Would she die a grisly death here in this room, under the cold, heavy blade of a Highlander, just like in her childhood nightmares? Or would he leave her to live while he went on in search of Richard and succeeded in killing the man she loved?

"But I'm not disappointed, lass," the Butcher said, cradling her chin in his calloused hand and lifting her face, forcing her to look at him. "Because tonight I stumbled on something much more appealing than a swift, clean death for my enemy. It's something that'll make him suffer much longer."

"You're going to kill me, then?"

Or perhaps he was referring to something else. . . .

Fighting against the knot of upheaval in her belly, she glared at him with hatred. "I am betrothed, sir, to the man I love. So if you mean to rape me, I promise you, I will scream my guts out—and you can kill me if you want to, because I would rather die a thousand agonizing deaths than be violated by *you*."

His eyes narrowed; then he swore something in Gaelic and let go of her chin. He strode to the tall wardrobe where her clothes were stored.

After tearing through the costly gowns of silk and lace, he threw them to the floor in the center of the room, then found a simple skirt of heavy brown wool. He pulled it from the wardrobe, along with drawers and stays, stepped over the other gowns, and thrust the articles at her.

"Put these on," he said. "You need to learn a lesson or two, so you're coming with me." He backed away and waited for her to dress in front of him.

For a moment, she considered her options, and thought it might be best to obey him, if only to buy more time. But when she imagined stepping into the skirt and lacing herself up in front of him—so that he could steal her away to the mountains and do Lord knows what with her—she could not do it. She would rather be beaten to a pulp.

Amelia squared her shoulders. She was terrified by this man, there was no denying it, but the intensity of her fury somehow overpowered her fear. Before she could truly contemplate the consequences of what she was doing, she had flung the clothes on the floor.

"No. I will not put these on, nor will I leave this fort with you. You are welcome to try and force me, but I told you before that I would scream if you touched me. So if you do not get out of my bedchamber this instant, I will do it. I promise I will scream and you will soon be dead."

For what seemed an eternity, he glared at her, clearly surprised and baffled by her rebellion. Then his expression changed. He took a slow step forward, and their bodies touched.

"So you're Winslowe's daughter," he said in a deep and quiet voice. "The famous English war hero."

She felt the Butcher's warm breath at her temple, and his tartan brushed against the front of her shift.

Her heart trembled at the nearness of him. He was like some kind of living, breathing mountain of muscle. She could barely think or breathe through the heady effect of his presence, so overwhelmingly close. "Yes."

"You're fearless, like him. I like fearless women." The Butcher took a lock of her hair in his hand, rubbed it between his fingers, then lifted it to his nose and closed his eyes. He seemed to drink in her scent; then he touched his lips lightly to her cheek and whispered, "And you smell good."

Amelia gave no reply. She couldn't think. All her senses were shivering with flames of terror and confusion. The heat was making her dizzy.

"Now take off your shift," he quietly said, "and do it now, or I will cut it off of you myself."

At last, she found her voice and reached for one last shred of courage. She lifted her eyes and regarded him steadily. "No, sir, I will not."

"Are you testing me, lass?"

"I suppose that's one way of putting it."

His gaze traveled over her face and searched her eyes; then he looked down at her breasts. She felt a curious sensation in her belly and tried to pull away, but he took hold of her arm and held her against him. His lips brushed against hers as he spoke.

"This is your last warning. I said take it off—and if you continue to defy me, I won't be held responsible for what I do to you next."

Amelia looked up at him and shook her head. "And I'll say it a hundred times if I have to. The answer is still no."

Chapter Two

Amelia would never forget the gut-wrenching sound of the fabric ripping in two, not as long as she lived. The torn garment dropped to the floor, and the chilly night air assaulted her bared flesh. She quickly hugged herself to cover her breasts.

"You should've done what I asked," he said, glancing briefly at her state of undress as he picked up the torn fabric, placed it between his teeth, and ripped it to shreds before her eyes.

He moved behind her and gagged her with a torn strip of linen, then tied a knot at the back of her head. His warm hands came to rest on the tops of her shoulders, and he spoke reassuringly in her ear. "I'll not harm you, lass, as long as you do as you're told. Can you do that for me?"

Clinging to the small suggestion of clemency she thought she heard in his voice, she nodded.

He crossed to the wardrobe, pulled out a clean shift, and handed it to her. "Now put this on, unless you want me to haul you out of here naked."

This time she obeyed. She quickly pulled the shift on over her head, then stepped into the drawers and donned the stays. Without a word, the Butcher stood behind her and laced her up tight.

After she pulled on a skirt and bodice, he used the

strips of her torn shift to bind her wrists behind her back. "Where are your shoes?" he asked, glancing about the room.

She tossed her head to gesture at the far wall, where she had placed them before retiring for the night. Under the portrait of King George.

The Butcher went to fetch them, glanced briefly up at the picture, then returned and knelt down before her. Setting his axe on the floor at her feet, he reached under her skirt and cupped her bare calf. The shocking warmth of his hand on her leg made her lose her balance, and she had to lean on his shoulder.

He lifted her leg and slid her foot into the shoe, then took hold of her other ankle and slipped the second shoe on, grabbed his axe, and stood. It all happened very quickly, without a single thought for stockings, and it left her shaken and distressed. She had never been naked in front of a man before, nor had a man ever put his hands under her skirt.

She looked up at him and sucked at the linen gag.

"I know it's tight," he said, as if reading her mind. "But I need you to be very quiet."

He bent forward, wrapped his muscular arm around her backside, and hoisted her up over his shoulder. The sudden movement stole the breath from her lungs, and she said a silent prayer that someone would see them on their way out and foil the escape, or that she would find an opportunity to alert a guard.

With his axe in one hand, the Butcher opened the door and moved noiselessly into the corridor, where Amelia found herself looking down at a dead soldier on the floor outside her chamber.

Stunned into silence, she stared numbly at the poor soul on the floor before she was carried down the stairs and through another dark corridor, past two more dead soldiers on the floor, and finally to a door at the rear of the barracks. She had not even been aware of its existence. How had this rebel known of it? Who had told him how to find Richard's bedchamber, and how had he learned that Richard was supposed to be here in the first place? It was only a last-minute call to arms that had resulted in his unexpected departure and the insistence that Amelia take his room to ensure her safety. A lot of good that had done.

Outside the barracks, a thick mist enveloped them. The Butcher carried her, kicking and struggling, up the grassy rampart toward the outer wall. When he set her down, she noticed a four-pronged hook embedded in the earth at her feet, with a rope tied to it. The next thing she knew, she was sliding down the wall on the Butcher's back, while grunting a number of unladylike protests.

Her feet touched ground, and she turned to look up at a prime piece of horseflesh, his shiny coat as black as night. He nickered softly and tossed his head. The breath from his nostrils shot out in white puffs of steam against the dark sky, and only then did Amelia realize that her captor was untying the binds at her wrists. He shoved his axe into a saddle scabbard and swung himself up onto the horse's back.

"Give me your hand," the Butcher said, holding out his own.

She shook her head angrily and bit down on the gag, which pressed sickeningly on the back of her tongue.

"Give me your hand, woman, or I'll come down there and thrash you senseless." He took hold of her arm and tossed her up onto the horse behind him, then kicked in his heels. The horse galloped forward, and Amelia had no choice but to wrap her arms around her captor's firm, muscular torso and hang on for dear life, or go tumbling over the side into the cold, dark depths of the river.

As it turned out, the Butcher's torso was very muscular indeed, solid as a rock, and Amelia was both troubled and preoccupied by his inconceivable strength. Nevertheless, she managed to stay somewhat focused and monitor their journey. She took note of all the landmarks along the way— the small grove of oak saplings, the stone bridge they'd crossed a mile back, and the long field with five haystacks, spaced evenly apart.

They must have traveled through the predawn darkness and drizzle for a full half hour before he spoke, and when he did she found it difficult to focus on anything other than the deep timbre of his voice and the way his long hair brushed up against her cheek when he turned his head to the side.

"You've been quiet, lass. Are you alive back there?"

All she could do was grunt with exasperation through the tight gag that was pressing down on her tongue.

"Aye, I know." He nodded, as if he had understood every word. "I was thinking about removing it, but something tells me you've been working up a mountain of complaints, so if it's all the same to you, I'll wait till we're somewhere more remote before I release that mouth of yours, so no one will hear your screeching."

"I won't screech," she tried to say, but it came out as a muffled grumble.

"What was that? You think I'm very wise? Aye, I think so, too."

She was tempted to punch him in the arm or pummel his back with both fists but decided against it, for he was a ruthless killer with an axe.

They rode through a grove of conifers and emerged onto another open field. Amelia glanced through the mist and spotted a tiny light in the distance. A lantern in a crofter's window perhaps? Or a company of English soldiers?

The possibility of escape screamed in her mind, and before she had a chance to strategize she was tugging at the foul-tasting gag. The fabric stretched just enough to slide down over her chin, and with a plan that went no further than swinging her leg over the back of the horse and dropping to the ground while they were still moving, she soon found herself dashing across the drizzly field toward the light.

"Help! Please!"

She was aware, of course, that the Butcher would pursue her but clung to the unlikely hope that he might topple off his horse and crack his skull open on a rock.

The sound of his feet hitting the ground reached her ears, her heart exploded with panic, and seconds later he overtook her. He wrapped his arms around her waist and threw her down.

The next instant, he was straddling her. She was pinned on her back with her arms up over her head.

"Let me go!"

She kicked and screamed and refused to yield. She kneed him in the stomach, struggled wildly for her freedom, and spit in his face.

The Butcher grunted and dropped his full weight upon her, holding her down with the stifling power of his arms and hips and legs. She could feel his tremendous masculine form—too close, too tight, too overwhelming. Hysteria spun through her mind, and she shouted with anger, "Get off me, you brute! I will not go willingly!"

The drizzle turned to rain, chilling her skin and soaking her hair while she fought with all her might. She blinked against the silvery drops that pooled on her eyelashes. Cool water sluiced over her bare thighs, for she had kicked her skirts up during the struggle. She continued to fight, punch, and slap at him.

It was not long, however, before her muscles grew weak against the uncompromising stamina of his brawn. She was perspiring heavily, breathless with exhaustion. She had nothing left.

The sky grew brighter. Morning was upon them.

"Please . . . ," she begged, hating that he had reduced her to this. If only she were stronger.

"You can't fight me forever, lass, though I admire your efforts to try."

She squirmed harder, but he had her arms pinned at her sides and at some point he'd curled a big leg around hers.

They were both soaking wet, drenched beneath the unforgiving rain. She looked up at his face and felt his warm breath on her lips. His dark-lashed blue eyes held her captive in some kind of persuasive dream. He was unbelievably handsome, and she could have wept at the unfairness of it all—that a devil like him could be blessed with such perfection. Clearly there was no justice in the world. She was doomed.

Relaxing her body and unclenching her fists, Amelia expelled a breath into the chilly dawn air. She had no choice but to surrender to him, at least for now.

He relaxed, too, and his nose brushed against her cheek. "Wise decision, lass."

She allowed the fight to drain out of her body, then felt the Highlander's erection, pressing against her pelvic bone. The shock of it nearly choked her, and her blood began to race. She knew it would come to this sooner or later, but not now . . . not yet. . . .

"Please," she said.

"Please what, lass?"

His lips swept across her mouth, and she made a small involuntary whimper.

"You're going to have to soften to me eventually," he said. "Wouldn't it be easier and more pleasant for us both if you did it now?"

"I will never soften to you," she replied, wishing she felt more in control.

He slid his hand down the side of her thigh, pulled his body closer to hers, and her insides began to burn. "Stop touching me like that," she said.

"Like what? Is there another way you would prefer?"

"I would prefer it not at all."

With those disarming blue eyes, he looked down at her in the dawn light. She wished she could escape his gaze, but again she was trapped in it. He was too much for her.

"That's better," he said as he began to lay soft kisses across her cheek.

"I don't know what you want from me." She closed her eyes at the touch of his lips.

"I just want you to yield."

Feeling helpless and defeated, she turned her head to the side and suddenly found herself gaping at a pair of animal-hide boots, less than two feet away from her face.

Startled out of her wits, she blinked through the rain to try to decipher if she was imagining things, but she was not. She was indeed looking at two hairy legs with wool stockings falling down around the tops of the boots, and a green plaid kilt reaching to the knees.

"God in heaven!" she shouted as the unexpected Highlander's raucous laughter disturbed the quiet dawn. She was completely done for now. All hope was gone.

The Butcher rose to his feet, and she was at least grateful to feel the crushing weight of his body come away from her, so that she could breathe again and get her mind out of that dangerous cloud of sensation.

"Should've known you'd be shaggin' some wench in a field," the new arrival said, "when you're supposed to be gettin' your arse in and out of Fort William." He looked up at the rainy sky. "Not much of a night for shaggin', though."

Still on her back, pressing the heels of her hands to her forehead, Amelia looked up through the driving rain at the second Highlander and, to her utter dismay, found herself looking at not one but *two* Scots, who were shoving the Butcher back and forth between them like a couple of schoolyard bullies.

"Get your fookin' hands off me," he growled.

God help them all, there was going to be a bloodbath.

She glanced uneasily at his axe in the saddle scabbard, twenty feet away. Perhaps she could get to it. . . .

Amelia sat up on her knees, but when she looked back at the three brawling brutes—and saw that the other two both carried pistols and claymores—she knew there was no chance that she could win an axe fight against them. They were warriors. It would be suicide.

"Well, did you get in and out, ye horny bugger?" the second Highlander asked. He stood at least six feet tall, with freckles, a red beard, and a shaggy mane of hair, which might have made him appear less threatening were it not for the diagonal scar that slashed across his face from eyebrow to nose. His eyes gleamed like two green marbles in the morning light.

Still laughing, he staggered away from the Butcher and withdrew a pewter flask from his sporran. He tipped it up, took a drink, and held it out.

The Butcher accepted it and guzzled deeply. "You referring to the wench or the fort, Gawyn?" he asked. "If it's the latter, I was in and out quick enough. Wasn't so quick with the lady, though."

He handed the flask back, swiped a hand across his mouth, and strode to where Amelia still sat in the grass, trying to assess the situation. He grabbed her by the arm and pulled her to her feet. "And she isn't just any wench," he told them. "She's a prize worth her weight in gold."

Amelia tried to pry his hand off her arm, but his grip was forged of steel. "Let me go," she ground out.

The first Highlander—a short, stocky, fair-haired Scot with the face of a bulldog—pulled a flask from his sporran as well. "She's feisty, I'll give her that."

"Aye, but she's quivering like a skinned rabbit," the other one said. "What'd you do to her?"

"I did nothing," the Butcher replied. "She's cold and wet, that's all."

"Well, she shouldn't have been rolling around in the wet grass," the tall one said. "Is she dim-witted?"

The Butcher led her back to the horse without answering.

"Why don't you just drag me by the hair?" she suggested irritably, still working to pry his fingers from her arm while her body shivered and her teeth began to chatter. "Isn't that what you barbarians usually do?"

The other two looked at each other and burst into a chorus of laughter, but the Butcher didn't crack a smile.

"We can't stay here," he said. "It'll be full daylight soon, and there are English patrols just beyond the forest." He lifted her into the saddle again, and looked up at her with clever eyes. "But don't get any ideas, lassie. One peep out of you and you *will* be skinned alive. I'll be more than happy to do the honors myself."

Just then, the thunder of approaching hoofbeats cut through the drizzly dawn. A fourth Highlander rode up and hopped off a pale gray horse while the animal was still trotting at a quick pace.

This latest addition to the unruly crew had long golden hair, and his eyes were two turquoise pools of malicious tenacity. He, too, was tall, enormous, and beastlike. "Did you kill him?" he asked, striding fast toward them.

The Butcher glanced at him briefly. "Nay. He wasn't there."

"Wasn't there?" The golden-haired Scot looked up at Amelia. She sat high in the saddle looking down at him while the Butcher wrapped a thin, coarse twine around her wrists and tied it tight. "Who's this, then?"

"She's Bennett's betrothed."

The rebel's brow pulled together in a disbelieving frown. "His betrothed? He has a woman? Bluidy hell, Duncan, why didn't you slit her throat?"

Amelia shuddered at the Highlander's unimaginable callousness while taking note of the fact that the Butcher had a name. It was Duncan.

"I thought better of it." He swung himself up into the saddle behind her.

A hostile antagonism sparked in the other man's voice. "You should've done it and left her head to rot in a box. What's wrong with you?"

The Butcher reached around Amelia to gather the reins in his fists. "You should know better than to doubt me, Angus. You know I do not falter. Nor will I, not as long as that English devil is breathing our Scottish air."

"Or *any* air." Angus stepped out of the way as the horse reared up skittishly.

"We should separate," the Butcher said, his voice a heavy blade that cut through the tension. "Keep your wits about you, lads, and I'll see you at the camp." He urged the horse into a gallop, and they darted forward, leaving the others behind.

They galloped for a short time across the sodden field, then trotted toward the shadowy fringes of the forest. The rain had softened, and the sky gave off an eerie pink glow.

Soaked to the bone, Amelia shivered. Without speaking, the Butcher wrapped his tartan around the both of them. She breathed in his rough, manly scent on the wool and felt the heat from the wide expanse of his chest at her back. She was thankful for that at least, despite the fact that this whole situation had her reeling with fear.

"What is it about you Highlanders?" she asked bitterly, her teeth chattering. "All you want to do is chop off heads and put them in boxes. Is it some kind of Scottish tradition?"

"It's none of your concern," her captor replied, "and I'll thank you not to ask that question again."

She was quiet for a few minutes while the warmth from the tartan slowly began to ease the chill in her bones.

"He called you Duncan," she said. "I heard him. Aren't you worried I'll tell someone your name and the true identity of the Highland Butcher will be discovered?"

"There are hundreds of Duncans in the Highlands, lass—so no, I'll not lose any sleep over it. And since you're asking more questions, are you not worried I'll change my mind and slit your throat after all?" He paused. "Since you know my name."

She swallowed uneasily. "Perhaps a little."

"Then you should stop asking questions you don't want to hear the answers to."

She gathered the tartan about her and tried to ignore the chafing burn of the binds at her wrists.

"I assume that was your famous band of rebels," she said, because she wanted to keep him talking. She wanted to know why this was happening and learn where they meant to take her. "I'd imagined there were more of you," she continued. "Because from the stories I've heard, you and your friends slaughter entire English armies in three minutes flat."

"You shouldn't believe everything you hear."

She turned her cheek to speak to him over her shoulder. "So it takes you longer than three minutes to slaughter entire armies?"

He paused. "Nay. Three minutes is accurate."

She shook her head at the mere idea of it.

"But we don't attack armies," he said, correcting her. "We're not daft."

"No. That is most definitely *not* the word I would use to describe you."

They crossed a shallow burn, where the horse's hooves splashed through the cool trickling water. Amelia hugged the tartan to her chest.

"What word would you use?" the Butcher asked, touching his lips to the back of her ear as he spoke and sending a torrent of gooseflesh across her neck and shoulders. He had an annoying habit of doing that, and she wished he would stop.

"I can think of a number of very vivid expressions," she said, "but I will not speak them aloud, because you still might change your mind and decide to slit my throat." She turned her cheek to the side again, and her nose almost touched his. "You see, *I'm* not daft, either."

She'd mocked him with her last words and was surprised to hear him chuckle softly in her ear.

"You seem too bright to be sharing Bennett's bed," he said.

"I told you before, we are engaged to be married, and the fact that I was in his bed . . ." She paused, not sure how to phrase it exactly. "It's not what you think. I was escorted to the fort by my uncle, the Duke of Winslowe, who is my father's heir and now my guardian. Richard was called away from the fort last night, and only wanted to ensure that I would be safe and comfortable."

"Well, at least you were comfortable."

She clenched her jaw against a sudden pulse of anger. "Until *you* broke into my room and interrupted my happy dreams of wedded bliss."

"There was no breakin' in, lass," he said. "I had a key."

"Ah, yes, the one you stole from the soldier in the corridor—the one you murdered in cold blood."

"That wasn't murder," he said, after a quiet pause. "This is war. The lad signed up for it, and it was a fair fight."

"No one signs up to die."

"Highlanders do, if the need arises."

She shifted in the saddle. "How delightfully courageous of you all. It's too bad you are committing treason when you perform these impressive acts of bravery."

He shifted, too. "You have quite a mouth on you, Lady Amelia. I can't deny I'm aroused by it."

Aroused. No man had ever said anything so bold in her presence, or taken such liberties with her before, and the shock of it made her cheeks turn scarlet. "Then I will close my lips," she said, "and keep them shut, Mr. Butcher. Because the last thing I want to do is arouse your passions."

"Are you sure?" She could feel the heat of his lips as he whispered in her ear, and the gooseflesh returned. It tingled across her skin, and she cursed her body's frustrating response.

"You seem like a passionate woman, Lady Amelia," he continued. "You might enjoy the lusty style of a Highlander's lovemaking. We're not like your polite English gentlemen. We're not afraid to grunt and thrust and use our mouths to pleasure our women."

A surge of heat shot through her veins. She felt a renewed urge to leap off the horse again and run all the way back to London, but she'd already learned her lesson in that regard. If she did that, he'd have her on her back in the grass again, and she didn't think she could survive another incident like that without losing control of her senses.

"I am not saying another word to you." She sat up straighter in the saddle, so that her back was no longer touching the solid wall of his chest, but it did nothing to cool the fires of anxiety that were coursing through her blood.

He leaned forward and whispered a warning in her ear. "You're wise to keep your mouth shut, lass, because I can only resist so much. Your lively little tongue might push me over the edge. *Ah,* look. Here we are—at my luxurious abode."

He reined in his horse.

Feeling shaken, Amelia fought hard to focus on their surroundings. His "luxurious abode" was nothing more than a cave—a cold, dark cavern cut into a steep-sided mountain, surrounded by moss and lichen-covered granite.

They truly *were* barbarians, living like animals in caves. A smoky mist curled ominously around the horse's legs.

"It's the Butcher's lair," her captor said, pulling his tartan away so that the cold morning air once again assaulted her damp skin. Tossing the plaid over his shoulder, he swung himself to the ground.

While she continued to stare at the pitch-black entrance to the cave, he pulled the axe from the scabbard, slipped it into his belt, and held his arms out to her. "Come, lass, I'll make a fire for us, and you can curl up in a warm bed of fur, and then I'll make a necklace for you out of all the pretty bones from the soldiers I murdered tonight."

She looked down at him in horror, not entirely sure he was jesting.

Just then, the golden-haired lion of a Scot who wanted to slit her throat came galloping toward them from the other direction.

The Butcher watched him approach with narrowed eyes, then spoke to Amelia with a firm tone of command. "Get off the horse, lass. My friend wants to kill you, so it'd be best if you waited in the cave while he and I talk it over."

The necessity of escape burned in her mind as she slid off the horse and hurried to the cave entrance. She stood for a moment just inside, waiting for her eyes to adjust to the reduced light, while the other Highlander arrived behind her and dismounted. She looked around for anything she might use as a weapon and began to tug frantically at her bonds.

Chapter Three

Angus MacDonald swung out of the saddle and landed with a heavy thud on the ground. His golden mane of hair, dishevelled and wet, fell forward over his brow, and his horse trotted away toward taller grasses.

"Damn you, Duncan," Angus said. "What was going through your bluidy brain? We've been tracking Bennett for the better part of a year. I thought we were of the same mind."

"We are." Duncan led his horse to a bucket of water outside the cave entrance.

He was not in the mood for this. He'd just killed five men and his clothes reeked of blood and filth and death. He wanted to go to the river and wash his hands and weapons, and clean the sweat and grime from his body. Above all, he wanted to lie down somewhere and sleep. For many, many hours.

"I didn't abandon the plan," he explained to Angus, his closest friend, the fearless warrior who had saved his life in battle more times than he could count. "But Bennett wasn't where he was supposed to be. That's the only reason he still lives." Duncan turned and faced Angus. "But if you cross me one more time in front of the others, I swear to God and all that is holy, I'll thrash you to within an inch of your life."

Angus stared at him for a long, hard moment before he turned toward the rock face of the hill and laid a scarred hand on the granite. He spoke quietly, his voice heavy with frustration. "I wanted his head tonight."

"And you think I didn't?" Duncan replied. "How do you think I felt when I raised my axe and found myself looking down at an innocent woman?"

Angus pushed away from the stone. "She's not so innocent, if she's engaged to that swine."

"Perhaps."

Duncan suddenly felt a pointed stab of irritation at the mere mention of her engagement, which disturbed his equilibrium. The woman had stirred something in him from the first moment. He'd been struck dumb by her penetrating green eyes and her bold and foolish bravery. He'd spent far too much time studying the lush curve of her breasts and her fiery red hair. She had thrown him off balance, and that sort of weakness was not an option. Not now, when they had come so far. He simply could not afford to become distracted.

"Perhaps? She's *English,* Duncan. She looked down at me like I was pond scum and she was the fookin' Queen of England."

"She's a proud one," Duncan replied. He lifted the heavy saddle off his horse and set it on the ground, then removed the bridle. "That's because she's the daughter of a great man. You'd know him as the Duke of Winslowe." He glanced knowingly at Angus. "Surely you remember him. He led a battalion at Sherrifmuir."

Angus's eyes widened. "The duke? The one my father almost killed on the battlefield?"

"The same." Duncan rubbed the flats of his hands over the sinewed flanks of his horse, wiping away the cool, moist lather while trying not to think about the famous colonel's daughter, who was waiting for him inside the cave.

Angus whistled. "Now I see why you let her live—at least for the time being." He frowned in confusion. "But she plans to marry Bennett?"

"Aye. That's why she was at Fort William—evidently dreaming of her future nuptials when I nearly lobbed off her head."

Angus paced back and forth in front of the cave entrance. "Is it a love match between them? Surely not."

"She claims it is."

"Has she fookin' met him?"

Duncan breathed deeply with frustration. He had no answer to that question, because any woman's betrothal to that animal Richard Bennett made no sense to him.

Angus faced Duncan squarely. "Do you think she knows what her fiancé did to our Muira? You don't think she might have put him up to it, do you? Because of what my father tried to do to hers on the battlefield?"

It was a troubling thought—surely not possible—but Duncan nevertheless gave it fair consideration before he shook his head. "Nay, I don't think so. She doesn't strike me as the ruthless type."

"What's the attraction, then?" Angus asked. "Why is she with Bennett?"

It was at least easy to imagine what had caught Bennett's eye. Not only was Lady Amelia the daughter of a duke, providing the highest social connections, but she also was beautiful beyond imagining.

Duncan found himself conjuring up images of what had happened between them in the field, when he had her on her back, squirming and rubbing up against him. She'd ignited his aggressions to such a shocking degree, it had taken every ounce of self-control he possessed to keep from taking her right then and there. It was difficult to say what might have occurred if Fergus and Gawyn hadn't arrived when they had, for he was still hungry for her.

Focusing his attention on the task of grooming Turner's coat, he reminded himself that he shouldn't be thinking about his prisoner that way and that he should avoid such thoughts in the future. She was an object to him. She was his enemy and his bait, nothing more. He could not forget that.

"I don't know," he said, "but I intend to find out."

Angus strode to the cave and looked in. "Then what? An eye for an eye?"

Duncan's gut churned. This was a dirty business, and he loathed it.

"I haven't decided yet." He left his horse to graze. "Go wait for the others on the ridge. I'll need some time alone with her."

"How much time?"

"A few hours at least."

He felt Angus's gaze on his back as he entered the dark chill of the cave.

"To do what, Duncan?"

"I told you, I don't know yet. But I'm tired and irritable, so just leave me in peace until I figure it out."

The fast-approaching Royal North British Dragoons were spotted in the distance by a young soldier, who was positioned on Fort William's high north wall.

"Colonel Bennett returns!" he shouted, and there was a flurry of activity in the courtyard below. Groomsmen hastened to fill buckets from water barrels, and foot soldiers lined up with their muskets on their shoulders, the straps of their haversacks slung across their chests.

The thunderous rumble of hooves signaled the time to open the gates, and the impressive mounted regiment of soldiers galloped into the fort.

Lieutenant-colonel Richard Bennett was the first to dismount. He withdrew the important contents of his saddlebags, then handed his horse over to a groomsman. Striding toward Colonel Worthington's quarters, Richard pulled off his gloves and removed his cavalry helmet.

His saber bounced against his thigh as he walked with single-minded purpose to address Worthington, for he had news to report. He'd burned another crofter's cottage, where he'd found maps, weapons, and letters from a number of known Jacobites.

A moment later, Richard was received by his commander. He was not prepared, however, for the unsettling image before him when he stepped through the door.

The snowy-haired Duke of Winslowe was seated in a chair, and the colonel was standing over him with a glass of brandy, which the duke seemed unwilling or unable to accept, because he was too distraught.

"Thank God you're back," Worthington said, turning from Winslowe. "Something dreadful has occurred, and we will need to rely on both your discretion and your resolve to set things right, Bennett."

"You have my utmost cooperation, Colonel Worthington."

"It concerns Lady Amelia."

Worthington paused, and Richard swallowed heavily, bracing himself for the news that the colonel seemed reluctant to report. "What has occurred?"

The commanding officer breathed deeply, then at last conveyed the details. "Your betrothed was abducted last night."

Richard stood motionless, clenching his jaw, until he could locate the composure and self-control required to speak calmly. "Abducted? By whom?"

"There is evidence to suggest it was the Butcher of the Highlands."

Richard's upper lip twitched. He took a step forward. "You are telling me that that savage has taken *my* fiancée from inside the heavily guarded, fully garrisoned stone walls of Fort William?"

The portly duke looked up at him and nodded. "My niece," he said. "My brother's only daughter . . . I have known her since she was a babe in her mother's arms. We must do something, Bennett. I was the one who brought her here, and if anything happens to that gel, I will never forgive myself."

Barely able to see beyond the scarlet rage that was burning his eyes, Richard gripped the hilt of his sword and backed away. "Who is responsible for this? Who was on duty last night?"

They both watched him with concern, and when they did not answer quickly enough, he shouted at them both, "*Who,* dammit!"

"They're all dead," the colonel replied.

Richard backed away toward the door. "I *will* find her," he said. "And when I do, I will cut that Jacobite traitor into a hundred pieces. Not just for Amelia's honor, but for my king and country as well."

Richard strode out of the room, crushing instantly the flicker of distress that had lodged in his gut, for he was not the kind of man who gave in to such weakness.

Amelia sat on the floor of the cave, fighting against an overwhelming sense of defeat. No matter how hard she tugged and wrenched at the thin ropes binding her wrists, she could not free herself. She was trapped like a helpless fawn in a wolf's den, and soon her captor would return and do what he'd wanted to do to her all along, since the moment he'd crept into her fiancé's bedchamber.

Then suddenly Duncan was there before her, kneeling down, pulling a knife from his boot. Terror exploded inside her.

"*Please,*" she said, tugging harder and more desperately

at the bonds. "If you possess the smallest shred of humanity, you will let me go. You must."

He raised the knife in the dim light, and just when she thought he was going to cut her throat, he sliced through her bonds instead. They dropped lightly to the ground.

"You're a fighter, aren't you?" He took both her hands in his and held them up to inspect the undersides of her wrists. "I admire your tenacity, but look what you've done to yourself."

A thin trail of blood was dripping down her arm. He reached for a cloth, dipped it into the pot of water that hung on a hook over the unlit fire, and touched it to her wrists. Gently he washed the blood away.

"Are you going to kill me?" she asked, glancing uneasily at the sword he carried. "Because if I am to be put to death, I wish to know."

He remained focused on what he was doing. "I'm not going to kill you."

She was grateful for the information, certainly, but was still a far cry from feeling reassured.

"What about the other Highlander?" she asked. "He doesn't seem to like me very much." She glanced toward the mouth of the cave.

"You're right. He detests the very ground you walk on." The Butcher folded the cloth and continued to wipe her forearm with the cleaner side of it.

"Why? Because I am English? Or is it because I am engaged to Colonel Bennett?"

Duncan paused. "I reckon both those things make him want to murder you where you stand."

The cloth touched a tender spot, and Amelia snapped her hand back.

Duncan looked at her intently, and somehow without a single word he persuaded her with his eyes to endure the discomfort without complaint. She found herself responding, as if she were being lured into obedience.

"Why do you both hate my fiancé so much?" she asked, striving to keep her mind sharp and clear while she offered her hand to Duncan again. She watched the water run in shiny rivulets over her raw, chafed flesh and focused on the movements of his hands. "What did he ever do to you, besides fight for our King in this war?"

Duncan's eyes flashed up. "*Our* King? Are you referring to the wee German laddie who sits on your throne like a puppet to parliament and speaks French?"

"He is the rightful King of Great Britain," she argued. "Which—in case you are not aware—according to the Act of Union, includes Scotland. But that is beside the point. It is my betrothed who is your target. Why?"

"It's not a topic I mean to discuss with you."

"Why not?"

"Because I doubt it's something you'd want to hear."

She shifted on her knees. "Why wouldn't I? It's the reason you took me prisoner."

The Butcher's eyes lifted, and he studied her carefully. "Aye, but are you sure you want to know *everything* about your fiancé? It might change how you feel about him. All your romantic dreams of your handsome Prince Charming on a fine white stallion would be crushed. Then what would you do? You wouldn't know east from west."

"Of course I am sure," she replied, refusing to be daunted by his patronizing tone. "Besides, there is nothing you can say that will change how I feel, because I know in my heart that Richard is a brave and noble soldier in this war. It is unfortunate that he is your enemy, but he does his duty for his country—that is all."

Duncan finished tending her wounds, balled up the cloth, and tossed it into the pot. "All right, then. I'll tell you the reason why you're here, though I cannot give you all the particulars, because it's best if you don't know the identities of the people involved. But what you need to know is this: Your betrothed is a tyrant, a rapist, and a murderer of innocent women and children. He'd burn every peaceful homestead in Scotland if he could."

She sat back and scoffed. "That is ridiculous. You are obviously mistaken."

"Nay, I am not." The Butcher rose to his feet and crossed to the other side of the cave where the food was stored. He seemed to be evaluating her expression in the dim light.

Amelia shook her head. "Yes, you are. I *know* Richard. He is a good man and an honorable soldier. He served under my father, who was also a good man and an excellent judge of character. He would never have given our engagement his blessing if Richard were unscrupulous. My father loved me and cared for me very much. He wanted me to be safe and happy. That's all he ever wanted, so you are wrong."

He had to be.

"I am not wrong."

"Yes, you are." She watched him tear off a hunk of bread from a loaf he withdrew from a basket. He crossed the cave and held it out to her.

"And you are a fine one to accuse another man of being a tyrant and a murderer," she said, accepting the bread. "You are the Butcher of the Highlands. Your acts of brutality are legendary, and I've seen them with my own eyes. Not only did you kidnap me, but you killed Lord knows how many soldiers on the way into my bedchamber, and you fully intended to chop off Richard's head once you got there. So I will not hear any more of this fictitious talk. You will not convince me that he is a tyrant when clearly I am looking at the very essence of tyranny, right here."

She stuffed the bread into her mouth and only then realized, with some anxiety, how boldly she had just spoken to the infamous Butcher.

He watched her chew and swallow, then turned in silence to the basket of food. He tore off another hunk of bread.

For a long time he said nothing, and she was uncomfortably aware of the massive broadsword at his side and the inconceivable strength in those muscular arms and shoulders.

Despite the fact that he was her enemy, she could not fail to acknowledge the inarguable truth that he was a magnificent specimen of manhood, a born warrior. In the field, she had been completely incapacitated by him, while he had seemed almost *pleased* with her efforts to fight him. That was probably what had prompted her to surrender.

But when he'd washed the blood off her arm just now, he'd shown that he was at least capable of some kindness.

"Get up," he said, with his back to her. "I'm in need of sleep."

"And what will you do with me while you are sleeping?" she asked. "Will you tie me up again? What if the other Highlander returns?"

She glanced uneasily at the cave entrance, which had grown bright with a shimmering morning mist, while the Butcher moved deeper into the den toward a bed of fur at the back.

"You'll be lying beside me, lass, nice and close."

Amelia tensed immediately. "I will not."

"You have no choice in the matter." He removed his leather scabbard and sword and placed it—along with the pistol—on the ground next to the fur. "Come to bed."

Come to bed?

"I am a virgin," she blurted out in a rush. "I do not

know if that means anything to you, it probably doesn't, but I would like to remain so."

He regarded her with displeasure. "You're saving yourself for Bennett?"

She wished there were another way to answer the question—a way that would not stoke the fires of his vengeance—but there was not. "Yes, I wish to save myself for marriage."

His eyes turned toward the light outside the cave, as if he was carefully contemplating her reply.

"If you leave me with my virtue," she added, "I promise I will . . ." She was not quite sure what to offer in return for such an act of kindness on his part. "I will give you five hundred pounds. Or rather, my uncle will."

Surely her guardian would honor that settlement.

The Butcher's eyes narrowed. "Save your negotiating. I've already decided to ask for much more than that."

She was pleased at least to be getting somewhere, to be speaking of practicalities regarding her release. "So it's ransom you want, then? In cash? Or land? Do you want a title? Because I am not sure my uncle has the power to grant that, but he could certainly—"

"I want no land, lass, nor do I seek a title."

"Then what *do* you want?"

The silence grew sharp and edgy while he stood in the gray hue of the morning light. "I want your betrothed to come and fetch you."

"So that you can kill him."

"Aye, but it'll be a fair fight. I'll let him defend himself before I cut him in half. Now, get up and come to me." He sat down on the fur with his back to the wall. "It's been a long night and I'm weary of talk. I want your warm body next to me, to ward off the chill in my bones."

She stood and approached him. "Are you not worried

that I might slip your dagger from your boot and slit *your* throat the moment you fall asleep?"

The corner of his mouth curled up slightly, as if he were amused by the notion. "I'll wrap my arms around you, nice and tight, and keep you very close—so if you move so much as a hair on that pretty head of yours, I'll feel it." He grinned. "I'll feel it right here, under my kilt."

She glanced around the cave and wished there were a way she could somehow avoid lying next to him—because she knew very well what he kept hidden under that kilt—but resigned herself to the fact that such hopes were futile. She had no choice but to surrender to the inevitable. She would have to lie next to him and try to sleep, for however long she could.

She sank to her knees, then stretched out on the soft fur. He lounged behind her with his back to the wall and wrapped his arms around her waist.

Her heart began to pound faster at the intimacy of their position as he pulled her close. She'd never lain in bed with a man before, not even Richard. He was too much of a gentleman to suggest any such thing before marriage. But here she lay this morning, with a huge Highlander pressed up against her backside.

He nuzzled her hair with his nose, and his touch sent tingles of awareness up and down her arms and legs.

"You're trembling," he said.

"I cannot help it. I'm cold."

But it was so much more than that. He was sexually bold. Decency and decorum meant nothing to him, and every move he made caused her to lose her breath. It all seemed carnal and primitive, beyond anything she'd ever imagined would happen to her in her proper, civilized life.

She realized suddenly that nothing in that life would ever be the same again. Not after this.

He inched forward, nestling his hips closer. Her heart quickened.

"You'll warm up soon enough," he said. "And you can stop your shivering. I'll not be groping you this morning, lass. I told you I was weary."

She tried to relax, but her body would not stop shaking. "I suppose I should thank you. . . ."

"*Thank* me," he said with surprise, lifting his head.

"Yes. For not depriving me of my virtue. I am grateful for that at least. Thank you."

He chuckled and tucked his knees into the backs of hers, then nuzzled the side of her head again.

"You shouldn't be too quick to thank me, lass," he said in a voice that grew quieter as he began to drift off. "Because I never promised you *that*."

Chapter Four

Sleep proved impossible for Amelia. The Butcher, however, slipped effortlessly into a quiet and restful slumber.

Clearly, the man's conscience was clear. He was not fretting about the men he had killed during the night, or the fact that he had kidnapped the fiancée of a prominent English military officer, who was likely hunting him down like a dog at this very moment. He was not the least bit concerned that she might outwit him and escape while he slept. No, the Butcher rested peacefully, serene and tranquil in his hidden lair, confident that his terrified prisoner would not rise up in a panic and stab him in the back if he inadvertently let go of her for even the smallest fraction of a second.

It was unlikely to happen, of course. He would indeed feel the slightest move on her part, for his arms were locked about her waist, pinning her against him. The mere sound of his breathing—so close, so steady and deep, like waves in the ocean—kept her riveted and still, for fear of waking him.

Silently, without moving a muscle, she let her gaze wander about the dimly lit cave, looking for something she could use as a weapon if an opportunity presented itself. She saw only the unlit fire and cast-iron pot, the basket of bread, some blankets, and his axe and broadsword, not far from where they lay.

Carefully she reached out to touch the axe, mostly out of curiosity, but felt the immediate, subtle pull of her captor's body. His hips pushed forward, and she froze, controlling her breathing, for he might not be so weary after a brief nap. He might decide he did have the strength, after all, to do more than just lie beside her. He might choose to help himself to her virtue and do all the wicked, lusty things he had talked about on the horse.

Her stomach flipped over suddenly at the memory of that conversation. She could not seem to purge it from her mind.

If only she could sleep. She would need her wits about her in the coming days and could not afford to be sluggish of mind.

A sudden *thump* outside the cave entrance caused her to jump. Her heart beat in her chest like some wild, fluttering creature as she stared wide-eyed into the mist for the other Highlander, who wanted to hack her to pieces and was probably coming to do it now.

But it was only the Butcher's big black horse, wandering freely outside the cave, his head bowed down to the ground as he tore at the grass with his teeth. Listening to the sound of the animal crunching, she let out an anxious breath and felt her captor snuggle closer, as if he sensed her unease and was urging her to relax.

A full hour must have passed while she lay staring with bloodshot eyes at the light outside. Then suddenly the Butcher stirred and drew in a deep breath.

"Ah, that's better," he groaned, tucking his knees up behind hers. "I feel good. Did you sleep, lass?"

"No," she curtly said, feeling the stiffness of his arousal.

He leaned up on an elbow. "Why not? Was the bed not

soft enough?" He paused and leaned closer, looking at her carefully. "How old are you, lass?"

"I am two-and-twenty. Not that it's any of your concern."

He ran his big hand over the curve of her hip and thigh, and she felt a strange, disturbing tension in her belly. "A grown woman, then. Worldly and experienced . . ."

She swallowed anxiously. "A grown woman, yes. And experienced enough to know a gentleman from a savage."

"Then you do not need any lessons from me about the difference between the two?"

"I certainly do not."

The Butcher paused, looking down at her legs while he gathered the heavy fabric of her skirts in his fist. Inching them up, little by little, until her bare calves were exposed to the knees, he said in a low, husky whisper, "That's too bad, lassie, because I'm an excellent teacher. And you smell very nice."

"Do I?" She voiced the reply in a blasé tone, despite the fact that her chest felt like it might explode.

Slowly, he nuzzled her shoulder with his chin, as if he was studying her response to his touch.

Amelia lay very still, resting her cheek on her hands, struggling impossibly to behave as if this were nothing to her. She would not react to his overtures, nor show fear or slap his hands away, for that might only provoke him. With any luck, a façade of boredom and indifference might douse the fires of his current inclinations—whatever they were.

"Aye, fresh as a spring daisy," he said. "*Very* tempting in the morning."

He continued to stroke her shoulder with his chin while her heart raced like a hunted fox.

"You, on the other hand, are *not* tempting in the least," she said. "Quite the opposite, in fact."

"Is it because of how we met? Without a proper introduction?"

She turned over to glare up at him. "You came to kill my betrothed, and you almost chopped off my head."

He let out a breath. "I knew I should have worn the silk jacket. Now I've spoiled everything."

Good Lord! Was he making fun of her? Or was he deranged?

"Get up," he said, vaulting lightly over her body, rising to his feet, and belting his scabbard around his waist.

Amelia leaned up on both elbows. "Why?"

She watched him pick up the axe and walk to the cave entrance, where he put two fingers to his lips and whistled. He then faced her—a godlike silhouette against the shifting mist, his kilt and hair wavering lightly in the breeze. "Because I intend to follow through with my devious and wily plot, of course."

"Will you send word to the fort that you are holding me captive?" she asked, still unsure what to make of him when he spoke like that.

He bent forward, picked up his saddlebags, stalked back into the cave, and began packing food. "Not yet. I want Bennett to worry about you for a few days."

A few days . . . Amelia examined the wounds at her wrists and remembered her frantic need to escape when she first set foot in this cave. She'd been the Butcher's prisoner for less than six hours and felt as if she'd skirted death and disaster at every turn. How would she continue to survive for another few days—and nights, too?

"What makes you think the full force of the English army isn't already searching for me?" she challenged. "How do you know Richard hasn't uncovered your tracks or learned of this hiding place? He has reason to interrogate people now. Surely someone will know this den exists."

"That's why we're leaving."

"Where will we go?"

"Further north. Higher into the mountains."

She glanced past him to the mouth of the cave again. "Will your friends be joining us?"

"They'll be close by," he answered, "but we won't travel together. That would make us too easy to track."

Just then, the two Highlanders they'd met in the rainy field entered the cave. The Butcher tossed a blanket to the tall red-haired one with the beard and freckled skin. "We're leaving," he said. "Pack everything. We'll meet at Glen Elchaig at dusk."

The Highlander began to roll up the blanket, his green eyes intense as he scrutinized Amelia. "Is she coming with us?"

"Aye."

He nodded at her. "I'm Gawyn." He gestured toward the other Highlander. "And the ugly one is Fergus."

Fergus belched and flashed a crooked, disquieting grin, which made her shrink back. "He's just jealous of my sensual appeal."

Deeply unsettled and striving to keep up her guard, Amelia rose to her feet and watched the rebels clear the supplies out of the den. They moved swiftly and efficiently while she stood back against the cold cave wall, keeping quiet, striving to avoid their attentions.

The Butcher tossed his saddlebags over his shoulder, then approached. "Time to go." He grabbed her by the elbow and led her out of the cave.

Scurrying to keep up, Amelia breathed in the briny scent of the fog as they emerged into the morning light. The mist shifted and rolled across the rocky hilltops, and she felt its chill upon her skin.

The Butcher saddled his horse while the other two Highlanders stuffed supplies into sacks and saddle pouches.

Amelia studied the craggy landscape, searching for some sign of the fair-haired one named Angus, but he seemed to have vanished into the mist. They were a dubious and shifty lot, these Highland rebels.

"You'll need to relieve yourself before we go," the Butcher said. "There's a rock there, and don't get any ideas about running off." He pointed toward a huge boulder, then turned away.

This is a nightmare, Amelia thought. *If only I could wake.*

A few minutes later, she finished her morning affairs and returned to where the others were waiting.

"Do I need to bind your wrists for the ride?" Her captor looked at her with challenge as he drove a musket into the saddle scabbard.

She touched the chafe marks on her wrists, still painful and raw, and shook her head. "No."

"You get one chance to earn my trust," he told her, "and if you disappoint me, I'll keep you bound and gagged until I kill your beloved, which could be some time from now, considering where we're headed."

She glanced up at the mountaintops and shivered. "I won't try to escape. You have my word."

"But can you trust the word of the English?" Fergus asked, swinging himself up onto the back of his horse and adjusting the powder horn he carried at his side.

"I could say the same about you Scottish rebels," Amelia tersely replied.

"Easy now," the Butcher warned in her ear, sounding almost amused. "You don't want to get into a political debate with Fergus. He'll wipe the ground with you."

Duncan wrapped his big hands around her waist, but Amelia slapped them away. "I know how to mount a horse," she said. "You don't have to toss me up like a child every time."

He backed away in mock surrender.

As soon as he gave her enough space, she placed her foot in the stirrup and mounted. The Butcher slung his shield across his back, then swung up behind her.

"I thought proper English ladies only rode sidesaddle," he said quietly, "because they like to keep their legs squeezed together, nice and tight."

Why did he constantly feel inclined to say such vulgar things to her? And why did he always have to breathe every word into her ear as if it were an intimate secret between lovers?

"As you know," she said, "my father was a colonel in the army. He might have enjoyed a son if he'd had one. Since he didn't, I was fortunate enough to be awarded the opportunity to play 'Dragoons' when I was very young, much to my mother's chagrin."

"He taught you to ride like a soldier?"

"Among other things."

"I'll keep that in mind."

He turned the horse in the opposite direction from which they had come, while Fergus and Gawyn made haste toward the east, choosing a different route to Glen Elchaig. She was not sorry to see them go, for she knew less of them than she did about the Butcher, who—to her great astonishment—had not yet harmed her, despite ample opportunity. The others she was not so sure of.

Then she looked up and saw Angus on his pale gray horse, watching them from the edge of a blunt outcropping. He wore his tartan like a hood over his head, and the ends of his long golden hair rippled like weightless ribbons in the breeze.

"There's your friend," she said suspiciously.

"Aye."

She watched Angus until he turned his horse in the other direction, disappearing over the ridge. She had the distinct impression he would not be far, however. For the duration of this journey, he would always be in the vicinity, watching from the mist, sending daggers of malice in her direction. She only hoped he was not waiting for the right moment to ride in and strangle the life out of her when the Butcher was not looking.

They rode in silence for a time, and she grew sleepy as the horse plodded along and rocked her back and forth in the saddle. Her head fell forward and she snapped it back up, shaking herself awake and fighting the urge to sleep, until the Butcher covered her forehead with his palm. It was surprisingly warm against her skin.

"Lay your head on my shoulder," he said.

She wanted to resist but was almost dizzy from lack of sleep and decided it would be best to comply, for she could not be much good to herself in such a state of fatigue.

The next thing she knew, she was dreaming about a ballroom, filled with orchestral music and swirling candlelight as she danced across the floor. The room was rich with the scent of roses and perfume. She wore powder in her hair, but her lips were painted a garish shade of red, and she winced at the blisters on her feet, which burned like hot pokers inside her tight shoes as she danced one minuet after another.

Then suddenly she was flying through the sky like a bird, over the mountains and into the clouds. Was this death? Or heaven?

She jerked awake. Heart pounding, not knowing where she was, she sat forward and grabbed onto the strong, steady arms that kept her from toppling off the horse.

The gentle thud of hoofbeats on the path brought her back to reality. She took in the unfamiliar surroundings—the canopy of branches and leaves overhead and the bright sky beyond. They were in the forest now, trudging over the soft, mossy earth. A flock of warblers chirped noisily in the treetops. "How long was I asleep?"

"Over an hour," the Butcher replied.

"An hour? Surely not."

"Aye. You were moaning my name and saying, '*Oh, yes, Duncan, yes, yes. Again, again . . .*'"

Amelia frowned over her shoulder. "You lie. I would never say that, and I barely know your name. You're just the Butcher to me."

"But you learned my name this morning, remember?"

"Of course I remember, but I wouldn't have said it in my sleep, unless it was to say farewell before I shot you dead with that pistol in your belt."

He chuckled, his body swaying back and forth with the easy movements of the horse. "You win, lassie. I confess. You weren't sighing my name. You were as quiet as the grave, sleeping like a corpse."

"What a lovely image." She hoped it was not a sign of things to come.

They rode in silence for a short while.

"Where are we?" she asked. "How much further?" They had not yet eaten, and her belly was grumbling.

"We're halfway there, but we'll stop soon to rest and eat."

"You have food?" Her mouth began to water.

"Aye. I can hardly let you starve."

"Well, thank you, I suppose."

"Don't be thanking me, lass. I only want to keep you alive because you're my bait."

They ducked their heads to pass through a dense thicket. Twigs and sticks snapped under the horse's heavy hooves, and the Butcher used his arms to shield Amelia's face and push back the branches.

"Will you answer a question for me, lassie?" he said as they emerged into a clearing.

"I suppose."

"How long have you known your fiancé?"

She breathed deeply, thinking back to those dreamy and idyllic days, so unlike what she was living now. "I met him a year ago in July, at a ball in London. He was serving under my father and they had both come home on leave. They couldn't linger long, however, because of the rebellion here in Scotland. All the troops had to return to their posts."

"So it's Scotland's fault your courtship was cut short?"

"In a manner of speaking, yes."

"Perhaps if you'd spent more time with your beloved, you wouldn't be marrying him."

Amelia turned slightly in the saddle to speak over her shoulder. "Let me make it clear to you, sir—I spent more than enough time with Richard Bennett, and I know exactly what I am doing. It is *you* who are ignorant of the man you deem your enemy, for he is a great war hero. He saved my father's life in battle, and were it not for the mortal wound he suffered in the spring, because he was shot by a Jacobite rebel like you . . ." She stopped for a moment, unable to go on. "For all I know, maybe it *was* you who killed him."

Duncan spoke with anger. "No, lass. I assure you it wasn't."

The vehemence of his denial was more than enough to convince her, so she let the matter drop. "At least he had one final, happy Christmas at home," she added, "knowing that I would be taken care of—that Richard would protect me."

She fully expected the Butcher to again point out that Richard had failed in the task of protecting her, but he said something else entirely.

"You were fortunate to have such a man as your father."

She turned quickly in the saddle. "Why would you say that? Had you ever met him?"

She couldn't explain it, but she felt an almost desperate need for some connection or link between this brutal savage and her father. She wanted to feel that her father was here with her, in some shape or form, wielding even the smallest influence over her captor.

But there was nothing extraordinary in the Butcher's expression. He remained cool and impassive. "I told you I fought at Sheriffmuir, so I know your father was a brilliant soldier and an honorable leader of men. It was a fair fight, despite the outcome that did not favor us." He paused, and his voice grew more serene. "I also know that after he recovered from his wounds, after the Christmas he spent with you, he returned to his post and tried to negotiate with the Scottish nobles in order to give them a second chance to accept the Union and agree to peace."

Her brow pulled together in surprise. "You know of his meetings and negotiations with the Earl of Moncrieffe?"

"Aye."

"How would you know about that?"

He laughed at her. "Highlanders talk to each other, lass, and so do the clans. We don't *all* live in caves, and we're not all illiterate brutes."

She faced forward in the saddle again. "No, of course not. My father spoke very highly of the Earl of Moncrieffe, who was a Highlander, like you. He said he was a passionate collector of Italian art, and described him as a harsh but fair man. He said his home was like a palace." She turned in the saddle again. "Have *you* ever met the earl?"

"Aye," the Butcher replied. "But things aren't as simple as you think. Here in Scotland, nothing is black and white. Your father might have judged the earl to be fair and civilized—a *gentleman,* according to your lofty definitions—but because he negotiates with the English and keeps his garden clipped and manicured like a puffed-up English estate, he has his share of enemies. Many Scots—the ones who want to fight for a Stuart king—view him as a coward and a traitor. They believe he only seeks to increase his landholdings, and there is likely some truth in that."

"What do *you* believe?"

He was quiet for a moment. "I believe every man has his reasons for doing what he does, for choosing one path, and not another. And no one can know what truly lives in another man's heart. You can judge him all you want from afar, but you'll never know why he does what he does, unless he trusts you enough to let you know it."

"So you don't think Moncrieffe is a traitor to Scotland? You think he has valid reasons to negotiate with the English?"

"I did not say that."

"So you don't really know the earl. Not like that."

He said nothing for a long time while the horse plodded through the clearing. "I don't think anyone really knows him."

And does anyone really know you? she wondered suddenly.

"Let's rest for a bit," he said.

They reached a shallow burn, and the Butcher steered his horse to where the water ran fast and clear. He waited until Turner finished drinking before he dismounted, then held his arms out to Amelia. She hesitated before accepting his assistance.

"Don't be stubborn, lass."

"I am not being stubborn."

"Then put your hands on me. I won't eat you alive, nor will I be overcome by my savage desire to deflower you."

Reluctantly, she laid her hands on the tops of his broad shoulders and slid smoothly down the solid mass of his body until her feet touched the ground. She stood for a few seconds, looking up at his face—all sharp planes and perfect angles. His lips were full and soft, and his eyes glimmered with unusual flecks of silver she hadn't noticed before.

"I don't suppose you ever rode astride with your beloved?" Duncan asked, his hands still resting on her hips.

She took a hasty step back, unnerved by his flirtatious tone. "Of course not. As I said, Richard is a gentleman. He would never suggest such a thing." She watched the Butcher tug the saddlebags from the back of the horse. "I wish you would believe me about that."

He pulled a jug of wine and some bread from the leather bag and sat down on a fallen log next to a weeping willow. "At least you're loyal."

"I have good reason to be, and I'll not stop working to convince you of that."

Her captor used his teeth to pull the cork out of the jug, then turned his head to the side and spit it out. "So that I'll let you go?"

"So that you will stop hunting Richard," she clarified, watching him drink. "He is a good man, Duncan. He saved my father's life."

It was the first time she'd used the Butcher's given name, and it did not go unnoticed. Something flickered in his eyes, and he frowned. "This discussion is beginning to grate on my nerves."

He tipped the jug of wine back and guzzled deeply, then wiped the back of his hand over his mouth. His expression burned with something wild and angry as he held the wine out for her to take. He stared at her, waiting.

After a moment, she reached for the jug. The stoneware was cold in her hands. She meant to take only a small sip, but when the full-bodied Scottish wine flowed over her lips and tongue she realized just how terribly thirsty she was and gave in to gulping and guzzling, just as he had done.

Never in her life had she drank anything so crudely from a bottle, but good manners had no place here, she supposed. Not with this man, who sat on a felled tree in a forest, looking like he wanted to either strangle her or wrestle her to the ground and have his way with her.

"Before I'm done with you," he said with grim resolve, "I'll make you see that your English officers in their fancy red coats can be just as savage as any Scot in a kilt."

She was taken aback, shaken by such an image, but the sound of approaching hooves interrupted any further discussion. She lowered the jug and spotted Gawyn and Fergus galloping across the glade toward them.

The Butcher stood, seized the wine from her hands, and walked toward them. "I thought you'd never get here," he said broodingly. "I need to take a piss."

With that, he shouldered past her, heading toward a dense grove of conifers.

"What do you want us to do with her?" Fergus shouted after him.

"I'm sure you'll figure something out," the Butcher replied, not bothering to look back before he disappeared into the curtain of branches.

Fergus leaped off his horse and smiled crookedly. Gawyn dismounted and stood behind her. She felt completely surrounded.

Suddenly it was quiet. *Too* quiet. Even the leaves in the trees seemed to be holding their collective breaths.

Wishing the Butcher had not chosen this, of all moments, to leave her alone, she turned to face the others. And then, as if matters weren't already unpleasant enough, Angus came thundering out of the bush at a full gallop. He swung himself to the ground, quickly recovering from the momentum of his charge with a few heavy, pounding footsteps across the grass, which brought him face-to-face with Amelia.

Hands clenched into fists at her sides, she did her best to be brave while the three fierce Highlanders surrounded her. It was not an easy task, however, when two of them looked like they wanted to eat her alive and the third looked ready to slice her in half.

Chapter Five

Duncan sat down on a boulder at the water's edge, took another sip of wine, then leaned forward to rest his elbows on his knees. Head bowed down, he wished there were enough booze left in the jug to get thoroughly soused, but even if there were, it would do him no good. There was no escaping what plagued him.

He'd thought it would all be over by now and that today he would return to that quietness he'd once known, before this war began. It was an internal calm he had taken for granted and perhaps never fully appreciated.

But life didn't always proceed according to plan, he had discovered. If it did, he would not be sitting on this cold rock with a half-empty jug of wine in his hand, his hair hanging loose in his face, while he struggled over what to do with a stubborn and impossibly beautiful woman who was devoted to his mortal enemy.

No, not just devoted. She was in love with him.

God, how he hated her for defending that monster. Yet when he woke up in the cave that morning, his desire for her was considerable, and for the second time he had had to crush the urge to flip her over onto her back and simply take her. He'd wanted to bury himself in her depths and prove that she was no longer his enemy's property. She was his now, because he had stolen her away.

But that violent need to conquer and possess was more than a little disturbing to him—for his contempt of men who used such force upon women was the very reason he was hunting Richard Bennett in the first place.

Duncan took another swig of the wine and watched the water flow cleanly around the rocks in the stream.

Perhaps this vile hurricane of wrath inside him was a fate he would never escape. He was, after all, the bastard son of a whore, and his father had been a cruel brute. Fierce passions and uncontrollable vengeance ran in his blood.

He had never questioned it before, but everything was more complicated today—because he had never had such trouble resisting a woman. Most Scottish lassies were fair game, and if anything, he was the one fighting *them* off. But this haughty, infuriating Englishwoman who despised him—and rightly so—reminded him that he was a man with hearty sexual desires. Politics and vengeance had nothing to do with it.

At least the others had arrived in time just now; otherwise he might not be sitting here sipping wine and watching the water flow. He might instead be back in the clearing, shaking some sense into the lady, spelling out, word for word, the gruesome details about her precious beloved. Giving her a lesson or two about villains and heroes.

He tipped the jug back and drank thirstily, then rubbed the heel of his hand in small circles over his chest to ease the ache that had suddenly lodged itself there.

He wondered if Bennett knew how lucky he was, to have the affections of a woman such as Lady Amelia. Not that he deserved her love, or *any* woman's love, for that matter. What he deserved was to have his fiancée ripped out of his world, severed from his life, quickly and harshly, without warning or any chance of restoration.

An eye for an eye.

Duncan lifted his head, accepted the heavy descent of his foul mood like a pounding hammer in his brain, and took another swig of wine.

Amelia wanted to run but felt as if her muscles had turned to stone. She was so terrified, she couldn't move or speak or breathe.

Angus, the blond one, stood in front of her, feet braced apart, his face a mere inch from hers—so close, she could feel the rapid beat of his breath on her cheeks. A sudden breeze gusted across the treetops and swirled around the glade, and her heart drummed against her rib cage.

Ridiculously, she said a silent prayer that the Butcher would return and stand between her and these three wild Highlanders. *Please, God . . .*

But God was not listening.

Angus tilted his head to the side and inhaled the scent of her skin, then let his dangerous gaze rake over her body. It was a deliberate attempt to intimidate her. She recognized it, and it worked—there was no doubt about that—but it also ignited her anger.

She had done nothing to this man, or to any of these rebels. She was an innocent victim in all of this, and she despised what they stood for. She loathed their foul, violent ways and their sick infatuation with bloodshed and brutality. No wonder England felt such a necessity to crush this Scottish rebellion.

"You won't kill me," she said, speaking the words clearly, in an effort to feel more confident.

"Are you sure?" he replied. His voice was unexpectedly soft and whispery.

"Yes, because you need me," she said. "I am your bait. Duncan said so."

Angus grinned with sinister intent. "Aye, that's because

he means to use you to settle a score." He glared at the other two, who had been watching the exchange with some concern, then slowly backed away.

Palming the hilt of his broadsword, he stalked off in the other direction. His horse followed, trotting obediently behind. When Angus reached the edge of the clearing he withdrew some food from his saddlebags, sat down on the ground, and leaned back against the gnarled trunk of a chestnut tree to eat alone.

"Are you hungry, Lady Amelia?" Gawyn asked.

She was oddly startled by the politeness of his address. "Yes, I am."

"Then you should eat." Fergus went to his horse and retrieved his own sack of supplies. "We don't have much— just a few biscuits and cheese—but it'll fill the hole in your belly until Gawyn can prepare a proper hot meal for you."

"A proper hot meal," she repeated. "I confess I am partial to the sound of that." Though she wasn't quite sure what it would entail, or if there would even be utensils. She imagined herself squatting by a fire, chewing flesh off the thighbone of something.

"Come and sit yourself down," Gawyn said, unfurling a tartan blanket and spreading it out on the grass. He offered her some dry-looking biscuits while Fergus poured wine into a pewter cup and passed it to her.

"Thank you."

They ate the biscuits in silence. Amelia watched the men uneasily, and they did the same to her, glancing frequently at her, then looking away. To avoid making any further clumsy eye contact, she let her eyes wander in all directions around the glade, wishing she knew the location of this place. She still clung to the hope that Richard was searching for her, or that she might still be able to escape when her captors were distracted, but where would she go? She could die out here in this deep wilderness.

She could starve or be gobbled up by a wolf, or be mauled by a wild boar.

Just then, out of the blue, Gawyn asked her a personal question. "So you were planning to get married, right inside the fort?" He studied her with a furrowed brow. "Your father's been dead only a month, lassie. Did you not think you should mourn him properly before you made such an important vow?"

Taken aback, Amelia reached for another biscuit. "You know when my father died?"

"Aye. Angus told us who he was, and your father was well known among the clans."

She sighed and returned to his original question. "Contrary to what you must think of me for behaving in such a way, I *did* think about my haste to marry. And I am still not certain it was the right thing to do, to dash off to Scotland so quickly after I buried my father. But something drove me here. My father had given us his blessing, and I believed it was what he would have wanted—for me to be safe and cared for. He didn't want me to be alone."

"But you had your uncle as your guardian," Gawyn reminded her. "And surely you have other folk you can call family. Do you not have any sisters or brothers, lassie? Or cousins?"

Hearing what sounded like pity in his voice, she glanced from one to the other, then turned her gaze across the clearing toward Angus, who still watched her like a starving animal. "I was an only child," she said, "so I have no brothers or sisters. I do have cousins who were willing to take me in, but I was never close to them, and I didn't want to be away from my fiancé."

She was quite certain Angus couldn't possibly hear what she was saying, yet he seemed to be listening from the other side of the glade, with a menacing scowl on his face.

Gawyn, who sat cross-legged, rested his elbows on his knees and his chin on his hands. "Aye, I know what you're saying, lass. True love can be a powerful thing."

Fergus shoved him over onto his side. "What the fook is wrong with you? She's talking about Colonel Bennett, you silly arse."

Gawyn righted himself. "I know that, Fergus, but love is blind. You know it as well as I do."

"I'm not blind," she told them. "I realize that my fiancé is your enemy, but as I told Duncan, this is war. Colonel Bennett is a soldier and has a duty to fulfill to the King. Besides, the two of you can hardly point fingers at him when you are known as the Butcher's untouchable rebels and you slaughter every helpless English soldier who crosses your path."

"Is that what they're saying?" Gawyn asked. "That we're untouchable?"

She glanced from one keen young Scot to the other and began to rethink her initial impressions about their savagery until a quick glimpse across the glade at the other one reminded her not to get too comfortable or take anything for granted.

"Why does he hate me so much?" she asked, still watching Angus.

"It's not *you* he hates," Fergus explained. "It's your betrothed."

"But his hatred spills over onto her," Gawyn clarified, turning his mossy green eyes in her direction. "He thinks Duncan shouldn't have let you live."

"I gathered as much."

"Don't get me wrong; he does hate you," Fergus said flatly, popping a biscuit into his mouth. "But who can blame him? Your fiancé raped and killed his sister."

All at once, the clearing seemed to spin in circles before

Amelia's eyes as she swallowed the breezy delivery of Fergus's remark like a jagged stone in her throat. "I beg your pardon?"

"Then he cut off her head," Gawyn added with an equal measure of nonchalance as he crunched down on his biscuit.

Speechless for a moment and shocked to the point of nausea, Amelia fought to form words. "You cannot be serious. I don't know what gossip you've heard, or what the Butcher has told you, but that cannot be true. If such a thing happened, my fiancé could not have been involved. You must have him confused with someone else."

Her Richard? Good Lord! He would never do such a thing. Not in a hundred years. They *must* be mistaken. They *had* to be.

The branches on the trees flapped and fluttered, and Duncan emerged. She turned to look up at him. His eyes were dark and grim.

"Pack up," he said to Fergus and Gawyn. "It's time to go."

Rising to their feet, they stuffed the food into the saddlebags and fled to their horses.

"Is this true?" Amelia asked, rising to her feet as well. "Is that why you are so determined to kill Richard? Because you believe he killed your friend's sister? And . . . and *violated* her?"

The last part was difficult to say.

"Aye, it's true." Duncan lowered his voice. "And those two talk too much."

Shock and disbelief coursed through her. She didn't want to believe what they were saying—they were her enemies—yet a part of her could not ignore the intensity of their hatred. Such an obsession with vengeance upon a single man had to be based on something.

"But how can you be sure it was Richard?" she asked, still clinging to the hope that it was a mistake or a simple misunderstanding. "Were you there? Because I find it very difficult to believe that he would allow such a thing to occur."

"It happened." He strode toward his horse.

"But were you there?"

"Nay."

Amelia scurried to keep up. "Then how do you know what happened, exactly? Maybe Richard tried to stop it. Or perhaps he was not aware that it was happening until it was too late. Did Angus witness it?"

"Of course not. If he'd been there, your beloved would already be dead." Duncan stuffed the empty wine jug into a saddlebag.

"Then how do you really know?" she demanded again, because she could not bring herself to believe it. She did not *want* to believe it. Every instinct and need inside her was urging her to deny it, because if it was true, she would never again trust the capacities of her own judgment—and she would doubt her father's as well, which would be heartbreaking, because she cherished his memory. He was her hero. He could not have been wrong about the gallant officer he encouraged her to marry. Her father was a decent man, and she had always trusted him with her happiness. He would never have promised her to a monster. Would he?

"Because you seem very sure of yourself," she said to Duncan shakily.

He paused and stared at her for a long, tension-filled moment until the impatience in his eyes slowly faded into something else—something reluctant and melancholy.

"I saw her head in a box," he said. "And there was a note, describing what happened, and why."

Feeling sick and dizzy, Amelia placed her hand on her stomach. "And what was the reason? I must know."

He lowered his eyes and gripped the hilt of his sword.

"I'm going to satisfy your curiosity, lass, only because I'm sure that once you hear the truth, you'll learn to hold your tongue and keep quiet—especially in front of Angus."

She waited, breath held, for Duncan's next words.

"Muira's death was a punishment meant for Angus's father, who is a powerful clan chief, a celebrated warlord, and a persistent, outspoken Jacobite. He was the one who raised the army that fought at Sherrifmuir, and he was also the one who shot your father down on the battlefield."

Amelia flinched. She had nothing to do with any of this—she hated war and killing—yet she was caught up in this tangled and dirty web of vengeance, as they all were. "You think Richard wanted revenge . . . because of me?"

Duncan removed a pistol from a saddle pouch and slipped it into his belt. "I don't know the answer to that. All we know is that Angus's father was standing over yours with his sword in the air, about to strike the deathblow, when your fiancé came riding out of the gunsmoke and clobbered him. Weeks later, Angus's sister was dead and evidently your father was approving your engagement."

"So you think he saved my father's life to secure his own rise."

"Aye."

"Do you believe also that my father was involved in this woman's death?"

"Nay. Your father was a good man. I know he was fair. I do not suspect him of such treachery."

She breathed a heavy sigh. "But you do not feel that way about Richard."

Duncan shook his head.

Amelia tipped her head back and looked up at the gray sky—a perfect circle framed by the treetops.

"I don't know what to say about all this."

She could make no sense of her feelings. She was in shock and felt very lost. The one man she believed would come to her rescue like a knight in shining armor was in fact being accused of horrendous acts of villainy.

"I feel very naïve," she continued. "I trusted my father to choose a husband for me, but now I must accept that his judgment may have been flawed. Who, then, do I trust? Who do I believe in?"

Duncan strode toward her. "You rely on your own judgment, lass. No one else's."

She pulled her gaze from the sky overhead and regarded his concerned expression. There was wisdom in his words, she knew it, but what seemed more relevant at the moment was the faint light of compassion she saw in his eyes, as well as the heavy beating of her own heart. She regarded him with curious wonder, let her eyes roam over the features of his face, and felt as if he understood what she was feeling.

He looked away, toward the trees. A muscle clenched in his jaw; his chest expanded with a deep intake of breath. Amelia stood rapt, stricken by the need to know—what was he thinking?

He moved closer. "You have much to learn about the world, lass."

More than ever, Amelia was shaken out of her comfortable, well-planned existence and had to accept that he was right, for none of this fit into her sheltered and clearly deficient realm of experience.

Then he reached out to her, and for some reason she was not afraid as he brushed his thumb across her lips. His eyes roamed over her face, a bird chirped in the treetops, then he leaned forward and gently touched his mouth to hers.

It was surprisingly comforting, which made no sense to her. No sense at all.

She immediately pulled away and backed up a few steps, but he followed. All her senses began to hum, and she felt as if she were dissolving. She couldn't think.

He looked at her with fire in his eyes, as if he were just as surprised by the kiss as she. Then he backed away and turned his attention to the saddlebags, pulling the cinches tight and gathering up the reins.

She wiped the moisture from her lips. "Why did you do that?"

He did not give an answer. He simply led the horse to the edge of the glade.

"I wish you would let me go," she softly said, following him. "I am innocent in all this. Whatever Richard did is not my fault. I know nothing of it. And I don't understand why Angus hates me so much, when he was the one who shot my father on the battlefield. He has it backwards. *He* is the one who wronged *me*."

Stopping under the shade of a tree, Duncan faced her. "There is no clear way to put into words the fury that consumes Angus. It's a fury that consumes us all, and you're just not capable of understanding."

She recalled the passionate fury that had swept through her when he entered her bedchamber. "Maybe you underestimate me."

"Nay, lass. You're an innocent. You'd have to enter hell on your own two feet before you could ever truly know of what I speak."

She saw something dark and disturbing in his eyes and frowned. "I am not sure I want to hear any more."

"Then stop asking questions. You know too much as it is." He strode toward her, took hold of her arm, and led her impatiently to the horse. "Do you want me to toss you up again, or can you do it yourself?"

"I can do it myself," she replied, no longer wishing to argue with him, at least not now, when he was so very cross and she was reeling with confusion over what had just occurred between them.

Nor could she purge from her mind what had happened to Angus's sister. She could not bear to think of that young woman's suffering.

At least now Amelia understood why Duncan and Angus both hated Richard so much. Their motivations to wreak havoc on the English were deeply rooted.

She mounted the horse, and Duncan swung up behind her. Soon they were trotting out of the clearing, heading north.

"Don't talk anymore," he said. "Just keep your mouth shut, because my patience with your questions is running short, and if you bring any of it up again, I'll be tempted to stuff another gag in your mouth."

Amelia shuddered at the firmness of his command.

The others had already left the glade. They had vanished into the trees like swirls of phantom mist, and Amelia was beginning to feel like a ghost herself. She felt as if she were disappearing into a world and a life she did not truly understand.

They reached Glen Elchaig at dusk, just as the moon was beginning its rise. Stars twinkled overhead, and a wolf howled somewhere in the distance.

The other Highlanders had reached the shelter of the glen before them and started a fire. Amelia inhaled the mouthwatering aroma of roasting meat and nearly leaped off the horse in anticipation of a hot meal.

"Is that rabbit I smell?" she asked, famished almost to the point of distraction, but not quite—for nothing could distract her from what had occurred in the glade earlier. She had not yet recovered from it.

"Aye. Gawyn is a master chef when it comes to a quick dinner. He can sniff out anything, kill and skin it in less

than a minute, and have it roasting on a spit before you
can blink twice."

Duncan urged the horse into a gallop, and she felt the
animal lift beneath her, as if they were taking flight. They
rode into the camp and dismounted, and the first thing
Amelia noticed was the stiffness in her legs from so many
hours in the saddle. She could barely walk.

Duncan tended to his horse while she approached the
hot, roaring fire. Sparks snapped and flew upward toward
the darkening sky while drops of grease from the roasting meat sizzled and hissed on the burning logs. She held
her hands out to warm them.

"Are you hungry, Lady Amelia?" Gawyn asked. It was
the same question he had asked earlier, with the same
proper address.

"Yes, I am. It smells very good."

He set about poking at the meat. He sniffed it like a
dog might sniff the air, and she suspected his nose was as
practiced as that of any famous French chef in Paris or
London.

Soon they were all crowded around the fire, gulping
down the tasty meat and sipping full-bodied cups of wine.
Amelia was relieved to have a cup, a plate, and a rock to
sit upon. She was not squatting, as she'd imagined she
would have to do. She was quite comfortable, in fact, despite her stiff muscles and numerous anxieties. She could
not deny that the tender rabbit meat was the best thing she'd
ever tasted.

Duncan was the first to finish eating. He rose to his feet
and tossed his plate and cup into a cauldron of hot water
over the fire.

"I'll take the first watch." He pulled his sword from the
scabbard with a wide, sweeping arc and left the fireside.

Amelia stopped chewing and watched him go. She was
still trying to make sense of what had happened between

them earlier, and why he had kissed her when he seemed to despise everything she stood for and thought her a fool for agreeing to marry Richard Bennett.

What surprised her most, perhaps, was how gentle he had been in that moment, which contradicted everything she knew and thought about him. She could not have been mistaken about the compassion she saw in his eyes, and she was grateful for that.

Returning her attention to the others, she found herself suddenly caught in the ice storm of Angus's frigid gaze. He had finished his meal and was leaning back on an elbow, cleaning his teeth with a small bone.

"I'm sorry about your sister," she said, summoning every shred of courtesy she possessed just to get the words out.

He frowned at her, then rose to his feet. "I did not ask for your condolences, woman, so you'd best keep your thoughts to yourself."

Like Duncan, he pulled his broadsword from the scabbard with an audible scrape of metal against leather, then stalked off in the opposite direction. The chill of the dark Highland night surrounded her like a cold fog.

"Pay him no mind, milady," Gawyn said. "He's just not over it yet."

"You mean his sister," she replied.

"Aye."

She finished her meal and set the plate aside. "No, I cannot imagine one would ever get over such a thing. What was her name again?"

"Muira."

Amelia turned her gaze in the other direction to the place where Duncan had gone. He was watching them from a rocky outcropping above.

"Will he come back before nightfall?" she asked.

"Hard to say," Gawyn replied. "He spends a lot of time alone these days."

"Why?"

"Because he's not over Muira's death, either."

Something shuddered inside Amelia as she digested the obvious suggestion that Duncan been involved with Muira, perhaps in love with her.

That would explain a great deal, she thought with a disturbing pang of discomfort when she imagined him loving a woman so deeply and devotedly that he was compelled to avenge her death by killing the man responsible.

Amelia's very own fiancé.

She took a deep breath and forced herself to concentrate on the simple task of wetting her lips while she watched Duncan on the outcropping above.

Almost instantly she chastised herself for caring one way or another about the circumstances of his life or his romantic involvements in the past. He was her captor and her enemy, and the fact that he'd kissed her and been understanding about her feelings changed nothing. It was a single moment that should not obliterate all the others.

She could not afford to become distracted by an attraction to him, no matter how confusing it was. She had to remain focused on survival and escape.

She took another sip of her wine and did not permit herself to look in his direction again.

Chapter Six

"I'm sorry, Lady Amelia," Gawyn said, "but Duncan says I have to bind your wrists for the night."

"You're going to tie me up again?" she asked. "Is that really necessary?" Her chafe wounds were only just beginning to heal.

"He says it's for your own good, because if you tried to run off you'd get lost and might get into trouble."

"I promise I won't run off," she insisted while she watched him pull the rough twine from a saddlebag, and winced at the recollection of being tied up that morning. "Where in the world would I go? We haven't seen a single soul for miles. I'm not stupid, Gawyn."

"Aye, but you might panic in the night," Fergus said, "or try to slit our throats while we sleep."

"Don't be ridiculous. I'm not a murderous savage."

Fergus smiled crookedly. "But you're in the company of savages, lassie, and don't you know our wicked ways are contagious?"

She watched his ruddy face while he wrapped the twine around her wrists, still raw and sore from the trials of the morning. "I am not sure, Fergus, whether you are serious or jesting."

He grinned again. "It'll give you something to think about, lassie, while you're floatin' off to dreamland."

* * *

The morning sun woke Amelia from a restless slumber, and she sat up on the bed of fur to discover the fire was already snapping and blazing in the pit. Eggs were frying on a pan.

"Gawyn, do you have chickens in your saddlebags?" she asked, looking down at her wrists and noticing that they were no longer bound. Someone had cut the ropes while she slept and she had not even been aware.

Gawyn threw his head back and laughed. "Chickens! Ah, Lady Amelia, you're a silly one."

She blinked a few times; then suddenly Duncan was standing over her, holding out a banged-up pewter mug. The sleep was not yet out of her eyes, and she had to crane her neck and squint to look up from his finely muscled legs and the folds of green tartan to his face, illuminated by the sun.

He seemed more attractive than ever, masculine and almost mythical, with one thick finger hooked through the handle of the dented mug, his other hand gripping the handle of his axe, his hair blowing lightly in the breeze.

"Must you always carry that thing?" she asked, tired of staring at the morbid weapon.

He tossed his head to flip his dishevelled hair off his shoulder. "Aye, I must. Take this and drink up."

"What is it?" she asked.

"Coffee."

Sitting up groggily, she accepted the steaming cup. Duncan sat down beside her.

Gawyn was busy flipping the eggs, and Fergus was some distance away, swinging his broadsword through the air, lunging forward mightily.

"Is he practicing for something?" she asked, sipping the coffee.

"Nothing in particular."

"Just the usual, everyday deadly skirmish, I suppose."

Duncan glanced sideways at her but made no comment.

"Was it you who untied me?" she asked. "I must have been sleeping very deeply not to have noticed."

"Aye, you slept soundly all night."

She kept her eyes on Fergus, still swinging his sword around. "And you could tell this from halfway up the mountain?"

"I came down when all was quiet," he told her.

"So you were skulking around the camp, watching me sleep?"

"Aye." He accepted another mug of coffee from Gawyn and blew the steam away. "I watched you all night, lass, and it's my duty to inform you that you snore like a bull."

"I most certainly do not!"

"Gawyn heard it as clearly as I." He raised his voice: "Didn't you, Gawyn? You heard Lady Amelia snoring like a bull last night?"

"Aye, you kept me awake, lass."

Amelia shifted uncomfortably on the soft fur and took another sip of coffee. "Well, I am not going to sit here and argue with the two of you about it."

Duncan crossed his long, muscled legs at the ankles. "Wise decision, lass. Sometimes you're better off just to yield at the outset."

She chuckled bitterly. "Mm, I learned that yesterday, didn't I? When you had me pinned to the ground in the rain."

Gawyn, who was busy cracking two more eggs into the pan, lifted his eyes briefly.

"At least you learned your lesson," Duncan said. "It's important to know when you've been bested."

Amelia shook her head at him, refusing to be provoked. "And what plan does the mighty conqueror have for his prisoner today?" she asked, determined to change the subject. "I suppose you're going to drag me higher up into the mountains? Although I don't really see the point in it, if you *want* Richard to find us. Which maybe you don't."

He glanced sideways again. "Oh, I do, lass. I just want him to suffer a bit longer with the angst of not knowing what's happening to you. I like to imagine him tossing and turning in his bed, night after night, wondering if you're dead or alive. Or thinking about how my axe is slicing your dress in two, and how you must be trembling and cowering at my touch, begging for mercy, and finally pleading with me to pleasure you senseless, again and again, night after night."

She shot him a disparaging look. "You're having delusions, Duncan, if you think that's ever going to happen."

He took a sip of coffee and kept his eyes fixed on Fergus, who was still practicing with his sword. "I'll be sending Bennett a message soon enough."

"A message? How? When? I haven't seen any goose quills within reach, or paper or inkwells for that matter. There are no desks in the immediate area, or post runners to deliver the dispatch."

He still did not meet her eyes. "As if I'd reveal any of that to you."

She accepted the plate Gawyn held out. "Fill your belly, lass," Gawyn said with an encouraging smile. "We've got a long day ahead of us."

She picked up the spoon and ate.

"How close were you to Angus's sister?" she asked Duncan later that morning, after they had packed their supplies and left the glen, the rebels spreading out on horseback in all directions like spokes on a fan. "Gawyn told me that—"

"Gawyn talks too much." Duncan's reply came down like a hammer.

Recognizing the note of impatience in his voice, Amelia cleared her throat and began again. "Perhaps he does, but we're alone now, Duncan, and I would like to know more about what happened. Was Muira's death what started this bloody rampage? Or were you known as the Butcher before that?"

He said nothing for a long time, so Amelia simply waited. And waited.

"I don't know who invented that name," he said at last. "It wasn't us. It was probably some adolescent English soldier who cowered behind a barrel when we attacked his camp."

"Someone who lived to tell about it," she added.

"And thought it clever to exaggerate."

Feeling a swift surge of hope, she turned in the saddle to search his eyes. "Exaggerate? So it's not all true?"

He paused. "More than enough of it is based on fact, lass, so don't get your hopes up."

They rode on. The horse's hooves plodded leisurely over the grass while a thick mist shifted and rolled across the mountaintops.

"But you still haven't answered my question," she said, "about Angus's sister. How close were you?"

His voice was quiet. "Muira was to be my wife."

Amelia had already suspected there was more to his vengeance than mere loyalty to a friend, but to hear him admit it openly was like a punch in the chest. She could not explain it. It shouldn't matter, but it did, especially now when she was relaxing into the warmth of his body and feeling safe and secure in his arms.

She looked up at the low cloud cover moving across the sky and suspected it would soon blot out the sun. A blackbird soared in and out of the vapor, and again she felt as if she had entered a different world, a place of complexity and sorrow. There was so much pain here—she felt it herself in so many confusing ways—yet at the same time there was divine beauty in these majestic faraway mountains. The air was fresh and clean; the rivers and streams ran clear as glass. Everything was so drastically, oddly contradictory and profoundly stirring to her blood.

For the rest of the morning after their conversation about Muira, Amelia and Duncan said very little to each other. He seemed to withdraw into a secluded mood of disinterest, which she tried to see as a blessing, for he was her captor and she was a fool to let herself feel sympathy for his circumstances, or worse—to believe that she was becoming attracted to him. It was best if they did not talk.

Later he left her alone for a short while. They stopped by a river to water the horse and eat a few bites of stale bread and cheese. Duncan did not eat with her, and in those fleeting seconds of freedom she glanced around and considered a hasty escape, but was hindered by the fact that she knew nothing of their position on a map, or what was over the next rise.

Better the devil you know, she told herself in the end, when she imagined darting into the mountains and finding a place to hide. What if she met up with a less hospitable band of savages? A different bunch of hooligans who might abuse her immediately? Or a vicious, hungry animal with fangs?

And so, she did not run away that afternoon. She merely sat quietly on a rock, waited for Duncan to return, and was greatly relieved to see him when he did.

That night after supper—in another glen that was very similar to the last—as Amelia lay down on the bed of fur by the slowly dying fire, she strove to stay calm by calling to mind happier thoughts. She remembered the raspberry tarts Cook used to make in their London house, the soft feather-down pillow she liked best, and the sound of her maid tiptoeing into her room early in the morning with breakfast on a tray.

She thought also of her father's gentle, soothing voice, his deep, merry laughter in the evenings when he smoked a pipe by the fire.

A painful lump of longing rose up in her throat, but she pushed it back down, for she could not fall apart now. She had made it this far. She would make it the rest of the way.

Pulling the blanket up to her chin, she closed her eyes and tried to get some rest. At least Angus was not present that night. He was scouting the forest on the far side of the glen.

As for Duncan, he was seated on a stony outcropping above, just as he had been the night before, keeping an eye out for danger. Though it was far more likely that he was simply making sure she didn't rise up in the night and bludgeon them all to death with a stone.

But could she actually kill a man if the opportunity presented itself?

Yes, she decided. *Yes, I could.*

With that morbid idea bobbing around inside her brain, she fell into a restless sleep, and woke in the night to the sound of quick footsteps and whispering.

Fear ignited in her breast. Instantly alert, she lay motionless, petrified with alarm.

"We'll be heading south in the morning," Fergus said, stretching out on the ground and pulling his tartan over his shoulders. "Back toward Moncrieffe."

Moncrieffe? The earl's residence?

She strained hard to listen. . . .

"But I thought Duncan wanted to bide his time," Gawyn whispered in reply.

"He did, but Angus spotted some redcoats at the loch. We need to turn back."

She heard Gawyn sit up. "Loch Fannich is less than half a mile away. Duncan didn't think we should pack up right away?"

Fergus sat up, too. "Nay, Angus said there were only five of them and their bellies were full of rum, and they were all asleep."

Gawyn lay back down. "Well, that's a relief."

"Maybe to you. But you didn't hear Angus and Duncan fighting over what to do with the lady." His whisper grew more hushed, and he leaned forward on an elbow. "I thought they were going to take each other's heads off," he said. "Angus wants to kill her tonight and leave her corpse outside the English camp."

Fear exploded in Amelia's stomach.

Gawyn sat up again. "But she's the daughter of a duke."

"Shh." Fergus paused. "We shouldn't be talking about it."

"What did they decide?"

"I don't know."

They were quiet for a moment; then Fergus settled down and drew his tartan over his head. "Either way, it's not up to us, so stop your blathering, you cockeyed nag. I need my sleep."

"As do I, you smelly arse. And it was *you* who started it."

An hour later, Amelia ran through the darkness, panting heavily, stumbling over rocks, and leaping over patchy hollows. Her skirts whipped back and forth with each harried stride, and her heart burned with wild, crippling panic.

She prayed that Duncan had not yet noticed her absence, or that she would not bash headlong into Angus, who was scouting the woods just ahead and wanted to deliver her corpse to the English camp. It was a terrible risk she had taken, for if her captors discovered her flight before she reached the English soldiers, there was no telling what they might do.

Please, God, let me find the camp. I cannot die here.

Then she felt a presence. . . .

The sound of footsteps across the glen, stealthily approaching, swift and fluid in the night, like some kind of phantom animal. They were coming at her from behind.

Or from the side . . . Or at a diagonal . . . Perhaps they were in front of her!

Dashing forward as fast as she could, she glanced over her shoulder.

"Stop!" the voice commanded.

"No, I will not!"

Before she could recognize anything in the heavy gloom, something smacked sidelong into her.

Thump! She hit the ground and her breath sailed out of her lungs. Fire lit in her veins as she comprehended what was happening. She was trapped again beneath Duncan's heavy body. Where had he come from? She was sure she had gotten away. Did he have eyes in the back of his head?

"Have you lost your mind?" he asked, rising up on hands and knees above her, his hair falling forward. He wore his shield on his back, his sword in the side scabbard, his axe tucked into his belt.

"Let me go!" she cried, more desperate than ever to escape and reach safety.

Her palm slammed down on a rock, and before she could form a single conscious thought, she had swung it through the air and struck Duncan in the side of the head.

He groaned and toppled over, cupping his temple in a hand. He fell onto his back. Blood oozed forth, between his fingers.

Horrified, Amelia scrambled to her feet.

He tried to move. He twisted and squirmed. Blood

poured everywhere, dripping over his knuckles and down his arm. God in heaven! What had she done?

She looked over her shoulder toward the edge of the forest, knowing the lake was not far beyond. There were English soldiers there. She could still reach them.

Indecision crippled her mind. She was shocked by what she had done to Duncan; she had not known she was capable of such violence. But what choice did she have?

He groaned again, then fell unconscious. Had she killed him?

Shaken, disoriented, and suddenly terrified that Angus would appear out of nowhere and make her pay for her defiance, she bolted for the woods.

She could not regret it. She had been abducted by enemy Highlanders. She'd had no choice but to save herself. At least now there was a chance she could survive and reach her own countrymen. She could see her uncle again and return to her home in England. Sleep in her own bed. Feel safe at last.

When she reached the trees, she skidded to a halt. It was pitch-black inside the forest. How would she ever find her way?

Her heart hammered in her chest; then suddenly she was racing blindly, whipping through the tangle of branches and leaves and sharp pine boughs that cut across her face. She fell so many times, she lost count, but each time she hit the ground she somehow managed to rise and keep going.

Panting, gasping for air, she refused to give up. She wrestled her way through the dark until she saw traces of moonlight through the trees. Mist on water. Sparkling ripples.

She flew out of the bush and collapsed onto her hands and knees on the grass. A campfire burned like a beacon on the beach. It was not far. There was a tent. There were horses and a wagon. Barrels. A mule. Sacks of grain . . .

Still on her hands and knees, she touched her forehead to the ground. *Sweet Lord, thank you.*

Amelia rose to her feet. She limped across the grass to the pebbly beach. This was victory. She had reached safety.

Weak and exhausted, she strode toward the English camp and tried not to think of the man she had left behind, unconscious and bleeding to death in the glen. She would try not to think of his pain, or the shock in his eyes when he realized what she had done to him. She would purge all thoughts of him from her mind. He was her enemy. She would think of him no more.

Chapter Seven

Five soldiers were asleep in their bedrolls inside the tent, and Amelia—holding the flap open with one hand—had to clear her throat twice before three of them startled awake. They leaped up in a disorderly fashion, and the next thing she knew she was staring from one pistol to another, three in total, all cocking simultaneously.

She gasped and shouted, "I'm English!"

The three on their feet took a wobbly moment to comprehend her words while the other two groaned in their beds.

"What's going on?" one of them asked, squinting at Amelia, who stood at the tent door next to a lantern.

"I am in urgent need of your assistance and protection," she told them. "I am the fiancée of Richard Bennett, lieutenant-colonel of the Ninth Dragoons. I was abducted out of Fort William by the Butcher of the Highlands."

"The Butcher?" The soldier at the far corner fought to untangle himself from his bedroll and groped around for a weapon he could not seem to find. "Bloody hell!"

God help them. God help them all.

"Please," she said. "I think it would be best if we left here as quickly as possible. I see you have horses. . . ."

"Damn right we do," one of them said, dashing for the

door and shoving her out of the way. "Where the hell is my horse?"

The distinct odor of rum on his breath wafted to her nostrils as he staggered onto the moonlit beach.

This was not good. She had imagined a disciplined brigade of fearless English heroes, on guard with arms at the ready, who would rise to the challenge of rescuing an aristocratic lady from the clutches of a known Jacobite rebel and enemy of the Crown. What she appeared to have stumbled upon, however, was an incompetent group of cowards and drunkards.

"Quiet, you imbeciles," another said from inside the tent as he lowered his weapon to his side. "The Butcher is a fairy tale. It's just a story invented by the MacLeans to keep us off their lands, and everyone knows the MacLeans are nothing but sheep stealers."

"I heard it was the MacDonalds."

"Well, *I* heard it was all true," said another. He was still lying in his bedroll but leaned up on an elbow to reach for a bottle behind his pillow. He tipped it upside down and shook it, but nothing came out. "My cousin saw him once. He was camped with the regulars outside of Edinburgh, and said the Butcher killed ten men single-handedly, then chopped off the head of the officer in charge and fed it to his horse."

One of them scoffed while a second one ran out of the tent and nearly knocked Amelia over as he passed by. She followed him onto the beach, where the fire was still burning. The first soldier was already galloping away.

"Wait!" she shouted, running after him.

"Oh, for the love of God," another said, emerging from the tent and swinging his pistol around. "Gutless fool. He'll ride straight into a tree."

Amelia turned to face him. "Who's in charge here?" she demanded to know. "Is it you, sir?"

"Yes." He staggered slightly and seemed to have trouble focusing on her face.

"What is your name and rank?"

He slowly blinked. "I am Major Curtis, at your service."

"I never took you for a poet, Jack," one of them said, tossing a handful of pebbles at him.

Frustrated beyond measure, Amelia spoke harshly. "I assure you, sir, the Butcher is true flesh and blood, and I believe . . ." She paused, looking back in the other direction. "I believe I may have killed him."

Saying it aloud made her feel sick to her stomach.

Another soldier emerged from the tent, drinking straight from a bottle. "This is a joke," he said. "Someone is having it on with us. Look at the dirty wench. She's no officer's bride. She's as grimy as a fishwife. I say we have some fun with her."

"It's no joke," she declared. "I was abducted out of Fort William. I am engaged to Richard Bennett, lieutenant-colonel of the Ninth Dragoons, and the Butcher and his band of rebels are not far from here. We must make haste to escape and report what has occurred."

The one with the bottle staggered repulsively toward her. "Come here, darlin'. Give me a kiss."

"Keep your putrid hands off me!" She backed up and stole a glance over her shoulder, looking for a way to escape. It occurred to her only then that she should have stolen the axe out of Duncan's belt. Why hadn't she? "Stay where you are, sir."

He charged fast, however, before she could even brace herself. His hands closed roughly around her upper arms, and his mushy lips attached themselves to her cheek. He sucked on her face, his wet tongue probing and licking.

The smell of his breath and body was sickeningly foul, and she grew wild with anger.

She swung her arms and tried to punch at him, but his grip was uncompromising. He was a large, heavyset man who could easily overpower her, even while intoxicated.

The others came out of the tent and began to whoop and cheer and applaud, entertained and goaded by Amelia's kicking and scratching.

"Let me go!" she ground out, but the next thing she knew she was flat on her back, struggling and shoving with all her might, while the vile, disgusting creature pressed his heavy body to hers.

"I'm next," she heard one of the others say, and then there was a dizzying, high-pitched ringing in her ears, drowning out everything but the sound of her own frantic heartbeats and the ferocity of her screams as she fought.

There were noises all around her, groans and crashes and terrible thudding sounds, and then the flabby heap of flesh on top of her took to the air. She watched him fly upward in an arc and land in the lake with a resounding splash.

She sat up, and there was Duncan, standing over her, feet braced apart, axe in hand, his broad chest heaving, his teeth bared like an animal. Their eyes met and locked, and he stared down at her in a crazed frenzy of murderous rage.

His hair was matted with blood, and his face was drenched with it, like a hideous mask of war paint. All she saw was the whites of his eyes, and her insides seized with shock.

The sound of splashing water drew her attention toward the lake.

With his claymore swinging in the side scabbard, Duncan strode to the water's edge. He waded into the dark moonlit waves, stalking after the soldier who had attacked her.

The man began to sob. "No, please, no!" He tripped backwards and plunged beneath the surface, then scrambled up and started swimming in the other direction, away from shore, kicking and flailing desperately in the waves.

Duncan pushed his way in deeper, not held back in the slightest by the resistance of the water. He raised his axe over his head.

Amelia rose to her feet in horror. She could not watch. She couldn't bear to witness the vicious slaughter of a man in cold blood, right there in front of her eyes, despite what he'd almost done to her just now.

"No, Duncan!" she shouted, taking an anxious step forward.

Her voice seemed to arrest him on the spot, and he looked down at his kilt floating in the water all around him. It was as if she had pulled him out of a trance.

He turned around, waded out of the lake, and whistled for his horse. Turner came trotting out of the trees without saddle or reins. Duncan slipped the axe into his belt and mounted the great black beast. He rode bareback to where Amelia stood in front of the tent, surrounded by three dead soldiers. He looked down at her and held out his hand.

She hesitated.

Then one of the soldiers moaned and rolled over behind her. She jumped and turned. Another began to drag himself across the beach, away from the camp, as if he were crawling toward safety in the bushes.

So they were not dead after all—although their leader, Major Curtis, was still thrashing about in the lake and would probably drown in the next few minutes.

"Come with me now," Duncan growled, "or take your chances with these men."

The one closest to her was rising up on his hands and knees, and the next thing she knew she had taken hold of Duncan's arm and was bounding up onto the back of his horse.

Duncan pulled the shield off over his head and handed it to her. "Put this on. Strap it to your back."

She did as he instructed, wrapped her arms around his waist, and they galloped out of the English camp toward the trees.

The precise moment they entered the forest, Amelia glanced over her shoulder and saw something speed by on the beach. It was Angus on his pale gray horse, his golden hair flying on the wind, his broadsword swinging over his head. He was galloping after the cowardly soldier who had been the first to flee the camp.

God help that wretched man now.

Then suddenly darkness laid siege to all that was visible, and they were whipping past branches and leaping over logs. It was quiet in the woods, except for the fast pounding of hooves on the ground and the snapping of twigs and dried leaves. The wind blew into Amelia's face, and she clung more tightly to Duncan's solid frame.

"Keep your head down," he commanded, and she buried her face in the soft wool of his tartan, which was draped over his shoulder, across his strong muscled back. She squeezed her eyes shut and willed her body to stop shaking, but it was no use. It was a delayed reaction to the terror of what had just occurred when that despicable man was on top of her, tearing at her clothes and slobbering all over her.

She clung more tightly to Duncan, overwhelmed by gratitude and relief—*thank God he arrived when he did*—but at the same time she was disoriented by the dizzying about-face of her emotions.

He was her captor. It was his fault she was here to begin with, and it was not so long ago that *he* had pinned her to the ground while she struggled and fought against him.

Somehow, however, what had occurred with the English soldier had felt very different, and she was hard-pressed to understand it in her panic-stricken mind. She had been both infuriated and alarmed when Duncan threw her to the ground in the field that first morning, but she had always felt as if she were being toyed with. She'd sensed that he was just biding his time, allowing her to fight and claw at him until she was depleted of strength. It had been his intention to wait for her to give up. To surrender when she was ready to surrender.

It had not been like that with the drunken soldier. He most definitely would have violated her. He would be doing so at this very moment if Duncan had not arrived and thrown him into the lake.

So what was she feeling now, exactly? Was Duncan her rescuer? Her protector?

No, that was not correct. He had stolen her from the safety of her bed in a guarded English fortress. He wanted to kill her fiancé. He had killed hundreds of men. He was a brutal, vengeful warrior and she was still not entirely certain she would not end up dead. He may have saved her tonight only because she was his bait. He still needed her to lure Richard into his trap.

Even so, she was not yet ready to loosen her grip, and if someone tried to separate her from him now, they would not succeed. She was holding on as if her life depended on it, and she didn't think she could pry her own fingers off him if she tried. She felt more safe here than she had back there on the beach—even in this wild, out-of-control moment while she was hurtling through the dark forest as fast as a musket ball.

She had no idea how long they galloped through the

trees. She didn't want to stop. She wanted to keep going, as far away as possible, but then she felt Duncan lean back and slow the horse to a trot. She opened her eyes.

"Whoa," Duncan said in that quietly commanding, authoritative voice.

They stopped in a moonlit glade, not far from a babbling brook.

Duncan was breathing hard. She could feel his chest heaving beneath her arms.

"Get off," he snarled.

She swung a leg over the side, dropped to the ground, and straightened the strap that held the shield on her back. He landed beside her and slapped his horse on the rear flank. The animal trotted to the water to drink.

Duncan faced her wildly. "Don't ever do that again!"

"I won't," she replied, not sure, exactly, what he was referring to. The escape in general? Or the moment when she bashed him in the head with the rock?

He put a hand over his stomach. "Ah, Christ. . . ."

He turned away from her and strode to a tree, where he bent forward and retched. Amelia watched him in horror. Was it because of what she'd done to him?

At least he was alive. She hadn't killed him. Thank God for that.

"I'm sorry," she said when he recovered himself.

He strode toward the rushing water in the stream, knelt down, and splashed water onto his face. After he washed the blood away, he cleaned his hands as well, scrubbing them together vigorously, violently, scraping at the skin with his fingernails.

"God help me, Amelia," he said in a low, dangerous voice. "I want to thrash you senseless. What were you thinking?"

She frowned at his broad back, for he was still crouching over the water. "What do you *think* I was thinking? I was trying to escape from my enemy and reach an ally—my own countrymen. It was hardly an outrageous plan, and you shouldn't be surprised. Angus wanted to kill me tonight. What did you expect?"

He glared at her over his shoulder. "I'll not let anyone kill you. I told you that already."

"But Angus seems to be at odds with your decision making in that regard."

"He'll do as I say."

"How can I be sure of that? I know nothing of him, or you for that matter. All I know is that you abducted me, and that you want to kill my fiancé, and that the entire English army is quivering in their boots right now because you are a wild, brutal savage with impossible strength who carries a big axe and wants to slay every last one of them in their sleep!"

He rose to his feet and stalked toward her.

She backed up in fright.

"Those men," he said in a low and threatening voice, "wanted to dishonor you. You shouldn't have gone there."

"I didn't know that when I left you! All I wanted was to feel safe again."

"You're safe with me."

Something inside her shifted and tipped over onto its side. "I find that difficult to believe."

"Well, believe it." He turned away to fetch his horse. "And I hope you learned your lesson tonight."

"I did," she admitted grudgingly. "I think."

He whirled around to face her again. "You *think*? Do you have rocks in your head where your brain should be?"

"What do you expect, Duncan? You're the Butcher, and you brought me here against my will. You abducted me and made me your prisoner!"

He stared at her in frustration. Animosity seethed in

his voice. "Aye, because I couldn't just leave you there." He raked a hand through his blood-soaked hair and spoke in a low growl. "If only you knew how badly I wanted to kill that soldier tonight. Seeing him on top of you like that, groping at you like some kind of animal, when clearly you did not want it. And the others, standing by and watching . . ." He shook his head. "I want to go back there now and finish what I started. I want to shove his head under the water and watch him splash and kick and die. Why'd you stop me?" Duncan's fists were clenching and unclenching.

"Because I . . . I couldn't bear to watch."

He seemed to be fighting some inner demon that wanted to break free. He wouldn't lift his eyes. Amelia stared at the top of his head, still matted with blood. His shoulders heaved with each breath.

She was still so unsure of him, so fearful of his explosive, hot-tempered nature. He had beaten those men insensible back there and still wanted to go back and do more damage.

And yet he wanted to do those things to protect her. To wreak vengeance on those who tried to dishonor her.

Or perhaps it was not *her* dishonor he wanted to avenge. . . .

"Thank you," she softly said, for she did not know what else to say. "Thank you for rescuing me from those men."

He looked up in anger—or was it remorse?—then put a hand to his head and staggered sideways. "Ah, bluidy hell."

She dashed forward and tried to grab hold of him under the arms but could do nothing as he sank heavily to the ground in a huge tartan-covered heap.

She leaned over him on her knees and slapped at his cheeks. "Duncan! Duncan!"

Good God! Sitting back on her heels, she pressed a fist to her forehead. He had just saved her from those awful men. She was alive and still in possession of her virtue because of him. What had she done?

An owl hooted in the treetops, and she looked up at the moonlit sky. She had no idea how to help him. They were in the middle of nowhere.

Then she heard a noise from beyond the glade—a cow lowing in the night. Perhaps there was a herd, and if there was a herd, there might be a drover, or even a crofter's cottage with a barn and a family with food and clean water and supplies. . . .

Rising to her feet, she looked down at Duncan unconscious on the ground, glanced briefly at his horse nibbling on the grass, then darted off in a run toward the sound she had heard and prayed it was not another troop of drunken English soldiers.

Chapter Eight

A faint, flickering glow illuminated a window. It drew her out of the trees and across a field to a small cottage, built of rough stone and thatched with hay. A ribbon of smoke trailed upward from the chimney to the clear, starry sky, and she heard again the sound of a cow lowing somewhere in the darkness.

Hoisting her skirts up to her knees, Amelia dashed across the uneven ground, then reached the door and rapped hard upon it. She'd already decided what she was going to say, for she had no idea what to expect from these Highlanders, or what manner of household she had chanced upon.

The wooden door creaked open, and she found herself looking down at a frail, elderly man in a kilt. He leaned over a rough-hewn wooden cane, and his snow-white hair flew fantastically outward in all directions, as if he hadn't combed it in a decade. His saggy skin was creased with deep grooves that looked as ancient as the bark on a two-hundred-year-old oak.

Amelia's hopes sank. She thought she might be greeted by an able-bodied young crofter, who would hurry to the glade with her and perhaps even carry Duncan to shelter.

"My apologies for disturbing you at this hour," she said, "but I am in need of assistance. My . . ." She paused,

then started again. "My *husband* is injured in the forest."
She turned and pointed.

The door opened more fully, and a young barefoot
woman stepped into view. She wore a plain white shift.
Her flaxen hair fell in loose curls upon her shoulders, and
she held a baby in her arms.

"She's English," the old man said in a scratchy, suspicious voice.

Then, to Amelia's incalculable relief, a younger, more
stalwart Scotsman appeared in the doorway. He was fair
in coloring and wore a loose nightshirt. "Injured, you say?
Whereabouts?"

"In the glade not far from here," she answered. "I can
take you there, if you will help us." She decided it would
be prudent to offer some additional information: "My
husband is Scottish."

The young man nodded. "No matter, lass. I'll hitch up
the wagon." He turned to his wife. "Put the kettle on the
fire and fetch some blankets."

He disappeared for a moment, then came back wearing a kilt, which he fastened over his shoulder while he
followed Amelia outside. She was uncomfortably aware
of Duncan's shield bouncing lightly at her back.

A short time later, they were rolling through the woods
on a rickety wagon with a squeaky axle, behind a stout
white pony who plodded along too slowly for Amelia's
current state of anxiety.

"It's just through there." She pointed toward the moonlit glade, then hopped down from the seat while they were
still moving. She ran ahead and found Duncan exactly
where she'd left him.

"Here!" she called out. "We're over here!"

Please, God, let him be alive.

Dropping to her knees, she touched his cheek. His skin
was still warm, and a strong pulse throbbed at his neck.

The wagon creaked to a halt, and the Scotsman hopped down. "What happened to him?"

Amelia paused, searching for a plausible explanation while the pony jangled the harness. "He fell off his horse and hit his head."

The Highlander glanced briefly at Turner, nibbling quietly on the sweet green grass, then leaned forward on a knee. He glanced also at Duncan's axe and claymore, then proceeded to examine his scalp. "It's a deep gash, to be sure, but at least he didn't split his skull wide open. Help me get him onto the wagon bed."

With a great deal of combined effort, they managed to lift Duncan and set him on a bed of hay in the back. Amelia climbed in with him and held his head on her lap for the short return journey to the cottage.

They reached the croft and slowed to a halt in front of the door. The young man lifted Duncan over his shoulder and carried him inside. A fire blazed in the hearth. The crofter's wife was now dressed in plain brown homespun.

"Gracious," she said, setting her sleeping infant down in a basket. "He's one strapping giant of a Highlander. What happened to him?"

"He fell off his horse and hit his head," her husband answered skeptically, giving her a sharp look.

"What's your name, lass?" the woman asked. Her tone was direct but not without kindness.

"Amelia." She decided not to mention her family name or title. They did not need to know she was the daughter of an aristocrat.

The woman stared at her curiously. "I'm Beth," she said, "and this is my husband, Craig. We're MacKenzies, and you met my father at the door. He's a MacDonald."

"I'm honored to make your acquaintance," Amelia replied, nodding respectfully at the old man who stood hunched over his cane in the center of the room, not looking at her. His angry, incredulous eyes were fixed on Duncan.

"Well, let's see if we can bring this clumsy Highlander around," Beth said, reacting casually to the tension in the room while she crossed to the rough-hewn table. "He's your husband, you say?" She did not meet Amelia's eyes.

"Yes. Can you help him?"

Beth exchanged another dubious glance with Craig, but Amelia could not concern herself with their suspicions now. All she wanted was for Duncan to wake up.

"We'll do our best." Beth picked up a plate and mashed its contents with a wooden spoon. "You said he was wounded, so I prepared an ointment of foxglove leaves while you were gone. This should do, but if it's a serious head wound, there might be swelling of the brain and there's not much anyone can do but wait and pray."

Amelia suppressed her fear, then glanced uneasily at the old man, who backed away toward the wall and watched her with dark, menacing eyes. The old man's expression harkened straight back to the terrifying nightmares of her childhood.

Later, when Craig went outside to tend to the pony and wagon, Beth looked Amelia in the eye. "Tell me the truth now, lass. He's not your husband, is he?"

She and Beth sat down at the table. "No."

Beth's father, the white-haired MacDonald, was sitting in a chair by the fire with his gnarled fingers folded over the top of his cane, glaring irately at her.

"Don't mind him," Beth whispered, leaning forward slightly. "He can't hear half of what anyone says anyway."

"He heard enough to know I was English."

Beth shrugged. "Aye. He's cautious, nothing more. So

how is it you know this big-boned Scot?" She gestured toward Duncan, resting quietly on the bed.

Amelia turned her gaze toward him and felt a sharp pang of anxiety. What if he did not recover?

"He stole me away from my fiancé," she carefully replied.

Beth's blue eyes narrowed with suspicion. "So the two of you are lovers, then?"

Amelia knew Beth did not believe that. She was just trying to draw out an explanation. "No, we are not."

The old man tapped his cane on the floor three times, as if he wanted something brought to him. Beth held up a finger.

"You can dispense with the secrets, lass," she whispered. "I know who this man is, and I know you're not his beloved."

Amelia fought to stay calm. "How would you know such a thing?"

She pointed at the round shield still strapped to Amelia's back. "That's the Butcher's shield. Everyone knows it holds the stone taken from the weapon of his ancestor—Gilleain na Tuaighe."

"Gillean of the Battle-axe," Amelia repeated, translating it into words she understood all too well from the legendary stories about the Butcher, who was descended from a famous warlord. She removed the shield over her head to examine it more closely and touched the polished oval stone in the center of the circle. It was pure white, with swirling veins of gray.

"It's a Mull agate," Beth said.

"It's very beautiful." But God help her now.

Beth nodded. "My husband noticed it when he followed you outside. Then he saw the basket-hilted broadsword your Highlander wore—with the tiny hearts engraved in the steel—along with the impressive black stallion you claim he toppled off of, and knew it was true. The man in the glade was the Butcher, and you were trying to save him."

Trying to save him . . . "Yes," she replied. "Yes, I must ensure that he lives."

"But you're not his beloved," Beth added. "I know that, too."

"How can you be so sure?" Amelia surprised even herself with the challenge behind that question.

Beth's eyes narrowed shrewdly. "Because his beloved is dead, lass, and from what I've heard, the Butcher buried his own heart in the ground with her on the day she died—at least the part of his heart that was capable of love. Now he fights for Scottish freedom. That's all that matters to him. Freedom and justice. Besides," she added, glancing at her baby asleep in the basket, "you're English. The Butcher would never give his heart to an Englishwoman. I mean no offense by it. It's just the way it is."

Amelia sat back in her chair, shaken by the depth of knowledge this woman possessed about the infamous Butcher—the specific details she knew about his weapons and ancestry and the grief inside him, which motivated him to fight and kill.

"You say he fights for Scottish freedom," Amelia commented. "But how does killing accomplish anything?"

She thought of her dear father, who had tried to negotiate peacefully with the Scottish nobles and had succeeded with many who were willing to lay down their swords and unite with England under one sovereign.

Beth stood up from the table. "Would you like some wine? I know my father will want a wee dram if he hears me talking of the past."

"Yes, thank you," she replied.

Beth went to the cupboard, retrieved a heavy stone jug,

and poured wine into three goblets. She carried one to her father, who accepted it with a shaky nod, then brought the other two to the table.

Beth sat down. "There are many Scots who believe fighting is the only way to preserve our freedom, because many remember a time when negotiations proved futile. Do you not know of Glencoe?"

Amelia shook her head. "I've never heard of it."

"Nay, most of you privileged English ladies wouldn't be told of such things. I can tell by your accent, lass. You're no kitchen maid. In any case, it happened back in '92, likely before you were born. Your King—that usurper, William of Orange—gave the clansmen an ultimatum to swear loyalty to his Crown or suffer the consequences and forfeit their lands. Most of them signed the document, but one of the MacDonald chiefs failed to meet the deadline, and not long after, his clan was massacred. They were taken out into the snow at dawn and shot dead. Few Scots have forgiven the English for that injustice, or the Campbells for that matter, because they did the dirty work. And now the Campbells support the Hanover succession." She leaned forward. "So naturally, there are more than a few Highlanders who are itchin' to pick up a sword or musket and fight for the true Scottish Crown."

"You are referring to the Stuart succession," Amelia said. "Is that why the Jacobites rose up in rebellion? Because of what happened at Glencoe? I thought it was because they wanted a Catholic on the throne."

Beth set down her goblet. "Ah, it's complicated, lass. Too much Scottish blood has been spilled over the centuries, and that blood still flows as thick as ever in the rivers and streams of this country. We *need* to fight," she explained. "We cannot help it. Our proud Highland men are brave and bold. They have warrior instincts coursing through their blood, and they don't like to roll over for a tyrant."

"King George is hardly a tyrant," Amelia argued.

"But your parliament can be," Beth countered. "I'm not even going to mention Cromwell," she whispered, "because if my father hears that name in this house, he'll be kicking over his chair and swinging his cane, and wanting to follow your Butcher out the door in the morning to kill a few redcoats for himself."

Amelia glanced at the weathered old Highlander, then back at Duncan, who had not yet moved. "Pray God he does wake by morning."

"Pray God indeed," Beth said. "Because if he does not, I promise you the clans will rise up like you never imagined and your precious German king will wish he'd never been born."

Amelia uneasily sipped her wine and pondered all that she had just heard. She had not known of the terrible massacre at Glencoe. Clearly, her father had kept that information from her.

To protect her, of course. Because in her world delicate young ladies of a certain sensibility were to be sheltered from such horrors.

She turned her tired eyes toward Duncan and realized yet again that there was much she did not know about this country. Its history and politics were far more complicated than she'd ever imagined, and getting more complicated by the hour.

"Do you know the Butcher's true identity?" she asked, sitting forward, still watching him. She was more curious now than ever about his life and upbringing. Had he been at Glencoe? Did he have family? Brothers or sisters? What kind of childhood had he known? Had he gone to school? Learned to read? Or had he only ever known how to fight and kill?

"No one knows where he comes from," Beth said. "Some say he's a ghost. But rumors abound that one of the rebels who fights at his side is a MacDonald who survived the Glencoe massacre. He was just a wee lad at the time, and his mother stuffed him into a trunk to hide him from the Campbells. He crawled out after it was over and watched her bleed to death in the snow."

Was it Angus she spoke of?

Beth tossed her head toward her father, who was quietly drinking his wine by the fire, and lowered her voice. "My father's nephews perished there, too."

Amelia's stomach turned at the thought of all those people dying so violently on that cold winter morning.

"What about the woman who was to be the Butcher's wife?" she asked suddenly. "Does anyone know who she was?"

Beth shook her head. "It's a well-guarded secret. But I reckon many young Scottish lassies would like a chance to help heal that damaged heart of his. The lads like to talk about his axe and his sword and the mystical powers in that ancient stone, but the lassies like to gossip about the power of what he keeps *under* his kilt." Thankfully, Beth changed the subject. "So you say the Butcher stole you away from your fiancé?"

"Yes."

Just then, the door burst open with a terrible crash. Beth screamed, and her father dropped his goblet on the floor and rose out of his chair with a threatening war cry.

In a blinding flash of tartan, Duncan, too, was off the bed and onto his feet, sweeping Amelia behind him with one arm while he drew his pistol from his belt and aimed it at the intruder.

The hammer cocked under Duncan's thumb. The whole world seemed to stand still as Amelia stared across the room at Beth's husband, Craig—trapped in a stranglehold with a knife to his throat.

Chapter Nine

Duncan, evidently, had recovered. Amelia, however, thought it might be her turn to take to the bed, for she was certain she was about to faint dead away at his feet.

"What's happening here?" he asked in a deep and threatening voice. He still held the pistol aimed at Craig, and his gaze flicked from Beth to the old man, then settled darkly on Angus, who kept Craig under control with the sharp point of his dagger. "Who are these people?"

Angus spoke to him in a clear voice. "I saw your horse outside, but this one I'm holding by the neck told me he never saw you, that he had no visitors. I knew he was lying to me, so I thought I'd take a look for myself."

"Of course I was lying," Craig ground out. "This man and woman are under my protection. I didn't know who the hell you were, and I still don't, you bluidy bastard. So until I do, you can rot in hell."

Duncan turned his head slightly, as if to ascertain that Amelia was safe behind him.

"I'm fine," she said. "These people gave us care. Truly. You have my word."

He reached up and fingered the pasty salve on his head, then sniffed the concoction.

"They helped the *Englishwoman*," Angus corrected in his usual antagonistic tone. "And I wouldn't be surprised to see a troop of redcoats galloping into the stable yard any minute now."

Duncan had not yet lowered his pistol. She noticed his long fingers close around the handle of his axe.

The old man glared petulantly at Angus. He raised his cane off the floor and pointed it at him. "Who are you, to break down this door and accuse this family of English sympathies?"

"I'm this man's friend," Angus replied, tossing a glance in Duncan's direction, "and he needs me to watch his back because he has more than a few enemies lurking about. Like this one here." He gestured toward Amelia.

"I brought him here to save his life," she argued. "He collapsed in the woods."

"It's no wonder," Angus said. "You clubbed him in the head with a rock."

All eyes turned to her. She met Beth's disappointed gaze, and her heart sank.

"Is that true, Amelia?" Beth asked. "Did you strike him down? Are you his enemy?"

She struggled to find the best way to explain herself. "Not exactly."

"Aye," Angus said, sounding all too satisfied with the convenient unfolding of events. "Did you hear that? She said 'not exactly.' Perhaps you should also know that she's the future bride of Richard Bennett, England's first and foremost executioner of Scots."

Wonderful.

"He is not an executioner," she tried to explain, needing to defend him. Or perhaps it was herself, and her choice of a husband, that she needed to defend. Either way, it did not matter. She'd just implicated herself and confirmed Angus's accusations—that she was an enemy of Scotland, and the Butcher's enemy as well.

"You didn't know that, did you?" Angus added, wrenching Craig roughly in his stranglehold.

"This woman is engaged to that swine?" Craig asked in a dry, gurgling voice.

Meanwhile, Beth said nothing.

Angus immediately released Craig, and he fell to his knees, gasping for breath.

"Aye," Angus said. "It's good to know which side of the border your sword falls on, crofter. What's your name?"

"Craig MacKenzie," he replied, rising unsteadily to his feet.

Beth's father relaxed and spoke in a more welcoming tone. "You're the MacDonald, aren't you? The one who survived Glencoe?"

Angus glanced dispassionately at Amelia and nodded.

The old man shared a long, meaningful look with him. "Get this brave lad a drink, Beth, and make it the best we have. Get the bottle of Moncrieffe whisky out of the mahogany chest."

Angus raised a smug eyebrow at Duncan, who at last lowered his pistol, released the hammer, and slipped it into his belt.

Amelia backed up in uneasy silence while Beth hurried into the back room. She returned with a bottle, retrieved four crystal glasses from her cupboard, and poured a drink for each kilted man. No one said a word. They strode forward, converging together around the table, picked up their drinks, and flicked them back in a single gulp. All four glasses hit the table at once.

"Another, Beth," Craig said.

She poured seconds, and the ritual was repeated; then each man slowly backed away to his respective corner.

Before he sat back down on the bed, however, Duncan paused a moment to stare questioningly at Amelia. Their gazes locked and held until he took a seat and rested his elbows on his knees.

Angus moved to the fire and warmed his hands while Craig rubbed at his neck, rolling his shoulders to work out the tension.

Beth's father sat down in his chair, nodding with pride and satisfaction. He was pleased to have the Butcher and one of his rebels in his home. "If you lads need supplies for your travels," he said, "whatever we have is yours for the taking."

Still standing over the fire, Angus acknowledged the offer with gratitude.

Duncan turned his questioning eyes toward Amelia again. She quickly shook her head at him, hoping to communicate that none of it was true. She was English, yes, and she was engaged to Richard Bennett, but she had brought him here to save his life—and for reasons she was not yet ready to explore, she needed him to know that.

"How'd you find this place?" he asked her.

"I heard farm animals and ran through the woods. You collapsed in the glade where we stopped. Do you remember? I didn't know what else to do."

"So you ran here, fetched help, then came back for me?"

"Yes. Mr. MacKenzie hitched up his wagon and I showed him where you were."

They all looked at Craig, who confirmed her story with a nod.

She noticed Angus looking over his shoulder at her, glaring with deep, smoldering hatred. He still did not trust her, and she did not believe it was possible to ever change that.

"It's the truth," Beth said. "That's what happened. And

there are no English soldiers on their way, at least not that we know of. All she wanted was help in tending to her Highlander."

"I told them you were my husband," she explained to Duncan.

Again he touched the salve that was packed on his head and winced slightly. "I am indebted to you," he said to the MacKenzies.

"It was the least we could do," Craig replied. "And you owe us no debt, friend. If anything, we are beholden to you, for what you do for Scotland."

Amelia observed that Duncan, in typical fashion, gave no response, and from that she surmised that fame and adulation meant nothing to him. He had his reasons for doing what he did—they were personal and private—and judging by what she'd seen of him these past few days, she was growing more and more certain that he took no pleasure in the killing. There was no joy, nor was it a simple, mindless frenzy of butchery.

That fact would come as a surprise to many people, no doubt. Most of the English population believed him to be a bloodthirsty savage, who attacked and slaughtered for the pure amusement of the kill. She had thought so herself. Before today.

"So is it true," the weathered old Highlander said to Amelia, "that you laid the great Butcher out, flat on his back, with naught but a rock in your hand? A delicate, wee lass like yourself?" He raised his wine goblet in a playful salute. "I'd wager more than a few Englishmen would be impressed by that feat."

Everyone chuckled, with the exception of Angus.

"This one is no delicate, wee lass," Duncan told them, keeping his eyes locked on hers. "And I promise you, I'll think twice about rubbing up against her again, especially in the dark. And I'd give the same advice to any man here who dares to try. She'll not yield to what she does not want, so you best keep your hands to yourselves, lads, or she'll be bashing your brains out before you can blink twice."

Everyone laughed, but a hush fell over the room when Angus interjected, "There's nothing funny about it. She was trying to reach the English camp at Loch Fannich, and she told them where we were. She'd just as soon see us all locked up in the Tolbooth as sit here and drink our fine Scottish whisky."

Everyone looked at her.

"That was *before*," she tried to explain. "Before I knew the kinds of men I had chanced upon."

She was still so very disturbed and shaken by the idea that everything she had previously believed about Scottish savages and English soldiers had been turned upside down. Why hadn't her father prepared her for any of this? How could he have raised her to believe that the world was black and white? That there was good and there was evil and England was incontestably good?

"Aye," Craig said, seeming to understand the deeper undercurrent of her words. "A red jacket with brass buttons and a pair of shiny black boots does not make a man worthy of your trust, nor does it give him honor."

"I know that now," she replied, dropping her gaze to her lap. "And I won't forget what I learned."

"That's wise of you," Beth added helpfully. "You can't judge a man's honor by the uniform he wears. That's just linen and wool. But to be fair, I've come upon my fair share of decent Englishmen in the past, as well as dishonest Highlanders who would rob you blind the minute you turned your back. The tide moves both ways, and don't you forget it." She reached for her goblet of wine and took a sip.

"So what are you doing with this haughty English lass?"

the old man asked Duncan. "Is it safe to assume you mean to use her to get to Bennett?"

"Aye," Duncan answered. "And I'd be grateful if you spread the word. I want him to know I have his woman, and that I'm stalking him straight to hell, to ensure justice is served."

Amelia trembled at Duncan's choice of words and could not help but think of Richard, whom she'd always believed was simply doing his duty in this rebellion. She'd always imagined him taking part in organized battles on an open field, but clearly—after what happened tonight—she had to accept that not all English soldiers were as noble as she'd imagined and it was quite possible that Richard had done some terrible things.

Craig lounged back in his chair and stretched his long legs out in front of him. "He already knows you're stalking him, which is why you haven't been able to catch him. He does his best to hide from you."

"He's a bluidy coward," Angus said in a low, bitter voice.

"You'll get no argument about that in this house," the old man said. "And you should both know that Bennett passed through Invershiel yesterday and he was on his way to Moncrieffe Castle to talk to the earl."

"The earl?" Amelia asked, feeling her hopes rekindle. "Are we on Moncrieffe lands now?"

It was difficult to imagine a lavish palace anywhere in the vicinity, with manicured gardens and servants and a fine collection of rare books and Italian art. Surely if she could reach the castle, the earl would remember her father and reunite her with her uncle.

"No, lass," Duncan said in a firm voice. "The earl is a MacLean, and we're on MacKenzie lands now."

"And thank God for that," Beth's father said. "That dirty MacLean is a bastard son of a whore and a traitor to Scotland. His father would roll over in his grave if he knew what his son had become. Mark my words, that faithless Scot will get what's coming to him."

"But what has he done to earn such an appalling reputation?" Amelia asked. Everyone shot angry looks at her, so she hastened to say more. "My father met him once, and he believed him to be a man of honor. He believed the earl desired peace with England."

Beth's father scoffed. "He'll give Bennett anything he asks for, if it means he'll have the ear of the King. All he wants is more land and more riches. He'll likely hand over the entire Moncrieffe militia to Bennett, to help him hunt down our Butcher and deliver his head on a spike to the Tower of London."

Angus paced in front of the fire. "The only head that'll see a spike any time soon will be Bennett's."

"God willing." Beth's father raised his glass and took another drink.

Beth quickly stood. "Well, I hate to break up the merrymakin', gentlemen, but it's morning. The cows will soon be whining, and the children will wake."

Craig stood. "What are your plans?" he asked Angus and Duncan. "You're welcome to stay here as long as you need."

Duncan stood, too. "We'll be heading out today, but we'd be grateful for some fresh provisions, and the lady could use a quiet place to sleep. She's had a long night, and I reckon she'd like to wash up."

"You can take the room in the back," Beth said. "The youngsters will be up soon, and I'll have them haul out the tub and heat some water for a bath."

Amelia exhaled with relief. "Thank you, Beth."

Duncan crossed to Angus and leaned close. "Where are the others?" he asked.

"Taking care of the camp," Angus replied. "They should be along shortly."

He glanced back at Amelia, then spoke privately to Angus again, but she strained to listen.

"Tell Gawyn to sit outside the lassie's window," Duncan whispered, "and guard the door as well."

"I'll see it done."

"And send Fergus with a message for my brother," he said in an even quieter voice. "I want him to know where we're headed."

He had a brother?

Duncan's eyes met hers only briefly, cool and unreadable, before he closed his hand over the hilt of his sword and walked out.

Hours later, after a deep and dreamless sleep, followed by a much-needed warm bath, Amelia finally felt more like herself, cleansed free of the grime from days in the saddle and the clammy residue of that disgusting English soldier who had assaulted her on the beach. She was just braiding her hair and pushing past the curtain that served as a door to the back room when she collided abruptly with Duncan.

"I thought you'd never come out of there," he said. A ball of fire bounced in the pit of her belly. She had been naked not five minutes ago, believing herself alone in the small cottage. She had not heard him enter and was unnerved by the possibility that he might have watched her bathe through a crack in the wall or listened to the dreamy cadence of her voice while she hummed. The framework of her stays felt suddenly tight and sticky over her breasts.

"And I thought I might have died and gone to heaven," she casually said, "when I thought I was actually *alone*."

His eyes gleamed, and danger bells began to chime inside her head, for it was difficult to ignore the sensual memory of his lips touching hers in the glade the other day. She found herself knocked off balance by her body's response to his nearness.

"I wanted to thank you," he said, "for what you did last night. You could've left me in the woods to die, but you came here instead."

"It's not as if I had any choice in the matter. I wouldn't have gotten very far on my own. And besides, those English soldiers . . ."

She did not need to explain herself further. He nodded with understanding, which left her feeling strangely displaced. The truth was, she was deeply relieved that he was still alive. Despite everything, she would never have been able to live with herself if she had killed him—especially after what he had done for her at the lake.

They were still on opposite sides of this war, of course—he was a Scottish Jacobite and she was an Englishwoman loyal to the King—but the personal antagonism between them seemed less absolute now. Less fierce. It seemed to be hiding behind shadows, and she wasn't quite sure how she felt about that.

He twirled the axe around in his hand, then slipped it into his belt. "You smell pretty, lass. Just like that first morning in the cave, when I had to fight my brutish urges to keep from ravishing you."

"And clearly your brutish urges have not diminished," she replied, throwing a veil of playful hauteur over her unease. "At least I was quick to don my gown just now; otherwise you might be in danger of another thump on the head."

He regarded her with amusement, his eyes like gemstones, and she felt the familiar embers of excitement burning into her skin, penetrating her nerves. It was as thrilling as fireworks.

"Do you mind if I go dip myself in your bathwater?" he asked. Without waiting for a reply, he began to unfasten his brooch and unravel his tartan. "Surely you'll appreciate it later when we mount Turner together. You'll prefer it if my whiskers are scraped off, so I don't scratch your tender skin when I'm straddled close behind you."

Why did he feel compelled to say such things? It made her heart beat fast with alarm.

She worked hard to speak in a detached tone while inching sideways to move past him, for they were wedged tightly between a cupboard and a chair. She was painfully aware of the thick muscles of his chest as her breasts brushed up against him, and as a result her heart catapulted into her ribs. She had to work hard to keep the hot stinging blush from her cheeks, for she would rather die than let him see what he did to her.

"That would be greatly appreciated," she said, "because you smell like sweat."

He chuckled softly, his tone low and sensual. "I was out in the yard with the lads, kicking a ball around."

"Sounds like a lovely way to pass the time."

"There are better ways."

He backed into the curtain. It fell gracefully closed behind him, wafted in the air for a second or two, then went still. Amelia was left standing there in the front room, aimless and deeply unsettled by the heavy pulsing of arousal in all her muscles and limbs. She felt like she was made of putty and all he had to do was touch her and she would soften and bend for him.

A few seconds later, she heard the sound of water sloshing about in the tub and knew he was fully immersed in her bathwater, naked, as she had been. Thinking about that—imagining the awesome spectacle of his nudity, and her very own water pouring over and caressing his thick, sleek muscles—was more than a little disconcerting.

She moved away from the curtain and looked around for something to do to keep her mind occupied, but this was not her cottage and even if it was, she wouldn't have the slightest idea what needed to be done. She was the daughter of an aristocrat, and she'd always relied on servants to take care of household chores.

Feeling uncomfortable and fidgety, Amelia wandered to the door and pulled it open. The sunshine was bright and warm on her face. She raised a hand to shade her eyes and watch the children, who were still kicking a ball around in the stable yard, when suddenly Gawyn's ruddy face appeared in front of her eyes.

"What are you up to, lassie?"

She nearly jumped out of her skin. "Gawyn! Must you startle me like that?"

"Duncan told me to guard the door," he said, "so I'm just following orders."

"I see," she replied, taking a deep breath. "Well, I am not attempting to escape. I had nothing to do, so I thought I would see what everyone *else* was doing."

"They're playing ball, lassie. And I didn't think you'd try to run off. I'm here to guard against the English. You never know when a red-coated thug might try to steal you back. I'm sure I don't need to remind you about the soldiers at the loch."

Amelia cleared her throat. "Well, thank you. I do appreciate your efforts."

He nodded courteously.

"Do you know what Duncan has planned for today?" she asked, in an attempt to make casual conversation. "Will we stay here another night?"

"Nay, lassie, we'll be heading out very soon, moving south toward Moncrieffe. It's a two-day ride."

"Moncrieffe?" Her heart went still in her chest at the possibility of traveling south toward a small orb of civilization in the middle of this wild foreign land. This was good news. Perhaps Duncan would release her to the earl—if in fact he intended to let her live, which she now believed he did. At least that was what he had promised last night. And this morning he seemed genuinely beholden to her for saving his life. Her welfare and happiness might even be a matter of honor to him now.

But then she remembered his primary objective, which had nothing to do with delivering her to safety, and felt a disturbing pang of uncertainty. He might be beholden to her—and he had certainly enjoyed flirting with her just now—but he was still stalking Richard, and when they arrived at Moncrieffe, Richard might have to fight for his life and his reputation in a savage, bloody battle for revenge.

"Thank you, Gawyn," she said before she retreated into the cottage and closed the door.

It was quiet inside. Almost too quiet. There were no sounds of water splashing, or the scraping of whiskers under a razor, which made her wonder if Duncan was asleep in the tub.

"Aye, lassie, it's true," he said from the back room, crushing that theory when his deep tantalizing voice reached out to her through the curtain. "We're riding south toward Moncrieffe today. I've no doubt you're glad to hear it."

"Indeed, I am," she answered, fighting to keep her tone light and easy. "Although it matters less now that I have enjoyed a warm bath," she casually added. "I feel quite rejuvenated and ready to take on the world."

"As do I," he replied, splashing in the water. "And I must confess, the pleasure of lying here in this warm tub—with the lingering scent of your sweet naked body surrounding me—has cured the ache in my head."

She crossed the room, listening. . . .

"So you'd best be on your guard, lass. You're in more danger than ever."

Her heart began to pound, and she hated the fact that he could evoke this anxiety in her. And he was doing it intentionally. Of course he was.

"You know," he continued, "I can't help but wonder

where my head was back at the fort, when I tore your shift from your body and tossed that skirt at you in such a hurry, telling you to get dressed. I let the moment pass without paying you the proper attention you deserved."

Pressing her ear to the curtain, she strove to keep her voice steady and composed. "I assure you, Duncan, I would not have welcomed your attentions in the least. So there is no point in punishing yourself. There were no missed opportunities. You can be sure of that."

She heard more sounds of water splashing; then the front door opened suddenly. Beth walked in with a basket of eggs and stopped dead in her tracks. She raised her eyebrows at Amelia and gestured toward the curtain, as if to say she knew exactly what she was doing and that she understood. That *yes,* Duncan was a superb specimen of manhood and it was only natural for Amelia—or any woman for that matter—to try to steal a peek at him while he was bathing.

Furious with herself for being caught in such an embarrassing position, Amelia exhaled sharply.

Beth set the basket of eggs on the table and walked out again. The door swung shut behind her, which caused the curtain to flutter. There was now a space between the curtain and the wall, which suggested a person in Amelia's position could peer through the crack. That was to say *if* a person was tempted.

She heard the watery splashes of Duncan rising up out of the tub.

Quickly she peered through, and could just as easily have been looking at a sculpted statue of sleek, shiny bronze, like Neptune rising out of the sea. Water dripped down the length of Duncan's spectacular muscled form in clean silver rivulets.

She'd never seen a naked man before. She'd seen works of art, of course, but never a true flesh-and-blood masterpiece of virility. And Duncan was most definitely that.

Lips parted, she stood gazing at his narrow tapered waist, his solid, firm buttocks and broad thighs. Her pulse burned with both shock and fascination, and even when she knew she should turn away, she could not. She was rooted to the floor, staring through the narrow space between the curtain and the wall, powerless to even swallow or blink.

Then, as the gleam of water streamed over the brawny bands of muscle on his shoulders and upper arms, she noticed the scars. Some were small, like tiny nicks in the flesh, while others were thick and deep. One was as long as her arm, from wrist to elbow, carved in the shape of a half-moon.

How many battles had this man fought and survived? Was he made of steel? He seemed invincible. No wonder he was such a legend. No one could crush or kill him, not with knife or sword or stone.

For some unbidden reason, she imagined him naked with a lover. *We're not afraid to grunt and thrust and use our mouths to pleasure our women.*

Her insides burned with heat. She had not forgotten those words, or how he had pressed his body to hers and pinned her to the ground on the morning of her abduction.

He had grunted and thrusted. She remembered every heart-stopping moment of it—every movement, every sensation. . . .

Duncan reached for his shirt, pulled it on over his head, then donned his tartan and belt, fixing the brooch in place over his shoulder. He was just reaching for his weapons when Amelia shook herself out of her stupor and realized he would soon push through the curtain. She backed away, looked around for something to do, nearly knocked over a milk jug with her elbow—then crossed to the basket of eggs on the table. But what to do with them?

The curtain swept open with a barely audible swish, but she did not turn. She could do nothing but listen to his light footsteps across the floor, coming closer . . . closer . . . approaching from behind.

The scent of him filled her head. It was not rosewater she smelled, however. It was just him and the musky smell of his clothes, the plaid and the leather. It was the smell of Scotland.

She felt his presence—so close, his chest touched her back. His hands came to rest on her hips, and her skin erupted in gooseflesh.

"You were watching me, weren't you?" he whispered in her ear.

There was no point in lying. He would know. "Yes."

Her bones seemed to melt beneath the sudden scorching heat of her skin.

"You've not seen a man naked before?"

She shook her head. "Of course not. That's not how we live where I come from. Ladies are sheltered from such things."

"Even after marriage?"

"I wouldn't know."

He did not move, but she could still feel his warm, humid breath in her ear. A strange pulsing began within. Outside her body, the whole world seemed to go silent and still.

Then at last he stepped back, and she exhaled sharply.

"We'll be leaving soon," he said, but she could not look up from the basket of eggs, nor turn around and meet his eyes. She was too mortified. She'd watched him bathe; she'd been aroused by the sight of his strong male body, and he knew it.

But at least this time, he was enough of a gentleman not to say anything more. He simply moved past her and walked out.

Chapter Ten

Richard Bennett stood up from the warm, rose-scented bathwater and wished he could enjoy the sensation of feeling clean, but he could not revel in it—not now, when he felt so damned irritable. He had traveled all day and half the night to reach Moncrieffe Castle but felt no further ahead in this frustrating chase. Amelia was still the Butcher's prisoner—if she was even still alive—and Richard had no idea where to look for them.

He turned and snapped his fingers three times at Moncrieffe's personal manservant, who appeared to be lost in a world of daydreams. "Hurry up, man! It's frigid in here!"

The servant hastened forward with a large linen coverlet stretched taut from hand to hand.

"I thought this place was supposed to be well-appointed," Richard said. "But I suppose it's impossible to get the dampness out of the air completely, this far north of the border. Does the sun never shine here?" He wrapped himself in the extravagant linen, but the chill of this putrid Highland air would not leave him.

"Indeed it does, sir."

Richard glanced over his shoulder at the earl's short, stocky manservant, who was backing away slowly. "You were looking at my scars, weren't you? And now you're struck dumb by the sight of them, and how hideous I am."

The man kept his gaze fixed to the floor. "No, Colonel."

Richard's annoyance waned slightly at the man's submissiveness. "Come now, be honest. You can't pretend not to have noticed. I'll not have a liar in my midst. Besides, I can take it. I've taken much worse. How do you suppose I came by them in the first place?"

Richard stepped out of the tub onto the polished plank floor, dripping water everywhere.

The valet cautiously lifted his eyes. "They look to be very painful, sir."

"Not at all," Richard replied. "I've had them forever. I don't feel a thing. It only vexes me when someone looks at them and reacts like you just did."

Richard rubbed the linen towel through his hair, scrubbing at his scalp to get all the water out. "So tell me, servant . . . what do you know of this infamous Butcher I have the pleasure of pursuing? Do the people of this country know he abducted an English lady out of her bed? Do they know she was the daughter of a great war hero, who once tried to help Scotland by negotiating for peace? One would think they would take that into consideration. Come now, servants hear things. How does the common crofter feel about the Butcher's tactics? There must be some who disapprove."

When the valet did not respond, Richard continued to openly speak his mind. "I know the earl is a civilized man—a gentleman, according to some. But what of the general populace outside the castle walls? Am I surrounded by enlightened people, or is this place crawling with Jacobites like the Butcher, who are hungry for English blood? Should I sleep with one eye open?"

The valet went to fetch Richard's robe, which was laid out on the four-poster bed. "I promise you'll be safe here, Colonel Bennett—inside the castle walls. And the door can be bolted from the inside."

Richard strode toward the valet, who was holding out his robe. "The door can be bolted, you say? So I am not so safe after all."

The valet nervously cleared his throat. "I wouldn't want anything to happen to you, Colonel. I am certain that His Lairdship wants very much to meet with you and discuss what the Butcher has done. He'll want to help in any way he can."

Richard dropped the linen coverlet on the floor and slipped his arms into the loose sleeves of his robe. "Indeed. It's no secret that the earl likes to help the King—at least when it proves to be profitable."

The valet bent to pick up the embroidered linen and folded it in his arms. "My master would never wish to see an innocent woman harmed. You'll have his full attention in the morning."

"Well, I should hope so," Richard said, tying the belt of his robe. "He profited greatly from his negotiations with the Duke of Winslowe in the spring, and it's that nobleman's daughter whose life is at stake. I would hope the earl will feel somewhat . . . *beholden* in that regard."

"*Beholden* . . ." The valet seemed almost panic-stricken. "Aye, Colonel Bennett. The earl understands debts and obligations. And he desires peace."

"Of course he does."

Exhausted and in need of a good night's sleep, Richard climbed onto the soft feather bed and laid his head on the pillow. "In the meantime," he said, "bring me some of that famous Moncrieffe whisky. I hear it's the best."

"Aye, Colonel. I'll have a bottle sent up right away."

"See that you do."

"How do you plan to confront Richard once we reach the castle?" Amelia asked.

She and Duncan were traveling through a shady forest,

alive with the chirping of finches, buntings, and warblers, all fluttering their tiny wings in the treetops. A soft breeze whispered and sighed through the leafy sycamores, like a gentle caress, and Amelia knew she was enjoying the peacefulness of this place far more than she should. This was not a quiet haven for the soul. It was the path that was taking them to Duncan's personal war, which was going to be hellish and bloody.

"It's no secret that the Earl of Moncrieffe does not support the Jacobite rebellion," she added, "and that he has pledged an allegiance to the King. Surely he has an army to fight against the threat you pose."

"Aye," Duncan replied, "but did you not hear what Beth's father said back at the cottage? That the earl's father would roll over in his grave if he knew what his son had become? That proud Scottish laird was an unwavering Jacobite, and he fought hard at Sherrifmuir and died there, along with many other loyal Scots who served under him. For that reason, Moncrieffe Castle is divided, and all we have to do is ride through the gate with our axes and claymores and we'll have two hundred men from the earl's army within minutes. Don't fool yourself. Your betrothed will have no protection there. The place is crawling with Jacobites who will be more than happy to feed him to us on a silver platter. In fact, I wouldn't be surprised if he was already dead when we arrived, which would be unfortunate, to say the least."

"Because you want to kill him yourself."

"Aye."

Amelia cringed inwardly. "Well, all of that is disappointing to hear, because when my father spent time at Moncrieffe Castle in the spring he believed the earl and the members of his clan were a civilized lot, and that they desired peace."

"Indeed they do, but how they go about achieving it is

where the differences lie. Some fight for it. Others just wag their tongues and profit from their signatures. But I am weary of this talk. Let us speak of something else."

Taking exception to his officious tone, she nevertheless strove to speak dispassionately. "What would you like to talk about? And let it not have anything to do with what happened back at the cottage."

"Why? Were you that excited by the overwhelming sight of my magnificent naked form, lass?"

Her veneer of dispassion became impossible to maintain—probably because she had been hard-pressed to think of anything *other* than his naked form since they had mounted the horse. The image of him in the tub had been striking erotic memory chords in her mind all morning, and no matter how hard she tried to ignore it, she could not suppress the stubborn, heated excitement it aroused in her.

"I told you that was the one thing I did not want to discuss. It's not suitable conversation for a lady."

"Then why'd you bring it up?" He paused. "I find it odd, how you English lassies always behave according to what's suitable. Don't you ever just want to live honestly, and not hide or bury your desires?"

"Are you suggesting I desire you, Duncan?"

He rubbed his nose lightly against the back of her hair, which caused an unwelcome torrent of gooseflesh to tingle between her shoulder blades.

"That's not the point," he replied, "and you know it, although I *do* think you find me fetching. How could you not?"

He was truly an unbelievable man.

"But if this fiancé of yours," he continued, "was always behaving so properly in your presence, minding his manners, how can you be sure you ever knew his true, honest self?"

She thought about that for a moment. "I have already admitted that it is quite possible I did not."

"There, you see? If a man doesn't say or act on what he truly feels . . ."

"But that is *my* point, Duncan. In England, we exercise self-control, which is why I feel more safe there, among people who behave properly according to a strict set of social rules, than with people like you, who act on their basic impulses."

"You prefer men who follow rules," he clarified, "like those soldiers at the loch?"

Amelia shifted uncomfortably in the saddle. He was challenging her basic beliefs again, which troubled her, because she was lost and alone here in this wild, foreign land. Her father was dead. If she did not have a civilized home to return to, how could she ever survive this ordeal? "Must we come back to that?"

"Aye, if you'll admit that being English and having good table manners does not make a man decent or give him honor."

Wondering if it was even possible to win an argument with this man, she pursed her lips. "All right, I will concede that point. How could I not? You are right. Those men were savages. How many times must I admit that to you?"

"The officer, too. He was the worst. Say it, lass."

"I already did," she replied irritably, "but I'll say it again, if it will make you drop the subject. They were savages. The officer especially."

Duncan leaned back. "Well done, lassie. You're making progress. Remember what I said to you that first day, when we stopped in the glade?"

Of course she remembered: *Before I'm done with you, I'll make you see that your English officers in their fancy red coats can be just as savage as any Scot . . .*

After a moment, he added, "But you should know that we have rules in Scotland, too. The clans are not without them. We follow the word of the chief."

"And *you* should know that not all Englishmen are like those soldiers."

As they rode on, she reflected upon the lesson Duncan was trying to teach her and knew he was right in many respects. One had to look deeper, beneath the layers of clothing and appearances—even beyond behavior sometimes—to truly understand a man's heart. She had always been aware of the principle intellectually, of course, but she had never been so challenged by the actual feat of understanding a man who was not from her world.

She pondered also what she had been through over the past few days—how she had been stripped bare in front of this Highland warrior, bound and gagged, abducted by force. She'd slept in a cave and eaten freshly killed rabbit. To top it all off, she'd almost bludgeoned him to death with a rock the night before. She had not known she was capable of any of that.

How then could she believe that she knew any man's heart when she did not even truly understand her own?

She thought of Beth and her children and their warm, comfortable home. It was a simple, peaceful life they led, yet Beth's elderly father had fought in many battles and lost loved ones in a brutal massacre initiated by her own countrymen.

Then finally, there was the image of Duncan—her fierce and violent captor—rising up out of a bath, dripping with glistening droplets of water. He was strong and rough and virile. A savage? Perhaps. But an impossibly handsome one, and heroic, in his own way. Intelligent, as well.

She thought again of all the evidence of his warrior life. . . .

"Are those scars painful?" she asked.

He paused. Turner tossed his head and shook his long black mane. "Aye. Sometimes one in particular will ache for no reason, and it will bring me back to the moment I was cut. I know every wound by heart—where I was when I received it, what army I was fighting for, and against. I can even recall the eyes of the man who slashed me, and whether or not I killed him in defense of my own life."

"What about the one that's shaped like a crescent moon?" she asked. "It looks like it must have been very deep. Where did that come from?"

He paused. "I fell down the side of a mountain when I was a lad. Tumbled and bounced like a stone."

She turned quickly in the saddle. "My word. How terrible."

"Aye, straight down the rocky side of a gorge. I broke my wrist, too, and had to set the bone in place myself."

She winced painfully, just listening to the story. "How old were you?"

"Ten."

"Good heavens. But why were you alone on a mountain? Was there no adult nearby to watch over you, or help nurse you?"

"Nay, I was on my own."

"But why? Did you not have a family?"

"I did, but my father believed in harsh discipline. 'From cradle to combat,' he always said. He's the one who took me to the mountains and left me there to find my way home."

Amelia did not understand this. Not at all. "Why would a father do such a thing? You could have died."

"He meant to toughen me up, and it worked."

"Obviously." She faced front again and tried to imagine the Butcher as a ten-year-old boy, fending for himself in the mountains with a broken arm. "How long were you alone like that?"

"Three weeks. That's why I climbed the mountain. I was trying to figure out where I was. But I got distracted when I heard a wolf howling at me."

"You must have been terrified."

"Aye, but a Scot knows how to deal with fear. We slay it, then take pride in the kill."

"My father once said that courage is not the absence of fear," she said. "It is how you behave when you are *most* afraid."

"Aye, your father was a wise man, lassie, and brave as well. You sure he wasn't a Scot?"

She chuckled. "I am absolutely sure."

"Pity for him."

Amelia slapped at a pesky midge on her neck. "What else happened to you during those three weeks when you were alone?"

"Mostly a lot of nothing. I wandered around, scrounged for food, tracked small animals, sometimes just for the mere pleasure of their company. I remember a squirrel who made things bearable for a few days. All I had was my knife, but I soon figured out how to make a spear and kill a fish, and then how to make a bow and arrow. I knew I was north of my home. That's the one thing my father told me before he galloped off and left me. So I simply followed the sun."

She looked up at the sky though the canopy of leaves overhead. "I wouldn't know which way to go in such a situation."

"Aye, you would, lass. All you need to know is that the sun rises in the east. You figure it out from there." His body curled into hers. "But you needn't worry about cluttering up your mind, trying to navigate by the sun," he said. "You have me to rely on, and I know exactly where we are."

"We are traveling to Moncrieffe," she said, waiting curiously for his reply.

"Aye."

She paused. "Will you release me into the earl's protection when we arrive? Is that your plan? To confront Richard, and then let me go?"

Please, God, let him say yes.

He nuzzled her ear again. "Nay, lass, I cannot promise you that, or anything else."

"Why not?"

"Because I don't know if your beloved will be there when we turn up at the gate. If not, I'll be keeping you till we find him. Or he finds us."

"I see." She strove to keep her emotions in check. "Well, perhaps he will be enjoying the Moncrieffe whisky so much, he'll decide to linger awhile."

"You should pray for it, lass."

Suddenly Duncan's body stiffened and Amelia's heart flew into a panic as a spear shot past their heads and penetrated the bark of a tree.

"What's going—?" But she didn't have a chance to finish the thought before the horse reared up and they both toppled backwards to the ground. She landed on top of Duncan with a heavy thud that knocked the wind from her lungs. He rolled her to the side, and before she could even look up he was on his feet, standing over her with his legs braced apart, axe already in hand, as his claymore came scraping out of its scabbard with a piercing and terrifying *swish*.

Chapter Eleven

Amelia's heart was still thrashing about in her chest when she spotted a small, golden-haired boy in a kilt crawling out from inside a hollow log. She glanced around to see if he was alone. He stood up and gaped at them, horror-struck.

"I thought you were the wolf!" he cried, and Amelia glanced down at the knife in his hand. His cheeks were smeared with filth, his hair matted.

Duncan slipped his sword back into the scabbard and strode forward, though he kept a tight grip on his axe. "What wolf do you speak of, lad?"

"The one who's stalking my pa's flock!"

Duncan stopped a few feet away from the boy. "Your father's a drover?"

"Aye. But it's been two days since I've seen him."

Amelia rose to her feet and brushed the flecks of moss and dirt from her skirts. Was this another ten-year-old boy abandoned by his father in the Scottish wilderness to learn how to survive alone? Perhaps he was so desperate, he'd hoped to kill them and skin them for dinner.

These Scots . . . She was trying to understand them, but sometimes, sometimes, she simply could not.

All at once, the boy began to weep, and she darted

forward to console him—but Duncan raised a hand to hold her back.

He slipped his axe into his belt. "Now, now, lad," he said in a firm voice. "You did well with your aim. It was strong and true." He knelt down on one knee.

The boy's frail little body shuddered with sobs. "I'm sorry; I didn't mean to!"

"No harm done. Now tell me what you're doing out here. You're separated from your father, you say?"

The child nodded, and his chin quivered while he fought to control his voice.

"What's your name?" Duncan asked.

"Elliott MacDonald."

Duncan gave Elliott a moment to collect himself. He waited patiently while the boy wiped his tears and stopped crying.

"Is your father on his way to the markets?" Duncan asked.

"Aye."

"Well, I know the drovers' trail. It's not far from here. We can take you to him."

Amelia carefully approached, and this time Duncan let her pass. "Are you all right, Elliott?" She bent forward and rested her hands on her knees. "Are you hurt, or hungry?"

Elliott glanced uncertainly at Duncan.

"It's all right, lad," he said. "She may be English, but she's a friend."

"She talks funny."

"Aye, that she does."

Amelia felt the tension drain out of the moment and smiled. "Yes, I talk funny in this part of the world, but I promise, you have nothing to fear from me."

The boy studied them both, his eyes darting from one to the other, then slipped his knife into his boot.

Duncan rose to his feet. "There's some sugar biscuits in my saddlebag." He tossed his head in the direction of his horse. Thankfully, the animal had returned after being spooked by the spear whizzing past his head. He was waiting by the tree, where the spear was still lodged in the bark.

Amelia gathered her skirts in her fists and pushed her way through the thick undergrowth of moss and ground cover. She reached the horse and took hold of the dangling reins, then led him back to where Duncan and Elliott were waiting. They sat down on the log while she dug into the leather pouches and withdrew the biscuits Beth had provided that morning.

"Here you are, Elliott," she said, offering him one.

The boy gobbled it up in a flash; then he burped and wiped his mouth.

"Beggin' your pardon," he said. "I haven't eaten since yesterday."

She handed him another biscuit, which he promptly devoured.

"A growing lad such as yourself?" Duncan said. "It's no wonder you swallowed both those biscuits whole."

She watched Duncan tousle Elliott's shaggy blond hair and wondered what the boy would do if he knew he was sitting next to the famous Butcher of the Highlands. Would Elliott run away, crying in terror and screaming for his father? Or would he be thrilled?

She compared Duncan's current behavior to his manner on the night he'd abducted her at the fort and found it all very confusing and difficult to comprehend. Who was the real Duncan? At the moment she felt no fear of him, nor anger. In fact, she quite admired the way he talked to the boy.

"Tell me about this wolf you were tracking," Duncan said to Elliott. "What does he look like?"

"It's a she," Elliott replied. "She has white markings, more than gray, which makes her hard to see. She blends in with the flock."

"Clever wolf," Duncan said. "Does your father know you're lost? Did you tell him you were hunting the white wolf?"

"Aye. He didn't want me to go at first, but I told him I'd come back with her fangs in my sporran."

"Have you seen her today?"

"Nay. That's the problem. I'm lost, and she's probably feasting on my pa's sheep right now, while I'm not there to watch over them. Me pa's probably pissin' mad."

"Sounds like you need to get back to your flock." Duncan stood. "Go help the lady mount, then get in the saddle with her. I'll take you through the pass, and we'll find your father."

The boy started off toward the horse but stopped and turned. "I should thank you, mister. Will you tell me your name?"

"It's Duncan."

"Are you a MacDonald?"

Duncan glanced briefly at Amelia and paused before he answered. "Nay, lad. I'm not a MacDonald. But I'm a friend."

The boy smiled knowingly. "You don't want to tell me, do you? Are you a fugitive?"

Duncan chuckled. "Something like that."

In fact, it was *exactly* like that. There was more than one reward out for the Butcher's head on a stick.

"You're not the Butcher, are you?" the boy suddenly asked, his eyebrows flying up.

Duncan glanced at Amelia again, then calmly replied, "Nay, Elliott."

"That's too bad," he said, "because I'm going to join the Butcher's band of rebels one day."

Duncan merely shrugged and spread his arms wide, in an expansive gesture, as if to apologize for being a nobody.

"Well, even so," Elliott said, turning back toward the horse. "I won't tell anyone I met you." He yanked his spear out of the tree. "And I'm glad my aim was off."

Cheerfully he waited for Amelia to collect the saddle pouches; then he offered his gentlemanly assistance when it came time to mount.

It took them two hours to reach the shepherd and his flock, which was passing through a fertile green glen under the glorious heat of the August sun.

Hazy beams of sunlight burned down from the sky, illuminating hundreds of white, cottony sheep while thick pearly clouds with heavenly linings sailed over the tall mountain peaks. A bird of prey soared weightlessly downward and shouted a call to another while dogs barked rowdily and bounded about on the valley floor, pushing the flock toward the noisy river.

The vast, emerald beauty of it all was almost too much for Amelia to comprehend. It aroused her sense of wonder and sparked her imagination as she breathed deeply the fresh aroma of the earth and vegetation, gleaming wetly under the brilliant sun. If she were an artist, she would preserve this scene on canvas, so that it would live forever in her memory. An odd thought, really, under the circumstances. Nevertheless, she studied every detail, determined to never forget what she had seen and how she had felt, beholding such heavenly splendor.

Elliott hopped to the ground and started running.

"Pa! Pa!"

The barking dogs alerted their arrival and came sprinting across the glen to greet Elliott.

The shepherd spotted them, too, and began to run.

Duncan—on foot, still leading the horse—stopped and watched the man drop to his knees and hug his son.

Amelia's heart warmed at the sight of the boy reunited with his father. Yet at the same time her joy mingled with a deep and painful melancholy as she thought of her own father and how she mourned the loss of him. What she would not give to dash across a Scottish glen right now and run into his safe, loving arms.

The fantasy caused a lump to rise up in her throat, but she fought to push it down and keep the unwelcome tears at bay. They would do her no good. Not here, and certainly not now.

The drover hugged his boy, then raised his long shepherd's hook to wave at them. Duncan started forward again, the horse followed, and Amelia swept aside all thoughts of her father. She turned her attention to Duncan instead, for she was, quite frankly, struck by the person he appeared to be at this moment—caring, helpful, and forthcoming. A kind and trustworthy man. One you would seek out if you needed assistance. Someone you could depend upon.

This was not the fearsome and brutal Butcher who had materialized out of her nightmares a few nights ago and abducted her into darkness. This was someone else entirely—which was a most bewildering thought.

"Good day to you!" the drover called out from across the distance. He wore a kilt, a quarter-length brown jacket, and a plaid bonnet with a feather stuck in it. "Elliott tells me he almost maimed you with his spear!"

"Aye," Duncan replied. "The lad is highly skilled. We're lucky to be alive to tell the tale."

The drover approached, stood face-to-face with Duncan, and spoke in a quieter voice. "I can't thank you enough for bringing him back to me. That lad is my life. He has no mother."

Duncan nodded. "Well, you ought to be proud of him," he said. "He's a brave one, no doubt about it."

The drover turned and looked over his shoulder at Elliott, who was laughing and chasing the dogs around. "Mm. He wants to fight. He'll not stand for any oppression, even from a wolf who's only looking for her next meal."

"I'll keep an eye out for her," Duncan offered. "Elliott described her to me. She has white markings."

"Aye, but I warn you, she's slick as muck, and she can sneak up on you. I've never seen such a clever creature, not in all my days as a drover."

"I'll remember your advice. Good luck with your flock, MacDonald."

Duncan began to turn the horse around, and Amelia nodded at the man, whose eyes were warm and friendly.

"Good day to you, lassie," he said, touching the brim of his bonnet as he looked up at her, sitting high in the saddle.

She decided it would be best to keep quiet and conceal her English accent. He couldn't help her anyway. If he knew who she was, he would most likely side with the Butcher— like everyone else north of the border.

"Good luck, Elliott!" Duncan called out over his shoulder. "I'm sure you'll catch her!"

"I will!" the boy replied. "And thank you for the biscuits!"

Duncan walked the horse for a few minutes, then stopped. "Push forward, lassie," he said to her. "It's time I joined you."

He slid a boot into the stirrup and swung up behind her, then gathered the reins in both hands.

Amelia had mixed feelings about his close proximity in the saddle with her again—with those strong hands gripping the leather reins and resting on her thighs.

They would move faster now, she told herself, trying to ignore his distinctive male scent as he kicked in his heels and urged the horse into a gallop. They would reach Moncrieffe sooner, and she would be one step closer to safety and the return of her freedom.

That was all she wanted. To be safe and free. To that end, she would continue doing what she'd been doing all along. She would stay close to Duncan in order to reach Moncrieffe Castle and find a way home. She would be brave until the moment when he finally let her go. And she would not think too much about his masculine appeal, or his maddening arrogance, or his teasing, tantalizing flirtations. Nor would she reflect upon how kind he had been to the boy and the drover, or how he had saved her, most heroically, from those horrid English soldiers on the beach.

No, she would not think of any of that. She would push those thoughts away. They were heading toward Moncrieffe Castle. That was all that mattered.

Late in the afternoon, when the air was humid and warm, they stopped at a shallow section of the river to cool themselves. Duncan was perspiring. His loose linen shirt was sticking to his back. He crouched down, dipped his hands into the water, rubbed them together vigorously, then splashed some cool droplets on his face.

A short distance away, Amelia removed her shoes. She picked her way barefoot over the pebbles, gathered her skirts up in a tangled bunch, and waded into the river, stopping when it reached her knees.

Duncan sat back. He stretched his legs out and leaned on both elbows, watching her bend forward and splash handfuls of water on her face and neck, as he had done. When she straightened, she closed her eyes and tipped her face toward the sky. Her copper-colored tresses reached all the way down to her sweet, tempting bottom.

She brushed her damp fingertips lightly down the length of her throat and across the tops of her breasts, seeming to delight in the featherlike sensation. Her cheeks were flushed from the heat, her skin dewy with perspiration. She parted her lips and wet them with the tip of her tongue. It was a slow, sensual, erotic gesture, and Duncan began to lose himself in an idle daydream.

In the quiet recesses of his mind, Amelia was standing nude in the river, while he was on his knees before her, half-submerged in the water, rolling his tongue around her pink nipples and probing her sweet navel. He relished the saltiness of her skin and the sweet perfume of her body, which filled his head with pulsating yearnings. Running his hands down the curve of her waist, he laid open-mouthed kisses across her belly and hip. His cock shifted and grew, and he closed his eyes on the pebbled riverbank, tipped his head back toward the sun, and inhaled deeply. The heat warmed his face and legs.

Abruptly he opened his eyes and shook himself.

"*Fook,*" he whispered, and stood up. She was the Duke of Winslowe's daughter. He shouldn't be thinking such things, nor should he be wasting time here in the middle of nowhere when Richard Bennett was still wreaking havoc in the Highlands.

"Get out of the river!" Duncan shouted. "It's time to go!"

Startled, Amelia turned to face him. "So soon? But the water feels so good."

"Put on your shoes," he said irritably. "We're leaving."

He did not look at her again until after she had mounted the horse. Then Duncan led Turner by the reins for at least half a mile before he finally swung up into the saddle to ride behind her.

At dusk, they set up camp near a single standing stone, high on a hilltop under the stars. It was a rare clear night without a single breath of wind. The moon was full—almost too brilliant to behold—and the mountains were sharp, pointed silhouettes against the deep twilight beyond.

Duncan started a fire and cooked the smoked pork Beth had packed for them, which they enjoyed with a hearty rye bread and a bag of juicy whortleberries he had picked in the forest.

When they finished eating, he reclined back against the tall stone and withdrew a pewter flask from his sporran.

"This, lassie, is Moncrieffe whisky, the very best in Scotland." He looked at it for a moment. "And Lord knows I need a good, deep swig of it tonight." He raised it in an informal toast, tipped it back and drank, then pointed the spout at her. "Maybe you should take a swig yourself, feel its arousing vigor, and then you'll understand why we're so proud to be Scotsmen."

She raised an eyebrow. "A well-made spirit is going to show me that?"

"Aye, lassie, and a whole lot more."

She looked at him with challenge. "I see what you are trying to do. You are trying to frighten me, and make me nervous about being here alone with you."

"You should most definitely be frightened," he said. "I'm a strapping hot-blooded Highlander with an axe, and I have needs." He paused and narrowed his enticing blue eyes at her.

She shivered at the suggestiveness of his tone but raised her chin defiantly, for she was determined not to show him any fear. At the same time, she sensed he was only trying to warn her to be cautious. He seemed determined to keep her at a safe distance.

He stretched out his legs and reclined back against the standing stone, then drank from the flask again. "*Ah,*" he groaned. "This is the best Scotland has to offer. How the earl does it I long to know."

"I find it difficult to imagine you longing for anything," she said. "Don't you usually just take what you want?"

He lifted his head. "Nay, lass. Otherwise, you'd be deflowered by now, and feeling very grateful for it."

She exploded in a dramatic show of affronted laughter. "It is absurd how confident you are."

"When it comes to my skills as a lover, there's nothing absurd about it. I'm very good at pleasing women."

"The famous Butcher," she pondered. "Good at lovemaking and chopping people in half. What an attractive set of skills you possess."

Amelia stared at the flask. She was thirsty, and there was nothing else to drink. And certainly the notion of sleeping like a baby had its appeal.

"I should prepare myself to be dazzled, should I?" She accepted the flask. "What if I swoon?"

"No worries, lass. You'll just tumble over sideways, and the grass is soft."

"You don't say."

Looking down at the flask, she swirled the contents around, then tipped it back and drank.

Well! She might as well have been swallowing liquid fire. As soon as the whisky shot down her gullet, a blazing inferno erupted in her stomach and she began to wheeze. "You call this fine?" She spoke like a raspy old man.

"Aye, lassie, it's stronger than the balls on a bull."

She squeezed her eyes shut. "And you enjoy this?"

Continuing to hold on to the flask, for she was determined not to be bested by this celebrated Scottish drink, she took a moment to recover. In a moment or two, she would try again.

Tipping her head back, she looked up at the stars, and soon her thoughts drifted back to the events of the day. She thought of Elliott and how he had survived alone in the woods for two days.

"The drover we met said Elliott didn't have a mother," Amelia mentioned. "I am without both my parents now, but at least when I was a girl I had a mother I could call in the night when I had a bad dream and she would come and hold me. I'll never forget how it felt to be held in her arms." She tilted her head to the side. "I don't suppose you ever had that, or ever had to call out for someone in the night."

He seemed relaxed while he lounged back against the stone, yet his eyes were as intense as ever. "I called out plenty of times, and my mother always came."

"You had nightmares? And a mother?"

"Despite what you might think of me, lass, I'm not the spawn of the devil."

A touch embarrassed by her comment, she took another drink. Again the whisky burned her throat, but it went down easier than the first time.

"It might surprise you to know," he continued, "that my mother was an educated woman of French descent. She taught me to read and write, and sent me away to be educated."

Amelia drew back slightly. "Indeed, I am surprised. You were educated formally? Where?"

"That's not a question I'll be answering."

Nevertheless, she tucked it away for later, because she wanted to know.

"How did your mother feel about your father's harsh discipline?" Amelia asked. "I can't imagine a scholarly woman would enjoy seeing her child treated with such brutality."

"Nay, she didn't like it, but she wouldn't dare speak against him."

"What about *you*?" she asked. "Did *you* ever try to defy him?"

"Aye, more than once, because I didn't always like what he did to me, or others. But he was my father and I respected him, and I'm the man I am because of him."

She took another drink and began to appreciate the subtle, aromatic flavors beneath the spirit's sheer muscular brawn.

"But what about right and wrong?" she asked. "Did he teach you anything about that? Or just how to fight and survive in the Highlands?"

He considered that for a moment. "That's quite a question, lassie. I cannot say for sure whether or not my father always did what was right, or tried to convey an adequate set of morals. In fact, I know sometimes he didn't. But maybe I know that because of what my mother taught me. She was a thinker and taught me to be one, too. My father, on the other hand . . ." He stopped. "He was just a warrior. Mostly muscle. Not much in the way of a conscience."

Just a warrior. . . . Not much in the way of a conscience. Amelia was shocked to hear Duncan say these things. "At least you had two different perspectives to influence your life. They both played a part in making you into the person you are today."

Indeed, she had seen two different sides of him over the past few days. She had seen a kind and helpful man who tousled a young boy's hair, while previous to that she had witnessed the Butcher's fury. She'd watched him toss an English officer into a lake, then pursue in order to kill.

A wolf howled in the distance, followed by a scuffling sound nearby. Duncan alerted to the sound. He picked up his pistol, which he had placed in the grass beside him. He cocked it and rose to his feet. Amelia stayed low, looking up at him.

Slowly he pulled the dagger from his boot and handed it to her.

She looked up at him curiously, and their eyes locked with a dark fervor as she wrapped her hand around the grip. He was giving her this weapon to protect herself should anything happen to him—or to help him fight, if need be. He was trusting her with it.

He pointed down at her, then at the tall standing stone, suggesting she move behind it. Silently he strode forward through the grass, away from the snapping fire. He stood with his back to her for a long moment, listening carefully to the sounds of the night.

There was another wolfish howl, but it seemed very far away, a mere echo, probably from the opposite mountain range. For a moment Amelia believed there was nothing to fear, until she heard the sound of movement swishing through the grass.

Her belly fired with panic. Was there never a moment's peace in the Highlands?

Duncan crouched low and pulled his axe from his belt. Amelia crawled behind the standing stone.

What if it was a wild boar? Or an enemy soldier?

Perhaps she should be praying to see a man in a red coat, marching toward them with his musket loaded or his bayonet fixed and ready for battle, but after what had happened back at the beach, she was not sure of anything anymore. All she knew was that Duncan was standing between her and this uninvited guest and, whatever the root of his motivations, he was ready to lay down his life to protect her.

The moonlight was bright overhead—so bright, it was easy to see the edge of the hillside. Peering out from behind the stone, Amelia watched with keen, focused eyes.

At long last, the intruder reached the crest of the hill and took a seat not ten feet away from Duncan, facing him squarely, and without the slightest sign of fear or aggression.

Chapter Twelve

"Don't move," Duncan said. He had not yet lowered his weapon.

Amelia was crouched behind the stone, her heart crashing like thunder in her chest, while she watched the extraordinary exchange.

"What does she want?" she asked in a whisper.

"She's curious."

It was the white wolf, sitting calmly.

None of them moved. Duncan was down on one knee, his pistol aimed squarely at the sharp-toothed beast while he held his axe low in the other hand. Amelia suspected he was ready to fling it through the air if the wolf suddenly charged, but for the longest time nothing happened—until Duncan slowly, carefully, sat back on his heels and lowered his weapon.

The wolf panted heavily in the cool night air, then closed her mouth and turned her head toward a sound, listening keenly. Satisfied that it was nothing, she let her mouth fall open again and resumed panting. After a while, she licked her chops and laid her chin down on her front paws, and watched Duncan with wide, blinking eyes.

Amelia came out from behind the standing stone. Duncan said nothing as she approached and knelt beside him. The wolf lifted her head and sniffed the air, then sat up again. Then, without warning, she turned and trotted away, down the hill.

Amelia exhaled with relief. "Did that really just happen?"

"Aye."

They sat for a few minutes, watching the spot where the wolf had disappeared from sight. Not a single blade of grass moved.

"But why didn't she hurt us? If she was afraid of you, or wanted to eat us for dinner, she would have growled or challenged us, wouldn't she?"

"I'd wager she had a full belly."

"I see." Amelia sat quietly for a moment. "So if she returns in the morning, there's still a chance we might become a meal?"

He slipped his axe into his belt and stood. "It's possible."

He held out his hand. Amelia took hold and let him pull her to her feet while she discreetly hid the dagger in the folds of her skirt.

"It didn't occur to you to shoot her, Duncan? Elliott probably would have wanted you to."

"I think the lad might have had trouble doing it, too, if he'd been here in my place."

Amelia stared after the wolf. "She was beautiful, wasn't she?"

"Aye."

Feeling the heat of Duncan's gaze upon her face, Amelia looked into the lustrous blue of his eyes and felt a little inebriated. A soft breeze—the first of the night—gusted past them and fluttered her skirts. She pushed a lock of hair away from her face.

"Come back to the fire," he said. Together they pushed through the grass to their little camp, and Duncan spread the fur out on the ground. "You'll lie with me tonight," he said, "in case she comes back."

Were it not for the wolf, Amelia would have fought him on that issue, but she did not think she would be able to sleep otherwise. And perhaps also she was feeling more relaxed because of the whisky, not to mention the knife she held in her hand.

She picked her way around the dying campfire to join him. Before they lay down, however, he eyed her shrewdly.

"I'll have the dirk now, lass."

She sighed. "You're not going to trust me with it?"

"Nay."

She paused a moment, then decided it was pointless to argue. Besides, after what had happened the night before, she didn't want to find herself in the position of having to choose between her freedom and Duncan's life. He had protected her from those soldiers and the wolf. She simply could not kill him. Not now. Not ever, she supposed.

She held out the weapon. He slipped it into his boot, then dropped lightly to his knees. "Let's get some rest."

They lay down together as they did in the cave that first morning. Amelia faced the fire, and he curled up behind her, tucking his knees into the backs of hers. He covered them both with his tartan.

"Are you comfortable?" he asked.

"Yes." Indeed, she was snug and warm, although she was a far cry from relaxed.

For a long time they lay there without talking, and just when she began to think she might be able to fall asleep, he spoke.

"Can I ask you a question, lass?"

"I suppose I can't stop you."

He hesitated. "Why did you say yes to Richard Bennett? You seem intelligent enough, and I don't think you're blind. You said you admired him because he was a gentleman, but there are scores of gentleman prancing about a London ballroom. Why him? Is it because he saved your father's life?"

She thought hard about all the possible answers to that question. She remembered the times Richard had called upon her and how dashing he had been in his clean scarlet uniform. She had been infatuated at the outset—quite inescapably. She was a young, inexperienced girl with romantic dreams, eager to be wooed by a brave and noble hero.

And her father had confirmed those first impressions and approved of the match. He was, after all, alive because of this handsome young officer, who had galloped across a raging battlefield, straight into the line of fire, to save his life.

"It's complicated," she said, "but I see now that I did not know him as well as I thought I did. All our encounters were polite and proper, and I had romantic ideas. My life before this was sheltered, and after my father's death I believe I was in a hurry to wed. I felt very alone and almost in a panic, so perhaps I *was* blind. I saw only what I wanted to see."

"You were looking for a replacement for your father," Duncan suggested. "You wanted the protection of a husband. You wanted security."

"Yes," she admitted, though it was a difficult thing to say. "Since I allowed you to ask me a question," she said, "and I answered it truthfully, may I ask you one, too?"

"You already asked me a number of them tonight."

"Just one more . . ."

He did not say yes, but he did not refuse, either.

Wetting her lips, she stared at the glowing embers in the fire. Her breathing was irregular, her body restless.

"Why have you not taken me, Duncan? If it's vengeance you want against Richard . . ."

He was quiet for a long moment; then he nuzzled her ear and spoke in a heavy, seductive voice that stroked her mind like velvet. "Maybe I still will."

She lay motionless, intensely aware of the ragged beat of her heart. She had not expected him to say that, but she was not horrified. Quite to the contrary, her body was melting irresistibly into the curve of his legs and torso and she was aching with a strange, unexplored desire.

"You shouldn't have brought it up, lass," he said. "Now my thoughts are wandering, and my hands want to wander, too."

Another breeze swept across the hilltop, hissing through the tall Highland grasses. A strange anticipation rippled through her belly; then he rolled on top of her, so smoothly and naturally, it seemed almost destined to occur. She felt the weight of his hips pressing into hers.

He braced himself high above her on both arms and looked down at her in the moonlight.

She could not move. She was immobilized by a host of emotions she could not begin to comprehend.

He began to swivel his hips in small circles, rubbing up against her. "I told you this morning that you were in more danger than ever."

"Please, Duncan . . ."

"Please what? Stop?"

She knew she should say yes or simply nod her head, but she was incapable of doing either of those things. The only thing she could make sense of was the fire coursing through her veins. She stared up at him with wide eyes until he slowly eased his upper body down and touched his lips to hers.

His open mouth and probing tongue melted every last

fighting scrap of her resistance. She knew she shouldn't want this, not with this man, but neither could she refuse the need to quench her desires.

He nudged her legs open with a knee while he continued to make love to her mouth with his lips and tongue. She moaned, feeling as if she were overcome by some kind of fever, then found herself gripping the fabric of his kilt in her fists.

"Tell me to stop," he said forcefully as he kissed the side of her neck, his movements growing more urgent.

Of course, she would do exactly that—she would tell him to stop—but something compelled her to let it go on for just a few seconds more. Her hips thrust upward on their own, and she kissed him in return, fiercely, angrily. Then at last she uttered a few words, in a desperate sigh of passion.

"Oh, Duncan, please stop."

"Say it like you mean it, lass, or I'll soon be inside you." He drew up her skirts, then slid his axe-roughened palm across the top of her thigh. She squirmed with pleasure.

His hand feathered over her knee, then to her hip and across her stomach. His voice was gruff and sexual. "I want to slide into you. I want to kiss your breasts and your thighs and your soft, naked belly. If you tell me you want that, too, lass, I'll undress you."

"No," she murmured, "I don't want it."

But she did. She couldn't understand it, but she did.

"Then tell me to stop, and do it quick."

She parted her lips to say it, but no words came out.

His hand moved slowly up the length of her sleeve and over her shoulder; then he brushed her hair away from her neck and kissed the tender flesh at the front of her throat. She sucked in a quick breath, still fighting against the desire that washed over her like ocean waves.

"What if I were a gentleman?" he asked, looking into her

eyes with challenge. "Like your Richard? What if I wore a velvet jacket and lace cuffs and shiny buckled shoes? What if I was the son of a wealthy duke or earl? Would it be all right then?"

"But you are not any of those things," she replied. "And he is not *my* Richard. Please stop, Duncan. Stop now."

He lay very still, looking down at her, saying nothing.

She squeezed her eyes shut and braced herself for the possibility that he might decide he did not wish to stop. Why should he? He was ten times stronger than she. He could simply take her by force if he wanted to. He could tear at her skirts and impose himself upon her, and there would be nothing she could do about it.

He rolled off her then, onto his back.

Knowing she had narrowly escaped ruination just now—and escaped her own unfathomable desires as well—she let out a breath and fought to recover her composure. It frightened her to think how close she had come to ravishment, and how desperately she had wanted him, and how amorous she still felt.

She lay still for a long time, staring up at the sky, afraid to speak or move. She turned her head and watched his profile and reflected very carefully and profoundly upon the fact that he had stopped when she'd asked him to.

"I'll trust you," he said, "not to bash me in the head tonight, or slip the dagger out of my boot and stab me with it." There was a hint of anger in his voice, and she wasn't sure if it was directed at her or himself.

"I won't," she replied. "And again, I am truly sorry for what I did to you last night."

"I'm only sorry that you are pledged to my enemy. If you were not, I wouldn't have to use you this way."

"Use me . . . As bait, you mean."

"Aye. That's what you are to me, lass. Nothing more. So do not think otherwise, just because I touched you and held you in my arms tonight. It was just lust—basic animal lust—and do not think that it'll make me forget what I mean to do."

Had he forgotten it? Was that why he was angry? Or did he think she was trying to distract him from that objective?

"You are referring to your desire to kill Richard."

"Aye."

She sat up and pressed the tips of her fingers to her throbbing temples. Heaven help her. She might as well have been the one knocked senseless the previous night, because her brains were clearly addled. She, too, had forgotten who they were and why they were here. She desired Duncan passionately and had lost sight of the fact that he wanted to use her to kill a man in cold blood.

"You still don't believe it, do you?" he asked. "You still think I'm mistaken, and that the people of Scotland have embellished the stories about your precious Richard. You're still loyal to him."

"That's not true," she said. "I do believe that I was too hasty in accepting his proposal. I recognize the fact that I was naïve and did not take enough time to get to know him. But if I've learned anything from all this, it is that I must think for myself and form my own judgments. Therefore I cannot, in good conscience, condemn a man based on what his enemies say. I must at least allow him the opportunity to answer the charges. When I see him again, I will most certainly give him that chance."

Duncan stood up. "The mere idea of you in the same room with Richard Bennett makes me want to vomit. I won't allow it."

"But even if he is guilty of those crimes of which you accuse him," she said, "that does not give *you* the right to kill him. Even the worst criminal deserves a proper trial."

Duncan's brow darkened with displeasure, and he began to pace.

"If Richard is guilty of something," she continued, "let him be arrested and dealt with according to the law. You should not darken your soul any further to ensure justice is served."

"But my soul is already destined for hell," he growled.

She shivered. "I don't believe that. There is always hope. People can change."

But did she truly believe there was hope where Duncan was concerned? He was the Butcher of the Highlands. He'd killed dozens of men.

They said nothing for a long time; then he shot her an irritated look. "You remind me of my mother sometimes. She was beautiful, and she was a stubborn idealist. She didn't approve of violence, and she worked tirelessly to convince my father that she was right and he was wrong."

"Did she ever succeed in convincing him?"

Duncan laughed bitterly. "Nay. That was a futile ambition. She and I both ended up bruised and battered over it. My father was a warrior. He had no interest in diplomacy, and I was stuck in the middle, between her and his crushing, iron fist."

Amelia sat back. Had Duncan protected his mother against his father's brutality?

Not wishing to provoke him any further than she had already, Amelia waited a moment for his anger to cool.

"My father was a warrior, too," she said in an effort to calm him, "but he could also be kind. He believed in peace."

"He was a soldier, Amelia. He fought and he killed."

She shuddered, for she had never thought of her father in that light, nor had she ever imagined him actually killing a man. She did not want to imagine it now. "He fought for what he believed in."

"As do I, lass, and for that reason, I cannot let your fiancé live."

The comment struck her hard, like a punch in the stomach. Alas, when Duncan had mentioned how he once tried to stand between his mother and his father's iron fist, Amelia thought she might be able to draw him away from his murderous quest. But looking into his eyes now and seeing the fury that dwelled there, she knew he could not be persuaded.

"Will you deliver me to Moncrieffe Castle?" she asked, needing to know how all of this would play out. "I know we are traveling in that direction, but even if Richard has left the castle and gone elsewhere, will you leave me there in the earl's care? The earl was a friend of my father's. Wouldn't it be best if—"

"Nay!" Duncan said harshly, facing her. "I will not leave you anywhere! Not while your fiancé still lives."

He breathed deeply for a moment, as if struggling to control his anger; then he moved around the fire. "You should sleep, lass, but I'm awake now, so I'll sit against the stone and keep watch."

He sat down, picked up the flask he'd left in the grass, but it was empty, so he tossed it onto the pile of saddlebags.

Shivering from a sudden chill in the air, Amelia lay down again and wrapped the fur around her. She closed her eyes and wondered miserably if she would ever feel sure of anything again.

The lass wanted him to spare Richard Bennett's life. How disappointed she was going to be when he ended it.

No, it would be much worse than that. She would see him as the savage that he truly was. She would be repulsed by the blood on his hands, and the stench of death and despair that followed him everywhere. She would loathe him, far more than she did now.

He should not have tried to slake his lust for her tonight. If he'd been listening to his brains instead of his balls, he would have kept her at a safe distance—perhaps even bound and gagged the entire time. He should not have revealed anything of himself to her. She knew too much as it was.

What was he to do, then? he wondered wretchedly as he watched her finally drift off to sleep. Let Richard Bennett live for the sake of her courtly, idealistic principles about order and justice? Let him continue to rape, murder, and destroy?

Duncan tipped his head back against the standing stone and stared up at the sky. If only he could feel some sense of peace again, or even hope to feel it one day in the future. Not long ago, he thought he would achieve it when Bennett was dead. All he felt now, however, was a heavy yoke of doubt and a deep, unfathomable emptiness.

He thought of his real mother then—the whore he never knew because she'd died giving birth to him—and the bishop who'd been slaughtered for his opinions on the matter of Duncan's existence in the world as a bastard child. That bishop should have known better than to pay insult to Duncan's father. He'd ended up without a head.

Perhaps this was Duncan's father's legacy and a continued punishment for his sins—a life of war and wretchedness for his doomed son who had inherited his wrath. All good deeds were rewarded, Duncan supposed, and all sinners were eventually escorted to hell.

Hours later, the sound of footsteps swishing through the grass startled Duncan awake. He had fallen asleep, sitting up against the stone.

His gaze darted to Amelia. She was resting quietly, wrapped in the fur.

Shaking off the heavy haze of slumber, he sat up.

Everything was as it should be. The bags were untouched. Turner was nearby. But then Duncan heard the faint whisper of footsteps again.

Slowly, with careful, hushed movements, he reached for his axe and closed his grip around the well-worn handle. If the wolf had returned to make a meal of them, he would not think twice. He would kill her. He would do what was necessary to protect Amelia.

He rose to his feet and moved without a sound around the ashes in the fire pit. The stars were all gone now, the sky a deathly black. Even the air was thick with the suffocating aroma of blood and doom.

The footsteps grew closer, and he moved forward like a cat stalking its prey. His gaze traveled from east to west, searching the landscape. He'd never felt more attuned to danger. He would protect Amelia, even at the cost of his own life.

The visitor appeared then, illuminated suddenly by the moon, which emerged from behind a wispy cloud.

"Elliott," Duncan said, lowering the axe to his side. "What are you doing back here? Where's your father?"

"He stayed with the flock," the boy said. "But I ran away. I followed you. I *stalked* you."

Duncan frowned. "What do you mean, you stalked me? Why would you do such a thing?"

"Because I know who you are. You're the Butcher, and you're a vicious killer."

A hot, burning star from the sky dropped into the pit of Duncan's stomach. He wanted to disagree, to say he was no such thing, but he could not speak. At least not those words.

"I'm going to kill you," Elliott said, drawing his sword. "Then I'll be a hero, just like you are."

Duncan shook his head. "You don't know what you're saying, Elliott. Put down the sword. Go back to your father and drive your flock to market."

"Nay, I want to take your head to London." He raised the sword and shouted a wild cry for justice, then dashed forward.

Duncan reacted on instinct. The boy came at him, and he swung his axe.

To defend myself. To protect my identity. To save Amelia.

Elliott's head flew threw the air, spinning like a ball kicked by a boy in a stable yard. . . .

The wolf watched with indifference from the crest of the hill, her tongue hanging out while she panted.

"Fook!"

Duncan startled awake and crawled away from the stone as fast as he could. He couldn't breathe! His stomach was churning with a sickening fire that was burning his guts. He crawled through the grass, needing to expel the contents of his stomach, but his body only heaved violently with a dry and pointless purge of emptiness.

"Duncan, what is it?"

He felt Amelia's hands on his back and tried to tell himself it was not real. It had not happened. It was only a dream. Elliott was not dead. The boy had not followed him here.

He put a hand on his forehead and collapsed onto his back. "Ah, Jesus."

"What happened?" she asked. "What's wrong?"

"It was a dream." He said the words aloud, compellingly, to convince himself.

He was sweating, gasping for air.

It was a dream. It did not happen.

Amelia cradled his head on her lap and pushed his hair away from his face. "It's all right now. It's over."

It took a long time for his heart to stop pounding, and when it finally did, he stared up at the sky but quickly closed his eyes and struggled against the unbearable memory of the dream.

Chapter Thirteen

The following morning, Duncan said very little. Amelia looked across the fire at him and felt as if she were looking at a stranger. He was exactly that, she supposed, regardless of the fact that he'd held her and kissed her and almost made love to her the night before. She wished she could push it from her mind, but the desire still lingered in her blood this morning like a treacherous fever, which made no sense.

How could she feel such pleasure with this man, who had kidnapped her and refused to restore her freedom by delivering her to safety? Despite her protestations, he still had every intention of killing Richard, and she could not understand such a hunger for violence and bloodshed. That was why the civilized world had courts of law—to decide whether a man was guilty of a crime, and to assign the proper punishment. This hunting and stalking approach—ending in the bloody slaughter of another human being—was barbaric. It was outside the realm of her understanding.

Nevertheless, her insides still burned with something. An eager, aching lust that shamed her. She swore to herself that she would do her best to conquer it.

That night, Duncan decided it would be best to keep his distance from Amelia. As a result, they ate in silence around the fire and when she tried to make conversation, he told her he had no interest in pointless talk. The truth was, it was simply too difficult to listen to the cadence of her voice, nor did it do him any good to watch the enticing movement of her lips when she spoke.

Later, however, not long after she fell asleep, he moved closer to the bed of fur and looked down at her. She lay on her stomach, with one long slender leg bent at the knee and drawn up into the thick tangle of her skirts. Her wavy hair was splayed out on the fur, shining like wild flames of fire. He recalled too easily the honeyed flavor of her lips and the soft texture of her tongue, swirling freely around his own. Growing agitated and resentful, he backed up a few steps and sat down on his haunches.

The moon was high in the sky. Cloud shadows moved swiftly across the quiet glen. There was a strong perfume of late-summer blooms in the air. In the far-off distance, thunder rumbled softly over the mountaintops.

He sat for a long time watching Amelia sleep while the curve of her hip played tricks on his mind.

With a soft moan, she rolled over onto her back and settled into a flauntingly feminine, seductive pose. Her breasts—too tightly confined by the stays, which she refused to take off, even at night—seemed to reach out and beckon to him lasciviously. Sexual hunger overwhelmed him, and he wished he could unlace all those constricting articles of clothing, slide her skirts down over her hips, and run his hands across her naked flesh. She lay before him like the embodiment of human sexuality, and he realized this was more a test of his strength than any violent swordfight on a battlefield.

The following day they stopped by a river to water the horse and eat a light lunch.

"Are you going to talk to me at all?" Amelia asked

when Duncan sat down on a low boulder across from her.

"Nay."

"Not even if I get down on my knees and beg?"

He shoved a piece of bread at her. "Do you want me to stuff a gag in your mouth?"

"No."

"Then don't be saying things like that."

They made camp in the forest that night, and Amelia was surprised when, after supper, Duncan lay down on the bed of fur next to her—for he had kept his distance the night before and had treated her with hostility through most of the day.

"What happens next?" she asked, hoping that tonight would be different. She had not enjoyed the tension between them, or the loneliness she felt, knowing he did not even wish to talk to her. "We've been traveling for two days. When will we reach Moncrieffe? Surely we must be close."

He covered her with his tartan and looked at her grimly. "Aye, lassie. This very ground belongs to the earl. We're an hour north of the gatehouse."

She leaned up on an elbow. The tartan fell away from her shoulder. "A mere hour? Then why have we stopped? We could be there by now."

His eyes were dark and indecipherable. "I wanted one more night with you, lass."

She took a moment to comprehend the meaning behind those words and thought again about how silent and brooding he had been all day. She had thought it was because he resented her for the things she said about Richard the other night and was surprised that he would stall the ultimate achievement of his victory.

"But you told me that you would never let me hold you

back from killing Richard," she said, "or distract you from it."

"Aye, and I resent you very much right now, so be careful what you say. I'm ill-tempered."

She swallowed uneasily. "I do not understand." He resented her, but he wanted another night with her?

Then suddenly her imagination was running riot and she was permitting herself to wonder if she might be able to sway him from his goal after all—that perhaps a small sliver of affection for her could become more important to him than the bloodshed he craved. Perhaps he might give it all up for the sake of her happiness. He was risking a great deal, after all, camping here for one more night, when Richard might be heading in the other direction at this very moment.

But then she understood, more realistically, that it was not an affection for her that had slowed their progress but a simple physical lust. She remembered how he had watched her throughout the day, and shivered with apprehension—a fear of something inevitable, something she might not be able to control or prevent.

"Make no mistake about it," he said. "I want my vengeance, and justice, too. Nothing can stand in the way of it. But when I achieve it, you'll not be able to look at me, lass. You'll see only the brutal savage that I am."

She felt a lump of dread rise up in her. Of course she wanted to reach Moncrieffe and return to her comfortable, civilized world, but the horrors of what Duncan felt compelled to do before he could release her did not bear thinking of. She did not want to imagine him committing an act of murder.

"I want this to end," she said. "I don't wish to be your captive. But must you really do it? Can you not have your vengeance another way? Report Richard to the authorities. Write a letter and demand an official inquiry."

Duncan chuckled bitterly at the suggestion, then reached up and pushed her hair away from her face. "I've enjoyed your company, lassie, and I'll miss you when you're gone."

Why would he not see reason?

He slid his arm around her waist and pulled her closer. "I've been aching for you all day, and try as I might, I can do nothing to slake my lust. I've never felt more savage than I do when I am lying next to you."

Shocked by his confession and flushed by the heat that was simmering inside her body, she pulled back and stared at him. But before she could utter a word, his mouth collided with hers, and he rolled over on top of her.

A breeze swished through the leafy treetops, and Amelia arched her back wantonly. The desire to hold him and be held by him was powerful, and her head began to swim. He cupped her breast and massaged it, and she gasped helplessly. She wanted the passion and intimacy, but at the same time she wanted to fight against it.

His tongue swept into her mouth; then he lifted her skirts, slid them up to her waist, and caressed her thighs. All that stood between them now was her split drawers, which he soon penetrated with skillful, probing fingers. She felt his whole palm slide between her legs, then stroke and knead her sensitive damp flesh. The pleasure became a kind of insistent ache, and she pressed her legs together, squeezing them around his hand.

"I'm just touching you, lass," he whispered against her lips, and she quivered with delight, even when she knew it would lead to so much more. This was seduction. He was luring her to a very dangerous place.

Her legs parted readily when he used the heel of his hand to pleasure her. Sensations rushed forward, and she thrilled at his touch. He tasted her with his tongue, then rose up on his arms and mounted her.

Her rational mind was telling her to put a stop to this, but her body refused to listen. Legs spread wide, she felt the silky tip of his erection, pressing against her. Everything was hot and wet, and she did not want it to end, even when she knew it was wrong.

"I want to take you now," he said, "but you must be willing."

Her chest was heaving. She hesitated to respond.

"If you do not want to part with your virginity, you must say so now."

"I don't know," she whispered. "I don't want to stop, but I always believed I would save myself for my husband."

Duncan gazed down at her in the firelight, then drew back and rested his forehead on her shoulder. He seemed to be taking some time to bring his desires under control.

"I'll not ruin you," he softly said, "but I can still give you pleasure."

She did not understand what he meant. All she could do was watch him inch downward on the fur and disappear under her skirts. She gasped in shock as he kissed her ankles, her knees, her inner thighs, then pushed her legs wide apart and plunged hard with his mouth and tongue into the folds of her womanhood.

She arched her back and sucked in a breath, reeling in a blind and mindless haze of rapture. "What are you doing to me?"

He offered no explanation, however, for his lips were very busy.

She soon forgot the question anyway, as she listened to the sounds he made with his mouth. Was this normal? Was this what all men and women did, or just the Scots?

Overcome by passion, she threw her head back and cried out. Her body began to quiver and shake, her muscles tensed, and a hot wave of fire splashed over her. She writhed like a trapped animal on the fur and pounded her fists on the ground. Pleasure like no other consumed her, even while she fought to resist it; then all her strength poured away.

After a time, he backed out from under her skirts and covered her body with his own. He held her close, and she felt strangely loved and protected. She didn't want to let go of him. She wanted to be held like this forever. She had never felt so close to anyone.

"What was that?" she asked, knowing that her emotions were not, at present, rational.

"I told you, we Scots like to pleasure our women." He pulled her skirts down to cover her legs. "But you should sleep now, lass."

She stared up at the sky, feeling as if she were in some kind of drunken stupor.

"I enjoyed it," she confessed.

"I know."

"But I should not have allowed it to happen. It was too much."

For a long time he said nothing. He simply looked up at the shadowy treetops against the night sky.

Then at last he spoke. "Aye, it was. And I should not have allowed it to happen, either."

They said nothing more to each other that night.

Duncan had not slept soundly in months, and feeling completely rested the following morning was a foreign, unrecognizable thing.

He woke to the perfume of the pines, the sound of swallows chirping in the treetops, and the pink glow of the sunrise beyond the forest, casting a pale light on his eyelids. Yawning, he stretched his arms over his head, then remembered, with a sudden stab of discontent, what would occur on this day. He would ride with Amelia to the castle and perhaps find Richard Bennett there, enjoying the many luxuries Moncrieffe had to offer.

Duncan's immediate reaction to the idea of Bennett being served at the castle made him want to go there straightaway, grab the dirty maggot by the throat, and toss him over the castle walls. But first he would drive a sword through Bennett's heart and remind him why he was dying: *Do you remember the girl in the orchard? This is for her. And it's for the woman you thought you might have for a wife. She'll never suffer what Muira did.*

Duncan sat up and looked around. Amelia was not beside him, however, nor was she within view of the camp.

Instantly alert, he rose to his feet and shouted, "Amelia!"

No answer came, nor was there any sign of another person within sight or earshot.

He surveyed the silent forest. Hazy beams of sunlight shone through the trees, casting long shadows on the ground. The new day seemed to be creeping up on him, moving surreptitiously along the mossy floor of the wood.

"Amelia!" he shouted a second time, striding forward more insistently into the mist, but his call returned only as an echo.

No, she wouldn't have. . . .

But yes, he knew that she had. "Fookin' hell."

Within minutes, he had saddled Turner, packed up the camp, and was shoving his axe into the saddle scabbard. He swung himself up onto Turner's back.

"Yah!" Duncan shouted, urging Turner into a gallop toward the edge of the forest, then to the southern fields beyond.

What time had she fled the camp? Duncan wondered anxiously. Had she reached the castle yet? And what if Bennett was there and had already issued orders to hunt down the infamous Butcher, who was in the immediate vicinity? Duncan might not even reach the castle gates before he was overtaken by enemy soldiers, and then what would he do?

Damn her. Damn her straight to hell. He should never have taken her from Fort William, because now the only thing he cared about was getting her back. He didn't care if Richard Bennett lived or died—only that he would never touch Amelia again.

In light of the current circumstances, Duncan could see only one way to accomplish all of those things. He kicked in his heels and rode hard toward Moncrieffe.

Chapter Fourteen

After an initial ordeal of terror and imprisonment, followed by a confusing and overpowering lust for her captor, that particular morning was the worst.

Amelia had woken up in a state of emotional turmoil. She took one look at Duncan asleep on the bed of fur—the most handsome man she ever laid eyes on—and realized she had to get away from him, because she had fallen hopelessly, passionately, foolishly in love.

Now she was stumbling across a field, weak and disoriented. Her shoes were wet from the dew in the grass, her toes numb from the chill. She was exhausted and breathless, for she'd been running frantically for almost an hour—first through the forest, then across these wide, rolling fields. She had no idea where she was; she had only the sunrise to guide her in any direction. She could be lost in the middle of nowhere for all she knew, for it was entirely possible that the castle was not located perfectly south of where they had camped the night before, even though Duncan had said they were north of it. She could have inadvertently passed it by and might in due course end up on the shores of the Irish Sea.

Surely he must have discovered her absence by now and begun his pursuit. He could come galloping across the fields at any moment and bring a swift end to her escape. If he found her, he would be furious. It would not be so pleasant between them after that. There would be no more kissing and caressing. He would likely tie her up and gag her from that moment on.

But it would not be so very different, she supposed, from the bonds of his sexual power, which had enslaved her in a mad, irrational desire and almost kept her from running this morning when she finally had the chance to escape.

She stopped and looked around, glanced up at the sun to try to ascertain her location and bearings. If she was going to survive this ordeal and return to the life she once knew, she would have to stop thinking about Duncan and set her sights on locating the castle.

It had been far more than an hour since Amelia had fled the camp in the woods. She was just resigning herself to the fact that she was lost when she reached the edge of a tree-lined field and a grand skyline of towers and turrets came into view.

Exhausted but clinging to newfound hope, she stopped in her tracks and blinked to focus her eyes on the impressive panorama of stone architecture, like a small city in the distance. On its outskirts she saw vegetable gardens, an orchard, a vineyard, a mill—all less than a mile away. Civilization at last. A world she knew.

She began to run, stumbling on blistered feet over grass that glistened with dew. White mist rose from the surface of a lake, but as she drew closer it revealed its true purpose as a defensive moat. The castle stood on an island. Its stone walls and drum bastions rose sheer from the water, and the tremendous gate tower was connected to the mainland by a drawbridge and an arched entrance.

Richard might be there now, perhaps with a small battalion of soldiers, stationed within. What would she do when she saw him? What would she say about the appalling stories she'd heard about him?

Would he ask if she had been ravished?

Breathless with exhaustion, she reached the bridge at last and crossed over, where she was met by a large, ruddy-cheeked guard dressed in a kilt and armed with two pistols and a claymore. He stood under an iron portcullis.

"Are you lost, lassie?" His voice was deep and intimidating.

"No, sir, I am not lost. For once, I know exactly where I am—at Castle Moncrieffe—and I wish to address the earl." She could barely speak through her breathing.

"And what's your business with my laird so early in the morning? He's a very busy man."

She spoke in a clear and steady voice. "I am Lady Amelia Templeton, daughter of the late Duke of Winslowe, who was a colonel in the King's army. One week ago, I was abducted by the Butcher of the Highlands, and I have just escaped. I am in immediate need of the earl's protection." It took every ounce of mettle she possessed to get the words out.

The Scotsman's smile faded, and his face went pale. "You're the colonel's daughter?"

Oh, thank God. "Yes."

He bowed to her. "Beggin' your pardon, milady. Come this way."

He led her through the wide, shaded archway, then into the blinding sunlight beyond, which beamed down on an inner bailey. It was a green, parklike space with a circular drive all around. To the left a high curtain wall with drum bastions blocked the view of the lake, and to the right a large square building cast a long shadow across the lawn. There were few people about.

Amelia and the guard walked quickly toward the main

castle, which was just as she'd imagined from her father's descriptions. Moncrieffe was a stately palace of classical elegance, and she could barely believe she was about to set foot inside it, after the trials of the past week. How strange it would be to walk on polished floors again, to behold works of art, to climb ornate staircases.

They entered the main hall and passed through an archway to a small reception room with elaborate wood paneling, a marble chimneypiece, and a fine collection of Chinese porcelain.

"Wait here, milady," the guard said, bowing again before he quickly departed, closing the door behind him.

Amelia once again felt the sting in her shoes from the blisters, so she hobbled to an upholstered chair, sat down, and clasped her hands together on her lap. She sat very still, taking a moment to close her eyes, catch her breath, and calm herself. None of this seemed real. She felt strangely detached from it.

It was quiet in the room, except for a clock ticking on the mantel. After a moment or two, she opened her eyes. She looked around at the furniture. The chairs and end tables appeared to be of French workmanship, while the carpet looked Persian. On the far wall there was a portrait of an ancestor—a fierce-looking man in an armored breastplate and kilt, with one hand on his sword.

The clock ticked on, and she did not move from her chair for a full ten minutes, though it seemed like an eternity. An eternity of stillness.

Finally, she heard footsteps in the hall and stood. The door opened, and a gentleman entered. He was of medium height and slender build, wore a green brocade morning coat with lace cuffs, black knee breeches, shiny buckled shoes—and upon his head a curly brown wig. He, too, was just as she'd envisioned from her father's descriptions, although she did imagine the earl to be taller.

If this was, in fact, the earl.

He looked very . . . *English*.

She curtsied.

"You are Lady Amelia Templeton?" he asked, and his Scottish brogue reminded her that she was still in the Highlands.

She noted with immense relief that the gentleman's voice was friendly and kind. There was nothing threatening or intimidating about him.

"Yes, and I am grateful to you, Lord Moncrieffe, for receiving me at such an early hour."

"Oh no," he said, strolling into the room, appearing rather concerned. "I am not the earl. I am Iain MacLean. His brother."

She shifted on stinging feet while struggling to hide her disappointment. "Is the earl not in residence?"

"Aye, he is here. But he is not yet out of bed. He'll need some time to at least put on a coat." Iain smiled apologetically.

"Oh yes, of course." She glanced at the clock. It was ten minutes past seven, certainly not the proper time for a call.

This was all very strange. She had been running for over an hour, having escaped an abduction. Her hair had not been combed, her skirts were soiled with mud—she could only imagine what she smelled like—and this man seemed to be wondering if he should ring for tea. What she really wanted to do was run to him and shake him and demand to know if he understood what she had been through.

"May I inquire," she calmly asked, "if Richard Bennett is here? He is lieutenant-colonel of the Ninth Dragoons, and I was told he was heading in this direction."

This felt utterly ridiculous.

"Aye, he was here," Iain replied, gesturing for her to sit down again. "He stayed only one night, however, for he was determined to find you, Lady Amelia. You should know there is a considerable search taking place on your behalf, even as we speak. Your uncle, the Duke of Winslowe, has offered five hundred pounds to anyone who delivers you safely back to Fort William. He's been most distressed by what has happened. As we all are."

Ah, sensible talk, at last, about the reality of the situation. This wasn't a dream after all. She had found sanctuary.

She exhaled sharply. "Thank you, sir. You have no idea how relieved I am to hear all of this. It is comforting to know I was not forgotten. I rather felt like I was in danger of disappearing forever."

Although she still feared that a part of her soul was lost in another place and would never be recovered.

He sat down on the sofa beside her and squeezed her hand. "You are safe now, Lady Amelia. No harm will come to you."

She took a moment to collect herself and hold back the tears that threatened to spill from her eyes. Her belly flooded with misery.

But no—it was not misery. She could not let herself believe that she was unhappy. She was safe now. The terror was past. She was no longer a captive in the mountains, or in danger of losing herself to that strange madness that had taken over her body. She had escaped successfully, before it was too late, and she would probably never see Duncan again. She should be happy. She *was* happy. She *was*.

"I must look a fright," she said shakily, managing a small smile.

There was compassion in Iain's eyes. "You look very tired, Lady Amelia. Perhaps you would like some breakfast and a warm bath. I can summon the housekeeper, and my wife, Josephine, would be happy, I'm sure, to offer her maid's services and lend you a clean gown. You look to be about the same size."

"That would be most kind of you, Mr. MacLean. I have long wanted to meet the earl, as my father spoke highly of him. Perhaps I could present myself to him in a more respectable fashion."

Iain smiled gently. "I understand. Please, let me show you to a guest chamber."

Amelia could have wept tears of joy after she enjoyed a private breakfast and was then shown to the bathing room, where she undressed leisurely and eased herself into a warm copper tub. The walls of the room were hung with green damask, and a rush mat covered the floor. White linen curtains, hung from a circular canopy above, surrounded the tub, while a strong, hot fire blazed in the hearth.

Mrs. MacLean's maid stood by to assist Amelia in bathing and dressing. She lathered her hair with herb-scented soap, massaged her scalp, then poured a gentle stream of water from a shiny brass pitcher to rinse it clean. She rubbed her skin with a soft cloth and washed her back, and afterward the maid dressed Amelia in a blue and pink gown of rich floral silk brocade, generously on loan from Mrs. MacLean.

The dress had a scoop neckline trimmed with lace. Its sleeves were tight, with deep cuffs below the elbow, and it boasted a boned stomacher of matching silk brocade. The buckled shoes, also of blue silk damask, were one size too large, but two extra pairs of stockings helped fill them out. Amelia felt as if she were dreaming all of this.

The maid piled her hair into an elaborate, towering construction and shook the powder generously until she blinked with burning eyes and sputtered and held up a hand to stop the assault.

It felt strange moving about in such a confining display of extravagance after a week of wearing nothing but coarse wool and loose linen, but when she viewed herself in the looking glass, glittering in silk and satin, and recognized what was familiar, she began to weep. The tears were strange, however. Her emotions were disjointed and rambling.

She longed desperately to see her uncle again and wondered when that blessed moment would occur. Perhaps then she would feel normal again.

A short time later, a liveried footman knocked at her door and said, "His Lairdship will see you now."

She followed the young Scot into the wide corridor, which took them to the main staircase, then downstairs toward the rear of the castle. They crossed over a bridge corridor with arched windows looking out onto the lake, which led out of the castle to the keep—a separate tower at the back, surrounded entirely by water.

Amelia wondered what questions the earl would ask. How much would he wish to know about her abduction? Would he ask the details of her capture, the specifics about Duncan's weapons, or his name and the names of all the rebels who followed him?

Would the earl force her to give an account of where she and Duncan had camped each night and who they encountered along the way? If she revealed that information, would the earl send an army into the forest immediately to hunt for Duncan and drag him to the Tolbooth?

Something raw and agonizing seized up inside her. She did not want to be responsible for his capture. Where was he at that moment? He must have known she would come here. Was he outside the castle walls, watching her pass by these very windows? Or had he escaped in the other direction, knowing that once she arrived at Moncrieffe, she would reveal all she knew and he would be pursued?

She hoped he realized the gravity of his predicament and had fled the other way. It would be best for both of them. She also hoped Moncrieffe would be as fair as her father believed him to be and that he would take all of Duncan's conduct into account. She was still in possession of her virtue, after all. Duncan could have deprived her of that, but he had not done so, and for that she would be forever grateful.

Amelia and the footman crossed a long narrow banqueting hall, then reached an arched door at the end with wrought-iron fittings. He knocked, then pushed the door open and stepped aside. Amelia entered a gallery with a polished oak floor, walls of gray stone, and a wide fireplace adorned with heraldic images in the spandrels. She moved fully into the room, and the door closed behind her.

The earl stood elegantly at the window with his hands clasped behind his back, looking out at the lake and park beyond. He wore a lavish full-skirted blue coat of French silk, heavily embroidered in silver, with frilled shirtsleeves extending from the cuffs. The tight knee breeches were gray, worn with knee-high riding boots, polished to a fine black sheen. Unlike his brother, he wore no wig. His hair was lightly powdered and tied back, the long queue spirally bound with black ribbon. She noted the decorative saber at his waist, encased in a glossy black sheath.

"My lord." She waited for him to turn around so that she could award him a proper curtsy.

When at last he did face her, she bowed her head, but the shock of familiarity shot into her stomach like a cannonball. Her gaze flew up as the urge to honor him with the customary curtsy fell to the wayside.

"You?"

Were her eyes deceiving her?

No, they were not.

It was Duncan. Butcher of the Highlands.

Or his identical twin. . . .

Her body shuddered as if she'd been punched, and she stood, breath held, fighting shock and disbelief. This was not real. It could not be!

Hands still clasped behind his back, Duncan—or the earl—strode ominously toward her, shaking his head. "Tsk-tsk, Lady Amelia. I am very disappointed to discover that Fergus was right in the end. 'Can you trust the word of the English?' he always said. I should have listened to him."

Feeling dazed and frazzled and still not entirely sure this was not Duncan's twin, she turned for the door, but he followed and pressed the flats of his hands against it before she could reach the handle. He stood behind her with his arms braced on either side of her while she tried in vain to tug, rattle, and shake the door open.

She called for a servant, but no one came to her aid. She might as well have been shouting into a void. When she finally gave up the struggle and tipped her head forward in defeat, Duncan nuzzled the back of her ear, as he had done so many times before, and she knew in that moment that this was the man she had come to desire so desperately. She had not gotten away at all.

"I would expect no less from you, lass. You were always a fighter."

His body brushed up against hers. Were it not for the memory of all too recent sensations and desires, she might have been able to keep her head, but this was impossible.

"I don't believe it," she whispered, closing her eyes. "How can this be?"

She felt as if she were back in that field in the rain on the first morning of her abduction—not knowing what kind of man she was dealing with, feeling powerless to escape. She had no idea what he meant to do with her now that she had run from him.

He pulled her away from the door, then circled around her and blocked the exit with his large, muscular form.

"I knew this was where you would come," he said, "so I rode hard from the camp. Did you enjoy your breakfast and bath? Is the gown fashionable enough for your sophisticated tastes?"

There was something diabolical in his eyes, and there was a hard edge to his voice that cut her to the quick.

"You are truly the earl? This is not a hoax?"

All at once, a hot and seething anger burned in her core. How could she have been so blind? And all that talk about her learning to trust her own judgment and see a man for who he truly was on the inside—how could he have said all that to her while he was masquerading as two different men, intentionally misleading and manipulating all who came into his sphere? Who *was* this man deep down? She had no idea.

"I am the great Laird of Moncrieffe," he said, spreading his arms wide, a gesture that flaunted the extravagance of lace at his cuffs. As he lowered his hands, a blue gemstone on his forefinger reflected the sunlight beaming in through the window. "But I am the Butcher, too."

"You lied to me."

All that had passed between them—the intimacy and tenderness she had felt in his arms, the trust that had begun to grow—it was all gone now, and she had never felt more foolish. With a sweep of her hand, she indicated his fashionable clothing. "What is all of this? I cannot believe you spent five days with my father negotiating for Scottish freedom, leading him to believe you wanted peace, while at the same time you were riding up and down the Scottish Highlands killing English soldiers?" She looked around the room, at the paintings on the walls. "Who else knows of this? You certainly pulled the wool over my father's eyes, as well as my own. Who else have you tricked besides me? Does your housekeeper know? The footman who just escorted me to this door? Is this a vast and bottomless conspiracy of treason?"

She thought of Richard spending the night here at Moncrieffe, enjoying the earl's food and whisky and his so-called hospitality. On the way to the guest chamber, Iain had told her that Richard had employed the earl's militia to ride out in search of the infamous Butcher. Richard was probably being lured on a wild-goose chase by now, on his way to the Orkney Islands or some other far-off place.

And was *any* of what Duncan told her about Richard true? She had no idea what to believe.

"No one at the castle knows," Duncan replied, "except my brother and his wife."

"Your brother, who was so kind, and arranged for my breakfast and a bath . . . He is a charlatan, too?"

Duncan frowned. "He's a good man and a loyal Scot."

She tried again to reach the door. "You are insane. You and your brother both."

Duncan seized her wrist. His big warrior hand gripped her like a steel vice. "I wouldn't do that if I were you."

She didn't bother trying to free herself. "Why not? Are you afraid I'll walk out of here and reveal your true identity to the world?"

It was a clear threat, uttered without subtlety or reservation.

His eyes narrowed, and he dipped his head to speak close in her ear. "I fear nothing at the moment, lass, because Angus is standing outside that door and he's been itching to slit your throat from the beginning. You'd be wise not to give him a reason to do it."

Chapter Fifteen

Amelia tugged her arm free and adjusted the fabric of her sleeve. "I despise you."

"It's your right to think of me however you choose, but I suggest you hear me out first."

She strode away from him, across the gallery toward the window. "Hear you out? What is there to possibly explain? You are a fraud. One week ago, you were a savage in a kilt, wielding an axe over my bed—the most sought-after enemy of England. This morning you are a gentleman, dressed in silks and ruffles and lace. You negotiated with my father, an English duke, who thought so highly of you and sang your praises to the King." She turned and faced him. "I will never forgive you for this. You have made a fool of me. When I think of the past few nights, and how you seduced me—"

"Seduced you?" He laughed. "You wanted it as much as I did, lass. If I remember correctly, you did mention that you enjoyed it." His eyes simmered with desire. "Don't lie to yourself. You need a real man inside you, instead of that polite English fop you think to call a gentleman, and do not insult me, or yourself, by trying to deny it."

She crossed to him and slapped his face. "You may be dressed impeccably. You may even be of noble blood, but clearly, you are no gentleman."

He stood motionless, barely reacting to the strike. Clearly this ruthless man was made of steel or stone.

She returned to the window and looked out at the lake. The light sound of his footsteps crossing the room sent sparks of awareness to all her nerve endings.

"I am more a gentleman than your betrothed, lass. You just haven't seen that side of him."

"Do all men have two sides?" she asked, feeling more lost and alone than ever. "Do you all have secrets? If so, how is it possible to ever know someone? Or to trust? Or *love*?"

She watched a duck fly low and skim the surface of the water in a smooth landing and fought ardently against the urge to weep and fall to this man's knees and beg for an explanation, so that she could understand what she was feeling. She was frustrated to the point of dizziness. Part of her still desired him, but she felt so confused over who he really was.

His hand came to rest on her shoulder. He stroked the back of her neck with his thumb, and all her defenses began to crumble.

"Are you not afraid I'll turn you in to the King?" she asked, retreating back to the war that still existed between them, because she was afraid to let herself give in to the passion.

"You won't do that, lass," he replied.

"How can you be so sure?"

"Because I know you care for me," he said, and her body grew warm with unease. "I felt it last night when I held you in my arms. A man learns much about a woman during such a moment."

Something compelled her to deny it. "That is not true."

Yet this morning, when she left him, she'd wanted to cry her eyes out.

He circled around her to block her view of the water and gazed down at her sagely. "And you call *me* a liar."

His voice was oddly hushed, and his eyes glimmered with shadows of desire that caused everything inside her to melt. Amelia lifted her face to his, and for a moment she stood apart, struggling to bury the memory of what had passed between them the night before, but the attempt was futile.

He pulled her toward him, her body flush against his, and pressed his mouth to hers. For a shuddering moment, the rest of the world ceased to exist. Arousal swelled within her, and she needed to touch and hold him, to beg him to make everything better, to deliver her from this torment.

Then a sudden, raw hurt reared up inside her and she pressed her hands to his chest.

"Please don't kiss me like that," she pleaded. "I may be your captive, but I am not your woman. I do not *want* to love you. So please, just let me go."

"It doesn't have to be so difficult," he gently urged. "All you need to do is follow your impulses."

"My impulses?" She glanced up at him with fire in her eyes. "What if my impulses are to run you through?"

Duncan slowly backed her up against the wall. His mouth found hers again in a second, tender effort to claim and possess. He kissed her deeply, then caught her up in his arms and held her close. The intimacy of it broke her will. His tongue rolled seductively around hers, and a wild frenzy of heartache and yearning racked her body. She was no match for him, and she hated him for that.

"What will you do with me?" she asked, still wishing she could push him away but failing in the attempt.

"I plan to keep you, lassie. I'll not let you run from me again." His voice was soft and husky, heavy with desire.

She could barely think now. "What are you saying? That you will never let me go? That you will keep me as your prisoner forever?"

He lightly palmed her breast. "Surely you know me better than that. I told you I wasn't daft. I'll not be letting you go, lass, because you'll be my countess."

She looked up. "I beg your pardon? You are suggesting that we should marry?"

His expression was darkly sexual. "Aye. I can't stomach the idea of you returning to your betrothed. He'll never put his hands on you again, not while I live. I mean to take you from him, and have you for myself."

"So this is about your vengeance?" she asked, needing to understand. "You wish to deprive Richard of his wedding day, as he deprived you of yours? Just to punish him? Is that it?"

"Aye, and I'll take great pleasure in it. I can't deny it."

Fighting to stay strong, she swallowed hard over the frustration and discontent she was feeling. "So by wedding me, you will again be using me as your weapon?"

The corner of his mouth curled up slightly in a predatory grin. "I'll be using you in all sorts of other ways, too, lass, and I promise we'll both enjoy it, just as we did last night by the fire."

Amelia pushed away from him and faced the door. "This is too much, Duncan. You cannot do this to me. You cannot make such a demand, nor can you expect me to forgive you for all that has occurred between us leading up to this moment. You abducted me, you bound me with ropes, you threatened my life, and you want to kill the man who is still, despite everything, my fiancé. You have no right to claim me as your own."

He scoffed. "You and your silly English rules. You will be my wife, Amelia, and I do not care what Richard Bennett thinks about it. It will not matter for long, at any rate."

"Because you still plan to kill him."

"I'll not rest until I have my justice."

She shook her head. "You do not have to do that, Duncan. You could simply let it go."

"Nay, I cannot."

She strode toward him. "Yes, you *could*. You refuse to do it only because you refuse to let go of your anger and hatred."

He crossed the gallery and stood in front of the hearth with his back to her. She waited for him to say something. Anything. To respond to her plea for mercy.

"You want to disarm me, lass. You want to temper my rage."

"Yes, I do. But do you consider that an undesirable quality—to be at peace, and without anger?"

He paused. She wished she could see his face.

"I cannot answer that. All I know is that you move me like no other woman. When I woke this morning and you were gone, and I imagined you rushing into the arms of that swine, I was enraged. I want you, lassie. I want you badly enough that I'll do anything to keep you for myself, and to keep you away from him."

"You'll do anything?" she said. "Even surrender your vengeance?"

He faced her at last and frowned.

Slowly, she approached him. "I believe that you are capable of compassion, Duncan. I've seen it in you. I've felt it in your touch. You did not deprive me of my virtue when you had the chance. That man who held me in his arms last night, he was kind and gentle and . . ." She stopped for a moment and redirected her thoughts. "I could never marry the Butcher. I cannot be a part of that world. I cannot turn a blind eye to death and murder, nor could I ever grow to care for you if you continued on this path of savagery."

There was still a hint of anger in his expression, but he seemed at least willing to listen. "Are you giving me an ultimatum?" he asked. "Are you telling me that you will not be my wife unless I lay down my weapons?"

She hesitated, uncertain suddenly about what she was alluding to, standing here on the brink of something very different from the future she'd imagined for herself. Was she truly negotiating a marriage? Or was she simply stalling for time so that she might escape him again? She had not had adequate time to consider this. He was still the Butcher and always would be. That history could never be erased. He would always live under the shadow of the dead. His heart would be forever scarred by the lives he had taken. . . .

"Would you agree to allow the courts to carry out justice and decide upon Richard's punishment, if he is found guilty?" she asked.

He scoffed in disgust. "You're telling me that you'd be willing to sacrifice your body and soul to *me,* a sinner bound for hell, in order to save that dirty piece of filth from the blade of my axe?"

God help her . . .

She nodded.

But did she truly intend to become his wife?

His eyes narrowed. "I'll not lie to you, lass. If I make this pledge, I will keep my word as a matter of honor. I'll not kill Richard Bennett. But this marriage—it will be a real marriage. I will have you in my bed, and you will give me children." He strode closer to her. "And I'd need a pledge from you as well. I have a responsibility to my clan and those rebels who have followed me. I need to ensure their safety and protection. I need to know you will not expose them."

She watched him warily. "You would insist that in return for your vow to spare Richard's life and allow the courts to judge him, that I would keep your secrets?"

"Aye." He stood with his hands at his sides, staring at her intently.

"What will Angus say?" she boldly asked, knowing that the question would unsettle Duncan. "He will not approve, so I will need you to protect me from him."

"I would."

Amelia was having trouble breathing. When she failed to give him an answer, he took hold of her chin and carefully lifted her face to study it. "But tell me this, lass. How do I know I can trust you?"

"How do I know I can trust *you*?"

They stared at each other while the light in the room grew dim. The sun had moved behind a cloud.

"I do care for you," he said at last, and she was surprised by the hint of vulnerability she sensed in his voice. It was not something she had heard before. "I mean to keep you safe, and you will be, if you agree to be my wife."

"I will be safe from Richard, you mean."

Duncan met her eyes. "Aye, and everything else that is unpleasant in the world. And one day I hope you will trust me."

Trust. The word shook her. One week ago, he had been consumed by only one ambition—to kill Richard Bennett. He was still consumed by the loss of his former betrothed. He could not possibly have been cured of that grief after only one week, just because he desired her physically and had proposed marriage to strike a bargain of loyalty. And he had been lying to her about his identity since the moment she met him.

"What about my uncle?" she asked. "He is my guardian. I could not possibly do this without his consent."

"I'll send for him."

"And do what?" she asked with sarcasm. "Win his esteem?"

Duncan's eyes lifted. "Aye. I saved you from the Butcher of the Highlands, didn't I? And I would wager your father would have been more than pleased if I'd asked for your hand when he was here in the spring."

She marveled at his confidence. "I have a dowry, you know. It's quite substantial."

"I care nothing about that, lass, but I'll take it. For the good of Scotland. We are agreed then?"

She took a deep breath and prayed that she was doing the right thing. "Yes, we are agreed."

He started for the door. "Good. You'll write to Bennett today and end your engagement, but do not seal the letter. I'll be reading it before it's sent."

"And what about trust?"

He shook his head. "Not yet."

She sighed forlornly, then said one last thing before he left. "I will oblige you in that, Duncan, but in the future . . ."

He waited for her to finish.

"If it is a docile wife you are seeking, you should know that you will not find it in me."

He faced her squarely. "I have no interest in a docile wife. I want *you*. And I like it better that you can defend yourself—even against the likes of me. On that note, you are mine now, so I'll come to your bed tonight. Will you receive me willingly?"

She lifted her chin. "As long as you don't bring your axe."

He grinned. "Just my hands, then. And my mouth. And one other thing."

"I suppose you are referring to your sense of humor?" she countered. "Or perhaps your boyish charm."

He stared at her with a slight glimmer of amusement,

then left her alone in the room to comprehend the shocking magnitude of what she had just agreed to.

Not only had she agreed to become his countess, she had given him permission to come to her bed tonight when they were not yet man and wife.

Would he take her virginity, or would it be like the other times? Would he stop if she asked him to?

Would she even *want* him to stop?

No, she decided. No, she would not. Despite everything, her desire for him was immense. After everything they'd done together, she belonged to him, body and soul, and tonight he would claim her as his wife in all but name. There would be no turning back. He would make sure of it.

She forced herself to focus instead on what she had achieved. She had bargained for a soldier's life, and she had won. Now it would be up to the King's army to decide his fate. Which was only right.

More important, she had bargained for the salvation of Duncan's soul, and for that she would have no regrets.

"They say they have never laid eyes on him," Major William Jones explained, feeling sick to his stomach as he emerged from the cottage, locked the door from the outside, and mounted his horse. "The wife claims he's nothing but a legend."

William's commanding officer, Colonel Bennett, reined in his skittish white horse. Bennett whipped him hard across the rear flank. "The Butcher is true flesh and blood, Major Jones, and these filthy Highlanders know it. They're Jacobites. Burn them out." His horse reared up and screeched alarmingly.

"But there are children inside, Colonel."

Bennett glared at him fiercely. "Are you questioning my orders, Major?"

"No, sir."

William feared he might vomit.

"Then do as I say and burn them out. There must be a window they can crawl out of, if they wish to live."

Colonel Bennett galloped away toward the stable and shouted, "Burn everything! Shoot the livestock and kill that mangy animal!" He pointed at the black and white sheepdog in the stable door, barking incessantly.

William fought to smother his agony. He looked up at the Highland mountaintops shrouded in mist, then at the clear water rushing brilliantly along the riverbed. His shoulders rose and fell with a deep, cleansing breath, which was necessary to discharge all independent thought, as he rode around the thatched cottage to ascertain that there was indeed a rear window. When he found it, he said a brief prayer for forgiveness, and for the safety of those inside, and then he lit the torch and tossed the flame up onto the roof.

Chapter Sixteen

Duncan entered his private study. It was dusty and cluttered with papers, paintings, and rare books, which were stacked in tall, tilting piles against the walls. A telescope on a tripod stood in front of the largest window, aimed at the sky to view the stars at night. A collection of busts lined the mantel, and the walls were hung with rich and vibrant Flemish tapestries.

In the center of the room, a set of rolled architectural plans stood vertically inside an open trunk. He had dragged the trunk there a month ago, searching for some piece of information he could no longer recall.

He sat down at the desk facing the small stained-glass window in the corner and pulled out a blank sheet of paper embossed with the Moncrieffe coat of arms. The light pouring in through the glass illuminated the page with a dappled rainbow of color. He reached for his quill, dipped it in the inkwell, and began a cordial and gracious correspondence, conveyed in the most exquisite penmanship possible while writing in such haste.

Lady Amelia Templeton, Richard Bennett's betrothed, had agreed to become his wife. He had claimed her as his own, and very soon he would bed her and draw soft cries of rapture from her lips.

In turn, he had agreed to spare Richard Bennett's life.

Disturbed suddenly, Duncan lifted the quill off the page, sat back, and looked around the room. He recalled a day he had once sat at this desk writing a letter to Muira, pouring out his heart and quoting love poetry. He had adored her, and his future had been filled with hope—not unlike what he was feeling at this moment. A strange condition indeed.

He supposed it was because, for once, shockingly, he was distracted from that grief. By making Amelia his wife he knew he would immerse himself in sexual pleasures, and he was anticipating those pleasures with great vigor and zeal.

But could he truly keep his word to her, lay down his weapons, and allow Bennett to live?

He idly tapped the soft tip of the feather quill on the page and gazed out the window. What if Bennett came here and demanded satisfaction?

Well. Duncan would simply have to exercise self-control and force himself not to run Bennett through. He could do it. He was a highly disciplined warrior. He would keep his hands off his weapons and focus instead on the effects of this less violent, altered form of revenge.

He was stealing Bennett's beloved, as Bennett had once stolen his own. It was an eye for an eye, as Angus had once said. And there was nothing to stop Duncan from presenting evidence to the Crown, which would instigate a court-martial and with luck, death by hanging. He had not promised Amelia anything about vengeance in that form. In fact, it was what she had tried to convince him to do.

So there it was—vengeance achieved from all angles. As an added benefit, Duncan would be satisfying his lust for Amelia. Her body, her innocence, and her virginity—it would all be his.

Sitting forward and dipping the quill, he continued the

letter. A moment later, he sprinkled it with sand and shook it clean, folded it, sealed it with wax, then rose from the desk and left the room. A liveried footman was standing in the corridor, waiting dutifully, as instructed.

"Take this to Fort William today," Duncan said. "It must be delivered to the Duke of Winslowe. No other man's hand. Do you understand this?"

"Aye, milord."

"Lady Amelia will also have a letter to be dispatched today, which I will need to see. Go and wait outside her chamber, bring it to me, then you will take the Moncrieffe coach to the fort and provide His Grace with a return escort."

The footman bowed to Duncan, then hurried down the corridor toward the stairs, passing Iain along the way.

Iain watched him go, then strode toward Duncan anxiously. "I hope you have a plan," Iain said, stopping outside the study door. He began to speak in an almost frantic whisper. "Because I'm growing tired of putting out your fires, Duncan. I've been waking every morning to find myself staring into the impossible consequences of your fury. A few days ago, it was Richard Bennett seeking Moncrieffe men to join his troops and hunt you down. Our own men! Today was worse. I was forced to receive the daughter of a great English duke, who wanted *you* of all people to protect her from the Butcher. What the devil was I supposed to tell her? Obviously, she must know the truth by now. It'll mean the gallows for us both."

Duncan glanced up and down the corridor to ensure there was no one about. "Come inside."

His brother walked into the study and glanced at the open trunk. "Could you not ring for a chambermaid, Duncan? This room is the very essence of anarchy."

It was no secret that Duncan's younger brother preferred order over chaos. He was exceptionally well mannered, highly intelligent and educated, and when faced with a choice, he never, under any circumstances, selected the path of greater risk. He detested conflict, had never held a sword or set foot on a battlefield.

And that morning he had reached the absolute pinnacle of panic when Amelia was announced—not five minutes after Duncan had come charging into the bailey like a cannonball.

"I like this room in its current state," he replied. "Sit down, Iain." Duncan gestured toward the settee.

Iain moved toward it but had to move a box of candlesticks in order to clear a space. He flipped back the tail of his morning coat and sat down. "Tell me what happened with Lady Amelia. What in God's name are we going to do?"

Duncan sat down at his desk. "There's no need to panic. She'll not reveal our secret. I'm confident she'll be loyal."

Iain's eyebrows flew up in disbelief. "She gave you her word, did she? Freely?"

"I did not threaten her, if that's what you think." He paused. "Well . . . maybe I did, but the lass is plucky and she threatened me, too. It was a fair fight. But now that it's done, I'll trust her not to betray me."

Iain frowned. "But how can you risk such a thing, Duncan? Bluidy hell! She just fled from you. She ran away in desperation, and the first thing she asked was whether or not Colonel Bennett was still here. She no doubt wanted to run straight into his arms and cry on his shoulder."

Duncan did not want to hear Iain's speculations, for they were pointless now. Whatever happened when she first arrived was of no consequence, because that was before she and Duncan had reached an agreement.

"Lady Amelia has agreed to become my wife," he said. "She'll be Countess of Moncrieffe as soon as the marriage can be arranged, and will not be able to speak against me as her husband. Her uncle and guardian, the

Duke of Winslowe, will soon arrive, and I am certain he will approve the match."

Iain sat for a long moment without moving. "You've already proposed to Lady Amelia? And she has accepted you?"

"Aye." Duncan stood and walked to the window. He bent to peer through the telescope at a mother duck and her ducklings, waddling along the banks on the other side of the lake. Quite unexpectedly, he felt rather buoyant.

"Are you sure it was not a ploy," Iain asked, "to make you let down your guard, so she can escape you again?"

Duncan straightened and looked up at the sky, dotted with fluffy white clouds. "I am not a fool, Iain. I know that she has feared me in the past, despised me, even. I cannot begin to make you understand what exists between us, but she gave me her word, and I gave her mine." He faced his brother. "You know, she is very much like her father. Do you remember the duke from his visit last spring? He was a decent and honorable man."

Iain continued to stare at him in shock. "But she's English, Duncan. The clan will not approve of an English countess. You already know what people say about you, since your negotiations with the duke. They say you only seek the King's favor to increase your lands and treasury. Now you want to marry an English duke's daughter? Besides all that, she's still betrothed to Colonel Bennett."

Duncan sat down again. "She belongs to me now."

His brother sighed and leaned back against the cushions. "Your prisoner, still?"

"Nay," he said angrily. "My wife." He regarded his brother with challenge. "There is something else I must tell you. Now that I have made this pledge, certain things are going to change."

Iain sat forward again. His brow wrinkled with curiosity. "What things?"

A knock sounded, and they both turned their attention to the door.

Angus walked in and stood with a tight grip on the hilt of his sword. His golden hair was tied back in a queue. He had shaved and changed his shirt.

"Did he tell you the latest news, Iain?" Angus asked, keeping his icy blue eyes fixed on Duncan. "That he's going to marry that English vixen, just so she'll keep her mouth shut?"

"Aye," Iain replied. "He just explained it to me."

Angus glowered at Duncan. "It would've been more prudent just to kill her, do you not think? It's what you should've done back at the fort nearly a week ago, and spared us all a lot of grief and effort." Duncan rose from his chair and strode toward Angus, who backed up and looked at Iain. "Did he also tell you he agreed to lay down his sword in exchange for her silence? And that he agreed to spare Richard Bennett's life?"

Iain shot a glance at Duncan. "Nay, he did not tell me that part."

"I was about to," Duncan explained.

He and Angus stood face-to-face in the center of the study. Angus spoke quietly. "Have you lost your fookin' mind, Duncan?"

"I know what I'm doing," he growled.

Angus paused. "But you shouldn't have to give up everything you've fought for. You cannot let her talk you into letting Bennett live."

"Don't tell me what I can and cannot do," he warned.

"The only reason you're not drawing your sword to defend yourself right now is because I'm guessing you mean to forget the promise you made and take up your sword again the day after you speak your wedding vows. At least that's what I hope."

Iain stepped in to interject. He was shorter than both men and for that reason had to look up to address them. "But it would be ungentlemanly," he said "to break a promise to a lady. Especially the daughter of a duke."

Angus glared down at him. "Ungentlemanly? Fook, Iain! You may dress like an Englishman, but the last time I checked, you were still a Scot. And you're forgetting that your brother stripped the lassie bare in her bedchamber and tossed her over his shoulder like a sack of turnips when he carried her out of the fort. Then he tied her up and threatened to skin her like a rabbit if she tried to escape. So I think it's a little late for good manners."

Iain swallowed uneasily. "It's never too late to be civil."

Angus leaned down close. "You never had the stomach for war, Iain. You always left that to others, so I suggest you stay out of this."

Iain's Adam's apple bobbed. He carefully backed away.

Duncan met Angus's cold, hard gaze. "I gave her my word. I'll not be breaking it."

"And what about your word to *me?*" Angus asked. "That together we would see my sister's death avenged."

Duncan felt an unexpected stab of guilt, which he quickly pushed aside. "I'll not defend myself to you."

A fierce moment of tension ensued; then Angus started for the door. "You may have pledged a vow to that Englishwoman, Duncan, but she heard no such vow from me. I owe her nothing."

Duncan followed him into the corridor. "Do not take this into your own hands, Angus. Leave Bennett to me."

Angus turned back. "Why? Does the fair English maiden mean that much to you? What about Muira? You loved her once. Can you forget her so easily? It hasn't even been a year."

There was the guilt again. He felt it in his chest. "I forget nothing. I only want to end the bloodshed. I'm sure it's what she would've wanted."

But did he really believe that? He had no idea. He had not even considered it until this moment. He had been considering nothing but his own needs and desires.

"My sister would have wanted to see Richard Bennett's head on a spike," Angus argued, backing down the length of the corridor. "But you've chosen that Englishwoman over her and your friends, as well." His brow creased. "What's happened to you, Duncan? Where is the man I knew—the brave Scot who fought beside me on the battlefield at Sherrifmuir? The fierce Highlander who raised his sword against tyranny and injustice? Have you forgotten everything your proud father raised you to be? Do you mean to forget Scotland, too?"

"I forget nothing," Duncan replied. "I'll have my vengeance. I've taken Bennett's woman, as he took mine."

"But what the fook do you plan to do with her?"

A knot of tension balled up in Duncan's gut.

Angus shook his head. "So that's it, then. You've made your decision, so I'll be leaving you now, because clearly, like your softhearted brother, you no longer have the stomach for war, either."

With that, Angus turned and descended the stairs.

Duncan backed up against the wall and pounded his fist repeatedly against the cold, hard stones of the castle corridor.

The letter to Richard was not easy to write, but it was almost done.

Amelia set down the quill for a moment and leaned back in the chair. What would her father have made of this decision? she wondered as she glanced about the former countess's lavish red bedchamber, where she was now situated and would forever remain.

Something told her that—without knowing of Duncan's dual identity, of course—her father would have been pleased to see her wed the great Earl of Moncrieffe. He was an aristocrat, after all, who lived in a luxurious palace and possessed more wealth than anyone could imagine. Her father might very well have chosen Duncan over Richard last spring, for Richard was the third son of a baron and would have been forced to rely on her dowry and her father's future generosity, if he'd survived, to provide them with the comforts to which she was accustomed.

Not that any of those customary comforts ever mattered to her, nor did they matter now. Nevertheless, this exquisite palace would be her home and she would spend the rest of her days here, knowing that she had at least steered the infamous Butcher of the Highlands away from his lust for blood and vengeance. She had used what power she had over him to temper his rage.

She thought about that particular power she possessed. . . .

She was not a fool. She knew he wanted to bed her, and that mutual sexual desire was the basis for everything. It was why he was willing to give up his vengeance for her. It had played a part in her own actions as well, for she wanted him. She could not deny it. She was aroused by his physical prowess and his own personal savage breed of heroics.

And so . . .

He would come to her bed each night to satisfy his appetite for her body, and she, too, would satisfy her own urges and curiosities. In a way, he would take his vengeance out on Richard through her. Through the ownership of her body. She had resigned herself to it, was even anticipating it—but at the same time it was a frightening notion indeed, to imagine the complete unleashing of that man's passions.

And her own, as well.

She sat forward and somehow managed to finish the letter.

A moment later, she was handing it to the footman outside her door, then donning a shawl to go and meet Josephine, Iain's wife, who had offered to take her on a tour of the castle and grounds. She imagined it was going to be very awkward, meeting this woman who knew everything about the situation, including the reasons why Amelia was suddenly betrothed to her brother-in-law.

Amelia hurried downstairs and entered the reception room where she had met Iain earlier that morning. Josephine sat in a chair by the window with an open book on her lap. She glanced up and closed it when Amelia walked in.

"I am pleased you did not get lost along the way," Josephine said, rising to her feet. "The corridors of the castle can be difficult to navigate."

Tastefully dressed in a modest blue silk gown, Iain's wife was prettier than Amelia had expected. Slender, blond, and blessed with a lovely smile, Josephine exuded a charismatic grace that helped to calm Amelia's nerves.

"Indeed, I hesitated after crossing the bridge from the keep, but in the end, I was able to find my way."

Josephine approached and held out her hands. "You'll learn every corner and crevice of this magnificent bastion before long. I'll see to it personally. I am very happy to meet you, Lady Amelia. You have no idea how pleased I was to learn that I would have a sister."

Amelia was surprised by how quickly she warmed to this woman's greeting when she had felt so unsure about her decisions and had not known what to expect from Iain's wife.

"We will stroll through the interior first," Josephine suggested, leading Amelia toward the door, "and then we will venture outdoors and become better acquainted."

The tour began with a return to the keep, where Josephine adhered to a courteous and leisurely pace through the banqueting hall, the heraldry room, the chapel, and finally into a central courtyard with a decorative stone fountain.

Afterward, they returned to the main castle. Amelia was shown through every cozy guest chamber—she lost count after seven of them—as well as the library, three drawing rooms, and finally the dining room, the kitchens, and the impressive wine cellar.

At long last, they exited the castle through a side door and made their way along a stone walk that led to the stables. The sun was shining, and Amelia lifted her face to feel its warmth on her cheeks.

"Let us be honest now, shall we?" Josephine said, linking her arm through Amelia's. "Clearly you are distressed. You're about to marry the Butcher of the Highlands."

Amelia exhaled heavily. "If only I could explain how difficult it has been."

"Please try, Amelia. You can tell me anything. I am a woman, and I will understand. I know the circumstances of what brought you here, and it cannot have been easy."

Josephine's understanding opened a floodgate of emotions and explanations. Amelia described Duncan's terrifying appearance over her bed at the fort and all the things that had occurred in the following days. She told Josephine about Fergus and Gawyn and Angus and how they had treated her. She described the details of her first escape to the English camp and what revelations had followed regarding her opinions about this country as well as her own. She also told Josephine about meeting the boy, Elliott, and how Duncan had been a very different person that day.

"That is the Duncan I know," Josephine said. "And I believe that is the man you will come to know as your husband. Not the Butcher. You will forget that other side of him. It is certainly not a side I see very often. He will win your respect and your love, Amelia. You must trust me in that."

Amelia swallowed over the jagged rock of uncertainty that had lodged itself in her throat. "I wish I could be so sure of everything."

"Give it time."

They strolled across the bailey to a sundial, which indicated the hour with precise accuracy.

"I must confess," Josephine said, "that I am pleased I can finally speak openly to another woman about my brother-in-law's activities as a rebel and a hero of Scotland. It has always been a well-guarded secret, but I am so pleased that I will not betray any confidences by regaling his efforts to fight for Scotland in every possible way. There are things I could tell you . . ."

"That would be helpful," Amelia replied. "I want to know all that is good about him, so that perhaps I will find this easier to manage."

They strolled along the perimeter of the castle island.

"Despite what you must think," Josephine said, "he is a good man and deserves his happiness. He has not known much of it in a long time." She described his grief over losing Muira, and her hope that when he found love again the weight of his sorrows would grow lighter.

Amelia pondered this new life and Duncan's obvious torment, as well as her ability to bring him out of it, as Josephine hoped. She had made considerable demands on him that morning, asking him to lay down his sword, believing it was in his best interest, and they had both entered into this arrangement hastily. She felt very daunted.

"Let me tell you some tales about his heroics," Jose-

phine began. "There is one particular story about his courage at the Battle of Inveraray, where he stormed the
Campbell stronghold like a wild Viking warrior of old.
And then I'll tell you how devoted and generous he is, as
laird of this castle. He gives work to anyone who wants it;
he shares his wealth and takes an interest in the lives of
those in his care. He does not allow for dishonor among
his people. A bad egg is punished or banished, and he has
the loyalty of all who serve him."

As they slowed their pace along the stone walk, Amelia listened to Josephine's homily and realized how very
little she actually knew about the complicated man who
would soon be her husband.

She wondered uneasily when her uncle would arrive
and what *he* would make of her decision.

And Richard, of course. She wondered when he would
receive her letter.

That night, they dined at opposite ends of the long table
with Iain and Josephine. It was a bountiful feast of oyster
soup, Cornish hens, fresh vegetables, and imported wine
from the south of France.

After a dessert of brandied peaches and cream with
chocolate truffles, they played cards in the blue drawing
room and conversed about theater and politics, laughed
over light gossip.

Amelia was astounded by the fact that everything was
so conventional, and there were times she felt almost
comfortable and was able to laugh genuinely, without
pretense. She felt more at home here than she did in her
own house since her uncle had taken up residence. It was
not that she did not love her uncle. He was a kind and
agreeable man. But he was older, and there was something very relaxed yet exciting about these young Highlanders. Even Beth MacKenzie and her family had made

Amelia feel at ease in a way she had not expected. The mood in their modest cottage had been cozy and without airs.

These Scots knew how to laugh and tease and ignore the rules that could sometimes suffocate a polite young lady of good breeding at a dinner party. Amelia did not feel suffocated this evening. Strangely enough, she felt free, easy, and astonished by Duncan's casual charm.

She recalled what Josephine had said to her that day: *I believe that is the man you will come to know as your husband. Not the Butcher. You will forget that other side of him. It is certainly not a side I see very often. He will win your respect . . .*

Indeed, when one was not in the position of fearing the gleam of his axe, his wit was vastly entertaining. Tonight, at least, there was nothing savage or barbaric about him. He was the very model of elegance and refinement.

She had a feeling, however, as she glanced at the clock, that things would be very different when he came to her bed.

At the mere thought of it, her heart began to flutter. She met his striking gaze from across the room.

The heat she saw in his eyes told her that it was time to retire.

Chapter Seventeen

Shortly after midnight, Amelia heard a sound in the corridor. Her belly exploded with nervous butterflies, but she made a silent vow that she would not cower. She would enjoy this and focus on the pleasures, of which she knew there would be many. She'd already experienced a number of them in the mountains, and her passion for Duncan was part of the reason why she'd accepted his proposal in the first place.

But there would be pain when she gave up her virginity tonight. She knew that, too. He was a generously proportioned and virile man. She sat up in the bed and hoped she would be able to accommodate him.

The fire had died down and raindrops pelted against the window. The room was lit by a single candle on the bedside table. It flickered when a knock sounded at the door.

"Enter."

The door opened, and Duncan strode in, carrying a candelabra with half a dozen candles. Shadows swung across the scarlet-draped walls. He closed the door behind him with a quiet click, set the candles down on the tall chest of drawers, and looked at her.

He still wore his dinner attire—the black velvet coat

with silver trimmings, gray waistcoat, and a white shirt with a ruffled lace collar and cuffs. His hair, however, was falling loose upon his shoulders in wild disarray, and for the first time since her arrival at the castle she felt as if she were looking at the rugged Highlander who had abducted her from her bed at the fort.

She wet her lips and tried to focus on something other than the rising tide of her apprehensions.

"Are you ready for me, lass?" he asked, still standing just inside the door.

Remembering her previous resolution to be brave, she said matter-of-factly, *"Yes."*

He approached the bed and shrugged out of his velvet coat. The movement showed his muscular shoulders and male brawn to shocking advantage. He folded the coat and draped it neatly on the back of a chair. Next he removed his waistcoat, then pulled his shirt off over his head, and Amelia was arrested on the spot, gazing up at his scarred bare chest and massive upper arms.

"You best be bracing yourself, lassie," he said, "for the enormity of what you're about to behold." His lips curled up in a teasing smile. "Come here now. Unfasten my breeches."

He held his arms straight out to the sides, and she found herself obeying his commands with curious amusement, for this was all new to her, and she did not know what she was supposed to do, or how she should behave.

She slipped out from under the covers and crawled across the bed. Sitting back on her heels at the edge, she released the fastenings on his breeches, which served to keep his enormous erection contained. She swallowed hard as the breeches fell open and her eyes took in the part of him that would soon break through her tender maidenhead. Her blood began to race.

"Take off your shift," he gently suggested as he slipped

out of his breeches, "and get in the bed, lass. I want to hold you close."

Seconds later, she was naked beneath the covers, feeling the cool sheets on her sensitive skin, while he slid in next to her. His large, callused hand brushed over her belly, and a flash of excitement lit her senses. She tried to stay calm as he rolled on top of her.

She did not spread her legs. He did not ask her to. She became very aware of his muscular inner thigh rubbing against the top of hers, his lips touching her cheeks in teasing, light kisses, then settling deeply, deliciously on her mouth. A tiny moan escaped her, and she ran her fingers through his hair, surprised that she could feel such desire when she was still so nervous about what was yet to come.

"Tell me when it is about to happen," she said, "so that I may prepare myself."

His lips brushed over her eyelids. "It's already happening, lass, and don't worry. You'll be ready. I'll see to it. I'll do nothing in a hurry."

With that, he bent lower and used his mouth to kiss and caress her breasts, her arms, her belly, her thighs—everywhere. His touch was light. His lips were moist, leaving her skin damp and tingly with a trail of sensitivity and rapture.

She, too, caressed his body with her hands. She ran her fingers up and down his battle-scarred back, down to the curve of his muscular buttocks, and lower, to his rock-hard thighs.

It went on for quite some time—this touching and loving in the candlelight—and soon she reached a quiet mood of tranquility, where her body seemed to melt beneath him like hot butter. She wiggled closer. Any rational thoughts seemed hazy and numb. All that existed in her mind was an awareness of his hands working over her body and the feel of his hot, bare flesh, tight against her own.

Unconsciously, she parted her legs and wrapped them around his hips, and felt an aching need from within her heated depths. He reached down with his hand and placed himself at her opening.

"You're slick and ready for me, lass, but you must tell me that you want me." He shifted his hips, positioning himself between her throbbing flesh. "I must have you when you're willing."

"Yes, Duncan, I want you. *Please*."

Something wicked flashed in his eyes. "Well, since you're begging . . ."

Her hips lifted, and with a deep groan of need he drove forward and plunged some two inches up inside her, stretching and filling.

She sucked in a sharp breath of shock, because there was pain. There was most definitely pain. He was very big, and she was tight and untested.

But she wanted it. She wanted all of it. And she felt very wanton. She could barely believe this was happening.

It was permission, at last, to surrender.

Duncan's whole being shuddered with both ecstasy and agonizing self-restraint as the swollen head of his desire reached only partway into Amelia's fiery dampness.

He wanted to push hard, fast, all the way in, to drench himself completely in her silky heat, but the rupture of her maidenhead—along with the sharp cutting of her fingernails into his back—caused him to hold still.

She clung to his shoulders. He lay unmoving, suppressing the pounding forces in his head, while he gave her a moment to grow accustomed to the penetration. A tear spilled across her temple.

"The pain won't last," he said, kissing her on the mouth.

"It's fine."

He looked into her eyes. "Aye, it is, lass. It's more than fine."

He trembled when he tried to breathe and had to take a moment to recover his capacities. Mere seconds was all it required before the pulsing in his loins began again. He pushed forward another inch, withdrew, then slowly thrust in again, steady and deep, until at last he stretched her enough to reach her womb.

She let out a small cry. He began to move carefully and gently inside her.

"I didn't want to hurt you," he whispered. "It'll feel better soon."

"It feels better already. It feels . . ."

He buried his face in her hair and whispered huskily, "What, lass? Tell me how it feels. I need to know."

She relaxed as he moved within. *"Exciting."*

It was a good thing, because he was quite sure he couldn't hold off much longer. There was a storm brewing inside him, and he wanted to thrust into her like a ramming bull. He wanted to hear her moan with rapture and delight, and feel her pulse around him as he climaxed mightily inside.

She parted her legs wider and raised her hips to move in harmony with each of his deep, finely tuned penetrations. Together they bucked and squeezed, seeking pleasures they had both been denying since the moment they first struggled against each other on that rainy field at dawn. There was violence in his movements now, but nothing else about it was the same, for she had finally yielded to him.

Suddenly, with a passionate jolt, Amelia cupped his buttocks and tensed beneath him. Her hips thrust forward savagely, and she gasped. He felt the quick pulsation of her interior, which squeezed around his rigid passions.

Their open mouths collided, and she twirled her tongue

around his. Without further hesitation, he gave in to the
heaving pleasures flooding through him, arched his body
upward, then pumped into her with a potent gush of release
that left him drained.

He collapsed on top of her and waited for the rhythm
of his body to return to normal while struggling to make
sense of this strange joy, when not so long ago his world
had been reduced to rubble and he'd given up on any hope
of restoration.

He felt stronger tonight, yet at the same time he wanted
to be gentle. Perhaps it was true. Perhaps his cruelty could
be tempered.

He rolled off Amelia and lay on his side, facing her in
the dim light. She curled up beside him.

"You belong to me, now," he said. "No other man shall
ever have you."

"Yes," she replied in a cool, somewhat distant voice
that quavered with uncertainty. "I am yours. And I confess, I am not sorry. It makes no sense. I hated you not
long ago. You hated me, too, when I ran from you. Is this
some kind of madness? Did you do something to me?"

"Aye, I did, lass. And I'll be doing it again as soon as
you're willing."

She laughed, and for a while they lay quietly in the
dim light, running their fingertips lightly across each other's bodies; then Duncan rose from the bed and crossed
the room. Amelia leaned up on an elbow to admire his
glorious nude form, gleaming with perspiration. He picked
up a brass snuffer and put out the candles he had brought
with him.

It was suddenly dark in the crimson bedchamber.
Amelia held out her arm.

"I think I am willing now," she said.

"As am I." He returned to the bed and climbed in.

They slept very little that night.

Fort William, the following day,
late afternoon

His Grace, the Duke of Winslowe, was enjoying a fine glass of brandy in his private chamber when a young soldier knocked on the door and entered with a letter, which he delivered to the duke on a shiny silver salver.

His Grace swept the letter off the plate, dismissed the man, then broke the seal and unfolded it. He squinted irritably, huffed in frustration, then searched his pockets for his spectacles, stuck them on his bulbous nose, and began to read.

When he came to the end of the elegantly penned correspondence, he tore the curly wig off his head and chucked it on the floor, as if it were suddenly infested with lice. "Good Lord. *Thomas! Thomas!*"

His tall, gangly valet came running into the room. "Yes, Your Grace?"

The duke rose from his chair. "It's Lady Amelia. She has been found! Pack everything immediately. We must travel to Moncrieffe Castle and leave within the hour."

"Pray God she is safe and unharmed."

The duke reached for his glass and tossed back the rest of the brandy in a single gulp. "My word, the whole world has turned upside down on its ear."

"How so, Your Grace?"

The duke stared at his devoted valet in utter disbelief and shook the letter in the air. "The Earl of Moncrieffe has asked for Lady Amelia's hand in marriage."

Thomas froze. "But she is already engaged to Colonel Bennett."

"I am quite aware of that, Thomas. I am not an imbecile. That is why I shouted your name twice just now. We must reach the castle as quickly as possible."

"I understand, Your Grace." Thomas swept His Lordship's wig off the floor, brushed it free of dust, and hastened from the room.

The duke rubbed a hand over his natural white hair— which stood on end in frizzy disarray—and strolled to the window. He looked out at the Scottish countryside and watched a line of soldiers training in the field.

"I believe that when I meet that man at last," he quietly said, "I will be tempted to brain him with a bottle of his own whisky. I don't care how fine it is. That man deserves a good thump on the head for taking so bloody long to declare himself."

Outside in the courtyard, an armed dispatch rider slipped Amelia's letter into a saddlebag and mounted his horse, with instructions to locate Colonel Bennett, who was heading north with the Moncrieffe militia toward Drumnadrochit.

The rider galloped out of the fortress gates with strict and rigorous haste, silently cursing the fact that he would have to answer to the despicable colonel while he awaited further instructions.

"Did you know that he defended you steadfastly to Angus," Josephine said to Amelia the next day, "and chose you over him?" They were crossing the drawbridge with baskets hooked over their wrists, on a mission to pick wildflowers in the orchard, even though the weather was quickly turning gray.

"No, I did not know that," Amelia replied with a frown. "When?"

"The day you arrived. Angus was not pleased to hear of your engagement. He felt Duncan was betraying Muira's memory, and Scotland, too, by laying down his weapons to make you happy. Angus takes great pleasure in war. He always has."

They stepped off the bridge and headed into the orchard. Their skirts swished through the tall grasses.

"How long have you known Angus?" Amelia asked, pushing aside her discomfort over the mention of Muira's name. Neither Amelia nor Duncan had talked about his former fiancée since the day they spoke of her in the mountains.

Josephine looked up at the sky. "I met Angus when he came here with his father to invite the MacLeans to join in the rebellion, over a year ago. Duncan's father, as I'm sure you must've heard, was a fearsome warlord. He was keen to join the cause, though Duncan opposed it."

Amelia was astonished to hear this. She'd thought Duncan was a passionate Jacobite, because that was part of the Butcher's notoriety.

"I knew that Duncan's father was a warrior," she said, "and that he died in the rebellion."

"Aye, and afterward, Duncan returned home to take his place as laird and quickly established himself politically as a Highland noble willing to support King George and give up the rebellion. You would know that, of course, because of your father's visit last spring."

"Yes, I am aware."

"Duncan desires peace and the safety of his clan above all. He does not sanction war and death for those in his care. But when he fights as the Butcher, it's personal." A gust of wind blew across the orchard, fluttering Josephine's hat ribbons.

Amelia felt a sudden pang of animosity. "Why are you telling me this?" she asked. "Do you think I am wrong to ask that he give up his campaign?"

Josephine considered it. "Nay, I don't think it wrong. I understand what you feel, and I would do the same in your position. I wouldn't wish for my Iain to be galloping about the Highlands picking fights with English redcoats, and I am glad he doesn't have a hankering for war, and never did. I only want you to know that it may take some time before Duncan is healed of that pain. He may feel some regret over his break with Angus. They were close. They've known each other since they were lads, and they've been through a lot together."

Amelia spoke defensively. "I did not ask him to give up his friend."

"Nay, and he wouldn't have done so, if it had been his choice. But it was Angus who broke the friendship. He's not one to give up a fight, and he doesn't have a pretty lass like you in his life to distract him from war."

Amelia felt a cold raindrop strike her cheek. "Will Duncan blame me for their quarrel?" she asked, feeling a rush of dread. "Will he resent me?"

"Not now," Josephine answered. "From what I can see, he's infatuated with you. But one day, he might regret the loss of his friend. Angus was there for him when Muira died. They shared the same grief. I suspect he'll regret it if Angus is not there to toast you on your wedding day."

They reached a patch of flowers on the far side of the orchard. Amelia bent to pick some daisies. "I am not sure what I can do about that," she said. "I don't wish to cause a rift between them, but Angus despises me. He would never listen to anything I say."

Josephine knelt beside her and tore some long stems from the earth. "I don't expect that anyone can do much of anything. Angus will have to resolve the matter himself and find a way to accept Duncan's decision. If he can't do that . . ." She rose to her feet and arranged the flowers in the basket. "If he can't accept it, he'll simply continue to live that hellish, unhappy life that Duncan has finally given up." She gazed meaningfully at Amelia from a distance away. "Do not mistake me, Amelia. Iain and I are both very pleased with how things have turned out.

We believe you are the best thing that's ever happened to Duncan."

"But really, I've done nothing." She glanced around the orchard. "What exists between us is very . . ." She did not know what to call it.

Josephine nodded. "I understand, but you must not give up hope that true love will blossom one day, now that you are pledged to one another, and you are able to see another side of him. Everything will change. The clothes make a difference, do you not agree? He's quite a distinguished gentleman when he puts some effort into it."

Amelia couldn't help but smile. "I must confess, I rather liked the kilt and the unkempt hair. I hope he doesn't feel it necessary to give that up completely."

Josephine chuckled. "Maybe you can convince him to wear his sword to bed on your wedding night, and nothing else."

They giggled naughtily and dashed back to the castle gates as thunder rumbled in the distance and murky clouds rolled across the sky.

Chapter Eighteen

The Moncrieffe coach rolled over the drawbridge and into the shaded stone archway of the gate tower. It was followed by a second coach, drawn by four magnificent grays and bearing the ancestral coat of arms of His Grace, the Duke of Winslowe.

The vehicles had been spotted by a scout. By the time the duke rolled into the bailey, Duncan and Amelia were waiting at the front door of the castle.

Duncan took out his timepiece and consulted it, then slipped it back into his coat pocket.

"Do you have somewhere else to be?" she asked.

"Of course not," he replied in an intimidating voice. "But your uncle is late, and my patience is wearing thin. I want you as my wife. He should've been here yesterday."

She was flattered by Duncan's impatience. He wanted her, and he wanted her now—not just in bed, but legally and officially. He wanted to speak vows before God.

Did she want that, too? Yes, of course she did. She'd already surrendered her innocence to him, and she might as well admit it to herself. She was hopelessly, desperately in love.

The ducal coach pulled to a halt in front of them, and a liveried footman hurried to lower the step. Wearing a garish green satin jacket and peach breeches, her uncle, plump as a pumpkin, emerged from the dark confines and squinted upward at the front of the castle before he set a shiny buckled shoe upon the step and hopped heavily to the ground. His perfume was overpowering. His black wig was tall and unwieldy, with ringlets that bounced as he walked.

"My darling girl!" He pulled Amelia into his arms and squeezed the air out of her lungs. "Thank God you are found, and you are safe!" He turned to Duncan. "I owe you a great debt, Lord Moncrieffe, for my niece's rescue. You have saved her from the Butcher's axe."

Duncan gave an elegant bow. "She saved herself, Your Grace. She is a remarkable woman. I did nothing but provide these stone walls as sanctuary."

Her uncle looked at her. "Are you all right, my dear?"

"I am fine."

He stood back and inhaled quickly. "I shall hear all about your ordeal soon enough," he said. "But first . . ." He faced Duncan again. "I am responsible for this young gel, Moncrieffe. She is my dearly departed brother's only child, and she means the world to me, so I must beg to ask, *why?* Why have you proposed this match between yourself and my niece?"

Amelia felt her smile drop. She moved closer to stand at Duncan's side and linked her arm through his, feeling grateful that he was not brandishing his axe today.

"She is already pledged to Lieutenant-colonel Richard Bennett," her uncle continued, "and this is highly inappropriate, to conduct yourself in such a manner."

"But Uncle . . . ," she protested. He did not know who he was speaking to!

His Grace swung a hand through the air. "Hup! Hup! Hush!"

Her teeth clicked together.

The duke tilted his wigged head to the side and raised

an accusing eyebrow at Duncan. "What do you have to say for yourself, young man?"

Duncan inclined his head and put a foot forward in a second, more elegant bow. "Forgive me, Your Grace. I have no excuse to offer, except to confess that I fell in love with your niece, and lost my head completely."

Amelia's head drew back in astonishment.

Her uncle turned his eyes to her. "The great Scottish laird fell in love, did he?"

"Yes," Amelia shakily replied.

"Just like that?"

"Can you blame me, Your Grace?" Duncan interjected. "Lady Amelia is like no other woman."

"My brother spoke well of you, Moncrieffe. I wondered if I'd ever be privileged enough in this lifetime to make your acquaintance and see for myself what sort of man you are."

"I'll leave that to Your Grace to decide," Duncan said, "if you will bestow us the honor of your company at dinner this evening."

"Of course I'll honor you with my company!" the duke shouted as he adjusted his wig. "Where else am I to go? We're deep in the wilds of the Scottish Highlands. I am fortunate I didn't get swallowed up by a hungry boar on the way here."

Amelia exhaled a nervous breath as they all entered the main hall together.

"Ah, Moncrieffe. I daresay this is the finest whisky in Great Britain and beyond." Winslowe swirled the amber liquid around in his crystal glass, then delighted himself with another deep draught.

Duncan lifted his own glass. "I am honored you think so, Your Grace. I'll be sure to send you back to England with a crate of my very best."

"You are a true gentleman, sir."

They had enjoyed a sumptuous dinner and dessert, followed by musical entertainment in the old banqueting hall, but now the hour had grown late. Only Duncan and the duke chose to linger on, sipping whisky by the fire in the library. The others had retired for the night.

"This is a fine castle, Moncrieffe. Quite old, I presume?"

"Construction of the keep and gate tower began in 1214," Duncan told him. "The main part of the castle, where we now sit, was completed in 1629."

Winslowe's gaze traveled about the candlelit room. "Indeed it is an architectural masterpiece."

They discussed architecture for quite some time, and Duncan promised the duke that he would show him the plans for future additions and refurbishments, which he kept in his study.

Then, at last, the time was at hand to discuss more important matters.

"So you claim to have developed feelings for my niece," the duke prompted, scrutinizing Duncan with a spark of challenge over the rim of his glass.

"Aye, Your Grace. It is my intention to love and care for her always."

The duke leaned forward in his chair. "*Love*, you say. I watched you this evening, Moncrieffe, and I do not doubt you are smitten, but I am not sure I would call it love." He sat back. "You are taken with her, naturally. She is a beautiful young woman. I see also that she returns your . . . *affections*. It was not difficult to make out. She is completely besotted." He leaned back again. "But it's all rather sudden, is it not? By my calculations, you proposed the very day she crossed your threshold."

Duncan wet his lips and thought long and hard about how he should answer the duke's challenge. Clearly he was a perceptive and insightful man. "I realize it may seem

strange to Your Grace, but I remember Lady Amelia's
father very well. I will always regard him with the highest
esteem. I recall also that he spoke with a great love for his
daughter. So if I may be blunt . . ."

Winslowe waved an inviting hand. "Please. I am curious."

Duncan set his glass down on the side table and rested
his elbows on his knees. "I have not had the pleasure of
meeting her former fiancé, Colonel Bennett," he said,
"but I do know of his reputation, and I feel it is my duty to
inform Your Grace that . . ." He paused to give the man a
moment to prepare himself for what he was about to hear.
"Richard Bennett is despised in this country, Your Grace.
He is regarded as a tyrant who knows no bounds when
it comes to oppression and brutality. Innocent Scots have
been slaughtered under his orders; peaceful homes have
been burned to the ground. So when I learned of your
niece's engagement, I could not bear the thought of her
marrying such a man, so I did not hesitate to violate your
country's rules of etiquette." He leaned back and stared
unshakably at the duke. "And for that I make no apologies."

Winslowe surveyed him carefully. "You are a willful
man, Moncrieffe, but I see that you are decent and forthcoming as well, so I, too, shall be blunt." He met Duncan's eyes. "I was surprised at my brother's decision to
allow his daughter to wed Colonel Bennett. I believe he
acted in haste to secure a husband for her before he departed from this world. Myself . . . ?" He sat back. "I am
not fond of the man. I have no concrete proof of any un-
seemly activities, mind you, but I simply do not care for
him. Call it instinct, a gut reaction, whatever you please,
but I recognize the fact that he has a cruel streak. I have
no doubt he can be charming when he wishes to be,
which is why Amelia was influenced in the beginning.

And when her father passed away—God rest his soul—
she was lonely and grief-stricken. I could not help but feel
that Bennett preyed upon that vulnerability. Amelia has a
generous dowry, and she is the daughter of a duke. Bennett wishes to advance himself, for he has few connections and is not a wealthy man." Winslowe waved a finger.
"He has a great talent on the battlefield, however, and
that is where he made too strong an impression on my
brother. He saved his life, you know. It was quite a heroic
feat."

"Yes, I've heard." Duncan tossed back the rest of his
whisky before he said something distasteful to His Grace,
which he might later regret.

"But with my brother gone," the duke continued, "Amelia's guardianship falls to me. I am all she has, and I will
not let her step into a future that promises unhappiness. I
believe you are genuine in your affections for her, sir, and
clearly you are a man of great wealth and personal integ-
rity. I will support your engagement, Moncrieffe, and if
Bennett sees fit to complain about it . . . Well, I am a duke
now." He raised his glass again. "I have some influence in
the world."

Duncan sat forward and shook his hand. "I give you
my word of honor, Your Grace, that Amelia will be happy
here. She will be treated with the utmost respect."

"Good man." The duke downed the rest of his whisky.

Duncan gave Winslowe a moment to enjoy the effects of
the drink before speaking again. "I hope it will not spoil
your evening, Your Grace, if I push the subject further."

The duke sat forward. "Push away, Moncrieffe."

Duncan nodded. "I spoke earlier of Colonel Bennett's
reputation and what I know of his military tactics. It is
my firm belief that the people of Scotland deserve their
dignity, and I mean to bring Richard Bennett to justice
for his crimes."

The duke's bushy eyebrows lifted. "You don't say. A formal complaint, you mean?"

"Aye. I can bring witnesses, and if you were willing to hear their testimonies, I would welcome your support."

The duke considered Duncan's request. "He is a celebrated war hero, Moncrieffe. The man has medals. It will not be easy. Certainly the army will not appreciate it. Nor will the King."

"Surely someone will see the truth in it, and be moved to do the right thing."

The duke crossed one stout leg over the other. "Perhaps. But if not—and if I choose to support you—it will be *my* reputation that will suffer. Imagine it, Moncrieffe—an eccentric English duke, new to his title, taking Scotland's side in a case against the King's army."

"A losing battle, to be sure," Duncan said.

Winslowe slapped his plump thigh and laughed. "Ah, you fearless Highlanders. How I admire your spirit, always so full of confidence and vitality, raging across battlefields with your swords and shields held high, even in the face of impossible odds. Ah, to be a Scotsman." He raised his empty glass. "And young again."

Duncan inclined his head at the duke and rose from his chair to go and bring back the decanter. He refilled both their glasses, then sat down.

"Let me tell you about my adventures at the Battle of Sherrifmuir," he said, "and then we can discuss what might be possible with the King's army."

Winslowe sat back and made himself comfortable, and they talked openly about warfare and politics until well past midnight.

"You're very late," Amelia said, sitting up in bed when Duncan entered her bedchamber. She had been waiting for hours.

"Aye." He set the candelabra down on the chest of drawers and removed his coat. "I've been busy, lass, winning your uncle's esteem. He thinks very well of me now, and I think well of him, too. He's a good man, like your father. We have much in common, and he supports our engagement. He said your father had been disappointed he'd not been able to arrange a match between us after his visit here last spring, and that, in your uncle's opinion, our marriage cannot happen soon enough."

"My father desired a match between us?"

She was surprised to hear this and felt a sudden rush of joy. With all her doubts and fears lately, especially regarding her own judgment and her recent decision to marry Duncan, it meant a great deal to know that her father had approved of this man as a potential son-in-law. Perhaps her father's spirit had been watching over her all along. She felt rather starry-eyed.

Crawling on all fours to the foot of the bed, she stood on her knees and hugged the tall bedpost where the velvet curtains were tied back with gold tassels. There was something different about Duncan's mood tonight. He seemed wound up tighter than a tallcase clock. His high spirits were almost contagious.

"You seem very happy," she said. "What else happened between you and my uncle?"

Duncan crossed to the window and looked out at the darkness. "I expressed my opinions about your former betrothed and told him that I mean to protect you from him, and your uncle did not dispute my views. He made it known that he never approved of your engagement to begin with."

Amelia was surprised to hear this as well. "He never told me that."

"He was respecting the wishes of your late father, even though it went against his better judgment. He's through with all that now, though. He will make his own judgments, and he will act upon his conscience."

Amelia sat back on her heels. "So that is why you are so pleased?"

He faced her. "Not just that, lass. Your uncle has agreed to help me bring Bennett to justice. He'll support an inquiry to investigate his crimes. As God is my witness, Richard Bennett will pay for what he did to my Muira."

Amelia felt a sudden jolt in her heart. She was pleased, of course, that he was choosing a more civilized path toward justice by leaving the ultimate decision of punishment to the army and the courts. It was exactly what she encouraged him to do on that final night of her abduction, and certainly, if Richard was guilty, he should be tried and convicted.

What troubled her was Duncan's unremitting desire for vengeance, fueled by his pain over Muira's death. Amelia shivered slightly, feeling the Butcher's elemental despair and his dangerous fury still lingering about. Clearly, all of that was not yet behind them.

"So you mean to continue with your vengeance?" she carefully asked.

He gave her a look of warning. "Let there be no accusation in your words, lass, because I break no vow to you. The promise I made was to refrain from using the blade of my axe to take Richard Bennett's life. I never agreed to let him go on raping and pillaging. What I do now is exactly what you asked of me in the mountains. I am doing it *your* way. The civilized way. I will leave his fate to the army and the courts."

He was right, of course, and she nodded. "I suppose you must do what you feel is right to avenge Muira's death," she said.

She recalled suddenly what Beth MacKenzie had said in the cottage: *The Butcher buried his own heart in the*

*ground with his beloved on the day she died—at least the
part of his heart that was capable of love.*

"It's not just for Muira," he said, "but for all of Scotland,
too. The man is a tyrant. He must be stopped." He passed by
the foot of the bed. "But let us not speak of Muira again."

"Why?"

"Because I do not *wish* to speak of her," he said irritably. He began to untie the ruffled cravat at his neck.
"Now take off your shift, lass. I am lustin' for you."

Still reflecting upon the hurt she felt over Muira's enduring presence in his heart—for it was a place into
which Amelia had not yet been invited, not *really*—she
watched his hands as he untied the loose knot.

And was this truly lust for *her?* she wondered, feeling
tempted to question him. Or was it lust for his long-awaited
vengeance?

He gazed at her with a hot, overwhelming sexuality.

She decided not to question him now. That would be a
foolish thing to do, for there was hunger in his eyes. He
looked ready to devour her, and it made her bones turn to
jelly, because whenever he had that particular look in his
eye, the sex was more passionate and satisfying than ever.

She realized at that moment how much of a captive
she still was—ensnared by the undeniable pull of his
sexuality. When he looked at her with those voracious
eyes, nothing else seemed to matter. The whole world simply disappeared.

A flashing moment later, he was there at the corner of
the bed, taking her face in his hands and pressing his
mouth to hers. She was astounded by how quickly she
could plunge into this role as his lover and forget everything else. It had been all she could do, over the past few
days, to distract herself from these feverish urges and desires. All he had to do was come to her, command her to
disrobe, and she obeyed.

He moved to the door, locked it, then returned to stand before her like a conquering warlord. "Lie back," he said, and she lay down crosswise on the bed.

He tore off his jacket with rough impatience and tossed it to the floor. His fingers moved in a blur of motion down the button fastenings of his waistcoat, which he threw on the floor as well.

Amelia leaned up on both elbows. Watching him rip the loose shirt off over his head, she could barely comprehend her desires.

She wanted to prove that he belonged to *her* now—that her power to enchant and possess matched his, and that he was just as much a captive as she.

Bare-chested, still in his breeches, he came down upon her in a fiery heap of masculine flesh. He lifted her shift—all this while kissing the tops of her breasts where her collar had fallen open. Desire burned in her depths, and soon her shift was off over her head. Nude at last, feeling no modesty, and baffled by this unhindered passion, she wiggled beneath him.

"You are mine now, Duncan," she found herself saying.

He drew back and stared at her. "Aye." Then he kissed her deeply and flicked his tongue over her nipples. Amelia moaned while he continued to lick and suckle and use his lips to blaze a trail of pleasure down her quivering belly.

She parted her legs and cupped his head in her hands. He inched lower still, and suddenly his face was in the damp hollow between her thighs, probing the depths of her womanhood with his lips and tongue.

She gasped with delight, her breath catching in her throat. Her blood quickened in response as he pushed ahead with his face, devouring her hungrily. He slid his hands under her bottom and lifted her off the bed to gain better access, and Amelia shuddered with pleasure.

He glanced up, and for a split second their eyes locked together. He moved up to mount her, then reached down and released himself from his bulging breeches.

A moment later, he was inside, thrusting and plundering, claiming her completely. All she knew was that she belonged to him, body and soul, and from this moment forward nothing could save her from this all-consuming desire to win his heart, and to make this marriage a true one.

A few hours later, Duncan woke to a quiet knock at the door. He turned his head on the pillow and saw that Amelia was sleeping peacefully, so he slipped out of the bed, making sure not to wake her. He walked naked to the fireplace where the enormous flames were dancing in the hearth, warmed his hands for a moment, then picked up his axe, which was hanging against the stones on the hook where the poker was normally kept. Stealthily, he crossed to the door and opened it.

Richard Bennett was standing there in the corridor. "She's mine. Give her back."

Without hesitation, Duncan stepped forward and cut Bennett down.

Duncan backed up, watched Bennett sink lifelessly to the floor, and felt a dark and sinister swell of satisfaction move through him.

He woke with a start and sat up in bed.

Amelia was still sleeping soundly beside him. All was quiet, except for the raindrops beating against the window.

His heart was racing. He glanced across the room at a few dying embers of fire in the grate, still glowing faintly. He placed a hand on his chest and felt again the wretched satisfaction he had experienced when he'd watched Richard Bennett die.

Disturbed by the dream, Duncan glanced uneasily at Amelia, rose from the bed, pulled on his clothes, and returned to his own bedchamber to sleep the rest of the night alone.

Chapter Nineteen

A week later, Duncan made love to Amelia on top of the covers with the bed curtains closed. They were surrounded by velvet, cloaked in darkness, and he gave himself over to the senses of touch, smell, taste, and sound. He lost himself in the ecstasy of her mouth, in the clever stroke of her tongue up and down the length of his passions, and in the sound of her hungry moans as she devoured his boundless desires. He simply could not get enough of her.

He closed his eyes and ran his hands through the silky locks of her hair and wondered if it was possible that she might one day succeed in removing him from that hellish black abyss of death. He'd not had any dreams of violence over the past week, yet it hardly seemed possible that it could continue this way—that he could live the rest of his life outside of that wretchedness, or that he deserved this pleasure.

The sex that night was like a haze all around him, and when he managed to open his eyes, she was coming down on top of him in the darkness, straddling him, sheathing him with her tight, lush heat. The intoxicating aroma of their lovemaking filled his senses, and he groaned as she began to move. He held her tiny hips in his hands, felt her hair sweep across his face, and thrust upward to revel in every forceful, pounding impact of their bodies coming together.

Afterward, following a string of explosive climaxes, he lay weak and sated, spread across the bed on his stomach like a dead man. Amelia covered him with her body. She weighed next to nothing, but he felt the pressure of her breasts on his shoulder blades and took great pleasure in the quiet reverie. It was like some kind of trance. He might even have fallen asleep. He was not sure. All he knew was that when he opened his eyes and felt the heat from her body on his back he could not help but think of the dream. . . .

He blinked a few times, then spoke softly. "He'll come here, you know."

"Who?"

"Bennett. He'll not let this pass." Duncan paused. "What will you do when you see him?"

She took a long time to answer, and Duncan felt his stomach turn over with dread.

"Nothing," she said at last. "We are no longer betrothed."

Duncan considered that careful, rather elusive reply. "If he comes here and tries to win you back, I cannot guarantee I'll be civil."

"But you promised not to harm him, Duncan. We have an agreement. You will leave his fate to the courts."

He wet his lips and fought to suppress the anger he felt at her desire to protect her former betrothed. Did she still care for him? Or was it something else? Was it Duncan she was trying to protect, by pulling him back from the precipice of hell?

"Aye. I will not break my word," he said. "But I will want you to see him for what he truly is."

She was quiet for a long time. "Why?"

"So that you will not regret the choice you made in a husband."

There it was. The truth.

She rolled off him and sat up. He felt the gentle stroke of her fingertips across his back, rubbing over the scars. He continued to lie on his stomach, facing away from her, staring into the blackness.

"I will have no regrets," she said, "if you keep your word to me. Despite how we began, Duncan, I do see goodness in you, and I desire you. You know that. Since we arrived here, and even before that, you have proven yourself to be a man of honor in so many ways, and I believe that in time we will grow to trust each other and care for each other very deeply. At least that is what I hope will happen."

Those hopes brought him no comfort, however, because deep down he still believed himself to be a savage and he feared that in time, when the initial heat of their passion cooled, she, too, would come to see that he was, and always would be, a warrior at heart. Like his father.

"I still do not think you understand me, lass," Duncan said. "You don't know the things I've done."

He had forgotten none of it. Not a single detail.

She hesitated. "I would prefer to put that behind us and begin anew. You are the Earl of Moncrieffe, and I will soon be your countess. Let us think of that and be hopeful about the future. The rest of it is in the past."

He pondered her words for a long time while she massaged his lower back. It relaxed him, made him want to sleep.

"Do you not worry about the violence in my nature?" he carefully asked.

"Perhaps, sometimes," she admitted.

Sometimes . . .

If she were wise, he thought wretchedly, she would worry about it every minute of the day.

Because he most certainly did.

* * *

A few days later, Amelia and Josephine took the coach to the village to deliver a cherry pie to Mrs. Logan, the miller's wife, who possessed a rare talent for the arrangement of flowers and had offered to decorate the chapel for the earl's upcoming nuptials.

But while the woman spoke of colorful blossoms and crystal vases, Amelia could barely concentrate on the conversation, for she was distracted by thoughts of Duncan and what had transpired in bed the other night, when he had revealed his concern that Richard would come to the castle to win her back. Duncan was worried that he would not be able to resist killing Richard.

She did not want Duncan to suffer with such self-doubt. She wanted to help him see that he was a good man and could put his past behind him. He was not like his father. She knew Duncan was not.

A knock sounded at the front door and interrupted her thoughts, as well as Mrs. Logan's presentation of the flowers. Briefly flustered by the intrusion, Mrs. Logan rose from her chair to answer it.

A tall, broad-shouldered castle guard stepped inside. He wore the MacLean tartan, and his hand was squeezing impatiently around the hilt of his sword.

"I have orders," he said, "to escort Lady Amelia back to the castle at once."

"Has something happened?" she asked, feeling a rush of panic as she stood. Josephine stood up as well.

"Aye, milady. The Moncrieffe militia has returned with the redcoats."

She took in a quick, sharp breath. "Do you mean to say that Colonel Bennett is here?"

"Aye. I'm to ride inside your coach with you, and I'm not to let you out of my sight until I deliver you safely to the gallery in the keep."

She strode to the door and saw more than twenty mounted clansmen waiting outside—all carrying shields, swords, and muskets. It seemed she had her own personal army of protectors.

She backed up into the miller's cottage. "Surely this is unnecessary. The lieutenant-colonel is my former fiancé, and we are not at war with his regiment, are we? Surely he just wishes to speak with Lord Moncrieffe and ensure that all is well."

At least she hoped that was the case, and she hoped Duncan would assure Richard as such. Then Richard could be on his way. Disappointed by her rejection, perhaps, but alive.

The tall Highlander shrugged. "It's not for me to say, milady. I'm just following orders. I'm to see you safely back to the castle."

She squared her shoulders. "Of course." She turned to the miller's wife. "I do apologize, Mrs. Logan. Perhaps we can continue this another day?"

"My door is always open to you, milady." The woman did her best to appear calm, but her cheeks were flushed with color.

A short time later, Amelia and Josephine were seated inside the coach, with the tall Highlander situated across from them. He kept his eyes fixed on the door at all times.

While the heavy vehicle rumbled along the road, no one said much of anything. The tension inside the coach was palpable. Outside, they were surrounded by a fierce contingent of Highland warriors on horseback, and it seemed as if they were driving straight into the very heart of a full-blown battle, already in progress.

Amelia hoped this was just a precaution and wondered what Duncan imagined would occur when she arrived. It was highly probable that Richard would wish to speak to her privately and ascertain that this union was of her choosing. Perhaps he was angry, or believed that Duncan had forced her hand. In that case, she would do her best to explain her change of heart and somehow make Richard understand that she was happy—otherwise he might feel compelled to fight for her, and that could lead to an awkward set of circumstances. She must do all she could to prevent him from saying or doing anything that might provoke Duncan. She would do her best to explain her feelings and convince Richard to leave.

As for the other issues regarding Duncan's official inquiry into Richard's alleged crimes as a soldier, which would be a full affront to his honor as an officer and a gentleman . . . Well, she hoped the charges would be laid at Fort William, not Moncrieffe, so that Duncan could be distanced from it.

The coach hit a bump and she bounced on the seat and wondered anxiously where her uncle stood in all of this. He had not mentioned Richard since he arrived, and he had been absent a great deal of the time. He had not asked Amelia how she felt about ending her engagement, nor had Duncan spoken of her uncle's opinions on the matter since that first night. They had both been curiously silent about Richard, which caused her some uneasiness now, as the coach rattled over the stone bridge and through the gate tower.

They emerged out of the archway into the bright, sunny bailey. She and Josephine sat forward and peered out the windows.

There was noise and confusion in the yard—kilted Highlanders shouting to one another, the clang of metal against metal as they practiced their maneuvers. Horses—restless and spooked by the sounds of battle—whinnied and reared up. In the east corner Amelia saw a splash of red as the coach rumbled by. It was a cluster of English soldiers, sitting together in the grass.

The coach pulled up in front of the castle door. The

Highlander who had been assigned to deliver her to the keep hopped out first, then took her firmly by the arm. He seemed determined to reach the gallery without stopping, and she had to pick up her skirts and scurry to keep up with him.

He led her through the front entrance hall and across the bridge corridor to the keep at the rear. They crossed the long banqueting hall and at last reached the gallery. The Highlander opened the arched door and pushed her through it. She stumbled inside; then the door swung shut behind her, and a key turned in the lock. The Highlander's footsteps disappeared down the length of the banqueting hall. Suddenly she was alone. All was quiet.

Amelia stood for a moment and stared at the keyhole, then abruptly turned away and walked to the window. She looked out at the calm lake and studied the reflection of the trees upon the water.

It was odd to imagine Richard being here at this moment. It was like a sharp, pungent taste of reality, the emergence of her old life, which had all but vanished over the past few weeks, as if it had never existed.

Only it was not the same life at all. The man she had once hoped to marry was accused of unspeakable crimes, and she would soon have to face him and try to see the truth for herself, when she had not been able to see it before.

What if she still could not?

And what was happening in the castle now? Was Richard speaking to Duncan? Was he angry? What would Duncan do?

Do you not worry about the violence in my nature?

Lord help her, she was certainly beginning to worry about it now, after being dragged out of the village by an army of Highlanders with muskets and spears. The whole situation seemed positively medieval, and her heart was racing with dread. What if something terrible was happening? Her hands began to shake as her mind swarmed with grisly images of Duncan in his kilt, splattered with blood, swinging his battle-axe through the air. She shut her eyes and pressed her fingers to her temples to block it all out.

Footsteps approached outside the door. A key slipped into the lock. The door opened, and Iain strode in.

She crossed to meet him. "Oh, Iain, thank heavens. Please tell me what's happening. Is Josephine all right? Where is Duncan? Has he spoken to Richard yet?"

"Not yet," Iain answered in a voice that seemed almost too casual under the circumstances. "Colonel Bennett is waiting in the library, and Duncan will be here soon. He wants you at his side when Bennett contests your engagement, which he fully intends to do."

"How do you know this?"

"Bennett announced it to the guard when he rode through the gate."

She laid a hand on her stomach. Lord help them all. But at least there was one promising factor in all this: Duncan would not wish to have her standing at his side if he intended to don his Butcher garb and slice off Richard's head. He knew how she felt about that, and he had given her his word.

"Did you speak to Richard already?" she asked. "Are you sure he wishes to confront Duncan? I'm surprised he did not ask to speak to me first."

"He did. It was the first thing he requested. Strode in here, bold as brass, and demanded a private appointment with you."

"And you said no?"

"Not exactly. I told him to wait in the library, that you were on your way back from the village, and he would see you then. I arranged for a small supper to be sent up."

"Thank you, Iain. But I believe all of this is quite unnecessary. If I could just speak to him, I would assure him that I am well, and that I genuinely wish to marry Duncan. If he heard those words from my own lips, I believe he would accept my decision and leave peacefully." She paused when Iain frowned at her. "Please, Iain, do not misunderstand. I do not wish to protect him. I only wish to do what I can to prevent an altercation. I am certain that he came here because he needs to confirm that I am safe. Do not forget, I was his intended bride and while under his protection I was abducted by the Butcher. You cannot fault him for coming here. You would do the same thing, I am sure."

"I do not fault anyone, lass. But Duncan will not let you be alone with Bennett. It is the unshakable truth. Do not even bother to ask."

She watched Iain for a moment to measure the strength of his resolve, then resigned herself to the fact that it could not be breached. She turned away and sat down on the long bench at the table.

She had no choice, then, but to abide by her future husband's wishes. He had his reasons to employ such excessive measures, she supposed.

Duncan walked through the door just then. She rose quickly to her feet. Their eyes met and locked.

"You heard Bennett is here?" Duncan asked. He was dressed in an extravagant full-skirted coat of gold, with heavy button ornamentation and a matching embroidered waistcoat, cut low in front to reveal the white, ruffled neckwear. On his head he wore a jet-black, full-bottomed French wig with a mass of curls that reached well below his shoulders.

The wig unnerved her. It was an accessory she had not seen him wear before. Had he worn it with her father?

She made careful note also of the dress saber, sheathed and belted at his waist.

"Yes, I heard," she replied. "I was dragged out of the miller's cottage, where I was looking at flowers for our wedding day."

She imagined that he might come forward, take her into his arms, and assure her that everything was going to be all right, that they simply had to get through this day and all would be well. But he remained just inside the door, his expression dark and menacing.

"You can return there tomorrow," he said flatly.

"Thank you. I will."

A heavy silence descended upon the room. Iain cleared his throat and shifted uncomfortably.

Duncan stood at the door, his eyes fixed on his future bride, while he fought to suppress the seething rage that was rising up inside him. Richard Bennett was here in his house. He'd just eaten his food and enjoyed wine from his private cellar. And he wanted to speak privately to Amelia.

Duncan took a few deep breaths and squeezed the hilt of his sword.

"We'll meet him in the banqueting hall," he said, remembering his promise to her and wishing—God, how he wished—that he had never made it. If he hadn't, Colonel Bennett would already be dead and there would be no need for talk.

Amelia nodded and stepped forward. She paused in front of Duncan and looked into his eyes. "Thank you," she said.

Thank you for what? he wondered wretchedly. *For inviting a rapist and murderer into my home, and agreeing to treat him with civility?*

Duncan held the door open for her, and she passed through it into the banqueting hall, which ran a length of seventy-five feet along the western side of the keep. The stone walls were hung with gilt-framed portraits; the floor was ebony oak, the furniture sparse. There was only one long narrow table in front of the hearth and a dais at the far end, with a single heavy chair in front of a rich, crimson tapestry.

His father had sat in that chair many times to hear clan grievances. He had always ruled with authority from that chair, and more than a few men had died by his sword in this room.

The duke was standing at the window, and Amelia stopped when she saw him. "Uncle, you are here as well?"

"Yes, my dear. Lord Moncrieffe requested it."

She looked up at Duncan and gave him a small smile, though he could see there was uncertainty in it.

He did not return her smile. How could he, when he was thrashing through everything that was bleak and vicious inside him? He was about to politely receive the disgusting piece of scum he had been hunting for the better part of a year. The scum who had raped an innocent woman—the woman he once loved—and mutilated her body. The scum who burned peaceful crofts and shot women and children for their mere knowledge of the rebellion.

That same man was about to walk into this hall and question Duncan's right to claim Amelia as his wife.

He took a seat in the chair. He lounged back in it, spread his legs wide while he gripped the armrests with both hands, for he needed to squeeze something.

"Get behind me, lass," he said, tossing his head, his mind smoldering with aggression, which he did not even bother to hide from her.

It was impossible now to act civil, to play the part of a charming, amiable gentleman, when his gut was churning with deadly hatred. At this moment, despite the fancy clothes and ridiculous wig he felt compelled to wear, he was a Scottish Highlander, a warrior, and a savage. He was chief of this clan, and he had been trained from birth to fight and kill in order to protect those in his care. It was taking every ounce of will he possessed to restrain the beast lurking inside him, lying in wait for his mortal enemy.

Amelia said nothing as she lifted her skirts and stepped up onto the dais. She stood just behind his left shoulder. Duncan sensed her apprehension, but that was not his primary concern. What consumed him most was his own self-control.

The duke remained by the window while Iain stood in the opposite corner. Duncan sat very still, staring straight ahead at the door at the far end of the hall, his battle-roughened hands opening and closing around the armrests, his warrior senses attuned to every sight and sound.

At last the door opened, and in walked Richard Bennett, Amelia's former betrothed. Heroic English officer. Rapist and murderer.

Chapter Twenty

When Amelia saw Richard for the first time since her abduction, something inside her lost its point of reference.

Her former fiancé was dressed in his impressive red uniform with shiny brass buttons. He wore tall black boots, polished to a perfect, brilliant sheen. He looked almost like her father in his younger days, and the recognition of that fact penetrated her convictions most disturbingly. Golden-haired and strikingly handsome, Richard carried himself with an impressive confidence as he walked the vast length of the great hall, his footsteps echoing up into the ceiling timbers, his gray eyes fixed on Duncan the entire time.

Fergus, Gawyn, and Angus strolled in behind Bennett and spread out across the back of the room.

Amelia's heart began to pound. She had not known of their presence at the castle today. What was their purpose? Why did Duncan want them here?

Richard stopped in front of them and gave the obligatory bow. Duncan, in all his silks and finery, sat on his throne like a great and powerful king, saying nothing.

For the longest time, no one spoke, and Amelia felt like her heart was going to explode out of her chest. She rested a hand on the back of Duncan's chair.

"I request a private conversation with Lady Amelia," Richard said.

"Your request is denied."

Amelia was uncomfortably aware of her future husband's flagrant show of disrespect. She glanced anxiously at her uncle, but he appeared to be taking it all in stride.

Richard's cheeks colored with anger, and his gaze shot to hers. "Are you all right, my dear?"

"Yes," she replied, unnerved by his familiarity. She had formally ended their engagement. She was no longer his "dear."

He turned his attention to Duncan. "You behave with dishonor, my lord."

"I'll behave any way I damn well please, Bennett, especially if it means you'll be troubled by it."

"Duncan . . . ," she whispered, seeking only to remind him of his promise to her.

He whirled around in his chair and glared up at her accusingly, as if she had just betrayed him in the worst possible way, then stood and hopped off the dais, slamming heavily onto the floor.

Though he was dressed in a sophisticated costume of silks and lace and wore a wig of shiny black curls, he walked with a dangerous, threatening swagger, circling around Richard like a carnivore assessing its prey. He palmed the hilt of his sword with a quiet, unbroken obsession. He had never, in her eyes, appeared more frightening.

Richard rotated a full circle, never taking his eyes off Duncan. Amelia stepped forward anxiously.

"Indulge me if you will, Bennett," Duncan said. "Do you remember a young Scottish lass by the name of Muira MacDonald?"

Oh, God. . . . She had thought Duncan would address the legitimacy of their engagement before anything else, but clearly she had misjudged his priorities. Foolishly so, she supposed. All of this had always been about one thing. Muira. It was why he had abducted her in the first place.

Her eyes turned to Angus. He stood against the far wall, watching the exchange with dark, sinister satisfaction.

"I do not recall any woman of that name," Richard replied.

"Think harder, Bennett. You took your pleasure with her in an apple orchard, against her will. You let your men take their pleasures, too; then you murdered her in cold blood. You sliced off her head and sent it home to her father."

Amelia sucked in a breath and glanced at her uncle. He seemed distressed by the explicitness of the account but strangely unsurprised.

"I know not of what you speak, Moncrieffe," Richard firmly said, "and I am here to challenge your betrothal to Lady Amelia Templeton. You are aware, sir, that when she arrived here she was already promised to me. Her own father, the late Duke of Winslowe, approved the match."

"Aye, I am aware, but now she belongs to me, and as a result, is under my protection. Do not forget, I saved her from the Butcher." He was still circling around Richard with his hand on his sword.

Richard followed his every move. "She was mine to protect, not yours."

Duncan stopped and changed direction, circling back the other way. "But your protection of women is rather selective, Bennett, do you not think? You seek to protect one, but not others. The lady deserves better than that."

He laughed. "And you think *you* can do better? That *you* deserve her affections? Clearly you are a brute, Moncrieffe, just like your father. You have no cause to accuse *me*—an officer in the King's army—of anything! I am here to ensure that she is safe, and from what I have seen thus far, it appears that you have coerced her into accepting your hand. You may even be in legion with the infamous Butcher of the Highlands yourself—in which case I will see you hanged for treason."

Duncan shook his head with loathing. "If anyone in this room is going to hang, Bennett, I assure you it will not be me."

"I have done no wrong," Richard insisted; then he tossed his head toward the window. "But your rebel clansmen led me on a wild chase into the north, while Amelia—miraculously—was being delivered back here."

"Miraculous, indeed," Duncan said with spite. "Now tell me about what you did to Muira that day in the orchard. Tell me about the message you sent to her father, the Laird MacDonald. I want my future wife to hear it straight from your own mouth."

Richard shot her a desperate look. "Do not listen to him, Amelia. He is trying to smear my good name only to have power over you, and therefore seek connections through your uncle. He means to distract you from his true purposes as a Jacobite traitor."

Duncan chuckled bitterly. "You're as good a liar as you are a murderer."

"Your Grace!" Richard shouted over his shoulder. Amelia's uncle strode forward. "May I have your word as a witness that the Earl of Moncrieffe has threatened me today, and that he has become involved in suspicious activities, and is an accomplice in the abduction of your niece, Lady Amelia Templeton?"

"I am witness to no such thing," her uncle replied. "The earl provided my niece with a safe haven upon her escape. That is all I know."

"Your Grace!"

When her uncle did not retract his statement, Richard changed the direction of his plea. "Amelia. Tell me now if this man has compromised you, or forced your hand in any way. If that is so, I will bring the law down upon him."

She spoke firmly, even though her head was swimming with fear.

"No, Richard, it is not true. I was not coerced. I accepted his proposal freely, and with love in my heart. So please, gentlemen, take your hands off your swords. If I mean anything to either one of you, there will be no fighting today."

"Amelia," Richard protested.

She stepped down from the dais. "Richard, I am sorry if my letter caused you pain. It was not my intention to hurt you. I will be forever grateful to you for saving my father's life on the battlefield, and I appreciate that you have come here to ensure my safety and happiness, but it is over now. I am sorry, but I do not love you. I love Lord Moncrieffe."

Something trembled within her.

Richard strode forward. "Amelia. This is absurd. The man is a Scot!"

She raised her chin. "There is nothing more to say, Richard. You must go now. *Please,* just go."

Duncan and Richard glared at each other for a tension-filled moment; then at last Richard made a move to leave.

Duncan stopped him with a hand. "Nay, Colonel Bennett. You will not be going anywhere just yet."

Please, no. . . .

"Take your filthy hands off me, you detestable Highland vermin. You're all alike." Richard looked up at her again. "Amelia, don't be a fool. You cannot think to marry this man. He is the son of a whore."

Anger reared up in her. "Richard, you forget yourself!

The earl's mother was the Countess of Moncrieffe, daughter of a French marquis and a great scholar and philanthropist."

Richard scoffed. "No, Amelia. Moncrieffe's father left his fine French wife for the village whore, and was excommunicated for it." He regarded Duncan as he spoke. "The great Scottish laird then butchered the bishop responsible, and was promptly reinstated as a good Catholic. When his whore died giving birth, he returned to his wife and brought his bastard son back to the castle. This is the man you wish to marry, Amelia—the son of a sinner, who is now most certainly burning in hell."

Her gaze shot to Duncan. "Is this true?"

His eyes were blazing. "Aye."

All at once, there was a startling scrape of metal from the back of the room and Angus came striding forward with his sword gripped in both hands. He drew the blade back over his shoulder. He meant to slice Richard in half from head to foot!

Angus crossed the full length of the hall with the fires of hell boiling in his eyes, and Richard stumbled backwards a few steps towards the dais, scrambling in a panic to draw his own sword.

Amelia bolted forward. "No, Angus! Please stop!"

In a lightning flash of movement, Duncan drew a pistol from under his coat, cocked it—and aimed it at Angus.

"Lower your weapon," Duncan said, his instruction a clear and certain order. "You'll not be killing this man today. I told you I'd have my vengeance—and have it I will."

"What about *my* vengeance?" Angus shouted with malice.

"You'll have it, too."

"When? And how?"

Her uncle—who had backed into the wall by the window when Angus charged across the room—offered a reply. "There will be an inquiry into Colonel Bennett's conduct," he quickly explained. "We have witnesses. I have spoken to a number of them since I arrived here."

Richard swung around and glowered at him. "Has everyone gone mad? Surely Your Grace does not mean to suggest that—"

"I mean every word I say, Bennett. Your methods are beyond the pale. You are a stain upon the King's name."

But Angus had not yet sheathed his broadsword. He still held it over his shoulder, poised to kill.

No one moved.

Angus turned to Duncan. "That woman has made you weak."

She shivered, while Duncan offered no reply. He merely stood with legs braced apart, his pistol still aimed between Angus's eyes.

Amelia could barely breathe.

"Fergus, Gawyn!" Duncan shouted over his shoulder. "Take Colonel Bennett to the dungeon and lock him up."

The dungeon? He had a dungeon?

It was only then—when the other two came scurrying across the hall to seize Richard and confiscate his weapons—that Angus lowered his sword and began to back away. Duncan, however, kept his finger on the trigger of his pistol.

"My men will not stand for this!" Richard shouted, struggling against Fergus and Gawyn's hold as they dragged him away. "I will have you shot, Moncrieffe!"

Duncan turned the gun on Richard. "Say one more word, Bennett, and I'll splatter your brains all over these walls."

They dragged him from the hall while Amelia fought to subdue her anxiety—not only from the shocking nature of her husband's threat just now but from all that had occurred in the past five minutes.

Overshadowing everything, however, was the fact that her future husband had kept his promise to her.

Duncan turned the gun on Angus again. "I'll have your word that you will not go against my wishes."

"My word?" Angus spit on the floor. "What good is any man's word when you just let my sister's killer live?"

"Muira will have her justice."

"But will I have mine?" Angus asked. "I wanted him dead, Duncan, and you're forgetting that not so long ago you wanted the same thing."

Angus headed for the door, and Duncan lowered the pistol at last.

Just then, four broad-shouldered clansmen entered the hall and blocked the exit. Angus laughed indignantly. He faced Duncan and spread his arms wide. "Are these men here to escort me off the premises?"

"Aye. I can't let you pay a visit to the dungeon, Angus, to simply do as you please."

The guards took hold of his arms, but he roughly shook them away. "No need to bother yourselves. I'm leaving this place, and I'll not be back. I've seen enough here today to turn my guts to ash."

He walked out. One of the guards looked at Duncan. He nodded to indicate an unspoken set of orders. The men followed Angus out of the keep to make sure he left peaceably.

Duncan turned to Amelia.

Her knees dissolved into clotted cream. She realized suddenly that her hands were shaking, and she returned to the chair and sank into it.

"Thank you," she said.

"For what?" There was a hard, contemptuous edge to his voice.

"For keeping your promise."

His blue eyes were cold as ice, and his shoulders heaved with barely contained fury. He pulled the wig off his head, dropped it lightly to the floor, then walked out of the hall without a word.

Chapter Twenty-one

Duncan entered his study, looked around at all the dusty books and rolled-up documents, his telescope in the window, and the portrait of his French mother over the mantel. He slammed the door shut behind him, then turned and rested his forehead against it. Closing his eyes, he fought to suppress his fury.

He had never felt such desire to kill a man. For a few unpredictable seconds, even his passion for Amelia was overshadowed by a blind lust for blood. He hadn't been certain he could resist the lure of drawing his sword from his scabbard and piercing Richard Bennett straight through his cold, black heart. Even now, when Duncan thought of what Muira had endured in the orchard that day, and what Amelia might have experienced as that man's wife, he wanted to wrap his hands around Bennett's throat and squeeze until every last drop of putrid life drained out of his body.

Duncan pounded his fist repeatedly against the door. He felt like he was being ripped in two. What sort of man was he? Was he the diplomatic aristocrat his mother had raised him to be? The educated scholar, who was pledged to marry an English duke's daughter? Or was he his father's son? A battle-scarred warrior, conceived in a whore's bed, seething with darkness and vengeance. A man who solved his problems with an axe.

He turned around, tipped his head back against the door, and tried to make sense of his duality and the savage warrior that existed within.

On the battlefield, he had never killed gratuitously. He had long been aware of the consequences of death. One person's demise had a ripple effect on the world. Others suffered and mourned that loss and were affected in ways only God could understand. Sometimes grief gave rise to compassion and kindness, depth of feeling, and an understanding of the soul.

Other times, it created monsters.

He was one such monster.

Richard Bennett was another.

Duncan opened his eyes and wondered suddenly—where had Bennett's cruelty come from? Did he have a whore for a mother? Or had someone he cared about been sliced without mercy from his life?

A knock at the door startled Duncan. He took a step away from it. Without waiting for an invitation, Amelia pushed her way inside. She closed the door behind her and leaned against it, facing him with her hands behind her back. Her cheeks were flushed, her eyes wide.

She was afraid of him. No wonder. She had seen the monster just now. He felt a terrible, crippling shame, which caught him off guard.

"Why didn't you tell me about your real mother?" she asked. "And that your father killed a bishop? It wouldn't have mattered—I choose to judge you for yourself—but I wish you had told me."

He had no answer. His head was full of thistles. He couldn't seem to think.

She did not press him, and he wondered how it was

possible that any woman could be so calm in a situation such as this. Why was she even here? He half-expected her to be down in the dungeon, apologizing to Bennett for the way he had been treated and begging him to take her home, away from here.

"That was difficult for you," she said.

Words spilled out before he could stop them. "I wanted to stab him through the heart."

She stiffened. "I could see that."

Neither of them spoke for a moment, and the silence seemed almost thunderous in his ears. He didn't want her here, in his private sanctuary. He wanted to push her from the room. But another part of him objected. Part of him needed her. Wanted her. Desired her.

Was this love?

No, that could not be possible. How could he feel so many different things at once? Hatred, anger, restlessness.

Sorrow.

"You resisted killing him," she continued as she moved away from the door, forcing Duncan to back up into the middle of the room. "And you prevented Angus from doing so as well."

Duncan let his eyes travel down the front of her gown, then back up again to the lush curve of her breasts, and finally to the gentle light of compassion in her eyes.

"If you hadn't been there," he said, "I might not have been so merciful. I've said it before, lass—you have a way of tempering my cruelty, of pulling me back from the brink. I hate you for it sometimes. But other times, I don't know what to make of it. Or of myself."

She closed the distance between them and laid her open palms on his chest. Her eyes were glossy, apprehensive— as if she didn't know what sort of mood he was in—and he felt an odd, confusing lust quicken his blood. A part of him still yearned for vengeance, but more than that, he wanted to make love to his future wife. The need was potent and fierce, laced with both anger and tenderness. It was complicated—far too complicated to understand. He simply needed to claim her now. That was all he knew.

His mouth closed over hers, and he kissed her deeply, cupping her head in his hands and plunging his tongue into her mouth. She moaned with pleasure. The sound of her arousal clouded his brain. He wanted her with a rock-hard passion that stifled all logic and seemed to make the whole world go silent.

An instant later, he was backing her up against the door, lifting her skirts, pulling down her drawers, and hastily unfastening his breeches.

She tore his coat off his shoulders, and he wondered why she was doing this. Did she understand the frenzy inside him that needed to be satiated? Was this for his benefit, or did she truly desire him at this moment, even after seeing his dark shadow self?

He slid his hand between her legs. She was already slick. There was no need for foreplay. He entered her smoothly, driving all the way in, and she clutched at his shoulders. He lifted her up off the floor. She wrapped her legs around his hips while he pounded into her, again and again, up against the door. It was both rough and intimate. Nothing existed for him outside of their coupling. He felt only the soft, damp lushness of her womanhood and the sweet, honeyed gift of her lips.

"Don't ever leave me," he said without thinking, but it was as if another man had spoken.

She climaxed quickly, and he came seconds later. It was over very fast. He was not proud of it, but at least they were both satisfied.

Carefully, he lowered her to the floor, but she clung to his neck for quite some time and held on to him. Again he felt ashamed, and he was not entirely sure why. It was not clear to him.

He did not move. He waited there inside her until his racing heart slowed and his breathing returned to normal; then slowly, he withdrew. He fastened his breeches and backed away. Her skirts fell lightly to the floor.

"How can you care for me?" he asked with a frown of disbelief. "You are a gentlewoman. Why do you want to be my wife?"

"I told you before," she replied. "I see goodness in you, and we both know there is passion between us."

He turned and walked to the window, stared across the lake at the fields and forests in the distance. "But what if I *had* killed your Richard in the hall just now? What if I had driven a knife through his heart, right in front of your eyes? Would you still see goodness in me then?"

"He is not *my* Richard," she said. "And you did not kill him."

No, but he had come very close, and part of him still wanted to.

Amelia crossed the room and sat on the sofa while he continued to look out at the calm lake.

"He denied everything about Muira." Duncan focused on the stillness of the natural world outside the window, because he did not want to confront the inner whirlwind of his rage. He believed that if he gave in to it now, there would be no turning back. "Do you believe I am wrong to imprison him?"

"No," she replied. "I believe he has acted with dishonor. My uncle believes it, too. He has just revealed to me some of the things he learned this past week, specific details that were very disturbing to hear." She sighed. "My uncle has spoken to many soldiers and Scots, and the King must hear their stories as well. And besides all that, I saw something in Richard's eyes today that I did not see before."

"What was that?"

"Lies."

He looked up at the sky and watched a blackbird soar against it. "Why did you not see it before, lass?"

"Because I was not a whole person before I met you," she continued. "I was naïve and sheltered and inexperienced, and I was consumed by the fear of losing my father and being alone. He is gone now, but look at me. I have survived, and I have discovered that I possess a mind and a reasonably strong will of my own. I survived *you*, didn't I?"

He turned and faced her. "But now you're consumed by your passions and the pleasures we share in bed. That sort of thing can blind a person, you know."

She smiled faintly and shook her head. "I am not blind, Duncan. I see your scars very clearly. They are deep and they are numerous."

He swallowed over a heavy swell of despair that rose up in him without warning. He was not accustomed to feeling such things. What had this woman done to him? "I do not want to disappoint you."

"You have not done so yet," she said without hesitation, which unsettled him, for he was not worthy of such confidence. He did not feel it in himself. "Quite the opposite, in fact," she added. "Especially after what I saw today. I know it was difficult for you."

"It was torture."

But there was so much more he could have told her—like how it pained him to turn on Angus, his closest friend, and how he had hated her in that moment for leaving him no choice.

But those were things he could not say. They were

feelings he did not welcome. Feelings he would have to bury, like so many other things.

He turned away from her and faced the window, and wondered how long this proper, civilized inquiry was going to take.

Later Amelia entered the library, where her uncle was pacing in front of the bookcases. "You sent for me?"

"Yes." He held out his hand and guided her to a chair, but continued to pace the room.

"You are troubled, Uncle?"

At last, he stopped and faced her. His cheeks were flushed with color. "I have been thinking about what I witnessed in the banqueting hall, and I have become most distressed."

Determined to stay calm, she folded her hands on her lap. "How so?"

He began to pace again. "I have not changed my mind about Richard Bennett. I still believe he is a villain and must be stopped, but something else has been poking and jabbing at me." He looked at her. "That savage who approached him with the claymore—the one they called Angus. Is he the Butcher, Amelia?"

She blinked up at her uncle in astonishment. "No, he is not."

He studied her carefully. "He is not the one who abducted you from the fort? You must be honest with me, gel, because if your future husband is in legion with such murderous rebels, I cannot, in good conscience, sanction this marriage."

She swallowed thickly. "I assure you, Uncle, that man was not the Butcher. He is a MacDonald, and he is an old friend of Duncan's. They fought together at Sherrifmuir, and Duncan was once betrothed to his sister. That was who Duncan was questioning Richard about in the hall."

"Yes, yes, I already knew about the young woman. Duncan shared many things with me. But when I watched that fierce Highlander advance across the room, I swear, my heart nearly gave out. I have never, in all my years, seen such fury."

Amelia had.

"I believe," her uncle continued, "that he would have slaughtered Richard before our very eyes if Moncrieffe had not been there to prevent it."

She looked down at her hands. "Yes, I believe you are right."

Her uncle went to a side table and poured himself a glass of claret from a crystal decanter. He took a drink, then paused a moment to let it settle his nerves. "So this MacDonald is not the savage who abducted you?"

"No, Uncle, I assure you he is not."

He faced her. "That is a relief, I must say."

She sat for a moment, then stood up and poured herself a glass of claret as well.

"What will happen to Richard?" she asked.

"That remains to be seen. I have sent a dispatch directly to the King with the details of my findings, and I have also informed Colonel Worthington at the fort. We sent a rider there today with news of Richard's incarceration here, and I suspect Worthington's forces will be here tomorrow to arrest him and take him back to Fort William. After that, there will likely be a court-martial."

"Will he be hanged?"

"It is difficult to predict," her uncle told her. "The man is a decorated military officer who has proven himself loyal to the Crown in countless situations in the past. These things can be . . ." He paused. "They can be delicate."

"Do you believe he will be found innocent of the charges, even with your influence and the testimony of the witnesses?"

"I cannot lie to you, Amelia. It is quite possible."

She lowered her gaze. "If that happens, Duncan will not be pleased, especially if Richard is reassigned to Scotland."

"I realize that, and who could blame him?"

She looked her uncle in the eye. "Have you expressed these concerns to him?"

"Not yet."

"Do you plan to?"

He turned and poured himself another drink. "I haven't decided yet."

Just before dawn, Amelia woke to the sound of birds chirping on the rooftop outside Duncan's window. A few stars still lingered in the violet sky.

She was lying on her side, nude but warm beneath the heavy coverlet. Duncan lay behind her, also nude, his knees tucked into the backs of hers, his strong arms wrapped around her waist. She listened to the steady pace of his breathing and wished all moments could be like this—intimate and quiet, without the immediate threat of war, revenge, or prisoners in dungeons.

They had made love with great tenderness the night before, and it was unlike any other previous sexual encounter. Perhaps it was the release of Duncan's goal to kill Richard. Perhaps now that he had faced him at last and resisted the urge, and Richard would be brought to justice, Duncan would find some peace within himself. She hoped he would be able to lay the pain of Muira's death to rest and allow himself to love again.

How quickly the world could change, Amelia thought. It was difficult to believe that not long ago she had imagined a happy future for herself as Richard's wife. It was frightful to imagine where she might be right now if things had not unfolded as they had. Would she be lying naked in Richard's arms?

Knowing what she now knew about his crimes against women and children, the thought made her skin crawl.

There was an eruption of noise just then. Voices shouting in the bailey. Someone blew a horn.

Duncan was out of bed in an instant, looking out the window. It was still dark outside, except for the faint pink glow of the sunrise on the horizon.

She sat up and hugged the covers to her chest. "What's happening?"

Without answering, he disappeared into the dressing room and returned in a loose shirt with his tartan wrapped around his waist. He belted it and pinned it over his shoulder.

It was the first time she'd seen him in his kilt since her arrival at the castle. His thick sable hair was long and dishevelled, just as it had been that first night when he stood over her bed, wielding an axe. He had not yet shaved; his jaw was stubbled.

Rugged and wild-looking, he dressed with deft speed, his hands working over buckles and brooches, his athletic legs taking him around the room with efficiency and purpose.

Amelia couldn't seem to make her lips work in order to speak through her alarm. He was the Butcher again. Transformed in an instant.

A knock rapped at the door as he pulled on his boots. He crossed to answer it. A kilted clansman stood outside, breathing heavily. "Bennett's escaped."

"When?" Duncan hardly seemed surprised. It was as if he viewed this as a natural consequence, typical of any rebellion.

"Ten minutes ago."

"Mounted?"

"Nay, on foot."

"Go. Saddle my horse and wake Fergus and Gawyn in the garrison."

The clansman departed at a run, and Duncan returned to the bed. He knelt and pulled a long wooden chest out from under it.

"Get dressed," he said, "and you are not to leave this room, do you understand? Lock the door behind me, and don't open it for anyone. *Anyone*."

He removed his weapons from the chest—his claymore in a scabbard, which he belted around his waist, his axe and pistol, which he loaded in front of her. Last, he withdrew his shield and slung it over his shoulder to hang at his back.

"That incriminates you," she said. "The stone—the Mull agate. There are tales about it."

He frowned, then set it back in the chest. "I'll find another." He handed her a dirk. "Take this." He pushed the chest back under the bed and made for the door.

"I'll send guards," he added, in a belated attempt to reassure her that all would be well; then he was gone.

Amelia scrambled out of bed and hastily locked the door behind him.

A key had been used in the escape. Someone in the castle had set Bennett free.

Duncan crossed over the bridge at a full gallop. The wind in his hair and the sound of Turner's hooves clattering noisily upon the stones sharpened his senses, focused his resolve.

The Moncrieffe militia was assembling and would soon follow and spread out across the fields. Others were searching inside the castle walls, some guarding the English soldiers, but Duncan knew that Bennett was gone and had escaped alone. The guard at the gate had confirmed it. He had looked Bennett in the eye as a knife plunged into his belly and twisted savagely.

That guard was now dead, and Duncan was no longer calm. Nor conflicted. He felt only one pure, unambiguous emotion. . . .

The sun was rising in the sky, and he had the advantage of both speed and knowledge of the terrain. He thundered across a dewy meadow toward the forest—any soldier's clear choice for cover—and charged into the shadowed growth. Once inside, he cantered through the wood, leaped over a fallen log, then reined his horse to a halt. He paused and listened.

A mourning dove gave a plaintive call, and a gentle breeze whispered through the leafy treetops. He closed his eyes and sat very still in the saddle, alert and focused. A twig snapped. Footsteps pounded over the ground. A hundred yards away perhaps?

His eyes flew open. Digging his heels into Turner's thick flanks, Duncan vaulted forward, deeper into the bush. Seconds later, he saw a flash of red to his left and wheeled Turner hard over.

Duncan ducked forward, keeping his head low to avoid the slash of branches while he nimbly pulled his axe from the saddle scabbard.

Bennett was running hard. He was out of breath. Panicked. He glanced over his shoulder.

Duncan gave a savage roar as Turner's heavy hooves pounded over the mossy ground. Then everything went dark and still inside Duncan's head as he leaned back and swung his axe through the quiet morning air.

Chapter Twenty-two

Duncan reined in his horse and dismounted. He strode back to where Bennett was huddled in a ball on the ground, hiding his face in the cradle of his arms. He was without his hat—for it had been sliced in two.

Duncan roughly shook him by the shoulder, as if to wake him from slumber, and Bennett responded by lying back in the moss and raising his hands over his head. It was a total, clear message of submission.

Duncan searched Bennett's belt and pockets for the knife he had used to kill the guard, located it, then wiped the blood off on the moss and slipped it into his own boot.

"You're the Butcher, aren't you?" Bennett asked.

"I am the Earl of Moncrieffe," Duncan replied. "Now get up."

Duncan paced back and forth, axe in hand, while Bennett rose on unsteady legs.

"I wouldn't have recognized you," Bennett said shakily. "You look different in the costume of a savage. That's why I thought you were the Butcher."

Duncan ignored the insult. "How did you escape?" he asked. "Who released you?"

"One of my own men. He had a key."

"Where did he get it?"

"I don't know that. I didn't bother to ask." The panic in his voice slowly began to subside.

Duncan continued to pace back and forth like a caged tiger. "You have to pay for your crimes," he said. "You cannot get away with the murder of innocent women and children. You cannot escape from it."

"I have done nothing but my duty," Bennett replied.

"Your duty to whom?" Duncan could feel his impatience mounting. "Your country? Your King? What about God?"

"God, King, country—it's all the same."

"Is that a fact?" Duncan stopped and fixed his eyes on Bennett. "Tell me something. You've fought in battles, as have I. You've killed many men, as have I. You've even saved the life of your commander, Amelia's father. But why do you hurt women and children? Why do you burn them out of their homes?"

"My duty is to crush this rebellion," he replied. "If that means I must wipe this country clean of all Jacobites, then that is what I will do."

Duncan took a deep breath, searching for calm. "Do you ever regret the things you've done?"

Do you wake up at night drenched in sweat, dreaming of your victims staring at you, watching you sleep? Do you see and feel the scorching flames of hell at your heels, and agonize over the blood you cannot wash off your hands?

"Never," Bennett replied. "As I said, it is my duty as an officer to serve the King, and I do so without hesitation. Or remorse."

Duncan looked away. He thought of his father's iron fist and the pain of that punishing, unrelenting hand as it struck bone—Duncan's own bones—in far too many lessons about discipline.

"Have you ever been wounded?" Duncan asked, thinking for a moment that Bennett simply did not understand the pain he inflicted upon others. "Have you ever felt real physical agony? Have you been shot, or cut, or beaten? Have you ever been a victim of another man's wrath?"

Bennett laughed. "Why all these questions, Moncrieffe?"

"I just need to understand. . . ."

"Would you like to see my scars?" Bennett asked. "I can show them to you, if you like. You can see where I've been wounded on the battlefield, and how I was once flogged to within an inch of my life."

Duncan eyed him with mistrust. "The British army does not flog its officers."

"No, but a father will flog a son to make a good soldier out of him."

Duncan pondered this. "You were whipped by your father?"

"Yes," Bennett replied. "Many times. But I cannot imagine it was any worse than what you endured, Moncrieffe. Let us not forget the bishop. Your father was not a man many people would defy. I'm sure you had a very stern and rigorous education as well, and did what you were told. Nothing to be ashamed of. I, too, was an obedient son."

It was true. Duncan had been raised with a firm hand, but he had also defied his father. At the age of thirteen, Duncan had walked in on his mother being slapped around the gallery. He had quickly sliced his father's arm open with a broken bottle, and it was a year before the man raised a hand to Duncan's mother again.

When it did happen, his father came away from that beating with a black eye. After the third, more violent confrontation with a bold son of seventeen, his father gave up the abuse completely.

"I'll be taking you back to the castle now," Duncan said,

returning to his horse and digging through his saddlebags for a rope, "where you'll wait for Colonel Worthington."

Bennett scowled. "Give me a sword, Moncrieffe, and let me fight you. It's only fair, after you stole my fiancée—no doubt gaining her hand by force, just as I gained the upper hand with your former fiancée. What was her name again? Mary? Megan?"

Duncan spoke in a low voice. "Her name was Muira."

"Well, Muira was a very pretty Scottish lass, and I made sure her last moments were exciting and memorable. She quite enjoyed herself, I believe. Pity you weren't there to see it."

Duncan faced Bennett and palmed the handle of his axe. "If I'd been there, Bennett, you'd be dead."

"Is that right? Then why aren't I dead now? Perhaps you don't truly have the guts for war. From what I understand, you like to negotiate in flowery drawing rooms, using your whisky to bribe for what you want. What happened to you? Your father was a fierce warrior. He must have been very disappointed with how you turned out. I'm still not sure why Amelia has taken a fancy to you when you are nothing but a weak and cowardly Scot and, I am quite sure, a dirty Jacobite as well."

Duncan voiced a warning. "You should shut your mouth." He thought of Angus suddenly and heard the low sound of his friend's voice: *That woman has made you weak.* . . .

Bennett smiled. "Why? Does the truth grate upon your delicate sensibilities? Here's another bit of grating truth for you, Moncrieffe." He took a step forward. "When these charges against me are dismissed—which they most certainly will be—the first thing I'm going to do is return to the Highlands. I will rape every woman along the way, burn every cottage, and then I will kill *you,* and every member of your household. I will take Amelia back to England with me where she belongs and make her my wife. I'll take her straight to bed on our wedding night and show her how a real man does it. At least then she will be an English whore. You might even hear her screams from your grave—but you won't be able to do a single bloody thing about it, because you'll be dead."

Rage detonated in Duncan's brain. There were flashes of light, an ungodly roar from somewhere over the tree-tops, and the next thing he knew he was staring down at Richard Bennett's head at his feet.

The body tipped forward and fell into him. He shoved it away, then stumbled backwards onto a tree. He dropped his axe to the ground, stared intently at the head and its headless body . . .

He quickly bent over to expel the contents of his stomach.

A few minutes later, he was standing on the other side of the clearing with his back to the red-coated corpse, looking up at the trees. He had no idea how long he stood there before Fergus and Gawyn came galloping along. He heard the vague sound of their voices, then felt a hand on his shoulder.

"What happened here?"

He met Gawyn's eyes. "Bennett's dead."

"Aye, we noticed."

Fergus was kneeling over the body. "Nice work, Duncan. But how'd he escape in the first place? You don't think it was Lady Amelia who set him free?"

Duncan pointed at Fergus from across the distance. "Say that again, Fergus, and you'll wish you were never born."

"I'll not say another word about it!" He raised his hands in surrender.

"What are we going to do with him?" Gawyn casually asked.

Duncan returned to the body and looked down at it,

and felt as if he were spinning into the hellish storm of his recent life—a storm that had never really moved out. Part of him was disgusted by what he had done, but another part felt satisfied. Deeply satisfied. He was drunk with the fulfillment of his vengeance.

What did that make him?

Stalking to his horse, he removed the empty saddlebag and handed it to Gawyn. "Put the head in this bag and take it to Kinloch Castle. Deliver it to the Laird MacDonald with a note saying that this is the English soldier who killed his daughter. Don't let anyone see your face."

"But who will I say did this?"

Duncan stared at him and experienced a moment of great clarity.

"The Butcher." He scooped up his axe and swung himself into the saddle. "Get rid of the body. He cannot be found on Moncrieffe land."

With that final order, Duncan kicked in his heels and galloped deeper into the forest, in a direction that took him farther away from the castle.

The search for Colonel Bennett continued for the next twelve hours, though Duncan did not take part. Nor did he return to the castle. Instead, he rode alone to the banks of Loch Shiel, reined in his horse, dismounted, and waded into the frigid waters—kilt, pistol, claymore, and all.

He kept walking until the water reached over his head, then dunked himself and remained there, submerged, his feet on the muddy floor of the loch, feeling utterly content to be swallowed up by the dark, bitter chill.

When he finally noticed an urgent need to breathe, he broke the surface, sucked air deep into his lungs, then unbuckled his weapons and let everything sink to the bottom.

He treaded water for a moment, immersed to the neck in the cold, then gave himself up to the gentle current.

Without the weight of the steel, his feet lifted. His eyes closed and he floated on the swells, dimly aware of the fact that he was drifting farther and farther away from shore.

He thought of Amelia and knew this would bring on the inevitable disappointment he had been anticipating since the beginning. It would fall as heavy as an anvil and crush everything. He had broken his vow to her, and she might very well view it as a violation of their marriage agreement. She might even leave him and expose him as the rebel that he was.

Strangely, however, he felt no despair, no aching regret over what he had done. All he felt currently was the cool water lapping up against his skin and the sway of his tartan, floating lightly all around him.

Was this the peace he had been searching for? Perhaps. Though he did not feel triumphant, nor did he wish to celebrate. His bones were going numb. He felt almost nothing at all, as if he were not a man but a mere element of the lake. He was composed of water, and he was floating.

Then he began to shiver and realized it was a stupid thought. He was very much a man with hot, pulsing blood in his veins—blood that was growing colder by the minute. He swam back to shore, staggered heavily out of the water, and collapsed onto his back on the pebbly beach, shivering.

He stared up at the white sky for a while, then found himself gazing up into two round, black holes.

Turner's flaring nostrils . . .

The great beast snorted and nudged him in the head.

"Nay, I've not gone to meet my maker." Duncan reached up and stroked the animal's silky muzzle. "But I don't feel alive, either. I don't know what I am."

He continued to lie there, wondering how long it would take for his clothes to dry, and for his conscience to truly pass judgment on what he had done.

It was dark by the time Duncan returned to the castle. He crossed the bridge on foot, leading Turner behind him, then handed him off to a groom outside the stables.

Duncan entered the main castle and went straight to his bedchamber but found it locked. He pounded on the door and heard Amelia shout from inside, "Who is it?"

He had told her to lock herself in. That had been more than thirteen hours ago. He raked a hand through his hair, displeased with himself. "It's Duncan. You can open the door now, lass."

Because Richard would not be coming back.

The lock clicked, the door opened, and Amelia flew into Duncan's arms. She wore a white dressing gown, and her tousled hair was wet, hanging loose upon her shoulders. She smelled of rose petals.

"Thank heavens you're all right," she said. "No one knew where you were."

He reached up to pry her wrists off the back of his neck and hold them low in front of him. "I'm fine, lass."

She led him into the room. The fire was burning low, casting the bedchamber in a shroud of warm, golden light. There was a tub in front of the hearth. Her maid must have come and gone, at least.

"Did they find Richard yet?" Amelia asked.

Duncan had had all day to consider how he would answer that question. In the end, he knew that honesty was the only option. Richard's head would soon arrive at Kinloch Castle—it was a mere two-day ride from here—and news of his death would spread quickly. There was no possibility of hiding what had occurred. Not from her.

"Nay, they did not find him," Duncan answered. "The militia is still searching, along with Worthington's men."

Before Duncan had a chance to say anything more, she came toward him, slipped her arms around his waist, and laid her cheek on his chest. "Oh, Duncan, how I missed you. I was so worried. I feared you would never return."

He stood motionless, bewildered, as she tugged his shirt out from inside his kilt and leather belt. She lifted it to bare his chest, then took a moment to study the cut of his muscles and the markings of his scars. Soon her soft, pink lips were brushing over his skin. Her moist breath made him shiver, and he lost all interest in conversation, despite the fact that there was so very much to say.

Her enticing wet mouth settled on a nipple, and she sucked greedily. His breathing grew heavy. She licked and teased both nipples for quite some time; then her eyes lifted and she gave him a smile of raw, sensual appeal.

He knew he should stop her, but he couldn't. He needed this physical sensation to bring him out of the strange, empty void he had been floating in all day.

She slid down the front of him to her knees and slipped her hands up under his kilt. She kept her eyes fixed on his the entire time as she stroked the muscles of his thighs, then took hold of his heavy balls. She caressed and massaged him. Finally, she lowered her ravenous gaze and disappeared under his kilt.

Duncan closed his eyes and tipped his head back as she took him into his mouth. Erotic pleasure flooded through him. The chaos of his life dissolved in the wet, luxuriant heat of her mouth and the ecstasy that coursed through his veins. She licked and sucked tirelessly, until he could no longer remain standing. He took her by the shoulders, pulled her to her feet, swept her up into his arms, and carried her to the bed.

He came down on top of her in a smooth blur of movement, needing to make love in a way he had never needed before. He kissed her deeply, thrust his eager, muscled hips into hers, then reached down and pulled her shift and his kilt out of the way.

He leaned up on one elbow and looked down at his erection, poised and pulsing hotly between her thighs. All he had to do was touch the tip of his passions to the dark, silky center of her womanhood and in one firm stroke he would be lost inside. But something held him back.

"Amelia . . ."

"Yes?" She wiggled impatiently, cupped his buttocks in her hands, and pulled him inside. He slid in all too easily. Heaven melted around him, rendered him immobile, speechless, but somehow he located his resolve and pulled out again. He rose up on all fours to look down at her.

He couldn't do this. Not now.

"I killed him."

She blinked a few times. "What do you mean?"

"I killed Bennett. I did it this morning. In the woods."

Her brow furrowed with confusion. He stared down at her in the dying firelight, waiting for her to say something. Anything. But she did not speak.

He rolled off her, onto his back.

"I don't understand," she finally said, sitting up and pulling her shift down over her legs to cover herself. "You told me they were still searching for him."

"They are."

"But do they know he's dead?"

"Nay."

She considered this. "So no one knows you killed him? Your militia is scouring your lands, searching for a dead man? Why didn't you tell me this before, Duncan? How could you let me . . . ?" She paused, and a hint of anger found its way into her voice. "What happened? Please tell me that you were defending yourself."

He could not lie. What he did was an act of rage, brought on by the nature of Bennett's threats and the horrors of his cruelties in the past. "Nay. He was unarmed. I had already taken his knife."

Duncan reached into his boot and pulled it out, then tossed it onto the floor with a noisy clang. It bounced end-over-end toward the wall.

She clutched at the neckline of her shift, holding it tightly about her neck. "If he was unarmed, why didn't you simply bring him back here and lock him up again?"

"That's what I meant to do. I had the rope in my hands, but . . ."

"But what?"

"Something came over me. I couldn't listen to the things he said. I can't even begin to explain it to you."

"Try."

Duncan swallowed over the bile that rose up in his throat. "He said vile things about you, lass, and about Muira—things I do not care to repeat. It started a fire in my head, and I lost control. I didn't even realize what I'd done until it was over."

She slid off the bed and went to stand in front of the window. "How did you kill him, Duncan?"

"I took off his head." It was the bitter, hard truth, delivered without hesitation, and strangely he felt no shame. He even reveled in the words as he recalled the silence in the woods—when Bennett had finally stopped talking.

For a long moment she stood without moving or speaking, and Duncan knew she was repulsed by what he had done. Sickened by it. As he had expected she would be.

Amelia faced him. "How do you feel about it? Are you at all troubled by what you did?"

He swung his legs to the floor and sat on the edge of the bed. "I wish I could tell you that I am. I wish I could say I'm drowning in guilt and remorse, and that I spent the day on my knees, praying for God's forgiveness, but that would be a lie, lass, because I do not regret it."

"You feel no remorse whatsoever?"

He looked up at her. "Nay. I'm glad I did it, and I would do it again if I found myself back there now."

She headed for the door, but he sprung from the bed and blocked her exit.

"How could you do something like that and feel no regret?" she asked. Her voice quavered with shock and anguish. "You had the chance to bring him back here so that he could face Colonel Worthington's court-martial, but you took it upon yourself to act as his judge and executioner. You killed an unarmed man in cold blood. I cannot imagine the savagery of it, not after the past few weeks, when I have seen another side of you—a side that gave me hope. I began to believe it might be possible for me to forgive everything else, and love you."

Love him.

His will collapsed, and he felt compelled to explain. The words spilled out of him quickly. "If it makes any difference, I didn't plan it."

She grimaced. "So you are telling me that you had no control over yourself? I am sorry, Duncan, but that does not make me feel any better. How can I be sure you won't lose your temper with *me* one day? How do I know you won't slice me in half as well, if I stir your anger?"

"That would never happen."

"But you just said you lost control. Your father lost control, too. He killed a bishop. You once told me that he was violent with your mother. How can I become your wife, knowing that you are so volatile?"

He strode forward to take her into his arms and convince her that he would never harm her, but she pushed him away. "Do not touch me. I feel as if I can smell his blood on you."

He frowned. "This is who I am, Amelia. I am a warrior. I was bred to fight, and I fight for my country. I fight to protect *you*."

"I don't want to marry a warrior. I want to marry a gentleman."

She might as well have stabbed him in the heart with a hot poker.

"You cannot close your eyes and pretend that war does not exist in the world," he said bitterly. "Men must fight to protect their freedom and their families."

"But there are other ways to fight!"

They'd had this argument before, and he was beginning to see, with great frustration, that it was not something they were ever going to agree on. She was disappointed in him now, as he'd always known she would be one day.

"Where is Richard's body?" she asked. "What did you do with him? He deserves a proper burial."

She would learn the truth eventually, so there was no point in keeping it from her. "I sent his head in a bag to the Laird MacDonald."

Her brows pulled together in shock. "Muira's father?"

"Aye."

"Oh, God! So was this just about avenging her death, then?"

"Nay, I told you before. I did it for Scotland, and to protect *you*. I couldn't risk letting him live."

She took a deep breath, and he knew she did not believe him. She believed he had done it as an act of revenge, nothing more. "What about the rest of his body? Where is he now?"

"I don't know. Fergus and Gawyn got rid of him."

She pushed past Duncan toward the door. "Let me out of here."

"Amelia . . ."

She flung the door open but turned back for one final

word. "We have shared many pleasures, Duncan, and you have been good to me. Despite everything—my own judgment included—I still have feelings for you, and for that reason I will not expose you as the Butcher. I will take your secret to my grave. But I cannot marry you. I cannot marry a man who takes a life and feels nothing. Even if you see it as a mere casualty of war, how can you not *feel* something?"

With that she fled from the room, and he was left standing in front of the dying fire, reflecting very carefully upon that question. It was a valid one. Where was his heart? How was it possible he could be so numb and dead inside? He slammed a fist hard upon the mantel, then sank to his knees.

Chapter Twenty-three

Moments later, in the privacy of her bedchamber, Amelia wept for the violent circumstances of Richard's death and the chilling, gruesome indignity of his severed head traveling in a bag to a neighboring Scottish castle as a prize. She didn't care what he had done. No human being deserved such treatment.

She wept also for her foolish, aching heart—the mad love she felt for the man who had committed this brutal act of savagery. Her disappointment was beyond measure, her heartbreak inconceivable. All her hopes for a happy life here at Moncrieffe—a life spent with her beautiful lover, who was, for a short time, the true mate of her soul— were crushed. He was not the man she'd believed him to be. She had put too much faith in him, in his ability to overcome his violent nature and embark upon a life of peace and diplomacy. His clothes, his home, his wit, and his charm—all of it was a mask he wore. He'd deluded her father with it, just as he'd deluded her.

Now she must conquer and lay to rest the passion she still felt for him—which made no sense, after what he'd just confessed. Yesterday he had told her that passion could blind a person. He was correct on that point. Every time she remembered the pleasure they shared in bed, her heart broke all over again.

Had he ever truly cared for her? she wondered suddenly. Or had all of this been for Muira?

The following morning at dawn, Amelia wrote a letter of farewell to Josephine, along with a brief note to Duncan, left them both on her desk for a servant to find, then walked out of the castle and stepped into her uncle's coach.

There was a chill in the air. Puffs of steam shot out of the horses' nostrils as they tossed their heads and nickered in the faint morning light. How quiet and peaceful it seemed.

Her uncle joined her a few minutes later with all of his bags and belongings, curious as to why they were leaving so hastily, without saying good-bye to Duncan. She explained that she had broken off her engagement and did not wish to discuss it. He stepped inside the coach, which bounced under his weight, and did not push her to say more, at least not yet. The door closed behind him. She felt very tired. He patted her hand and said he would listen when she was ready to speak of it. Amelia could only nod.

The coach pulled away from the castle, and she did not dare look back.

The minute Duncan opened his eyes to a blinding ray of sunlight shooting in through the window, he knew he had lost her.

By some inexplicable means, he had slept through the night, but it was a night haunted by dreams of corpses and blood, and the scorching fires of hell burning at his skin. He dreamed of Amelia, too—watching him from a balcony above while he sank deeper and deeper into a sea of flames beneath a smoky sky. She waited until he was immersed to the neck in fire, then turned and walked away. She did not look back, and he remained there, staring after her, floating on the fiery swells.

He sat up in bed and rubbed the heel of his hand over his heart. There was a dull, muffled ache inside him, like distant roaring thunder. He looked at the window. The sun was just coming up.

Then he saw the note—a sealed letter, slipped under his door sometime during the night or that morning. From Amelia, no doubt. An acute sense of panic gripped him. He swallowed over a debilitating swell of dread, then went to retrieve it:

> *Duncan,*
>
> *By the time you read this, I will be gone. My uncle is taking me back to England. I am sorry to leave without saying good-bye, but I am certain this is the better way. I do not wish to ever see you again. Please honor that wish.*
>
> *Amelia*

He tried to breathe, but his lungs felt tight. She was gone, and she did not want him to follow. She did not wish to ever see him again. There was no hope for forgiveness. The tenderness she had begun to feel for him was no more. It was dead, annihilated, and he was the only one to blame, for he was the one who had killed it. He had slaughtered their love in a savage, bloody massacre. He had murdered someone he'd promised to spare.

An unarmed man in cold blood. Sliced his head off with an axe, and stuffed it into a bag.

It was an unquestionably brutal act of savagery.

But still—*still!*—Duncan could not bring himself to regret it. Even now, he would do it again. He would do it ten times over to protect her. He would sacrifice everything—her love and, in turn, all present and future happiness—to keep that vile monster from ever touching her. Even if it meant never seeing her again.

Duncan crossed to a chair and sat down, tipped his head back, and listened to the steady ticking of the clock while everything inside him went quiet and still.

"Will you speak to me, Duncan?"

Duncan looked up from his book and saw Angus standing in the open doorway, waiting for an invitation to enter the study.

"Come in."

Angus entered and stood for a moment, looking around the untidy room. "Iain's worried about you," he said. "As am I. You've not left these rooms for five days."

It was true, but he'd needed time to think. Time to ponder and reflect upon his purpose in the world, the source of his strength, and the value of the sacrifice he had made.

He was glad Angus had come. There was much to discuss.

"I regret some of the things I said and did," Angus told him, "especially in the banqueting hall. I was not fair to you, Duncan. I should never have doubted you."

Duncan closed the book and set it aside, rose from the chair, and shrugged into his green silk morning coat. He adjusted the lace at his sleeves, then approached his old friend. "Did your father receive the package I sent?"

"Aye, and let me assure you, there was dancing and a feast like no other. You should've been there, Duncan. I wish you were."

Duncan merely nodded.

"But *you've* not been celebrating," Angus noted as he adjusted his tartan over his shoulder.

"Nay, I have not." He waved Angus into the room and poured him a glass of whisky.

"But you did the right thing, Duncan. Do not think otherwise, not even for a minute. Bennett got what he deserved, and Scotland thanks you for it. You shouldn't be punishing yourself. You deserve a medal." He accepted the glass Duncan held out.

"I have no regrets, Angus." Duncan sat down on the sofa.

Angus's eyes narrowed, and he stared at Duncan skeptically. "I'll argue that point, because I believe you have one very big regret—the loss of the colonel's daughter." He swallowed the whisky in a single gulp and set the glass down on the corner of the desk next to a tall stack of books.

Duncan crossed one leg over the other and looked toward the window. His silence seemed to stir Angus's impatience. He began to pace the room.

"You're better off without her, Duncan. Surely you know that. She left you, for God's sake. What kind of woman . . . ?" He stopped and took a breath. "We've been through a lot together, you and me. And despite our differences lately, I consider you my friend. I respect your leadership and your strength and your skills on the battlefield. You've saved my life more than once, as I've saved yours." He paused. "Come back to us, Duncan. Forget about the Englishwoman. She was not worthy of you. She was in love with that worm, Bennett, and defended him until the end. You can do better. All you need is a pretty little Scottish lass to turn your head and remind you that you're a proud and strapping Highland warrior." He paused again and took a breath. "Make no mistake, I loved my sister, and I'll always be indebted to you for what you did to her killer, but it's time for us both to move on. Pick up your weapons again, Duncan. Don your tartan and carry your shield with pride."

Duncan frowned at him. "Pick up my weapons? For what purpose?"

"What other purpose is there but to fight? The rebel-

lion has withdrawn, most of the Highlanders have retreated to their farms, yet the English are still here. We
need to drive them out of our country once and for all,
while we still have their fear in our hands. Bennett's head
in a bag is already spreading a wave of terror through the
English garrisons. I say we continue our rampage until
they retreat completely, back across the border."

Duncan considered this. He gazed out the window at
the clouds in the sky and recalled the Butcher's rampage
of terror in the past. It had been effective, there was no
question of that, and with Bennett's death the Butcher's
infamy would only grow.

Yet there were other things to consider. There was the
small matter of his conscience, and his dreams, night after night. . . .

He met Angus's gaze. "I believe I can exert more influence through the Moncrieffe title. I have the ear of the
King, and despite what has come to pass between Amelia
and me, I am certain that her uncle, the duke, will continue to support my efforts to establish peace, if I choose
to step forward and make a case for it."

Angus scoffed. "Winslowe will not hear a single word
you say after what you did to his niece. I'd be surprised if
she hasn't already told him who you are and how you abducted her in the dead of night, and threatened her life. An
army of redcoats could come marching in here any day
now. Which is why I suggest you don your tartan and ride
out of here while you still can. Iain can take your place
here. He's more suited to this kind of life than you are."

"Amelia will tell no one," Duncan said. "She gave me
her word."

Angus scoffed bitterly. "You trust her word, do you?
The word of the English?"

"Aye, I trust it."

"Be sensible, Duncan. Use your head."

A wave of anger washed over him, and he stood. "How do you expect me to be sensible? The woman I wanted as a wife is repulsed by me. She thinks I'm more of a monster than that raping, pillaging pig Richard Bennett. For all I know, she could be carrying my child, and I will never know."

Duncan could hear the sound of his heart thudding in his ears. Perhaps Angus could hear it, too, because he took a sudden step back.

"And I do not even have my weapons," Duncan continued. "They're at the bottom of Loch Shiel."

"Fook, Duncan. What are they doing there?"

He pinched the bridge of his nose. "I cannot say. I barely remember. All I know is that they were weighing me down and I probably would've drowned if I hadn't let them drop."

"But your father's sword—he passed it down to you."

"It's a hundred years old," Duncan told him. "You think I don't know that?" He strode to the window and slammed his fist down on the stone ledge. "I think I've lost my mind."

For a long time he stood there, looking out at the lake; then he felt Angus's hand on his shoulder.

"Fight, Duncan. It's what you were born for. It'll restore your sanity. Trust me in that, and come with me today."

Duncan shook his friend's hand away. "Nay! It will only make me more of a madman. I cannot do it. Something else has to be done."

"What are you saying?"

He faced Angus. "I'm saying it's time I retired the Butcher. I did what I set out to do. I killed the foul bastard who raped and killed Muira. Now, I'm done. I'll kill no more."

"Duncan, listen to me."

"Nay! I will not listen to another word! Go and tell Fergus and Gawyn to meet me at the cave. We'll talk about what must be done. You are all free men, and if you wish to continue on your own, I will not stop you, and I will do what I can to protect your identities. But I will not be joining you. I'm done, Angus. I'm going to do what I can to get Amelia back."

Angus frowned.

"I love her. I will not live without her."

He loved her. *Loved her!*

Angus took an anxious step forward. "You're making a mistake. She's English, and she doesn't understand the way we live."

"She understands more than you think, Angus. Now go, please. I'll come to the cave tomorrow at dusk. The only thing I have left of the Butcher is the shield. I'll bring it, and I'll offer it to you, if you wish to continue the fight. If that is your choice, I'll pledge my loyalty to your cause. You are my friend, Angus, and I will never betray you. But I will not be joining you."

Stunned, Angus nodded as he backed out of the room. Duncan sank into a chair, looked up at the portrait of his mother, then cupped his hands together and pressed them to his forehead.

There. It was decided. He was going to lay the Butcher to rest and fight some other way. And somehow . . . somehow . . . he was going to earn Amelia's forgiveness. Somehow he would redeem himself in her eyes and win back the gift of her respect.

Chapter
Twenty-four

Duncan stood inside the mouth of the cave, where he had taken Amelia on the morning of her abduction, and waited for his eyes to adjust to the chilly gloom. He looked at the dried-out fire pit and remembered how she had crouched over it, bound by coarse ropes, trembling with fear. He had sliced the ropes from her wrists, done what he could to ease her fears, and wiped the blood from her wounds.

An odd thought, really, for *he* had always been the one with blood on his hands, and he had not yet been able to wash them clean. He never would, he supposed. Not completely.

I cannot marry a man who takes a life and feels nothing.

Over the past few days, he'd had time to reflect upon the wisdom of those words, and what he'd learned about himself was the very thing that gave him hope for absolution—because he *had* felt something. A great deal, in fact. He might not regret taking Richard Bennett's life, and he would do it again if the circumstances were the same, but the despair . . . It was present and it was potent. He had always grieved and mourned for the pain endured by every living human being, even Bennett, who was beaten ruthlessly by his own father—a situation Duncan understood all too well. They had much in common, he and Richard Bennett. And yet they were not the same, for Duncan derived no pleasure from the pain of others. He did what he could to prevent it. That was why he fought—to protect the freedom and safety of his countrymen and -women.

And Amelia. Especially.

But in so doing, he agonized over every life he took on the battlefield, even in the defense of his own. He wished the world were a kinder place, a gentler place, and that was why he was here tonight.

Duncan lifted his shield off his back, knelt down, and reached into his sporran for the small flintbox he had brought with him. A moment later, he was stretched out on his back, running a finger over the shiny agate in the center of the shield. The stone sparkled dazzlingly in the firelight.

He would present this shield to Angus tonight, because Angus would wish to carry on the Butcher's campaign. Duncan was certain of it. He would not interfere with Angus's choice to continue that fight, but he would offer him another option first. . . .

Horses approached. Riders dismounted just outside. Duncan closed his eyes and took a deep, cleansing breath. Everything would be different now.

He heard his friends enter and join him at the fire. Then he opened his eyes and looked up—straight into the eyes of an English redcoat, and three others crowded around him, with muskets cocked and aimed at his head.

His gut seized, for he recognized the leader instantly.

He was the one who had tried to rape Amelia on the beach. The one Duncan had let live.

"Good work, men," the pasty redcoat said with a foul-mouthed grin. "Looks like we caught ourselves a Butcher." Then he swung his musket by the barrel and struck Duncan hard in the side of the head.

Fort William, midnight

Amelia woke to a frantic knocking at her door. Heart suddenly racing, she sat up and squinted into the darkness. "Who is it?"

"It's Uncle!"

Recognizing the distress in his voice, she slid out of bed and hastened across the room in her bare feet. She unlocked the door and opened it. "What's happening? Are we under attack?"

He stood in the narrow corridor wearing only his nightshirt and cap, his finger hooked around a brass candleholder. The flame flickered and danced wildly in the drafts. "No, my dear, it's not that. It's something else. Good news, actually. They've caught the Butcher."

A horn blew from somewhere in the compound. There were voices shouting. Footsteps tapping up and down the stairs. Amelia stood in the doorway, staring mutely at her uncle, not entirely certain she'd heard him correctly. There must have been a mistake. They had caught someone else, an imposter. Not Duncan.

"Where is he?" she asked.

"He's here. They just brought him in on the back of a wagon, half-dead from the sounds of it."

"Have you seen him yet?"

"No, but I thought I should tell you right away, because surely it will give you some peace of mind to know that your abductor will finally get the justice he deserves for what he did to you, and countless others."

She backed unsteadily into the room. "Half-dead, you say? What happened to him? How in the world did they catch him?"

And was it really him? If it was, did they know he was the Earl of Moncrieffe? Had he been dressed in silks and finery when they took him? But no, he couldn't have been, or her uncle would have said something. News like that would shake the very foundations of the fortress, and the entire country as well.

"Information was delivered to a small English camp on Loch Fannich," he explained. "The soldiers learned where he would be at a certain hour, and sure enough, that's where he was—living in a cave like the savage barbarian that he is."

"Yes . . . ," she said, feeling almost dizzy with shock. "That's where he took me on the morning of my abduction."

Her uncle moved fully into the room, set down the candle, and pulled her into his arms. "I am so sorry, Amelia, that you endured such torture, but you are safe now. That despicable savage will be locked in a cell and chained to a wall. He will never be able to hurt you again."

She blinked a few times and fought to stay calm. Locked up? Chained to a wall? Her emotions careened dizzily. She could not bear to think of it. Despite her need to turn down Duncan's offer of marriage, she had never desired his imprisonment or his suffering. She would never wish to see pain inflicted upon him.

And what did her uncle mean . . . half-dead? What had they done to Duncan?

"Are you all right, Amelia? You look ghostly white. Sit down. I'll send for some brandy."

"No, Uncle. I do not need to sit. I must see him."

"See him? But surely you do not wish to see the man who—"

"I do wish it," she argued. "If you will wait outside, I will dress quickly."

"But why, Amelia? Do you not think it would be best if—"

"Please do not oppose me, Uncle. I need to know if it is truly him."

Winslowe took a step back and sighed. "Oh, it is indeed the Butcher, without a doubt. Not only was he carrying the famous shield with the Mull agate, but the officer who captured him had encountered him before and barely escaped with his life. He survived only because he was a strong swimmer."

Amelia whirled around to face her uncle. "A strong swimmer . . ." *God, no.* She could not stomach any more of this. What kind of strange destiny had befallen them? "Did this officer mention a woman who was there as a witness?"

"No. He said the Butcher appeared out of nowhere and hacked their tent to pieces while they slept."

"Is his name Jack Curtis? Major Curtis?"

Her uncle studied her curiously. "Yes, but how would you know that?"

She felt a dark, simmering rage burn in her guts and wanted very much to speak to this allegedly brave survivor, who had neglected to mention the part *she* had played in his unexpected dip in the lake that night.

"Because I had the distinct *dis*pleasure of meeting Major Curtis. I was there on the beach when the Butcher attacked. I can attest to the fact that this English officer is a scoundrel and a liar." She was breathing hard now and could barely suppress her fury. "If you must know, he only lives because I pleaded with the Butcher to spare his life."

"You were there?"

"Yes. Major Curtis was drunk and attempted to disgrace me in the worst possible way."

Her uncle gasped. "Good Lord, Amelia."

"But the Butcher came to my rescue. That is why he attacked the camp. He arrived in the nick of time and saved me from certain peril."

Her uncle's eyes filled with sorrow and regret. He strode forward and took hold of her hands. "If only I had taken better care of you. Clearly there is much you have not shared with me about your experiences as that man's captive. What hardships you must have endured."

"Yes, there were quite a few, but I cannot lie about it. The Butcher was indeed my abductor, but he was never cruel. He never hurt me." She paused. "There are still so many things I have not told you."

"But will you tell me one day?" he asked. "Will you ever trust me with all that you have endured?"

She stared at him for a long moment, realizing that her greatest suffering was happening right now. "Perhaps I will. But not tonight, because I must see him, Uncle. And I must see him alone."

Duncan's identity would soon be exposed to the world, Amelia thought miserably as she was escorted down the stairs to the prison by a guard in a red uniform. As soon as her uncle saw Duncan, he would recognize him as her former fiancé—the charming and amiable Earl of Moncrieffe. Duncan's double life would be revealed and the sky would come crashing down. She, too, might be charged with treason for keeping his secret.

Her stomach turned over. It was a wonder no one had recognized him yet. Colonel Worthington would certainly know Duncan on sight. He had dined at the castle more than a few times over the past year. Dozens of the soldiers stationed here had taken refuge there as well on a number of occasions. They had offered their assistance just this week in search of Richard. A search now called off, of course. News of his severed head arriving at Kinloch Castle in a bag had reached Fort William two days ago, and the Butcher had never been more fantastically notorious.

The guard beside her slowed his pace as they approached the cell at the end of the corridor. She trembled slightly, not knowing what to expect. Her uncle had told her that Duncan was half-dead. Part of her hoped it would be a case of mistaken identity—that it was not really Duncan at all. But to wish for the punishment of an innocent human being, wrongly accused, was beyond the scope of her conscience. She did not wish that. She could not.

At last they reached the cell door and she rose up on her toes to peer through the small barred window. There, lying facedown on a hay-strewn floor, was a brawny, kilted Highlander. His wrists were locked in iron manacles and chained to the wall. His long, black hair covered his face, making identification impossible, but there was no need to see his face. Amelia knew every inch of his body and recognized the familiar green MacLean tartan. There was no doubt in her mind that it was Duncan—asleep or unconscious. Perhaps even dead.

Her blood quickened. She turned to the young guard, who was fumbling clumsily with his keys, searching for the right one.

"Hurry, please."

"My apologies, milady." He found it at last and unlocked the heavy wooden door. It squeaked on rusty hinges as he swung it open. "No need to be frightened of him," the guard said. "He may look like a monster, but he's chained up and in no condition to do you any harm. I suspect he'll be dead by morning, and if not, he'll be just as dead when they hang him."

Amelia's heart throbbed in her chest, but she strove to maintain an appearance of calm as she entered.

"Take a good look at him," the guard said. "Then I'll see you out safely."

She turned to him. "I shall require a moment or two. There are a few things I wish to say to him. In private, if you please."

His head drew back. "Of course, milady. I understand. I'll leave you to do just that, but I won't be far. I'll be right here in the corridor. Call out if you need assistance." He closed the door and left her alone in the cell.

Heart-wrenching agony nearly choked her as she regarded Duncan, unconscious, on the floor. His hair was matted with dried blood. His left hand was bruised and misshapen, swollen the size of a turnip. There were cuts and contusions on his legs. She knelt down and gently touched his shoulder.

"It's me," she whispered. "Please speak to me, Duncan. Can you hear me? Can you open your eyes? Can you move?"

No response.

She leaned down closer and pulled the wavy locks of his hair aside to whisper in his ear, "Duncan, wake up. Please, wake up."

All of a sudden he jerked and tugged at the chains, flipped over onto his back, kicked his legs, and fought for a few brief seconds, until he realized the extent of his injuries, and groaned. He grimaced and writhed violently on the floor.

The guard was bursting through the door in an instant. "Are you all right, milady?" There was panic in his voice.

"I am fine," she replied. "The prisoner woke up, that is all. Now leave us, please. Now!"

The guard reluctantly backed out and closed the door.

"Try not to move," she said to Duncan, keeping her voice as quiet as possible so the guard would not hear the echoes of her despair. "You're hurt. Your hand seems to be broken."

But there was so much more than that. She now found herself beholding the gruesome horror of his face, cut and swollen beyond recognition. His nose was broken, his cheekbone mangled, his lip cut and inflated. This at least explained why no one knew him. Even her uncle would not make the connection. Not in this state.

"My God, what have they done to you?"

"I don't remember." He struggled to breathe. "Ah, God, my ribs."

"They found you in the cave," she told him. "The one who captured you was the soldier who attacked me on the beach. He has identified you, Duncan. I am so sorry. It is all my fault. If I had not run away that night . . ."

He fought to breathe steadily and seemed to gain some command over the pain. "Nay, do not say you're sorry. This is my fault, and no other's. You did nothing wrong, lass."

She could not bear it any longer. She touched her forehead to his shoulder and wept. "What can I do? How can I make this better?"

"You've already given me what I wanted. Just seeing your face and hearing your voice is enough. I thought you'd already returned to your own country, and that I'd never see you again. I thought you hated me."

She lifted her face. "Of course I do not hate you."

"But you must accept now that I am a savage. You wanted a gentleman, but what gentleman is ever as bloody and broken as this?"

"No."

"Can you forgive me for all the things I've done?"

"Yes," she heedlessly answered, without hesitation. Without even thinking. "I forgive you, but I cannot bear to see you like this."

He shook his head. "If I die here tonight, it'll be a better death than any other, knowing that you do not hate me, and that you are safe from Bennett, and in the care of your uncle. He is a good man. Let him take you home, and know in your heart that I wouldn't change any of this."

"Please do not say these things."

"I must say them while I can, lass. I need you to know that I have no regrets, and because of what you taught me, there may be some hope for me in the afterlife. If you could send for a priest . . ."

She shook her head. "No!"

She looked over her shoulder, worried that the guard might have heard the distress in her voice. "I am not going to send for a priest. I am going to get you out of here somehow. No one knows who you are. If I can only get you back to Moncrieffe Castle . . ."

He closed his eyes and shook his head. "The Butcher might have been able to slay twenty men and carry you out of here with one hand, but I am broken now, lass. I'll not be slaying anyone, and I'll not be leaving this place."

She sat back on her heels, stared at him furiously, then stood. "Yes, you will, because I will not give up. *Guard!*" she shouted. "Let me out of here! And for God's sake, be quicker with your keys this time!"

The door to the officers' quarters burst open, and five uniformed soldiers marched in with muskets at the ready. "Major Jack Curtis, you are under arrest."

Curtis, who was seated at a table with four other officers, quickly stood. The others stood up as well, all of them startled by the commotion.

"What are the charges?" Curtis asked incredulously.

"Drunkenness and attempted rape." They swarmed around him, confiscated his pistol and sword, and seized him by the arms.

"I demand to know the name of my accuser!"

"The Duke of Winslowe, on behalf of his niece, Lady Amelia Templeton. Tsk-tsk, Major. Trying to have your way with a noblewoman? Shame on you."

They dragged him out of the room and escorted him roughly to the prison.

Sometime during the night, a surgeon entered Duncan's cell, and after he was gone, Duncan dreamed of angels and his mother's pearls and Amelia's mossy green eyes. He felt her hands upon his wounds, healing his bones, and was vaguely aware of her softly kissing his forehead, washing his face with clean, warm water, and rising occasionally to keep the red soldiers from his door.

He was alone, of course, chained to the wall. None of it was real. Amelia was not in the cell with him. She was somewhere else. But he slept soundly that night. And he felt no pain.

Chapter Twenty-five

Amelia fought to stay calm and focused during the night as she paced in her room. She could not allow herself to give way to melancholy or helplessness. She could not fall into the trap of weeping or lamenting. If she fell apart, she would accomplish nothing.

Duncan was injured and imprisoned, but at least he was alive. It was something to be thankful for when the circumstances of his capture could have easily resulted in a different outcome. All was not lost. As long as he was alive, there was hope, and where there was hope, there was still a chance to save him.

Perhaps she could state his case to Colonel Worthington and explain how Duncan had always treated her well and how he had rescued her from Major Curtis's abominable attack on the beach. They might consider those facts and offer some leniency in his sentencing. If they were not willing to release him of all charges, perhaps they would at least spare his life. Instead of the noose, he could be taken to the Tolbooth, and perhaps one day . . .

All her thoughts seemed to be whirling about in her brain like dry leaves in a storm. She sat down on a chair, then immediately stood up again and paced.

Perhaps she should appeal to her uncle for help. She had already revealed what had happened with Major Curtis at the lake, and her uncle had taken steps against the major with great effectiveness. He was now in custody. But could she confess everything to her uncle and reveal Duncan's identity?

No, she quickly decided. That would not be helpful. They might accuse her uncle of being a spy, for he had spent time at the castle. Some might even suggest he had colluded in planning Richard's death. She, too, could be charged with treason if her knowledge became known. How would that help anyone? It certainly wouldn't help Duncan. Iain and Josephine would then be implicated, and Duncan would die a miserable death, knowing his family would suffer for his crimes.

She pressed her fingers to her throbbing temples and squeezed her eyes shut. Forcing herself to breathe slowly, she decided it would be best to keep Duncan's identity a secret, even if the Butcher was sentenced to death. If it did come to that, Iain would inherit the title, and perhaps they could stage the Earl of Moncrieffe's death weeks later. . . .

Stop it, Amelia. Stop it!

Why was she even thinking such things?

She went to the bed and flopped down on her back. If only there were more time. All she had managed to do thus far was arrange for the surgeon to visit Duncan's cell and give him some laudanum for the pain, and she was still torturing herself over her refusal to send for a priest, when that was all he had asked for. Just that one thing, so that he might repent for his sins before the final moment of judgment, and be forgiven and depart from this world with some feeling of peace.

She should not have denied him that.

She had been selfish and insensitive.

A moment later, she was standing at the foot of her

bed, staring blankly at the wall. She did not even remember rising to her feet. She chewed on a thumbnail.

Did Iain know Duncan was here? Had he been alone in the cave when he was captured? Where were Fergus and Gawyn and Angus?

Again, she considered sending for a priest, when what she really wanted to do was spirit Duncan out of there. To circumvent the time-consuming legalities that may or may not work in his favor, and act quickly and aggressively.

But how? He was a prisoner in an English garrison. He was locked in a cell, chained to a wall. She was not a ruthless, axe-bearing warrior who possessed the strength and skill to break out of such a place and abduct someone in the dead of night, as he had once done.

She could think of one man, however, who did possess those skills.

Her heart began to race. Was it even possible?

Yes, of course it was. It *had* to be.

But if she was going to do anything to help Duncan, she could not waste another minute deliberating it. She would have to decide on a plan and set it in motion straightaway.

She would travel to Moncrieffe Castle at first light. Once she got there, she would enlist Iain's help to find Angus, and then she would say and do whatever it took to set aside their differences and unite in this one common goal—to save Duncan's life.

Angus MacDonald rode across the drawbridge at Kinloch Castle and dismounted. He had left this place in high spirits not long ago, after the unexpected arrival of Richard Bennett's head in a bag. For days, Angus had celebrated with his father, the chief, and the warriors of his clan. Feeling jubilant, Angus had raised a glass and spoken in honor of the great Butcher of the Highlands, a noble and courageous Scot.

Angus had not known, however, that a few days later Duncan would disappoint him so absolutely and choose a woman—*an Englishwoman*—over his desire to fight for Scottish freedom.

Nor had he imagined that he, Angus Bradach MacDonald, would ever be capable of such malice and treachery.

He laid a hand on his gut, which had been churning since daybreak. He felt as if he'd eaten a plate of rancid meat but knew it was not so simple as that. This was not something he could purge. It was something very ugly that would follow him through the rest of his life and deep down into the fiery depths of his grave.

He walked to the stables, delivered his horse to a groom, and strode to the great hall, which was silent and empty. There was a grim sort of gloom in the air. The celebrations were over.

He looked up at the MacDonald heraldry hanging from the stone walls—the crests and banners and tapestries. He was proud of his ancestry, devoted to his clan, and had made a vow to himself two days ago: that no woman would ever exert such influence over him as that woman had exerted over Duncan.

Angus was a warrior—loyal to clan and country. He would be chief here one day, and for that reason, such blind passion could have no place in his life. He would take a wife, of course, in order to produce an heir—but by God, she would know her place. And she would most assuredly be Scottish.

He turned and looked at the cross, carved deep into the stone of the hearth, and stood for a long time, staring at it, until a noise caused him to look up. A small bird was trapped inside the hall. It flew around the rafters and fluttered desperately in the highest peak of the ceiling.

Angus looked down at the floor and felt suddenly as if he were sinking through the stones. He had been so angry with Duncan. But what had he done?

He knelt down on both knees, cupped his hands together, and bowed his head. "Merciful God," he whispered, "I pray for your forgiveness, and for the strength to endure the shame of my sins."

Then he heard the scrape of a sword at the back of the room and turned to see the dark glimmer of wrath in his father's eyes. His father, his chief, the man he revered more than any other . . .

He knew.

And he, unlike God, would not merciful.

Amelia stepped out of her uncle's coach and looked up at the massive stone façade of Moncrieffe Castle. The wind was gusting and whipping at her skirts. Her hat ribbons flew wildly around her face. She reached up to hold the hat in place and tried not to think about where Duncan was at that moment, or what torture he might be enduring, as she hurried from the coach to the castle entrance. Instead, she rehearsed her speech in her mind. She had much to accomplish here today, and she could not afford any emotional outbursts or thoughts about possible catastrophes. She could not allow herself to become distracted from what had to be done.

The housekeeper met her in the entrance hall. She spoke awkwardly. "Lady Amelia, we were not expecting you. The earl is not at home. His Lairdship left for Edinburgh yesterday."

Amelia managed a courteous smile. "Edinburgh? On important business, no doubt. In that case, please inform his brother that I have arrived."

The housekeeper curtsied and hurried from the hall.

A short time later, Amelia was shown into the gallery. She walked through the door expecting to meet with Iain and Josephine but found herself staring also at Fergus and Gawyn. They stood before the fireplace, wide-eyed and surprised to see her.

"Gentlemen." She removed her gloves. "I am pleased to find you both here. Something terrible has happened. I came as quickly as I could."

"Aye, we know all about it," Fergus said with a note of contempt.

She looked curiously at Iain. "You know?"

He nodded, and Gawyn approached. "Lady Amelia, I'm pleased to see you as well. Did you come from the fort? Did you see Duncan? Is he alive?"

"Yes, he still lives."

There was a clear exhalation of relief in the room. Josephine rose from her chair, came forward, and embraced Amelia, who was still trying to understand what all of this meant. They knew. Were they already planning how to extract Duncan from the prison?

"I thought you'd be halfway to England by now," Josephine said.

Amelia held her close. "No. I couldn't leave." She stepped back and held both of Josephine's hands in her own. "I've been at the fort for days, not knowing if I did the right thing by leaving here. Then last night there was a terrible commotion in the compound, and my uncle told me they had captured the Butcher. I was beside myself with despair. I didn't know what to do, so I came here straightaway."

"How is he?" Iain asked with concern. "What have they done to him?"

"Do they know his identity?" Fergus asked.

Amelia shook her head. "No one knows who he is,

at least not yet. But he is not well, Iain. He was badly beaten, which is a mixed blessing, I suppose. It's why he is unrecognizable."

Josephine stepped back and covered her mouth with a hand. "Poor Duncan."

"They'll hang him, I suppose," Iain said.

"Yes," Amelia replied. "That is their intention, which is why I came so quickly. We must get him out of there somehow, and the sooner the better."

Fergus circled around the table. "You think it's an easy thing to do, lass—to break a Scottish rebel out of an English prison?"

She met his gaze directly. "Duncan managed to break in and carry me out on his back. Perhaps we can do the same for him."

Fergus scoffed. "You're lighter than a daisy. He's heavier than an ox, and chained up besides."

"He may be able to walk," she argued, refusing to be daunted. "His worst wounds are on his hands and face."

"There's still the wee issue of getting him free of the prison," Fergus said. "The place is crawling with redcoats, and with the notorious Butcher as a captive, I suspect they have their watch doubled or tripled."

Amelia took a deep breath. "Yes. I realize it will be difficult. But as I said before, Duncan managed to get in quietly."

In fact, he had slit a few throats to get inside. He had been ruthless. There had been no mercy. Was she willing to condone such methods to save his life?

"Where is Angus?" she asked. "Would he be willing to take such a risk? I could give him instructions and tell him exactly where Duncan is being held, and I have, in my trunks, three red uniforms that might be useful. I took them from the laundry before I left this morning. I doubt they've been missed yet."

A heavy silence descended upon the room. They all exchanged troubled glances.

"What is it?" she asked. "What's wrong? Has something happened to Angus? Don't tell me . . . has he been captured, too?"

"Nay, lass, he wasn't captured, but something did indeed happen to him," Gawyn said, "and we're all still recovering from the shock of it."

She frowned. "Tell me."

"He turned on us, lass. He's the one who told the English soldiers where Duncan would be."

She felt the blood drain from her face. "I beg your pardon? Are you sure? No, it cannot be true. Angus hates the English. Why would he do such a thing?"

"It's unforgivable," Gawyn said.

"He'll rot in hell," Iain added.

"But are you sure it was him?" Amelia asked. "Perhaps you are mistaken."

"Always giving everyone the benefit of the doubt," Iain said. "I admire that in you, Amelia, but in this case there can be no doubt of it. He's the only one besides me who knew where Duncan would be that night. Angus was supposed to bring Fergus and Gawyn to meet him in the cave, to discuss the future of the Butcher's campaign, but he went to the English soldiers instead. A boy who was spying for us saw him there, and rode hard to tell his father, but it was too late."

"But why would Angus do that?"

"He was angry with Duncan. He believed his actions were a betrayal to Scotland."

"Because he proposed to me," Amelia finished for Iain—once again feeling as if this was all her fault. "But I broke off our engagement," she told them. "I had already left him. By all accounts, it was over, and he killed Richard, which is exactly what Angus wanted."

"Aye, but Duncan was going to give up his crusade as the Butcher," Iain told her. "He didn't want to fight any longer, at least not with his axe."

She took a moment to ponder this news. "He was truly going to give it up?"

Josephine nodded. "Aye, Amelia. He couldn't live with any more blood on his hands. He told Angus he was going to retire the Butcher for good."

Amelia bowed her head in sorrow for all the pain he was forced to endure because of her, especially now, when he was England's prisoner, tortured and sentenced to death. She sat down on a chair, then lifted her gaze and looked pleadingly at Iain. "We have to get him out of there. Everything he did, he did to protect others and fight for their safety and freedom. He cannot die. He deserves a chance to live."

"But how, Amelia? How do we get him out?"

Her thoughts returned to the one thing he had asked of her. "All he wanted," she said, "was to speak to a priest. He wanted to confess his sins before he died. I denied him that, because I could not bear to give up hope that I could save him. But I think it's time I respected his wishes."

"That's very kind of you, Lady Amelia," Gawyn said, "but it does not bring him back to us."

"No," she said, "but I believe if we can get a priest into his cell, we may be able to deliver him to a safe haven, without ever hurting a single soul."

Chapter Twenty-six

Father Douglas arrived at Fort William on a Wednesday. His coach, drawn by three impressive chestnut geldings, rolled through the village of Maryburgh and passed through the fortress gates at noon. He was greeted by a young sentry, then escorted into the officers' mess for a hot meal of pork stew and rye bread, followed by fruitcake and sweet cream for dessert.

He had the pleasure of meeting Colonel Worthington in his private chambers after the midday meal. The colonel offered him a glass of claret and informed him that the Butcher of the Highlands had been tried for treason that morning and had been found guilty.

His sentence was as followed: He would be removed from Fort William in five days. He would then be transported to the Tolbooth in Edinburgh, where he would remain, incarcerated, for twenty-seven days. On the twenty-eighth day, he would be hanged.

Colonel Worthington was against such a public and lavish display. He believed there would be a riot, not to mention the fact that the risk of escape during the transfer was too great. He believed the Butcher should be put to death at Fort William as quickly as possible, but sadly, politics prevailed and the King's advisors wished otherwise. They'd communicated their instructions for the Butcher's imminent capture and death six months ago.

"It is why I am a soldier and not a politician," the colonel said with a heavy sigh as he sipped his claret. "I have no interest in showmanship. I want only results, without such pointless fanfare."

Later that evening, Father Douglas was escorted to the prison by two heavily armed guards. They unlocked the cell door and waited outside while he heard the Butcher's confession.

The following morning, a whistle blew. Two guards woke inside a prison cell, chained to a wall. Their heads were throbbing, their weapons gone. A third guard dashed through the corridor to the Butcher's cell. "Wake up, you cockeyed fools!"

While the two soldiers sat up groggily, the one outside fumbled with his keys, dropped them on the floor, bent to pick them up, then unlocked the Butcher's door and pushed it open.

His wide-eyed gaze fell upon the priest, Father Douglas, chained to the wall and gagged with a wad of green tartan. He was fast asleep and wore nothing but his linen shirt. His robes were gone.

The guard hurried to free him. He unlocked the manacles and pulled the gag out of the priest's mouth. "Are you all right, Father Douglas?"

Father Douglas pressed a hand to the back of his head and groaned. "My word, someone must have clubbed me." Then he noticed his current state of undress. "Why am I half-naked? Where are my robes?"

The guard looked around in dismay. "It appears you've been robbed, Father."

"By whom?"

"Who else but the Butcher?"

Father Douglas frowned up at the guard. "But I came here to listen to his confession. He was shackled to this wall and was supposed to be on death's door. How could he have accomplished such a feat? And where is he now?"

The guard helped Father Douglas to his feet. "If I were to hazard a guess, I'd say he's halfway to Ireland."

"I suppose I should be thankful," Father Douglas said, "that he took my robes and nothing else. I'm relieved to discover that I am still in possession of my head."

"The Almighty must have been watching over you," the guard said.

"Though it appears He was watching over someone else, too—the prisoner who just escaped."

The guard helped Father Douglas out of the cell. "Have no worries, Father. Justice will prevail. It always does where villains are concerned."

They slowly made their way up the stairs. "But we're on Scottish soil, young man. Some might take issue with your opinions and call the Butcher a hero."

"And you, Father? What would you call him?"

He took a long time to consider the question; then he chuckled. "I am inside an English prison, but I am still a Scot by blood. So I suppose I will simply call him lucky."

Sitting at the edge of the glade not far from the Mac-Kenzies' cottage, on the banks of a cool, babbling brook, Amelia tried to make sense of the extraordinary events of her life. A few days ago, she had fled from an English garrison where Duncan was incarcerated, leaving him behind—alone—all the while hoping that she might find the help she needed in order to free him.

Now she sat by this stream in the Scottish interior, praying that her plan had not gone awry and that Duncan would somehow survive.

She lifted her eyes and looked around. This was the very place they had stopped after escaping the English soldiers at Loch Fannich. It was where she had first seen Duncan in a different light, just before he collapsed at her feet as a result of the head wound she had inflicted upon him. She had run off and left him alone that night, too, in search of help from others.

Something caught her eye at that moment—a flash of gray on the other side of the stream. *Duncan?* Her heart skipped a beat, however, as she recognized the visitor.

Strangely unafraid, Amelia sat motionless. The wolf sniffed around and soon caught Amelia in her gaze.

How odd and incredible to again be so close to a creature of the wild. Amelia wished she had something to offer the wolf but knew that would be a mistake, because it would only encourage her to return and perhaps discover that the MacKenzies had a stable full of plump, juicy animals.

But it was not wrong to enjoy the wolf's company, Amelia decided, while she marveled at the fact that she felt so very safe in her presence.

Suddenly, however, the wolf lifted her head. Her ears pricked; then she darted in the other direction. She flew into the bush and vanished as quickly as she had appeared, leaving Amelia to wonder if she had imagined the entire thing.

The forest grew quiet again until a clear rustling began behind her, followed by the sound of hooves on the moss. She turned quickly and stood.

Was she dreaming? Twice now had her eyes deceived her?

No, this was real. She was looking at Duncan, fierce and dangerous, sitting atop a chestnut gelding, dressed in his familiar green tartan. His thick sable hair was wild and windblown, his left hand wrapped in a splint. His eye was still blackened but less swollen. He looked almost himself again, and he was alive. He was free.

"You're here," he said, in that deep Scottish brogue she had come to know so well. His expression was stern.

She could not speak. Her heart was racing, for despite all the pleasures they had shared and her knowledge of his wealth and aristocratic blood, he was still a brutish and intimidating beast of a man when he wished to be.

She swallowed hard and forced words past her lips, for she was not about to let him break her. He had never managed to do it before, and he was not going to do it now. "Yes. And you got away."

"From the English—aye." He tossed a leg over the back of the horse and swung himself to the ground. "I was told you played a role in the plan to break me out of there. That it was your idea to bring Father Douglas to my cell so he could lend me his robes."

She wet her lips. "Yes. And he was happy to oblige."

"But you shouldn't have taken that risk, lass. If anyone finds out, there will be a price on your head. You could be charged with treason." His eyes flashed with anger. "What were you thinking? You put yourself in harm's way, and it makes me want to tie you up again, lass, just to keep you safe and contained."

Amelia glowered at him. "Contained? Honestly, Duncan, you still think I am that naïve, frightened captive who needs your worldly wisdom and protection. What will it take to convince you that I am no longer that woman? I have learned a great deal about the world, and I am absolutely self-sufficient. I left you, didn't I? I was not afraid to walk out and live my life on my own terms. So do not dare to ask me if I have stones in my head where my brain should be. I am perfectly capable of making my own decisions and doing what I think is best."

A muscle clenched in his jaw, and his eyes narrowed. "Woman, you make me wild. You know that, don't you?"

"Yes, and I don't really care. You can be as wild as you wish to be. I will not be afraid of you."

For a long moment he stared at her as if he was deciding whether or not he should argue; then he strode to the other side of the glade.

"Your plan worked well," he said diffidently, and she breathed a sigh of relief, for it was a clear white flag. "Father Douglas was helpful, and he didn't seem to mind the manacles too much."

"And Fergus and Gawyn?" she asked, choosing not to gloat over her victory, for she knew how hard it was for Duncan to surrender this way. "Are they safe as well?"

"Aye. They escorted me out through the main gates, and as soon as we were clear of the village we left the coach behind and each took a horse. We thought it best to separate."

"So that you'd be harder to track."

"Aye. But if anyone finds out about this, lass . . ." He turned to face her, and his eyes communicated a warning.

She smiled. "I know, I know. There will be a price on my head. Have it your way, then. If that happens, I will need protection."

"From a very powerful man."

Amelia laughed. "Yes."

At last he crossed to her and took hold of her upper arms. "I owe you a great debt, lass. You were very brave, and you saved my life."

She laughed in tearful disbelief. "And you saved mine."

Ecstatic, rapturous, too happy to even think, she threw herself into his arms and nearly knocked him backwards onto the grass. "I thought I'd lost you."

He regained his footing and held her tight. "And I thought

I'd never see you again, but you must ease up on my ribs, lass."

She stepped back, and they stood in the center of the sunny glade, staring at each other for the longest time. Then at last his mouth found hers, and he kissed her hungrily. His hands roamed over her body and ignited her desires.

"I don't want to ever let go," she said, holding his face in her hands. "I was miserable without you. It's why I couldn't leave Scotland, and why I asked my uncle to remain at the fort. I dreamed of you every night, and I wasn't sure I had done the right thing when I left you. I wanted to go back and ask if we could begin again. I wanted to talk more about what happened with Richard—but then the news of his head in a bag arrived at the fort, and everyone was talking about the ferocious Butcher of the Highlands. I was confused, and then my uncle knocked on my door, and . . ." She could not finish the thought.

Duncan kissed her mouth, cheeks, and forehead. "You must know," he explained, "the reason I was there at the cave that night was to surrender my shield. I told Angus that I wouldn't do it any longer, that I would never take another life. The last thing you said to me was that you couldn't love someone who took a life and felt nothing. I wanted to tell you that I *do* feel things. Too much, in fact. Everything I've done will follow me to my grave. I've felt wretched for a long time, but I didn't know how to change it."

She touched his cheek. "When I went to Moncrieffe in search of help, Iain and Josephine told me what happened between you and Angus, and I knew I had to get you out." She bowed her head. "I am so sorry for all of this. You would never have been captured if it weren't for me."

He shook his head. "Nay, lass. I'm not sorry for anything. If it hadn't happened the way it did, I wouldn't be here with you now, feeling worthy of your affections."

She rose up on her toes and kissed him.

"But am I truly worthy, lass?" he asked when she withdrew from the kiss. "I broke the vow I made to you. I killed Richard Bennett."

She looked at him with anguish in her heart. "I believe you had your reasons, Duncan, and you must somehow forgive yourself." She spoke the words with conviction, although a part of her was still wary of him and probably always would be. He had lost control of himself and killed a man. He had killed many men.

"I did have my reasons," he said, "but I need you to understand something, if we are going to be together." He touched her cheek with the back of a finger, then strode to the water's edge. "I learned something about Richard Bennett on the day I killed him," he said, kneeling down and splashing water on his hands.

"What was that?"

He paused. "I learned that he and I were very similar, almost like mirror images of each other. The same, but opposite."

"How so?"

"We were both warriors, both raised from birth to fight and survive and endure pain."

She frowned. "But you are nothing like him, Duncan. Because that man I almost married remembered his own pain, and he wanted to hurt others to make up for it, or to satisfy some dark hankering for revenge against the world." Duncan rose to his feet and faced her, so she continued. "But I know now that the only thing you ever wanted was to prevent the suffering of others. You thought you wanted revenge, but what you really wanted was to stop Bennett from doing all the bad things he wanted to do to good people."

"Similar," Duncan said, "but different." He strode closer. "But most of all, I couldn't let him do those bad things to *you,* lass. I'll never tell you the things he said before I took his life, but I did what I did to protect you."

"You did it for me?" she asked, still feeling a small niggling of doubt, deep in her core.

"Aye."

"But what about Muira?"

He stopped before Amelia and frowned. "What about her?"

Amelia looked away, toward a weeping willow that dipped its branches into the water; then she slid her gaze back to Duncan's face, marked with cuts and bruises. "When we were together one night, you told me that you did not want me to ever speak Muira's name. I have felt your love for her between us, Duncan, but I cannot let it keep us apart any longer. I must understand how you feel about her, and about me."

"There is nothing to understand," he said, bewildered. "I loved her once, but she's gone now. I know that."

"But do you still love her?" Amelia asked. "And will you ever care for me the way you cared for her? Because I cannot compete with a ghost."

"Compete?" He looked at her as if she had just grown whiskers and a beard. "I don't want you to compete, lass. I just want you, plain and simple."

She sighed. "But that is exactly the problem, Duncan. You *want* me. You desire me. I've always known that, and I have enjoyed your passions as well as my own. There has never been any doubt that there is lust between us. But . . ."

"But what, lass?" He seemed genuinely confused.

She did not know how to say it, how to explain herself, how to make sense of this, or demand what she truly wanted.

Then Duncan grimaced and took her chin in his big hand and shook his head at her, as if she were completely daft. "I didn't want to speak of Muira that night," he said, "because I didn't want to imagine losing you the way I lost her. I couldn't bear the thought of it. That's why I didn't want to be reminded of it. But you're the one I love now, lass, with all my heart. And if it weren't for you, there'd be nothing left of me. At least now there's something beating in my chest. I feel like I can finally have what I once wanted for myself—a peaceful woman for a wife, and a lusty one, too."

"You love me?" she asked, realizing she'd not heard a single word he'd said after that little declaration.

"Aye, of course I love you, you ninny. Do you have stones in your head where your brain should be?"

She laughed out loud, but he was no longer listening. He was gathering her up into his arms, crushing her mouth to his in a fierce kiss that left her breathless with desire.

"I do love you, lass," he said. "And I mean to keep you, too. Will you be my wife and never run from me again?"

She felt completely besotted. "I promise I never will. I'd have to be a fool."

He held her tenderly in his arms. "And I promise to be the gentleman you've always desired. That will be my vow to you, from this day forward."

She smirked and shook her head at him. "I don't want to marry a gentleman," she said. "I want to marry a Highland warrior. It's what I've always wanted. I just didn't know it."

"Well, perhaps I can be both, just to be safe."

"You are already both of those things," she told him. "And what sacrifice do you want from me, Duncan MacLean? Can I be your English wife? Or should I adopt a Scottish brogue?"

He smiled. "You can be whatever you like, lass, as long as you continue to be lusty."

"So is it safe for me to be happy now?"

He thought about it. "Mm . . . not quite yet, but very soon."

"How soon?"

He kissed her on the mouth while he unhooked her bodice. "When you're naked and on your back right here in the grass, crying out my name, begging for more."

She laughed. "Then I suspect I shall be happy in a few short minutes from now."

He inclined his head. "Surely you know me better than that, lass. It'll be more than 'a few short minutes.' "

She slid her hands up under his kilt and was very pleased to discover just how ardently and enormously this handsome Highlander loved her. And true to his word, a short time later—but not *too* short a time—he was sliding into her with great strength and skill and she was trembling all over with rapture.

Author's Note

Scotland, in 1715, was in the throes of rebellion over the English succession. Queen Anne had died without an heir, so the Crown passed to a German prince, George of Hanover. Scottish Jacobites (*Jacob* is Latin for "James") believed the rightful king was Prince James Edward Stuart, whose father, James II, had been removed from the throne in 1688 because he was Catholic.

The history books show that the MacLeans, under Sir John MacLean of Duart Castle, were among those who rallied support for the Jacobite uprising in 1715. The MacDonalds joined in as well, along with the MacGregors, Camerons, and MacLachlans, among others. Under the leadership of the Earl of Mar, an army of twelve thousand clansmen set out to fight for the cause. By September, Mar had taken Perth, but the English stronghold at Stirling, under the command of the second Duke of Argyll, still stood between the Scottish Jacobites and the English border. Mar's military expertise was no match for Argyll's, and his hesitation in marching forward cost the Scots their victory.

Meanwhile, the MacLeans, Camerons, and MacDonalds marched unsuccessfully on Inveraray, and in November joined Mar at the Battle of Sherrifmuir, where they suffered terrible losses and failed to restore a Stuart monarch to the throne.

These battles provided the turbulent political background for *Captured by the Highlander* and set the characters in motion, pitting Highlanders and Englishmen against each other in acts of vengeance and quests for justice.

All the main characters in the book—including Duncan MacLean, the "Butcher of the Highlands"—are fictional, though many of the events surrounding them are true, including the fact that the London government took drastic measures against the Scots who took part in the rebellion. Some were spared, by pledging allegiance to England, but others were executed or sent to America, and many peerages and estates were forfeited to the Crown.

True also is the fact that individuals took vengeance on one another. One Scottish Whig—a Campbell of Ardkinglas—tracked and followed a MacLachlan for five years until he shot him dead in 1720.

The ancestor of my hero was also a real person: Gilleain na Tuaighe, Gillean of the Battle-axe, who fought ferociously at the Battle of Langs in 1263 and defeated a fleet of invading Vikings. I was inspired by his story, along with the notion that the MacLeans were sometimes known as "the Spartans of the North." This stirred my imagination in regards to Duncan's childhood and upbringing.

As far as my red-coated villain is concerned, he, too, is pure fiction, though loosely based on a real British soldier, Lieutenant-Colonel. Banastre Tarleton, who, interestingly enough, was known as "The Butcher." He was famous for his violence and brutality during the American Revolution.

Castle Moncrieffe is fictional but modeled loosely after Leeds Castle in England—post the additions of 1822 and even some twentieth-century renovations—though I took some artistic liberties with a few decorative and architectural details.

Duart Castle is the true MacLean stronghold. It still stands today and is located on the Isle of Mull. Similarly, Fort William was a real English garrison, and its ruins are visible not far from Inverlochy Castle in the Highlands of Scotland.

If you enjoyed Duncan's story, I hope you will look for Angus MacDonald's story, *Claimed by the Highlander,* coming next month.

I invite you also to visit my Web site at www.julianne maclean.com to learn more about my books and writing life. I enjoy hearing from readers, and you can contact me via e-mail through my Web site.

By the time Gwendolen reached the battlements and took aim at the invaders on the drawbridge below, the iron-tipped battering ram was smashing the thick oak door to bits and pieces. The castle walls shuddered beneath her feet, and she was forced to stop and take a moment to absorb what was happening.

The frightful reality of battle struck her, and all at once, she felt dazed, as if she were staring into a churning abyss of noise and confusion. She couldn't move. Her fellow clansmen were shouting gruffly at each other. Smoke and the smell of gunpowder burned in her lungs and stung her eyes. One kilted warrior had dropped all his weapons beside her and was crouching by the wall, overcome by a fit of weeping.

She stared down at him for a hazy moment, feeling nauseated and light-headed, as cracks of musket fire exploded all around her.

"*Get up!*" she shouted, reaching down and hooking her arm under his. She hauled him roughly to his feet. "Reload your weapon, and fight like a Highlander!"

The young clansman stared at her blankly for a moment, then snapped out of his stupor and fumbled for his powder.

Gwendolen leaned out over the battlements to see below. The MacDonalds were swarming through the broken gate, crawling like insects over the wooden ram. She quickly took aim and fired at one of them, but missed.

"To the bailey!" she shouted, and the sound of dozens of swords scraping out of scabbards fueled her resolve. With steady hands and unwavering spirit, she reloaded her musket. There was shouting and screaming, men running everywhere, flocking to the stairs . . .

"Gwendolen!" Douglas called out, stopping beside her. "You should not be here! You must go below to your chamber and lock yerself in! Leave the fighting to the men!"

"Nay, Douglas, I will fight and die for Kinloch if I must."

He regarded her with both admiration and regret, and spoke in a gentler voice. "At least do your fighting from the rooftop, lassie. The clan will not survive the loss of ye."

His meaning was clear, and she knew he was right. She was the daughter of the MacEwen chief. She must remain alive to negotiate terms of surrender, if it came to that.

Gwendolen nodded. "Be gone, Douglas. Leave me here to reload my weapon. This is a good spot. I will do what I can from here."

He kissed her on the cheek, wished her luck, and bolted for the stairs.

Hand-to-hand combat began immediately in the bailey below. There was a dreadful roar—close to four hundred men all shouting at once—and the deafening clang of steel against steel rang in her ears as she fired and reloaded her musket, over and over. Before long, she had to stop, for the two clans had merged into one screaming cataclysm of carnage, and she could not risk shooting any of her own men.

The chapel bell tolled, calling to the villagers to come quickly and assist in the fight, but even if every able-bodied man arrived at that moment, it would not be enough. These

MacDonald warriors were rough and battle-seasoned, armed with spears, muskets, axes, bows and arrows. They were quickly seizing control, and she could do nothing from where she stood, for if she went below, it would be suicide, and she had to live for her clan.

Then she spotted him. Their leader. Angus the Lion, fighting in the center of it all.

She quickly loaded her musket and aimed, but he moved too quickly. She could not get a clear shot.

A scorching ball of terror shot into her belly as she lowered her weapon. No wonder they called him the Lion. His hair was a thick, tawny mane that reached past his broad shoulders, and he roared with every deadly swing of his claymore, which sliced effortlessly through the air before it cut down foe, after foe, after foe.

Gwendolen stood transfixed, unable to tear her eyes away from the sheer muscled brawn of his arms, chest and legs, thick as tree trunks—just like the battering ram on the bridge. There was a perfect, lethal symmetry and balance to his movements as he lunged and killed, then flicked the sweat-drenched hair from his eyes, spun around, and killed again.

Her heart pounded with fascination and awe. He was a powerful beast of a man, a superb warrior, magnificent in every way, and the mere sight of him in battle, in all his legendary glory, nearly brought her to her knees. He deflected every blow with his sturdy black shield, and swung the claymore with exquisite grace. She had never encountered such a man before, nor imagined such strength was possible in the human form.

She realized suddenly that her mother had been correct in her predictions. There was no possibility of defeating this man. They were all doomed. Without a doubt, the castle would fall to these invaders and there would be no mercy. It was pointless to hope otherwise.

She moved across the rooftop to the corner tower where her bedchamber was housed, and looked down at the hopeless struggle.

This had been far too easy a charge for the MacDonalds. To watch it any longer was pure agony, and she was ashamed when she had to close her eyes and turn her face away. She had wanted so desperately to triumph over these attackers, but she had never witnessed a battle such as this in all her twenty-one years. She'd heard tales, of course, and imagined the evils of war, but she'd had no idea how truly violent and grisly it would be.

Soon the battle cries grew sparse, and only a handful of willful warriors continued to fight to the death. Other MacEwen clansmen, with swords pointed at their throats, accepted their fate. They laid down their weapons and dropped to their knees. Those who surrendered were being assembled into a line at the far wall.

Gwendolen, who had been watching the great Lion throughout the battle, noticed suddenly that he was gone, vanished like a phantom into the gunsmoke. Panic shot to her core, and she gazed frantically from one corner of the bailey to the other, searching all the faces for those gleaming, devilish eyes. Where was he? Had someone killed him? Or had he penetrated the chapel to ravage the women and children, too?

She spotted him, at last, on the rooftop, clear across the distance, standing on the opposite corner tower. His broadsword was sheathed at his side, and his shield was strapped to his back. He raised his arms out to his sides and shouted to the clansmen below.

"I am Angus Bradach MacDonald! Son of the fallen Laird MacDonald, true master of Kinloch Castle!" His voice was deep and thunderous. It rumbled mightily inside his chest. "Kinloch belongs to me by right of birth! I hereby declare myself laird and chief!"

"Kinloch belongs to the MacEwens now!" someone shouted from below. "By Letters of Fire and Sword, issued by King George of Great Britain!"

"If ye want it back," Angus growled, stepping forward to the edge of the rooftop, "then raise your sword and fight me!"

His challenge was met with silence, until Gwendolen was overcome by a blast of anger so hot, she could not control or contain it.

"Angus Bradach MacDonald!" she shouted from the dark, outraged depths of her soul. "Hear me now! I am Gwendolen MacEwen, daughter of the MacEwen chief who won this castle by fair and lawful means! I am leader here, and *I* will fight you!"

It was not until that moment that she realized she had marched to the edge of the rooftop and drawn her saber, which she was now pointing at him from across the distance.

Her heart pummelled her chest. She had never felt more exhilarated. It was intoxicating. She wished there were not this expanse of separation between them. If there were a bridge from one tower to the other, she would dash across it and fight him to the death.

"Gwendolen MacEwen!" he shouted in reply. "Daughter of my enemy! Ye have been defeated!"

And just like that, he dismissed her challenge and addressed the clansmen in the bailey below.

"All who have taken part in usurping this castle and are in possession of lands that did not belong to you—you must forfeit them now to the clansmen from whom ye took them!"

Gwendolen's anger rose up again, more fiercely than before. "The MacEwens refuse!" she answered.

He immediately pointed his sword at her in a forceful show of warning, then lowered it and continued, as if she had not spoken.

"If that clansman is dead or absent today," he declared, "ye may remain, but I will have your loyalty, and you will swear allegiance to me as Laird of Kinloch!"

There was another long, drawn-out silence, until some brave soul spoke up.

"Why should we pledge loyalty to ye? You are a Mac-Donald, and we are MacEwens!"

The Lion was quiet for a moment. He seemed to be looking deep into the eyes of every man in the bailey below. "Be it known that our two clans will unite!" He pointed his sword at Gwendolen again, and she felt the intense heat of his gaze like a fire across her body. "For I will claim this woman, who is your brave and noble leader, as my wife, and our son, one day, will be laird."

Cheers erupted from the crowd of MacDonald warriors below, while Gwendolen digested his words with shock and disbelief. He intended to claim her as his wife?

No, it was not possible.

"There will be a feast on this night in the Great Hall," the Lion roared, "and I will accept the pledge of all men willing to remain here and live in peace under my protection!"

Murmurs of surrender floated upwards through the air and reached Gwendolen's burning ears. She clenched her jaw and dug her fingernails into the cold rough stones of the tower. This was not happening. It could not be. Pray God, this was still the dream, and she would soon wake. But the hot morning sun on her cheeks reminded her that the dreams of a restless night had already given way to reality, and her father's castle had been sacked and conquered by an unassailable warrior, and he intended to make her his bride and force her to bear children for him. What in God's name was she to do?

"I do not agree to this!" she shouted, and the Lion tilted his head to the side, beholding her strangely, as if she were some sort of otherworldly creature he had never encountered before. "I wish to negotiate our terms of surrender!"

Her body began to tremble as she waited for his response. Perhaps he would simply send a man to slit her throat in front of everyone—as an example for those were bold enough, or foolish enough, to resist. He looked ready to do it. She could feel the hot flames of his anger from where she stood, at the opposite corner of the castle.

Then the oddest thing happened. One by one, each MacEwen warrior in the bailey below turned toward her, and dropped to one knee. They all bowed their heads in silence, while the MacDonalds stood among them, observing the demonstration with some uneasiness.

For a long time Angus stood upon the North Tower saying nothing, as he watched the men deliver this unexpected defiance. A raw and brutal tension stretched ever tighter within the castle, and Gwendolen feared they would all be slaughtered.

Then at last, the Lion turned his eyes toward her.

She lifted her chin, but his murderous contempt seemed to squeeze around her throat, and she found it difficult to breathe.

He spoke with quiet, grave authority. "Gwendolen MacEwen, I will hear your terms in the Great Hall."

Not trusting herself to speak, she nodded and resheathed her saber, then walked with pride toward the tower stairs, while her legs, hidden beneath her skirts, shook uncontrollably and threatened to give out beneath her.

When at last she reached the top of the stairs, she paused a moment to take a breath and compose herself.

God, oh God. . . .

She felt nauseated and light-headed.

Leaning forward and laying the flat of her hand upon the cool stones, she closed her eyes and wondered how she was ever going to negotiate with this warrior, who had already defeated her clan in a brutal and bloody campaign, and claimed her as his property. She had nothing, *nothing,* with which to bargain. But perhaps she and her mother could think of something—some other way to manage the situation, at least until her brother returned.

If only Murdoch were here now . . .

But no, there was no point wishing for such things. He was not here, and she had only herself to rely on. She must stand strong for her people.

She took one last look at them. Angus the Lion had quitted the rooftop and returned to his men. He was giving orders and wandering amongst the dead and wounded, assessing the magnitude of his triumph, no doubt.

A light breeze lifted his thick golden hair, which shimmered in the morning light. His kilt wafted lightly around his muscular legs, while he adjusted the leather strap that held the shield at his back.

He was her enemy, and she despised him in every way, yet she could not deny the awesome power of his strength as a leader.

Just then he glanced up and saw that she was watching him. He faced her squarely and did not look away.

Gwendolen's breath caught in her throat. Even from this distance, he had the ability to hold her captive in his gaze. Her knees went weak, and something fluttered in her belly. Whether it was fear or fascination, she did not know. Either way, it did not bode well for her future dealings with him.

Shaken and agitated, she pushed away from the wall and quickly descended the tower stairs.